VIRAL

About the Author

Mike is the author of children's fantasy series *The Imaginary Friends Saga*, and the creator of many ridiculous videos on YouTube. His shows include *A Week On* and *Infomercialism*, and he has amassed more than 125,000 subscribers who like to see him miserable as he suffers through fad diets and naff infomercial products. He currently lives in Bedfordshire with his wife and cat. *Viral* is his first adult novel.

VIRAL

MIKE JEAVONS

Unbound Digital

This edition first published in 2019

Unbound

6th Floor Mutual House, 70 Conduit Street, London W1S 2GF

www.unbound.com

ISBN (eBook): 978-1-91261-869-9
ISBN (Paperback): 978-1-91261-868-2

Cover design by Mecob

Printed and bound in Great Britain by Clays Ltd, Elcograf S.p.A.

For Gracie

Dear Reader,

The book you are holding came about in a rather different way to most others. It was funded directly by readers through a new website: Unbound.

Unbound is the creation of three writers. We started the company because we believed there had to be a better deal for both writers and readers. On the Unbound website, authors share the ideas for the books they want to write directly with readers. If enough of you support the book by pledging for it in advance, we produce a beautifully bound special subscribers' edition and distribute a regular edition and e-book wherever books are sold, in shops and online.

This new way of publishing is actually a very old idea (Samuel Johnson funded his dictionary this way). We're just using the internet to build each writer a network of patrons. Here, at the back of this book, you'll find the names of all the people who made it happen.

Publishing in this way means readers are no longer just passive consumers of the books they buy, and authors are free to write the books they really want. They get a much fairer return too – half the profits their books generate, rather than a tiny percentage of the cover price.

If you're not yet a subscriber, we hope that you'll want to join our publishing revolution and have your name listed in one of our books in the future. To get you started, here is a £5 discount on your first pledge. Just visit unbound.com, make your pledge and type JEAVONS19 in the promo code box when you check out.

Thank you for your support,

Dan, Justin and John
Founders, Unbound

Super Patrons

Todd Allis
Virginia Anderson
Cayden Andrews
Stuart Ashen
Heather Bain
Amy Banner
Mona Stephanie Benedetto
Allison Bennett
Ian Bradburn
Antony Brown
Hannah Brown
Patrick Brown
Chip Bush
Rick Bush
Stu Cameron
CarlosVanVegas
David Carreiro
Danielle Crain
E R Andrew Davis
Susan Downes
Jimmy Du
Dan Fearon
John Fenderson
Sarah Flaherty
Francesca Framer
Ethan Gates
Chase and Erin Gilley
Joël Golay
Traci Gondek
Philip Gonzalez
Alison Goodhew
Christopher Grimshaw

Kevin Hague
Muro Hana
Kelly Harris
Zico Harris
Jonny Hart
Andrew Heaton
Charles Hellings
HiP.P
Thomas Holme
Jack Hopkins
Antony Horner
Meghan Hrncir
Tuba Hung
Tina Jackson
Grace Jeavons
Janet Jeavons
Neil Jeavons
K a m e o ✻
Andy Kimberley
Chris Kirman
Satu Kumpulainen
Nicola Lahoud
Ross Laing
Ellis Langley
David Law
Nathan Lewis
Corinna Liller
Jamie Macgregor
Paul Mackay
Ian Marchant
Frances Marnane
Andreas Mayerhofer
Kristin McKenna
Leigharna Mckenzie
Caz Mitchell
Lyall Moffitt

Andrew Mortimer
Matthew Nelson
Daniel Nethersole
Philippa Neville
Carl Newby-Hughes
David Nutty
Joshua Oxenford
Andy Pandini
Nathan Pearson
Kyle Pelegri
Rebekah Pellerin
Bethany Person
Ryan Picton
Mike Plant
Alexander Potehin
Laura Quin
Jennifer Reid
Jon-Carlos Rivera
James Rogers
Samantha Rose Howard
Beth DBT Sargent
Shayna Shaw
Jesse Shearer
Dominic Smith
Stuart Staines
Gina-Rose Stewart
Hope Swinn
Stephane Tanguay
Brad Tashenberg
Glyn Tebbutt
Emily Thomas
Mike Scott Thomson
Mikael Torslund
Christopher Valenze
Tyler VanNatta
Ryan Walterson

Rich Wareham
Stacey Watkins
Margaretta Westerman
Phillip Wilson
Ben Yates

Chapter One

From the paper pinned to the brightly lit office wall, my own face grins back at me. I have a sour, forced smile, my eyes are wide, and it isn't my body the face is attached to, it's Jabba the Hutt's. Above the image, in big white letters, it says 'Chadda the Slut', probably the worst pun I've ever seen considering my name's Chad, not Chadda, and I'm about as far from a slut as someone could possibly be.

So, the joke's on them, I guess.

I pull the page from the wall and throw it into the black bag on my cleaning cart. Binning Photoshopped pictures of myself has become a regular part of my job (last week it was Fat Bastard from *Austin Powers*), but when it's not that, it's a fart machine sewn into my overalls, or my mops stolen, or my shoes covered in glue and dipped in glitter. Working at IATech has set an all-new bar for workplace bullying. I haven't experienced treatment like this since I was sixteen and did my two weeks' work experience on a building site. At the time I thought being sent to find a tin of tartan paint was pretty rough, but it's nothing compared to the weekly torture I face here. The obvious way to tackle workplace bullying is by telling your boss, but when your boss is the one doing the bullying, and also happens to be your own brother, there's fuck all you can really do about it.

I move through into the next office and there are three Chadda the Sluts lying on a bank of desks in the middle of the room. I scoop them up and screw them into a tight little ball. If I could roll my eyes any further I'd be able to see my own brain. It's always the same photo that's used too, taken from a shitty family holiday to Brighton in 2006 a few months before Dad left. My loving brother uses it because my face is red and I have three extra chins. We were only in Brighton a week but it felt like a month and it rained every day. The best thing about it was the little arcade in the hotel we stayed in, where I managed to get the top score on three out of the five machines they had. My brother screwed me over though by resetting the machines on the last day and erasing all evidence of my achievements. Twat.

1

I can't say I'm surprised that the way Sam treats me in everyday life has bled into how he treats me at work; I've had twenty-two years to figure that out. The day I learned to walk, he pushed me over into a pile of dog shit. Not that I remember, but Uncle Jeff told me about it a few years ago, and it does sound like something Sam would do. He has this look in his eye which shows how much he loves torturing me, making me uncomfortable. The more I squirm the more it feeds him.

Including when he gave me this stupid fucking job. He acts like I should be honoured to clean his toilets and vacuum his carpets, but there's nothing I'd rather *not* be doing, and he knows it.

I guess I could quit, but Mum says she'll cut off the internet if I leave another job. She might be bluffing, but it's not a risk I'm willing to take. One day I got home and told her I was going to jack it in because Sam put toothpaste in my cheese sandwiches, but she said I had to suck it up and stick with it because my brother had pulled a lot of strings getting me this job and it would make him look daft if I left a month after joining. Like I give two shits about whether Sam looks daft or not (he does, with his stupid haircut and lumberjack shirts) but I do care about making sure Mum doesn't cancel the broadband.

I open the door to the break room, which they call the chill-zone because they're all pretentious douchebags, and there's a bunch more pictures of me stuck to the walls. And the vending machines. And the sofas. And the pool table. I tear them all off and stuff them into the bin bag. In the corner of the room, there's a guy asleep in a hammock, and even he has a picture stuck to him. Is he a part of this operation? Did Sam have him pin the pictures up in the break room, only he got tired, took a quick nap to recharge his batteries? I pick up a bottle of cleaning spray and hold it up to his face. All it would take would be a quick squirt into his eyes, or his mouth – that might make him think twice about doing stupid shit like this again. But I know it wasn't him – it was undoubtedly the biggest tosspot in the entire business, my brother – so taking it out on this prick would be a waste of energy. I lift the picture gently from his chest and spray a little bleach onto his expensive looking trainers instead.

I move through the building, pushing my little cleaner's cart from room to room, removing Chadda the Slut pictures from the walls, wafting a cloth over the occasional desk or railing. It's hardly rewarding work, but it's not too far from home and it gets me out of the house. Not that I particularly want to be out of the house, but the twenty minute walk there and back stops my belly from getting any bigger, so that's something to be grateful for... I guess.

I make my way down and past the restricted section which covers most of the first floor. It really isn't as cool as the name would suggest. I saw inside once, when I was given a tour of the building on my first day and they let me peek through the door. It's full of machinery and nerds and is apparently the only area which doesn't require cleaning. God knows why it's all such a huge secret. All IATech does is design AI programmes and crappy robots that stand and greet people in hospitals, so who really cares if I wipe some drool off of the desks or not? I did try using my pass to get in once, but it flashed red and beeped so I ran away and pretended to clean the toilets.

I head back down to the ground floor and push my cart into reception. The receptionist ignores me and the security guard sneers. In front of the revolving doors is the chest, arms and head of a robot on top of a shiny silver pole. I'm allowed to clean the pole (which is why it's so shiny) but God fucking forbid I ever touch the robot itself. It's supposed to greet people when they enter the building, but apparently it started to get a little too talkative, so now all it does is wave and smile at people. Its face is that of a real woman projected onto it from behind, her perfect teeth always on show. It looks more like something you'd expect in a theme park ride, but they seem to think it's important for an AI company to show off what it can do as soon as you walk through the revolving doors.

The main atrium of the building is huge, with everything made of glass – the walls, the tables, even the ceiling. The idiots who decorated it said it creates a better sense of team spirit, but all I see is a hundred extra places I have to clean after people smear their greasy hands over everything. On the far side is a giant wall of TVs all fixed together to make one massive screen, playing a mixture of techy things, social media feeds and twenty-four-hour news channels. It's eight o'clock in the evening and most people have gone home, but there are still a few workaholics (aka arse-lickers) sat at their desks, bathed in blue light from their multiple monitors. I pass one guy, and he looks up at me through his long hair and laughs. I grab the Chadda the Slut picture stuck to the wall beside him and sigh loudly because I can't think of anything clever or funny to say.

I water the plants and vacuum the floor, which pisses off the people still tapping away, but I have a half-arsed job to do, so I ignore them and try to make it look like an accident when I knock into their chairs.

To the far side of the open space are the owners' and managers' offices, but because the place is so edgy and cool they haven't given themselves job titles. The first glass office I come to has *Barry Richmond* in the centre of the glass door, as if everyone is meant to know who the hell Barry Richmond is. I pretend to dust the glass desk, then move into *Jilly Adams'* office and do the same. The next office belongs to *Samuel McKenna*, my brother, but his door is locked, so I can't pretend to work in there. Sam never locks his door, because 'locks create boundaries' apparently, but it's obvious why he's decided to do it for the first time since I started working there. Hung on the back wall of his office is a giant, ten-foot canvas of Chadda the Slut.

I hold my access card against the lock and it flashes red, so I bang on the door with my fist and a loud *clang* echoes through the room. A few heads pop up from behind their monitors, but they soon duck down again when they see me scowling.

'Fuck's sake, Sam,' I yell as loud as I dare.

The working plebs pop their heads up again like scared little groundhogs. Somebody snorts a laugh.

'Is Sam still in?' I ask. The heads dip back down.

Sam's laptop is still on his desk, and he doesn't go anywhere without his precious laptop – *the source of his power*, as he calls it, because of course that's what a complete twat would do. He likes to remind me that it cost more than I make in six months. Doesn't see the irony of putting a shitty little alien head sticker on the top and ruining it though.

'Sam, you knobhead!' I yell, this time loud and angry enough that no heads pop up. Instead, a door on the opposite side of the room bursts open and a big bloke with arms almost as fat as his enormous thighs strides over. His neatly trimmed beard quivers like a defensive porcupine's quills.

'Calm it down, Chad,' he says, his voice so deep that I reckon dogs would probably struggle to hear it.

'I am calm,' I say.

'Lower your voice.'

'It is low!'

'Lower. Your. Voice.'

'Is this any fucking better?' I whisper.

He places his hand on my shoulder, his sausage fingers wrapping around me like a vice. 'I think you need a little time out,' he breathes.

'No, I'm not a child!' I whine.

My brother steps out from behind a bank of desks and smirks. 'That's debatable,' he says.

I sigh and his smirk turns into a grin.

'He's fine, Bill, leave him with me.'

The big man releases his grip and grunts.

'I'd rather go with this guy than stay with you,' I say.

'That can be arranged,' says Bill.

Sam shakes his head and his floppy hipster hair slaps the side of his face. 'That's fine, thanks, Bill.'

As the giant stomps away, I turn to face Sam. 'Take that stupid picture down.'

'You didn't say please.'

'Please.'

'No.'

'Sam!'

'Hmm, I think you're forgetting your place here.'

'I don't give a shit about my place.'

'And that's the problem, which is why I'm trying to remind you.'

'Just fire me if I'm such a massive issue.'

'Tempting, but having you around is too much fun.'

'Can you please open the door?'

'It's fine, I cleaned it myself earlier.'

'Please.'

'Nah.'

The inside of my chest is hot, like there's a motor in the bottom of my stomach spinning, getting faster and faster every time the prick's stupid smug smile gets wider. He's like some mutant plant who feeds off of my pain and discomfort, and right now he's being shovelled with nourishing shit.

I clear my throat and take a deep breath. 'Please—'

'Let me stop you there,' he says. 'Because I'm not interested in hearing whatever bollocks you have to say. You're only here because I'm doing Mum a favour, not because IATech needs you. If it was up to me, you wouldn't have even made it through the door, so shut the fuck up and accept when you have a good thing going.' I clench my fists, open my mouth to speak, but the twat raises his hand inches from my face and keeps talking. 'I don't want to hear it. You work four hours a day doing some of the easiest shit I've ever seen, and you make damn good money doing it, so you can go home and wank yourself sore and play MMOs with your non-existent friends for fuck knows how long.' My nails dig into my palms. He carries on. 'If I want to decorate my office at my business with a stunning piece of art, then I will. So, shut your fat fucking face, go have a little cry in your little caretaker's cupboard, and get on with your menial little job, so I can go home to my nine-bedroom house and fuck a real-life girl with tits even bigger than yours.'

I don't know why, but for the first time in my life I hit my brother. It's not a cool right hook kind of punch, more of a flailing of arms in his direction, but I manage to land a solid hit right in the middle of his nose, and it goes with a really satisfying crunch. His eyes widen (even wider than mine) and he steps back, propping himself up with his hand on his office door. Blood drips from his nose and he winces as he touches it. His expression darkens, and my stomach drops as steam practically vents from his ears.

But he doesn't hit me back. I guess I have the crowd that's gathered to thank for that.

'That wasn't clever,' says Sam, taking a tissue from his pocket and delicately dabbing his nose.

'I'm sorry,' I say. My heart is racing and sweat streaks down my face.

Sam nods at the crowd and smiles. 'It's okay, everyone, back to work. Just a couple of bros having a little disagreement.'

'Your nose—' says one girl, but she stops as Sam raises his eyebrows.

'Back to work,' he says.

The crowd filters back into the office, and Sam turns back to face me. I push my back as tight into my cart as I can and hold my breath.

'That includes you,' he says. 'Back to work.'

'I'm sorry,' I say.

He snorts and swipes his pass against the reader, unlocking the door. 'You will be,' he says, walking into his office and sliding into the chair behind the large, glass desk.

I could follow him in and apologise again, but I don't know what to say. He opens his laptop and smacks the keyboard, probably in the same way he'd like to smack me. Trying to speak to him may be pushing my luck.

I push my cart out of the atrium and into my caretaker's cupboard. The place always stinks of bleach, so I try not to spend too much time in here, but today it's been covered from floor to ceiling in Chadda the Slut pictures so I can't exactly just dump my stuff and go. After five minutes of snatching and shredding my head is woozy but my cupboard is back to normal, with my little shelving unit filled with cleaning stuff, the hooks holding my brooms and the air vents by the floor back on show.

I'm supposed to work four hours every night, from six until ten, and it's only half-eight, but my whole body is shaking and I might throw up at any point. I take off my ugly blue overalls and hang them on the back of the door, then slip out of the building while the giant security guy tries to chat up the receptionist. At least the robotic greeter waves me goodbye. At least she cares.

By nine o'clock I'm home and Mum must be asleep, because she doesn't come looking when I jump onto my bed and scream into my pillow until my throat's sore. My heart hammers and my entire body is tense. I can almost hear the blood rushing through my veins, so I hum loudly as I strip down to my boxers and kick my clothes into a pile by the wardrobe. I guess this is how a cage fighter feels after kicking the shit out of an opponent, all hyped up and ready to burst with an erection the size of a tree trunk.

I switch on my PC and the room fills with a blue glow. I always feel so calm in my room, my little sanctuary where no other person is allowed. When Sam and I were kids, it was the one place he was never allowed to follow me (under Mum's instructions) so it was my only escape from his constant arseholery. But tonight I feel like he's followed me in, his fists raised and his eyes constantly on me.

Tonight's also the first time I don't feel powerless. For the first time in twenty-two years I've stood up to him (kind of – I didn't even mean to hit him, but still), and it surprised the shit out of him. Well, it surprised me too – the only thing I ever hit before was our cat after it bit me, and I felt really bad about that for weeks afterwards. It's dead now (not because of me). There's a strange sensation bubbling inside of me. I am now Chad McKenna, puncher of faces!

There's only one thing I can think of to release some of that pressure building inside me, and that's to open an incognito window on my web browser and go to town. It doesn't take long to find a decent bit of porn – two girls making out while shoving a dildo into each other. They're moaning like they've both been given the news about their parents' death, but I still blow my load into a tissue in under two minutes.

I take in a deep breath and sigh. My heart slows and my muscles relax, and I fall from my desk chair and collapse onto the bed. I'm sweaty and tired, but everything about the world is different now. I'm no longer Chad McKenna, constant victim to his older brother, I'm now Chad McKenna, puncher of bullies, defeater of worlds. Actually, if I cast my mind back to the incident in the atrium, I'm pretty sure I saw Sam cry. A twenty-six-year-old man, one who owns a huge international tech company no less, crying because his little brother smacked him on the nose.

What a fucking pussy.

The next morning (well, afternoon) starts like every other. I wake up around two, lie staring at my phone for an hour, get up and eat some crisps, think about showering but don't because I can't be arsed, spray with deodorant instead and finally get dressed. I don't need to get dressed, but it makes me feel a little bit better, like slightly less of a slob, while I browse the internet and make bitchy comments to people beneath YouTube videos. Never anything *too* bad, mind, I just like to pick out the small errors in videos and imperfections about the way they look. Pointing out other people's faults makes me feel a little better about myself, and right now I feel great.

In the background I stream a pirate copy of the movie *The Layover* starring Alexandra Daddario and Kate Upton. It's a pretty shitty movie but for some inexplicable reason I'm drawn to it. I must have seen it a dozen times.

At 5.30, right as I'm thinking about putting on my trainers to head to work, Mum comes home and hammers on my bedroom door.

'CHAD,' she grunts. 'Chad, chad, chad.' Uh oh, she sounds like a train, which means she's not happy about something.

I make sure my desk is clear of crusty tissues and my private browser window is closed and I clear my throat. 'Yeah?'

My door swings open and Mum steams in. 'I've just spoken to your brother.'

My forehead feels clammy. I have this incredible gift where my sweat levels can go from completely dry to absolutely drenched, and right now I feel like an Olympic swimmer fresh out of the pool.

'Oh,' I squeak.

'Oh indeed,' huffs Mum. 'Why did you do it?'

'Do what?'

'Don't play ignorant with me, Chad. Why did you hit him?'

'I didn't. I mean. I did, but he put pictures of me up all over the office.'

'And you thought that was a good enough reason to break his nose?'

My eyes widen. 'I broke his nose?'

'Yes.'

I fight back the urge to smile, but it's like a massive sneeze begging to come out, and I think Mum realises because she slaps me on the side of the head.

'What is wrong with you?'

'Nothing.'

'Everything, more like. Your brother gives you this job out of the kindness of his heart and this is what you do to him?'

'Mum, there is nothing kind about his heart whatsoever.'

Mum stares at me, which means she's either working out what to say next or resisting the impulse to slap me again.

'You will apologise to him tonight, do you hear me?' she hisses.

'For what?'

'Chad, please, you must be able to see what you've done here.'

'Yeah, I can. I hit my brother, the guy who has been torturing me for years. I didn't mean to hit him, but I did, and there's not much I can do to take it back now.'

Mum stares again, this time for so long it gets uncomfortable. It's like she's frozen to the spot.

'Fine,' I say. 'I will apologise to him.'

'Good,' she says. 'Now get a move on, you don't want to be late for work.'

I slip into the IATech building just before six o'clock and half smile, half grimace at Bill, who watches me with narrow eyes as I pass him and shuffle down the first of two corridors behind reception. As I push open the door to my cupboard and close it behind me, the security guard's booming laugh bounces from wall to wall.

I suppose they're still laughing over what happened yesterday. I mean, I'm not surprised, I've heard Sam is a complete prick to most of the people who work for him, so it probably put a smile on more faces than just mine to see him with a broken nose. If even the security guard is laughing about what happened, then Sam is surely not going to try and get back at me. I imagine he's too scared, he's finally realised that I can stand up for myself, and who knows what I might do next? He even told on me, and he hasn't done that since I pissed in his shoes when I was six. I bet I don't even see him for the rest of the week and I won't even need to apologise to him!

I pull my overalls over my clothes and zip them up to my chin. They're not the most comfortable piece of clothing I've ever worn, but I purposely chose a size too big so it wouldn't hug my belly like a wetsuit. Today, I feel so proud that I hold my head high and I puff out my chest and feel like I can do whatever the fuck I want.

At six o'clock I pull my little cart out of my cupboard, loaded with empty bin bags and bottles of cleaning crap, and wave my cloth at things. I still have a job to do, after all. Someone's left a stinky shit in the ladies' which takes three flushes to get rid of completely, and there's a little pile of powder on the side of one of the small kitchenettes, but it turns out to be sugar and for a moment I'm a little disappointed I'm not about to uncover a hidden drug ring within IATech.

I push my cart into the chill-zone and empty the bins in the corner. I feel so good I even make sure the new bin bags are attached properly and won't collapse as soon as somebody drops in some rubbish. That's how generous I'm feeling. The chill-zone is empty, so to reward myself for ten minutes of hard work I pop a pound into the vending machine and enjoy a well earned bag of Skittles in the hammock.

The door opens and I throw myself to my feet to pretend that I'm dusting the table. A girl walks in and awkwardly smiles as we make eye contact. It's like for one tiny moment she considers backing out of the room, but instead she clears her throat and fills up a paper cup from the gurgling water cooler.

'Hi,' I say. I wouldn't normally say anything, but I recognise her as being fairly new so she might not have had time to hear about my reputation just yet.

'Hello,' she says.

'Working late?'

'Yeah, kind of.'

I casually throw my last orange Skittle at my mouth but it clicks as it hits my front teeth and bounces off my bottom lip onto the floor. It's cool, I don't think she notices.

'You're new,' I say.

'Yeah.'

She has pretty eyes and nice blonde hair and I look at her butt and thankfully she doesn't catch me as she necks her water.

'I'm Chad,' I say.

'Yeah, I know,' she says, and she looks away.

A lump forms in my stomach. She must have seen the Chadda the Slut pictures. Shit.

I screw up my Skittles packet and toss it into the bin bag on my cart. She definitely notices when I miss this time.

'Your brother is Samuel McKenna, right?' she asks.

The lump in my stomach leaps up to my throat.

'Yeah, yes, um, he is, yeah,' I coolly say.

'I heard about what happened with you two.'

I lean against my cart but it rolls slowly away so I stand up straight. 'Yeah?'

'Yeah,' she says. She shifts awkwardly and the lump moves back down again. 'Listen, you didn't hear this from me, but you might want to just… go home.'

'What do you mean?'

She drops the paper cup into the bin beside the water cooler. 'Just go home. Right now.'

'Why?'

'Because—'

The timing of the chill-zone door opening is infuriating, because the appearance of two plebs from the warehouse makes the girl stop talking and awkwardly turn away from me.

'Look who it is,' says the taller of the two plebs.

'It's the wanker,' says the shorter.

'You what?' I ask.

The girl widens her eyes in my direction, then leaves the room without saying a word. I want to call after her, but the taller one steps towards me and blocks my view of the door.

'You're a wanker,' he says.

'Big fans of Sam, are you?' I ask.

'No, but you must be. At least from what I can tell, it's hard to get a good look when it's so small.'

My mind ticks around but I don't get the reference. It must be something to do with Sam's broken nose, a warehouse reference I don't understand or some sort of inside joke.

'Good one,' I say, nodding and smiling, and the two plebs burst out laughing. 'Anyway, I've got stuff to get on with, see you later.'

I push my cart out of the chill-zone and down the corridor flapping my cloth at anything that might gather dust. Railings, door handles, little internet ports about six inches from the floor. What sort of super modern tech company has use for wired internet in this day and age? I pass the restricted section and make my way towards the atrium.

Slap slap slap slap.

I stand still and hold my breath to listen.

Slap slap slap slap.

What is that? It sounds like a mouse chewing on a mouth full of gum, except way louder and never ending.

Slap slap slap slap.

'Nnnnngh,' comes a voice I definitely know.

Whatever it is, it's a sound I haven't heard before at IATech, but I swear I recognise it. I'm having a flash of deja vu. Is it from a movie I've seen?

Slap slap slap slap.

So familiar...

I push my cart to the end of the corridor and it opens up into the atrium. The usual arse-lickers are sat at their desks, but something seems off. Their faces aren't pressed against their screens, instead they're gathered in small groups, talking and occasionally looking over my head.

Slap slap slap slap.

One of the arse-lickers spots me and they scatter like startled rats. Are they still talking about my victory over the bully known as Sam McKenna? Is it really such a big deal to these people, and they now see me as one of their equals (or even a superior)?

'Nnngh, come on,' says a voice from behind me.

And now I know where I've heard that sound before. The voice, the soft slapping, the groaning.

I turn and crane my neck back to look up at the enormous wall of monitors that makes up a giant screen against the atrium wall. No longer is it displaying social media feeds and twenty-four-hour news channels – it's displaying me. My cheeks are red, my shirt is off and I'm pounding my dick so hard it looks like I'm trying to start a fire.

I'm practically staring into the camera lens as I breathe like a woman in labour, my left hand clicking on the mouse on my desk.

It's webcam footage taken from last night, and it's playing on the big screen for the entire company to see.

'What the fuck is this?' I scream. 'Stop watching! Everybody stop watching right now!'

I run up and down the centre of the atrium like an excitable kid at a wedding, except I'm swearing a lot more and I'm filled with murderous rage.

'Sam!' I scream. 'Sam, get out here!'

For the second time in as many days I feel like I will hit my brother. In fact, it's safe to say I'll do a lot more than just hit him when I get my hands on him. Right now the only thing going through my mind is that I want Sam dead, right here in his precious office building.

'Have you seen Sam?' I screech at one young programmer who's cowering at his desk.

'No,' he says, and he starts crying. That's what you get for hiring kids straight out of school I guess.

'Has anybody seen my brother?' I yell.

Silence. All except for the *slap, slap, slap* of my hand against my dick.

I run over to another guy at his desk and slam my hands clumsily on the keyboard. 'How do I delete this?' I ask, my eyes clouding over until all I see is a haze.

'I don't know,' he chokes. 'It's been uploaded to the intranet, only the person who posted it can delete it.'

'You're a nerd, just delete it!'

'I work in customer service.'

'Fuck's sake!'

I run back and forth, hitting screens and keyboards and mice in some sort of attempt to stop the video. I wince as I hear myself groan with pleasure, there's a moment of silence, then the video starts over from the beginning.

'Sam!' I scream. I pound both fists on his office door, which is of course locked and empty. 'Sam, if you're here then you better fucking come out and turn this shit off! I will kill you!'

I grab a chair from a nearby desk and swing it above my head. I have near superhero strength right now, so I easily slam the legs into the door, shattering the glass with one hit. I drop the chair at my feet and blink as my eyes struggle to focus on the tiny shards littered through the room. I stare at my hands in one of those *I can't believe my own power* moments from movies, then the sound of my pleasured moaning snaps me back around and I bolt over to Sam's desk.

Luckily Sam has left his laptop open, so I mash the keyboard and it boots up. I fumble around for what feels like forever, clicking icons on the desktop until I finally find the intranet and click into Sam's profile.

There's the video, the thumbnail of me with the tissue around my cock, with the words EDIT and DELETE beside it.

'Chad, what the fuck are you doing?' bellows the enormous security guard.

'Nothing,' I say, which sounds fucking stupid considering the circumstances.

The guard strides towards me, his footsteps crunching on the glass, and he stretches out his massive hand.

I don't think, I just click DELETE and the video disappears from Sam's profile. I don't care what happens next, so just let the security guard grab me by the shoulder and drag me out of my brother's office as the sound of me jerking off stutters and then stops.

At home that night, I can't fall asleep. All I see whenever I close my eyes is my belly jiggling as I knock one out, the crowd of people laughing and sneering as they watch me on the fifty-foot screen. This is a whole new low for Sam. Even Mum thinks I'm lying when I tell her about it. I know he's good with computers, but never did I think he'd be able to hack my webcam. I mean, why would I think that? It's sick. Who wants to watch footage of their own brother jerking off and then upload it to their own company's internal server? What possible joy could he get out of that?

I spend the night researching revenge porn (after sticking a plaster over the webcam lens, obviously) and find that I have a pretty decent case against my brother. All I need to do is report it to the police and then Sam will forever be known as the creepy guy who recorded his own brother having a wank.

But then again, I've deleted it. Surely Sam's removed all evidence that the video ever existed and told his employees to deny having seen it. Sam is co-owner of a multimillion pound AI company, if he wanted to permanently delete something then I've no doubt he would know how to do it.

And then what would that make me? The loser who makes up weird sexual stories about his brother.

Fuck knows it's not like I need another reason for everybody to hate me.

Chapter Two

As seven o'clock rolls around, the morning sunlight creeps into my bedroom through the gaps in the curtains. Mum is clattering down in the kitchen, probably making herself a cup of tea. My phone buzzes (wow, I never get texts!) but it's just her.

Can you come down here please? X

My head throbs and my eyes ache, so I pull myself up from my desk and fight back the urge to throw up. I shuffle out of my room and downstairs.

'Morning, sweetheart,' she says. It's amazing to be called a nice name like that.

'Hi,' I say. I drop into a chair at the wooden breakfast table and bury my head into my arms.

'How are you feeling?'

'Tired.'

'I'm not surprised. I could hear you typing all night.'

'Sorry.'

'It's fine.'

I lift up my head but I don't say a word. Mum leans against the kitchen counter and her eyes are on me, but she's looking at me like you'd look at a kitten struggling to walk.

'What's up?' I ask.

'Your brother is here.'

'Where?'

'In the lounge.'

I stand up and the chair groans against the tiled floor. 'Okay, see ya.'

'Wait, wait,' says Mum, stepping forward and placing her hand on my shoulder.

'Wait for what? I don't want to see that prick.'

'Chad!'

'Well, he is.'

'Look, I know what you claim he did is bad—'

'I'm not *claiming* he did anything, I'm telling you what happened. Why would I want to see him after he humiliated me?'

'Perhaps it was a misunderstanding.'

'Mum, no, he's taken things too far this time. How can you justify that?'

I plop back down on the chair and slouch down until I'm nearly completely beneath the table.

'Maybe he wants to apologise,' says Mum. 'I'm sure he realises he crossed the line and he wants to make amends.'

'You don't make amends for what he did. You go to prison for what he did.'

'Chad...'

'It's true, Mum. I could have him locked up for what he's done.'

'Chad, no...'

'Yes, Mum. This isn't just him being a naughty big brother this time. He's not pushing Play-Doh up my nose or wiping Nutella on my bedsheets while I sleep this time. He recorded me in my bedroom, naked, and broadcast it to his entire company.'

Mum stares at me. I try to stare back but I can't.

'What?' I grumble.

'At least listen to what he has to say.'

'No.'

'Please. For me.'

I sigh and shake my head. I hate it when she says that.

'For me.'

'Fine. But if he comes up with a load of bollocks about—'

'CHAD.'

'Sorry – a load of rubbish about it being a prank or banter or whatever then I'm going to lose my sh... mind.'

'Just give him a chance. Do you want a cup of tea?'

I follow Mum into the lounge and she hands Sam a cup of tea. He's sat in the armchair Dad used to sit in, his laptop bag at his feet. He watches me as I perch on the edge of the sofa, but I make sure to avoid looking at him – that'll show him that I'm still mad.

'I know you're still mad at me,' he says.

Nailed it.

'But I wanted to let you know that there aren't any hard feelings.'

If I'd taken a sip of my tea this would be the point where I'd spit it out.

'What do you mean no hard feelings?'

'About my office door. I know you were frustrated about our little disagreement, so I just wanted you to know that it's okay, I forgive you.'

'*You* forgive *me?*'

'Yes.'

'But I'm not sorry.'

Mum sighs. 'Chad...'

'I'm not. He put a video of me naked on the IATech intranet. Dozens of people saw it. One guy literally pointed at me and laughed.'

'Samuel, did you post the video?' asks Mum.

For the first time I look at my brother. I know what's coming, so I take satisfaction from seeing the white strips stretched across his bent nose.

'Of course not.'

'Liar!'

'Woah, woah, where's this come from?'

'You're a fucking liar!'

'CHAD.'

'I'm sorry, Mum, but he is. I'm sick of Sam being a complete tosspot and getting away with it every time. He posted the video and he knows it. Just look at his smug face.'

'This is just my regular face.'

'And everybody falls for it,' I say. My ears are hot and my heart is thundering inside my chest. 'You included, Mum. I haven't done anything to deserve this.'

'I admit that maybe I do take things a little too far sometimes,' says Sam.

'Sometimes?' I shriek.

'Let your brother speak,' says Mum.

I grunt and flop back into the sofa.

'I can be a little overzealous,' says Sam with his stupid mouth. 'I don't mean to, but I realise I can get a little carried away. I want us to get along, I really do, so I promise to try and give you a break.'

'You promise to *try*?'

'Absolutely.'

'How fucking noble of you.'

'CHAD!'

'Mum, I'm sorry, I just can't listen to this. I can't believe I'm the only one who sees him for what he is. He's a slimeball. He doesn't believe what he's saying right now. All he does is look after himself, he doesn't care about me unless I'm the brunt of one of his stupid jokes—'

Sam puts his hand up and my voice catches in my throat.

'Actually,' he says, leaning down to pull an envelope out of his laptop bag and handing it to Mum. 'I thought that this might be a good time to give you this.'

Mum cautiously takes it and for a moment I panic. Have I forgotten her birthday again?

'What's this?' she asks, turning it over in her hand.

'Open it,' says Sam, and he shoots me a smug smile.

Mum tears open the envelope and pulls out a sheet of paper. As she reads it her eyes redden and she brings her hand to her mouth.

'Is this real?' she splutters.

'Of course it's real,' says Sam. 'I want to make sure you're okay, Mum. Both of you.'

He can't contain how smug he looks as Mum dives across the lounge and wraps her arms around him. As she cries into his shoulder, Sam stares at me.

'Chad, look,' says Mum, letting go of my brother. She hands me the paper and I read the first line.

This letter confirms the total repayment and any incurring charges for the mortgage held by Ms Mary McKenna, totalling £205,328.08, for the property at 3 Belwin Road, Hemel Hempstead.

Mum pulls Sam in for another hug and she wails.

'You paid off Mum's mortgage?'

'It's the least I could do,' he says. 'I just want you two to be comfortable, you know.'

Sam smiles at me and I glower back at him. What is he playing at?

Mum finally lets Sam go and I pass her back the letter. She rereads it over and over.

'You really didn't have to,' she says.

'I wanted to,' says Sam.

'It's such a lot of money.'

'You're worth it. You both are.'

Uggggghhhh! I want to break his neck!

Mum wipes tears from her face and stands. 'I need to make a few calls. Give me a minute, okay?' she says, trotting from the room.

I spot a hair on the carpet and focus on it. It doesn't do much to distract me from my brother, whose eyes are burning into me.

'So,' he says. 'Isn't it nice that Mum no longer has to worry about money?'

'I guess,' I mumble.

'Come on, Chad, lighten up.'

'What am I supposed to lighten up about?' I say. A trickle of sweat runs down from my forehead. I can't imagine what shade of red I must be right now.

'This is good news,' says Sam. 'Great news!'

'Yeah, very unexpected,' I say. 'You're a true hero.'

'Yes, I suppose I am.'

I will kill him.

'With this new and improved Sam, does it mean you won't post any more videos of me to the IATech intranet?'

Sam nods. '*I* won't post any more.'

'What do you mean?'

'Hm?'

'I hate it when you play dumb like this.'

'Who's playing dumb?'

'Well then you *are* dumb. What do you mean *you* won't post any more?'

'Because *I* don't need to.'

'What does that mean?'

'You'll see.'

'No, Sam, I don't want to see. Please, don't upload the video again.

Take off whatever malware you've put on my computer and leave me alone.'

Sam looks over his shoulder to make sure Mum isn't within earshot. She's talking excitedly elsewhere in the house.

'I already have everything I need from you,' he whispers.

'What do you mean?'

'This isn't over. Not even close.'

'What isn't over?'

'I think you're more than aware,' he says, pointing to his nose.

'Sam, I didn't mean to hit you, okay. Do you want me to apologise? Will that make you stop this?'

'Stop what?'

'There you go again, playing dumb. I don't know what you're trying to prove by paying off Mum's mortgage, but you can stop now. You win, okay? I'm sorry I hit you, I didn't mean to, I just got carried away.'

Sam smirks at me.

'So can we please drop this now? I don't want to keep going on like this. What you did with the video was out of order.'

'It was funny though, wasn't it?'

'No!'

'Yeah, it was. It is.'

'What do you mean *is*? You deleted it, right? It's gone?'

Sam laughs. 'Not even a little bit.'

'Sam, please—'

'Nope, too late for begging.'

'I'm not begging, I'm asking.'

'Whatever you call it, I don't want to hear it. People need to know what a disgusting little cretin you really are. Mum might feel sorry for you, but she won't forever. Once you hit thirty and you're still a virgin living at home wanking to shit porn she'll wake up and realise what a loser her darling little boy actually is.'

My fists ball so tight my knuckles crack. I do everything I can not to break his nose all over again, and he can tell, because he grins that stupid fucking grin he always does whenever he thinks he's winning.

'This coming from a lame coder who piggybacked off his uni mates to get to where he is,' I say. 'Your office is in an industrial park in Hemel Hempstead, you're hardly in Silicon Valley.'

Sam snorts a laugh. 'And this is exactly why that video isn't going anywhere. You need to learn your place. You can't talk to me like that and expect to get away with it.'

'Listen to you, you sound like a fucking dictator. Heil Sam,' I say, sticking my arm up in a salute. 'You might have your little army of drones lapping at your feet, climbing over each other to lick your arsehole, and call you sir, but I don't need that. You're deluded. Just because you can afford a big house and an expensive car it doesn't mean you're better than me. What are you doing, compensating for your small cock?'

Sam laughs. 'Whether I'm compensating or not, at least my cock isn't all over the internet.'

'What you've done is illegal, Sam. I could have you arrested like *that*,' I try to click my fingers but they slip and make a tiny *fft* sound.

'Mm, probably best if you don't do that, Chad.'

'Just watch me.'

'I'll watch. And I'll laugh when they find no evidence.'

'There's evidence.'

'Which I can permanently remove.'

'And dozens of witnesses.'

'Who are on my payroll.'

I say nothing. I want to punch him and kick him and shout and swear and do everything to him to make him suffer. Just like he's making me suffer. But I do nothing, I just look at him and suck in the sadness which wants to burst out.

'That's it,' says Sam. 'Do the right thing. Accept this punishment and learn from it. The sooner you realise that I'm the man of this family now, the better. Do as I say and it will all go away. Pull your finger out, sort your life out and stop being a cave-dweller.'

I wipe my face and clear my throat. My eyes flick up and I follow the little lines in my eye fluid.

'Nothing to say for yourself?' asks Sam.

'No,' I say.

'You sure?'

I shake my head.

Sam takes his phone from his jeans pocket and fiddles with it for a second, before flipping it around to show me. It's my video.

'Sam, please.'

'Know what website this is?'

'It's the IATech intranet.'

'Nope. Look again.'

I grab the phone from Sam's hand and close the video file so I can see the website it's playing from. The first thing I spot is a familiar bright red logo with a white play button in the centre. The title is *loserjerksoff.mp4*. Below the video there are seven comments and 200 views.

'Why the fuck have you uploaded it to YouTube?'

Sam snatches the phone back. 'I haven't. But sometimes videos have a habit of spreading by themselves. Remember that woman in the Chewbacca mask?'

'I don't give a shit. Take it fucking down.'

'Sorry, not my problem.'

'Do the others at IATech know about this?'

'They don't have to know.'

'You're such a dick!'

'You're not helping yourself.'

'Why are you doing this? Why do you have to keep torturing me?'

'It's just so much fun.'

'Please, take it down, I'll do anything. I'll work for you for free.'

Sam scoffs. 'You think there's a chance in hell you're allowed back at IATech after you smashed up my door? You're lucky we're not pressing charges.'

'*You* pressing charges? You record me in my room, you upload it for everybody at work to see, you upload it to YouTube, you pay off Mum's mortgage to somehow put me down even more, now I'm fired. All because I punched you?'

Sam says nothing, he just slips the phone back into his pocket and nods.

'You're a dick. I'm never going to forgive you for this,' I say. I stand up and storm out of the room, past Mum who has a huge grin on her face, and stomp upstairs to my bedroom.

The first thing I do is log into YouTube and, with great resentment, search for *loserjerksoff*.

Seven results. All the same video, all with views, comments, likes, dislikes.

loserjerksoff.mp4

208 views

2 likes

11 dislikes.

7 comments.

Fuck's sake.

I check the account to see who uploaded it. *loserjerksoff003.*

'FUCK YOU, SAM!' I scream.

Below the video is the report icon, which I click to bring up a short form. I fill in some information, select 'sexual content' and click submit.

I want to just sit here and seethe, but there are six more videos, all with hundreds of views, dozens of comments and likes (but mainly dislikes). Each video has been uploaded by a variation of *loserjerksoff* with the number at the end slightly different. *loserjerksoff004, loserjerksoff006, loserjerksoff007* (ha). I scroll through some of the comments beneath the videos:

Ew, wtf did I just watch?

must be some good pr0n

That is even more disgusting than Two Girls One Cup.

Reddit sent me.

Does it grate cheese?

sick trolololololol.

I report each video, but the nausea in my stomach and the thumping in my head mean I can't take any satisfaction from it. Slowly, one by one, the videos disappear from YouTube. By midday, all signs of *loserjerksoff.mp4* have gone, but by no means has the boiling rage inside me gone along with it. If there was ever any chance that Sam and I could have a normal brotherly relationship it's now completely out the window. There's no turning back for us now. And the thing is, I don't really care. He's been a dick to me for years, so it doesn't make a difference to me that we're sworn enemies from this day forth. It might make Christmases a little weird, but I can deal with that. Christmas is crap anyway.

Now I just need to make sure that the video is removed for good.

Date: 23 September 13:11
From: ChadMcKenna_baws@hotmail.co.uk
To: barryrichmond@ia-tech.co.uk;jillianadams@ia-tech.co.uk
Cc: samuelmckenna@ia-tech.co.uk
Subject: Removal of sensitive material on IATech servers

Good morning,

Hoping you are well. I am writing to you to inform you that sensitive materials have been uploaded to the IATech servers. The material in question is a short, 90 second video featuring myself in a compromising situation, which borders on pornographic in nature.

The video is titled loserjerksoff.mp4, or another similar variation. It was uploaded to your intranet sometime after 9.00pm on 21 September. I would be most grateful if you would consider removing this material from your databases to ensure it does not cause me any further unwarranted distress.

Please confirm in writing that the offending material has been removed and the appropriate action has been taken regarding the individual who uploaded the original file.

Kind regards,

Chad McKenna

Date: 23 September 14:22
From: barryrichmond@ia-tech.co.uk
To: ChadMcKenna_baws@hotmail.co.uk

Cc: samuelmckenna@ia-tech.co.uk;jillianadams@ia-tech.co.uk
Subject: RE: Removal of sensitive material on IATech servers

Chad,

*This is a personal grievance and one which you must take up personally
with Sam. Please do not contact us again with this.*

Barry

Date: 23 September 14:29
From: ChadMcKenna_baws@hotmail.co.uk
To: barryrichmond@ia-tech.co.uk
Cc: samuelmckenna@ia-tech.co.uk;jillianadams@ia-tech.co.uk
Subject: RE: Removal of sensitive material on IATech servers

Dear Barry,

*As the offending material is currently located on the IATech servers, then
it is a company matter and must be dealt with immediately. Please adhere
to my request as soon as possible and confirm back to me once it has been
removed.*

Kind regards,

Chad

Date: 23 September 15:02
From: jillianadams@ia-tech.co.uk
To: ChadMcKenna_baws@hotmail.co.uk
Cc: samuelmckenna@ia-tech.co.uk;barryrichmond@ia-tech.co.uk
Subject: RE: Removal of sensitive material on IATech servers

What is the video of?

J

Date: 23 September 15:04
From: ChadMcKenna_baws@hotmail.co.uk
To: jillianadams@ia-tech.co.uk
Cc: samuelmckenna@ia-tech.co.uk;barryrichmond@ia-tech.co.uk
Subject: RE: Removal of sensitive material on IATech servers

Hi Jillian,

It's a private and SENSITIVE video which needs to be completely removed. Please confirm once this has been actioned.

Kind regards,

Chad

Date: 23 September 16:39
From: ChadMcKenna_baws@hotmail.co.uk
To: jillianadams@ia-tech.co.uk
Cc: samuelmckenna@ia-tech.co.uk;barryrichmond@ia-tech.co.uk
Subject: RE: Removal of sensitive material on IATech servers

Hi,

Did you have an update on this?

Chad

Date: 23 September 17:03
From: ChadMcKenna_baws@hotmail.co.uk
To: jillianadams@ia-tech.co.uk
Cc: samuelmckenna@ia-tech.co.uk;barryrichmond@ia-tech.co.uk
Subject: RE: Removal of sensitive material on IATech servers

Any information on this would be great. This is very time sensitive.

Date: 23 September 17:10
From: samuelmckenna@ia-tech.co.uk
To: ChadMcKenna_baws@hotmail.co.uk
Cc:
Subject: RE: Removal of sensitive material on IATech servers

lol nice try

Date: 23 September 17:12
From: ChadMcKenna_baws@hotmail.co.uk
To: barryrichmond@ia-tech.co.uk;jillianadams@ia-tech.co.uk
Cc: samuelmckenna@ia-tech.co.uk
Subject: FW: Removal of sensitive material on IATech servers

fyi see below

Date: 23 September 17:10
From: samuelmckenna@ia-tech.co.uk
To: ChadMcKennabaws@hotmail.co.uk
Cc:
Subject: RE: Removal of sensitive material on IATech servers

lol nice try

Date: 24 September 10:22
From: jillianadams@ia-tech.co.uk
To: ChadMcKenna_baws@hotmail.co.uk
Cc: samuelmckenna@ia-tech.co.uk;barryrichmond@ia-tech.co.uk
Subject: RE: Removal of sensitive material on IATech servers

Had the IT team take a look, couldn't find anything like that. Rest assured there is no such video on our intranet.

J

Date: 24 September 10:27
From: ChadMcKenna_baws@hotmail.co.uk
To: jillianadams@ia-tech.co.uk
Cc: samuelmckenna@ia-tech.co.uk;barryrichmond@ia-tech.co.uk
Subject: RE: Removal of sensitive material on IATech servers

Thank you! Can I please get something in writing with regards to how the offending party is going to be dealt with.

Thanks,
Chad

Date: 24 September 16:57
From: barryrichmond@ia-tech.co.uk
To: ChadMcKenna_baws@hotmail.co.uk
Cc: samuelmckenna@ia-tech.co.uk;jillianadams@ia-tech.co.uk
Subject: RE: Removal of sensitive material on IATech servers

Please don't contact us again.

Date: 24 September 17:02
From: ChadMcKenna_baws@hotmail.co.uk
To: samuelmckenna@ia-tech.co.uk
Subject: FW: Removal of sensitive material on IATech servers

Twat.

Date: 25 September 11:14
From: samuelmckenna@ia-tech.co.uk
To: ChadMcKenna_baws@hotmail.co.uk
Subject: RE: Removal of sensitive material on IATech servers

;)

Chapter Three

I feel good. That stupid video has gone forever and now I can move on with my life and never have to deal with my arsehole of a brother ever again. I can get a new job, doing something that I love, and I can move out and know Mum is safe and the whole world is amazing. The autumn scene outside my bedroom window is like a postcard (well, if my curtains were open and I could actually see it) and now I even have more time to catch up on some well earned Netflix bingeing and Minecraft Let's Plays.

But fuck it, today seems like a good day to troll people, so I stick on *The Layover* and fill a few comments sections with insults. I even whistle while I work, because today is just that good of a day.

At least it is until I receive notification from Tom Maron, a douchebag from my old school. He's tagged me in something which turns out not to be a crappy game invite.

It's my video, right there on Facebook.

OMG is that Chad McKenna? Why the fuck have you uploaded this you sick freak?

I taste bile, which gives me just enough notice to turn my head so I projectile vomit over the carpet and not my computer monitor.

In the time it takes for me to spit the remains of whatever I last ate (roast chicken flavour crisps don't taste nearly as nice coming out as they do going in) two more people have posted beneath the video, and both are people I went to school with.

Holy crap it is! Chad McKenna what is wrong with you??
Daisy Williams
Well this has just put me off having hotdogs for lunch, thanks Chad.
David Smith

My first instinct is to write back, explain that it wasn't me who uploaded the video, it was the work of my sick and twisted brother. At school I was always known as the weird kid and stuff like this isn't going to help change anybody's perception. I start to type, but shake my head and mash delete. My side of the story can wait, so I click the report button above the video and flag it for being sexual.

Sam has even gone to the trouble of uploading the video via a bunch of brand new Twitter accounts all with loserjerksoff in the name, and tagging them with a load of trending hashtags. He obviously hasn't got any real work to do if he can afford to spend time setting up fake profiles. Thankfully the video is gone from Twitter in less than five minutes.

I direct message Tom, Daisy and David and write a whole essay explaining my side of the story, but I guess I was a dumbarse for expecting any kind of sympathetic response, because all I get is a tirade of abuse and insults in return.

An hour later and the video is back on Twitter. Even more this time, all on fake loserjerksoff accounts and filled with hashtags. Somehow they all have retweets, too. Why would people want to retweet this shit? I report the tweets as soon as I find them, and they're gone almost straight away, but ten minutes later and it's back once more, then gone almost instantly after I report it. It's a never-ending cycle.

I log into YouTube and it's back on there, as well. About a dozen of them, all called *loserjerksoff.mp4* and uploaded by variations of the name.

loserjerksof034
_loserjerksoff005
loserjerks.off002
loser-jerks-off001

I report every single one, and this time I don't even bother looking at the comments. There are only so many times you can read that you're a disgusting, fat pervert without it starting to get to you.

I log in to a few of my favourite forums and ask for help. They once got a headteacher sacked because he made a paedophile joke on Twitter eight years ago by spamming hundreds of local sites and Facebook pages with screenshots. If anyone is able to get something done it's those basement dwellers. My request is simple enough; help me get rid of the video.

But even their replies follow the trend.

Fuck off perv, go sort out your own mess!

Fucking marvellous.

I Google *loserjerksoff.mp4* and almost throw up again when the results load. Thirty pages of links to my video, all on different video hosting websites and embedded all over social media. Facebook, YouTube, Twitter, Dailymotion, JWPlayer, Blip, Vimeo, Pornhub (I guess that one makes sense, still pisses me off though).

'You prick,' I say to myself. 'You absolute prick. I fucking hate you, Sam. Can you hear me? Are you listening to me through my webcam?' I pull the plaster from the camera on my monitor and stare into it. I'm like a hot ball of pure rage coated in a slick layer of boiled sweat. 'You need to stop this. You fucking win, Sam, okay? This is enough. Stop. Please!'

And I vomit again.

I spend the rest of the day searching for and reporting videos. Unsurprisingly the porn sites are the hardest to remove the video from, but I quickly realise that if you report them as being kiddie porn they're taken down pretty much instantly. Not that it matters; they're reuploaded again almost straight away anyway.

I don't eat, I don't piss, I don't do anything other than switch from site to site reporting videos. My stomach aches, my back hurts and my wrists crunch as I hit the keyboard harder and harder with each video reported. My eyes burn and my arse-cheeks are numb, but I don't let any of my ailments slow down my quest to get the video removed. I don't care how many times Sam uploads it, I will be right behind him at every step. He'll get bored sooner or later. He has to. Surely he needs to do some actual work at some point.

I make sure to screengrab every single video. I don't particularly want evidence that videos of me wanking were uploaded to every corner of the web, but they will help when it comes to the case against Sam, because there is no way I'm letting him get away with this. As soon as I'm done removing the videos I'm going straight to the police.

My inbox bloops as a new email comes in. I don't recognise the sender's name, but a lump forms in my stomach as I spot where it's from.

Date: 26 September 03:12
From: 01001000@ia-tech.co.uk
To: ChadMcKenna_baws@hotmail.co.uk
Subject: I can help you

Sir

I can help

Respond

In no way is this the sort of email I would usually respond to, and if it wasn't for the IATech email address I would click delete without hesitation, but… who is it? After everything that has happened, why would somebody at IATech want to help me? Did Jillian find something hidden on the intranet after all, and she now secretly wants to help me without Sam finding out?

My shoulders slump. I'm not that lucky. It's probably Sam trying to screw around with me even more. He'll be sat at his desk right now, probably trying to watch me through my taped up webcam, laughing and high-fiving himself because he knows the stress he's causing me.

Fuck you, Sam, I'm not playing your game any more.

I delete the email and fall asleep in my chair.

The next morning when I wake up, my neck is stiff and my head is cloudy. I slowly push myself up and my entire body creates a symphony of snapping and cracking sounds.

The screensaver bounces around on my monitor. My mouth is dry and sticky, but before I go to grab a drink, I check whether Sam has uploaded any more videos.

A Google search brings up more than 200 pages of results.

I heave but nothing comes up. My throat burns and I cough.

The video isn't just on video hosting websites any more. There are now gifs of me embedded in people's blogs, their Tumblrs, their Facebook pages, their Twitter feeds. I find the video on a blog about yoga, a Facebook page about veganism, a website that sells toy cats made out of cat hair. Why the fuck are these people posting this?! I click on a website called *The Daily Bullshit* and I'm greeted with the headline *Masturbation Floods the Internet*. A blog called *From The Web* has posted *Top 10 Comments On Loser Jerks Off*. I read a fifty-tweet-long thread on Twitter where people are trying to guess the name of the porno I watched.

There are more than fifty versions of the video on YouTube alone. The most popular one, uploaded by *loser.jerksoff035*, has received more than 10,000 views. Of course I report it, but it feels like just as quickly as I have one removed another pops up in its place.

Shortly afterwards I find the first reaction video. Two lads wearing sunglasses sat in front of their laptop being tricked into watching my video by their fucking mate. They're grossed out, obviously, pretending to throw up in their hands and daring each other to watch until the end. When I finally blow my load they jump up and down screaming like they've just won the fucking lottery.

Throughout the day more and more reaction videos appear. Apparently it's hilarious to get your grandma to watch me spaff into a tissue and record her grimacing and wondering why their idiot grandson chose this path in life. It does get over 100,000 views in less than an hour though.

And there are memes. So many memes. I'm already sick of seeing my face edited onto different things thanks to Sam, but now the entire internet is doing it as well. And they're all shite, except for one where my spunk is replaced with kittens flying out of my dickhole. That one's quite funny, but I report it anyway.

My hand aches from the amount of times I press the report button, but I can't stop. I can't let this be my legacy.

What else can I do? Am I supposed to chase this video around the internet forever? Do I let Sam upload video after video until it engulfs the entire internet? Do I just sit back and continue reporting things whilst reaction videos and memes pop up even faster than the re-uploads of the video itself?

I have no choice. I have to report it to the police.

I've already done enough research to know what to do next, and thankfully it just involves completing another online form. There's no way I could deal with having to talk on the phone right now anyway, I always panic on the phone and end up saying stupid things. I once had to ring to order a pizza when the Domino's site was down and I accidentally tried to order a cheeseburger. Needless to say I never ordered from that Domino's again.

There are two options on the website, *Online Scams and Viruses* and *Fraud and Cyber Crime*. I click the second option, then fill out the form, making sure to make it sound every bit as horrible as it is. I include every tiny little detail, and make sure to add the name SAM MCKENNA as often as I can.

As soon as I hit 'Submit' my heart beats heavily against my ribs. I've never reported anyone to the police before, and it feels wrong because he's my brother, but I can't let him continue doing this. It's going to ruin my life.

A moment later I receive an email:

Date: 26 September 13:36
From: 01001000@ia-tech.co.uk
To: ChadMcKenna_baws@hotmail.co.uk
Subject: Please to help you

Please sir

I am wanting to help you

You must take notice of this

Respond sir

Date: 26 September 13:48
From: ChadMcKenna_baws@hotmail.co.uk
To: 01001000@ia-tech.co.uk
Subject: RE:Please to help you

Who is this?

Date: 26 September 13:49
From: 01001000@ia-tech.co.uk
To: ChadMcKenna_baws@hotmail.co.uk
Subject: RE:Please to help you

We to explain

Meet us 0300

IA Tech

Date: 26 September 13:52
From: ChadMcKenna_baws@hotmail.co.uk
To: 01001000@ia-tech.co.uk
Subject: RE:Please to help you

Seriously, who are you? I was fired, how am I supposed to get into the IAT-ech building?

Date: 26 September 13:53
From: 01001000@ia-tech.co.uk
To: ChadMcKenna_baws@hotmail.co.uk
Subject: RE:Please to help you

Access restored

Meet first floor

Date: 26 September 14:10
From: ChadMcKenna_baws@hotmail.co.uk
To: 01001000@ia-tech.co.uk
Subject: RE:Please to help you

Sam, I'm not dumb. You're trying to get me caught in the restricted section, you know I don't even have access. Not falling for it.

Date: 26 September 14:11
From: 01001000@ia-tech.co.uk
To: ChadMcKenna_baws@hotmail.co.uk
Subject: RE:Please to help you

Not Sam

Access to all areas granted

If it's not Sam, then who is it? Could it really be somebody helping me from inside IATech? Who would do that? It can't be Jillian – there's no way she'd ask me to meet her in the office. Could it be that new girl who warned me to go home the day Sam first uploaded the video? Maybe. But again, why would she risk everything by arranging to meet me at the IATech building?

It has to be Sam. It's the only logical explanation. He has some new plan to humiliate me or have me arrested and the only way for him to do that is by me going to the IATech offices even though I no longer work there. Of course he'll tell people that I broke in, that's assuming I make it past the receptionist, the security guards and the cameras to begin with.

What a cock.

Date: 26 September 14:45
From: ChadMcKenna_baws@hotmail.co.uk
To: 01001000@ia-tech.co.uk
Subject: RE:Please to help you

Nice try Sam. Not falling for it.

Date: 26 September 14:46
From: 01001000@ia-tech.co.uk
To: ChadMcKenna_baws@hotmail.co.uk
Subject: RE:Please to help you

https://h01100011.ia

I hover the mouse cursor over the link. It doesn't look like any sort of link I've ever seen before. Am I currently having a conversation with a scammer who's about to reveal that his uncle, the King of Iceland, wants to transfer a million pounds to me? Or could it just be a good old fashioned virus waiting to infect my computer?

Fuck it, at this stage what do I really have to lose?

I click the link.

A web page loads up. A black background with what looks to be a live security feed with four separate images in the centre which I recognise instantly as the IATech building. In the bottom corner is the current date and time.

The top left image is reception. A delivery driver is handing something to the receptionist. Top right is outside the entrance, where the big security guard is smoking a cigarette. Bottom left shows the atrium, where the hordes of nerds are working. Bottom right shows one of the board rooms, where Sam, Barry and Jillian are sat talking around the long table in the centre of the room.

I gawp at it for I don't know how long while the workers of IATech have no clue I'm watching. If this is Sam, then he's going a bit fucking far to try and trick me.

Date: 26 September 15:22
From: ChadMcKenna_baws@hotmail.co.uk
To: 01001000@ia-tech.co.uk
Subject: RE:Please to help you

How do I know if this is real? Do something on the camera to prove it.

Date: 26 September 15:23
From: 01001000@ia-tech.co.uk
To: ChadMcKenna_baws@hotmail.co.uk
Subject: RE:Please to help you

What would we do?

Date: 26 September 15:25
From: ChadMcKenna_baws@hotmail.co.uk
To: 01001000@ia-tech.co.uk
Subject: RE:Please to help you

Set off the fire alarm.

No more emails come in as I watch the security feed, unblinking. I study Sam's movements, trying to work out if he's somehow checking his phone or reading his emails in some way.

Nothing happens. Minutes go past, and IATech continues with its day to day activities like it does every other day. The delivery driver has left reception, the security guard has returned from his cigarette break, and Barry is showing Sam and Jillian some information on a spreadsheet.

I feel like I've been holding my breath the entire time. My chest is hot and my back twinges from leaning in so close to the screen.

Then, flashing lights. People stand up from their desks, alert to something I can't see. The security guard strides into the atrium and shouts something, flailing his arms and pointing. Sam, Barry and Jillian quickly leave the board room.

An email lands in my inbox.

Date: 26 September 15:31
From: 01001000@ia-tech.co.uk
To: ChadMcKenna_baws@hotmail.co.uk
Subject: RE:Please to help you

You see

For the next ten hours I do nothing but search for videos, report videos, eat crisps and repeat. It's strange that I haven't yet heard anything from the police, but they're probably just investigating the case before they swoop in and arrest Sam.

There isn't much I can do about the memes. I report them where I can, but there are just too many for me chase around the internet.

Every five minutes I switch back to the CCTV feed at IATech, just to check it's real. I even go as far as ringing the reception desk to see if the receptionist picks up, and as soon as I hear 'Hello' I hang up and suppress a giggle. A moment later I watch the feed as she picks up the phone and shakes her head at the point I hung up.

At five o'clock some of the workers go home, but most of them don't leave until at least seven. The real brown noses stay until nine, and by ten only the uber nerds and blokes who hate their wives and bratty kids are still there.

Sam is the first of the big three to leave, a little after 10.30. Barry is next at eleven, followed by Jillian ten minutes later. For most of the evening they had been on a video conference speaking to a bunch of Japanese blokes. I really wish I could hear them.

Midnight passes and I chug two energy drinks, which is a mistake as I can hear my own heartbeat and I'm ninety per cent certain I'm about to have a heart attack. I lie on the bed staring up at the ceiling, and after an hour or so my heart rate lowers and the sweat on my neck dries up.

Mum's asleep when I sneak out of my bedroom at almost half-past two. I'm twenty-two years old, for fuck's sake, too old to be sneaking out of my Mum's house, but these are exceptional circumstances. I haven't done this in years, but I still remember where all of the creaky floorboards are on the stairs, and I make it to the downstairs hallway without making a sound.

I slip on my trainers, grab my jacket and old IATech passcard, and head out into the night, making sure to close the front door as lightly as I can.

Chapter Four

It takes me less than quarter of an hour to arrive outside the IATech building. It sits in the centre of a large industrial park, right across from a van rental company with a pair of enormous warehouses on each side. IATech sticks out like a sore thumb – it's a new building with glass walls, lots of angles and lights everywhere. It looks like a kid designed it using Lego bricks and Christmas lights. It definitely doesn't belong in a grotty industrial park twenty miles outside of London, but Sam always insists it's affordable and has good transport links. Not that I care, I can walk to work every day.

Well, I *could*.

I hide behind the big, fancy IATech logo in the centre of the only patch of grass for a mile, and I assess the situation.

And my assessment is, I have no idea what I'm doing.

I wish I'd asked my mystery helper what the plan actually is, because then I wouldn't be sat behind a massive sign in the freezing cold wondering what the hell I'm supposed to do next.

I slide my phone out of my pocket and hold the screen close to the ground to hide the light. It's 2.59am.

One of the revolving doors at the front of the building spins and I fall flat on the ground. If somebody drives into the industrial estate behind me, they'll see me instantly and I'll be fucked. There's no way I'm talking myself out of this mess.

I pull myself along the damp grass and peek my head around the concrete base of the IATech logo. A security guard I don't recognise lights up a cigarette, illuminating his face in an orange glow.

Now what? Any second a delivery lorry is going to pull up behind me and call the police and congratulations Chad, you're now Butch the Slaughterer's prison bitch getting thirty-two stitches in your anus after being passed around C block.

My phone buzzes in my hand. I hold it close to my chest and open up the text message which came in.

From: 01001000

43

Enter on the signal

What signal? Will a light shine onto the clouds with a giant fucking arrow accompanied by an airhorn which repeats NOW NOW NOW?

The guard's radio crackles. He drops the cigarette and stubs it out with his foot, then holds the radio up to his face. He mumbles something I can't quite make out. The radio hisses and the guard takes off running, first along the front of the IATech building, then he disappears down the side.

I stare at my phone. Is that the signal? It must be the signal. Give me a signal that that was the signal! Fuck it, I stand up and run towards the building. By the time I reach the nearest door my chest is tight and it's agony to breathe. My knees are about to give way and there's a ringing in my ears.

Holy shit I'm unfit.

I push open the revolving door and almost collapse into the building. Luckily there's no receptionist working at three AM, but the robotic greeter lifts her head and smiles at me. She raises her arm and waves, but not in the usual 'hello' way, but in a more, 'go down this way' kind of way. It's probably just a glitch, but I head down the left side corridor she seemed to be gesturing towards anyway.

I walk on my tiptoes and try to slow my breathing. There's a distant tapping of fingers on keys, which means people are still in the building.

Footsteps approach, so I duck into the nearest office. I think it belongs to HR, but it's dark and empty so I can't tell. It does smell a lot like biscuits though, which is why I think it must be HR.

As the footsteps die down I sneak back into the hallway. By now the news of my departure from IATech will have spread through the entire company, so there's no way I can let even a single person see me.

Somebody coughs and I panic. My heart leaps up into my throat and I have the irrational urge to cough back, like a weird version of yawning in response to somebody else's yawn. I clasp my hand over my mouth and make a guttural scream in a pathetic attempt to suppress it. The only thing I suppress is my dignity as all I end up doing is blowing snot over the back of my hand. I gently push open the door to my old caretaker's cupboard and wipe myself down with a rag. I shake my head as I throw the rag into an old bin bag, even though I'd love for somebody to start wiping desks with it.

This isn't me. This is way out of my comfort zone. Why the hell did I think sneaking back into the company I was fired from two days ago would be a good idea? I play video games and insult people in YouTube comment sections, I don't creep about and break into buildings with no plan at three o'clock in the bloody morning. I'm doing exactly what my brother wants with this, he'll be sat at home right now watching this whole thing on his forty-foot TV and having a laugh with his six girlfriends and pet Komodo dragon (I don't think he has a Komodo dragon, but it seems like a good pet to imagine a complete prick to have).

I should go home. If I hand myself in to the security guard now then he might even let me go as a result of my honesty. You know, a light slap on the wrist and wink as he says 'Oh, you little scamp'.

My phone buzzes in my pocket. It's my mystery helper again.

From: 01001000

Enter R&E on floor 1 immediately

But what if it isn't Sam? None of this feels like something Sam would do – he doesn't think that far ahead. He's the sort of person who would empty his bowl of cereal onto my head (he did that once), not the sort of person who would spend time planning a convoluted plot in an attempt to… I don't know what. If Sam's plan is to have me arrested he could have easily done so when I broke his office door, he didn't need to do… whatever the hell this is.

It must be the girl. It *must* be. She warned me once, she might be trying to warn me again. Does she work in the development team, so knows how to hack the system and send mysterious messages and set off the fire alarm? She might even know where the video is stored and want to help me delete it forever.

From: 01001000

IMMEDIATELY

Fuck it. What have I got to lose?

I open the cupboard door and stride down the corridor, keeping my head low and making sure to stick close to the walls. I turn into the stairway and climb up to the first floor, then poke my head around the corner to make sure I'm alone.

I plot my escape route in case anything goes wrong. There's a fire escape at the bottom of this corridor and through the warehouse, but if things get extra dicey I could duck into the bathroom opposite and squeeze out the window. It would only be a thirty-or-so-foot drop into the bushes, I could survive that, right?

Let's hope it doesn't come to that.

I step out into the corridor and up to the door that leads into the restricted section. It isn't reeeeeally called the restricted section, I just call it that to make it sound cooler – it's actually the Research and Engineering department, but it may as well be the restricted section as bugger all people are allowed anywhere near it, especially me.

I hold my pass up to the card reader. Any moment now the alarms will sound and the entire building will be swarming with police. I hold my breath. I tense up. I wince.

The light turns green and the door opens.

'Fuck me,' I say, maybe a little too loud.

A wave of nausea sweeps through my body. My hands shake and my heart beats in a weird pattern which is probably Morse code for *what the fuck are you doing, Chad?* It's the exact same feeling I had as a kid whenever I snuck into Dad's room to steal his stash of porn mags he hid under the bed.

The restricted section looks exactly like the rest of the building; white and sterile with glass walls and no personality. There is a low hum, like a distant generator is doing its thing, but more importantly there is no sign of any employees.

I turn the first corner and press my face up to a glass door. Nothing of interest inside, just a bunch of computers and piles of paper. The next room isn't much different, except there's a long table along one side with circuit boards and other computer parts spread across the shiny surface.

I turn the next corner and face a long, bright corridor. On each side are glass doors spaced evenly apart, with each room looking like the next stage along a robot's life. The first room is full of metallic limbs all hung from the ceiling like a futuristic abattoir. The second has torsos, along with poles leant up along the far wall, like the one I'm allowed to clean in reception. The next room is full of heads, all missing the faces which would usually be projected onto the front from inside. Why the hell do they build them with ears on the side? It's not like they need them, all it does it make them look like faceless ghosts all lined up waiting to catch the bus.

The next room is filled with the completed robots, all stood to attention like an army waiting to march into battle, except they all have poles instead of the lower half of their bodies, so they're not exactly going to march anywhere soon.

The last door at the end of the corridor is different from the others. It's wide and heavy and is completely white so I can't see through. There's even a passcode reader to the right-hand side, with black lettering above it that reads *1X*.

I've come this far, I may as well swipe my card and see what happens.

The door opens.

Sweat pours down my face at a rate so fast I can hear it dropping on the tiled floor like little patters of rain. This room isn't like the others; it's dark and grey and warm. The ceiling looms above with pipes and vents criss-crossing in every direction.

The hum is so much louder. There are rows of what look like huge computers in the centre, with the only light source in the room being the hundreds of blinking LEDs across the front. Along the walls are units, shelves and metal worktops. It looks less like a tech business and more like a mad scientist's lab.

I reach the end of the wall of computers and poke my head slowly around. At the far end are three rows of machinery I don't even want to try and describe. It's like something you'd see in a movie where they build spaceships, except smaller and right there in front of me. There are robotic arms with pincers, conveyor belts and giant vats of... something. There's a strong smell of iron and my mouth completely dries up.

I almost shit myself as a loud *eeeeeee* rings through the room. I leap back into defensive position, which is similar to something from a Jackie Chan movie, but probably not really, and I hold my breath.

Eeeeeeeeeee. Ft ft ft ft ft ft ft. Eeeeee urrrrrrr.

I spot the cause of the screech and I wait for my heart rate to return to more human levels. A printer beside a bank of desks is spitting out a single sheet of paper.

I tip toe away from the computer wall and stare down at the printer as the paper lands on the desk in front of me. The colourful flickering LEDs allow for barely enough light for me to read the text:

Sir

Please assist

Disable the firewall by pressing the following keys on the server panel –
H37L – control unit –

D6, C1, A9, A7, B2, C9, B6,

We can then do as you require

I spin around on the spot. Apart from the hum, the room is still. Is somebody watching me? Are they keeping themselves to protect themselves? They're going to huge lengths to stop me from seeing them. Does that mean I already know who they are?

'Hello?' I whisper.

Nothing.

'Will this delete the video from the servers?'

Unsurprisingly, still nothing.

I step away from the desks, moving my legs so slow I may as well not be moving at all. It takes me five whole minutes until I'm once again beside the wall of computers. I stare at the printed sheet in my hand, and the words jumble together until they stop making sense.

I turn my head from side to side. Where am I supposed to start? There's a panel right beside me, but there aren't any buttons on it labelled with letters and numbers. What if I push something and it locks me in or calls the police? What if there's a self-destruct button? I've seen enough movies to know that shady companies have them installed in case of emergencies.

At the top of the panel is *F11A* in big black letters. The next panel along has *F12A* at the top. The one below that has *F12B*.

That must be the number of each system. Or computer. Or server. I have no idea what I'm looking at, but somebody clearly does.

I reread the note and spot *H37L* is printed in bold font.

That must be the panel I have to use! Not giving a fuck about the noise any more I pace around the computers. I pass panels starting with D, E, G and then B, and for fuck's sake, who didn't put these bloody things in alphabetical orde— THERE IT IS!

I lunge at the panel marked *H37L*, and sure enough there are large, coded buttons arranged in a rectangular formation, a bit like a keyboard where every button makes different farmyard animal sounds except without the pictures. I hold up the note. All the buttons listed are there, so I push them in sequence, making sure to leave dramatic pauses between each one.

I'm expecting something to happen. A hiss as a trapdoor opens or a thundering crash as that fucking video is deleted forever and ever. But no. Nothing. Not even a beep to let me know I've done it properly.

'Is that it?' I ask.

But all I get in response is silence.

'What else do I need to do?'

Still nothing.

I stomp back over to the printer and stand gawping at it like when Grandma tries to work out the DVD player. I push a couple of buttons, but I don't know what I thought would happen.

'Do I go now?'

Nothing. Whoever is supposed to be helping is just being rude now.

The room plunges into darkness and my stomach does that thing where it feels like you've swallowed a bowling ball. Or is that just me? It's where it sinks and feels full and sends a charge through your entire body.

A red light in the corner of the room flickers on, washing everything in an Amsterdam glow.

That's when the machinery on the far side of the room roars to life. I hold my hands to my ears, but it still doesn't stop me from screaming in pain. I've never heard anything so loud, and I'm convinced both of my eardrums burst. I would check my palms for blood but it's just so fucking loud.

I run out of the room and slam the door shut behind me, but it doesn't do anything about the noise, as it turns out it isn't in the slightest bit soundproof. I need to get out of this place before security come up and find me and they call the police and Sam gets exactly what he wants.

I walk as briskly as my legs will allow down the long blank corridor of the restricted section, doing my best to ignore the army of robots in the first room who are all now switched on, their projected faces smiling at me as I pass. Even the decapitated robot heads are grinning like the inside of a medieval executioners dungeon for sadists.

I shove open the door to the restricted section and the machinery is still churning and groaning and screeching. In the nine months I worked at IATech I never heard anything even close to the sound it's making. Imagine a tank being crushed by a swarm of giant hornets and you're about halfway there as to how loud this thing is.

Still, it's not quite loud enough to cover the yelling from behind. I turn on the spot and the security guard is charging down the corridor towards me. This is how it must feel, I think, to be in the African savannah and see a rhinoceros in heat barrelling straight at you – except I'm in an office building in Hemel Hempstead and I'm close to shitting myself.

I dive through the door opposite and leap down the stairs four at a time, bouncing from the wall half way down and ignoring the pain in my shoulder so I can propel myself to the ground floor. The guard is catching up to me fast – I can hear his hooves pounding against the steps and his voice grunting and huffing.

I almost tear the door from its hinges as I burst out into the ground floor corridor. I barely stop myself from slipping on the tiled floor and bolt in the direction of reception. Sweat streaks from my face and my chest is literally on fire, but I ignore the desperate urge to lie down and give in as the guard gets closer and closer.

'Stop right there!' he booms.

'No,' I reply for some reason, although it comes out as more of a strained whine.

'Chad! Stop!'

I reach reception and pass the greeter robot. I'm sure I hear somebody say 'Don't stop, Chad,' but I'm delirious with adrenaline so it must be my own mind, though I listen to it anyway and shove my way into the revolving doors. They spin agonisingly slow, but just enough for me to squeeze through and plop outside, where I collapse into a sweaty, messy heap. This is it, this is all the security guard needs to catch up to me, in a second he'll be on top of me and pinning my hands behind my back, and I'll receive a taster of the sort of treatment a guy like me will be receiving in prison. I tense my whole body and I close my eyes.

But the pain doesn't come.

I roll over and open my eyes. My deep pants are pathetic, I sound like a crowning first time mother, and my heart is about to burst through my ribs and land on the ground beside me.

It all slows as my wide eyes meet the narrowed, hate-filled eyes of the security guard. He's trapped inside the revolving doors, neither inside the building nor out. No matter how hard he shoves and barges at it, it doesn't budge in the slightest.

I slowly push myself to my feet. This only angers the guard even more.

'You stay right there!' he screams.

This is my chance, this is where I can say an action movie one liner and be a badass. This is it.

'No, thank you,' I say.

It's something.

I turn and walk briskly away.

It's a little after 4.00am by the time I arrive home. I sneak inside, crawl upstairs and bury myself beneath my bedsheets, where I plan on staying for the rest of my life. My chest may implode or I may shit out my lungs or my feet might burst, but at least that fucking video is gone from the IAT-ech servers and I no longer have to worry about Sam spreading it like a cancer throughout the internet. When I eventually muster up the energy to unravel myself from my cocoon, I'll delete the remaining videos from whatever website they've been uploaded to, this entire incident will be behind me, and I can move on with never speaking to my spiteful piece of shit brother ever again. Sorted.

Chapter Five

'Chad?' says Mum.

I don't move. Maybe she'll go away if I don't move.

'Chad? Wake up.'

I fake a snore and tighten my grip on the bedsheets.

'Chad,' she says, louder this time. 'You need to wake up.'

I grunt.

'Mr McKenna,' says a man's voice from close by.

My eyes snap open and I scramble into a seated position, allowing my covers to slip from my head.

Mum is perched beside me. Behind her are two uniformed police officers, both staring down at me with looks in their eyes that suggests I'm about to be shot dead right here in my bed.

'We need to speak with you Mr McKenna,' says the nearest officer, his Eighties pornstache vibrating.

'Okay,' I mumble.

I slide out of bed and follow Mum and the two police officers downstairs. My mind is cloudy, like my brain's been stuffed with cotton wool, and my calves feel like I've run a dozen marathons.

The police officers lead me into the lounge, where Sam is sat in the chair waiting. Great. The first officer sits on the sofa and gestures for me to sit beside him. The second stands over by the TV while Mum hovers in the doorway.

'I am Sergeant Johnson,' says the officer with the pornstache. 'This is PC Graves.'

'Am I under arrest?' I ask. I always see people in movies ask this, so I figure it's the done thing.

'Why should we arrest you?' asks PC Graves, raising her head so that she can look down on me.

I shrug and Sam lets out a little snort.

'Mr McKenna, where were you between the hours of 3 and 3.40 this morning?'

'In bed.'

'Liar,' says Sam.

'Please, Mr McKenna. If you can't remain silent we will ask you to step away,' says Officer Pornstache.

'Okay,' says Sam, sinking back into the chair.

'Mr McKenna, I'll ask you again,' says PC Graves. 'Where were you between the hours of 3 and 3.40am?'

I give everyone my best puppy dog expression. Both officers scowl at me (slightly less than Sam is, admittedly) but there is something about the way I'm sat in my lounge and not in the back of their car that makes me wonder whether they know or not.

Fuck it, let's see how far I can take this.

'In bed,' I say.

Sam shakes his head.

'Can anybody confirm that?'

I look up at Mum.

'Well, me,' she says. 'He's barely left his room for the past two days.'

PC Graves flicks open a notepad and scribbles something down. 'Mr McKenna, is it true that you were recently sacked from IATech?'

'Yes,' I say.

'What was the reason for that?'

'Because *he* spread a video of me around the internet and I got angry,' I say.

'What was the nature of the video?'

I look at the floor. 'Personal.'

'What were you doing in the video?'

'I was… it was personal. I filled in a form online about this, it's all on there.'

'Okay, well we can follow up on that down the line. At the moment we need to figure out what happened last night, okay?'

'Okay, yeah, well I was asleep.'

'There is a security guard at IATech who places you at the scene.'

'What scene?'

'The IATech building.'

Fuck.

'Oh right. Why would I care about IATech? Like you say, I was sacked.'

'Do you know why the security team would say you were at the IATech building this morning?'

I shake my head. 'There is that one guy who hates me. He's the one who dragged me out when I *accidentally* broke the door to Sam's office. I did call him some names, so maybe he has it in for me.'

'What did you call him?'

I glance at Mum, then at the floor. 'Twat and stuff.'

PC Graves writes down *twat and stuff* and I hold in a smile.

'Can't you just take a look at the CCTV footage?' asks Mum. 'Surely it's as easy as that. If Chad was there then you'll see that he was there.'

'There is no CCTV,' says Sam.

My heart does a flip.

'From exactly 2.59 until 3.24am every single security camera at IATech was disabled.'

Thank you, my mysterious helper!

'Is somebody helping you?' asked Sam.

'Helping me what?'

Sam smirks, and I put on my best dumb expression.

'If you were there, the lack of CCTV evidence isn't enough to save you,' says Officer Pornstache. 'There's a witness. There is also forensic evidence we can take. Fingerprints.'

'He worked there,' snaps Mum. 'Of course his fingerprints will be there.'

Officer Pornstache keeps his eyes on me. 'Things will be a lot easier for you if you just tell us why you were at IATech last night.'

'I wasn't.'

'Chad, enough of the bullshit,' says Sam. 'You were there to try and get rid of that video. Someone's obviously trying to help you, God knows who, seeing as you don't have any friends. We'll find out soon enough, so just tell us.'

'I was at home all night,' I say, so cool and calm I almost want to offer a high-five to the entire room to commend me on my awesome acting skills.

PC Graves and Officer Pornstache exchange a look and PC Graves stands.

'Thank you for your time, Mr McKenna,' she says. 'I trust that should we have any further questions you will be happy to cooperate?'

'Of course,' I say.

'Ms McKenna, apologies for disturbing you.'

The two officers leave the room as Sam shoots me the darkest glare I've ever seen. He steps towards me and leans right in so that his face is inches from mine.

'I know it was you,' he says. 'And I know you've had help. You might have fucked things up for us temporarily, but it won't last. I'm going to prove it, and when I do you are going to suffer like you've never suffered before.'

'I wasn't—'

Mum walks into the room.

'Hey Mum, I've gotta go,' he says, his voice light and carefree like the manipulative prick that he is.

'Okay, darling. Do you want something to eat?'

'No thanks, Mum, busy day today,' he says all light and chipper and dickheadish.

I spend the next seven or eight hours searching every corner of the internet for *loserjerksoff.mp4*. I search Google, Twitter, Facebook, YouTube and every video hosting website I can think of. I even resort to searching on Yahoo and Bing – that's how desperate I am.

It feels good. I can see the number of videos decreasing in real time as sites pull the videos almost as soon as I report them. Now that the file is deleted from IATech's servers, Sam won't be able to carry on uploading.

The memes continue to spread, but who really gives a shit about memes? I mean, nobody, right? I might as well try my best to take down as many as I can anyway.

I will win this war!

A notification pops up on Facebook, so I click through to it and see that somebody has tagged me against an article on the BBC website. Usually it would be from my Auntie Cathy, she tags me in anything she finds online related to cats, but it's not from Auntie Cathy. It's from my old school mate Tom Maron.

*This is **Chad McKenna**! lololololol,* says his comment, right below the

Daily Mirror article titled 'Loser J*rks Off – Who Is The Mystery Masturbator?'

Here comes that puke again.

LONDON – *If you've spent any time online over the past 24 hours then chances are high that you have seen the latest 'viral' video in the form of Loser J*rks Off, a ninety-second video featuring a young man partaking in the lewd act of self-abuse. The video, originally uploaded by the user loserj*rksoff, first started to spread in a virus-esque fashion around midday on 23 September, and has quickly infected blogs and websites around the world.*

Since the original discovery users have been searching for the video in what is being referred to as Jerk Hunting, or 'Junting'. While each individual upload is only viewed an average of 200 times before it is either blocked or removed, Reddit users have calculated that approximately 150,000 versions of the same video have been uploaded to the internet thus far, with an estimated 120,000 videos still remaining. This has resulted in over 30,000,000 cumulative views to date, with no sign of the momentum slowing down, as 100 new uploads of the video are discovered every three minutes.

*Accompanying the unedited video is a viral sensation we have never seen on this scale, even surpassing 2016's Chewbacca Mom. If you have somehow managed to avoid seeing the unedited video, there's no chance you have avoided the various accompanying virals and memes based on Loser J*rks Off.*

*Little is currently known about the identity of loserj*rksoff, the original uploader of the material. It has been speculated that the video is the result of a virus, or the work of an online 'hacktivist' group, but to date no specific group has taken responsibility.*

Even the BBC has been victim to the attack, with the popular iPlayer platform having already been targeted for several hundred uploads of the video. What may have started as a joke has quickly escalated to unacceptable levels, as the video has reportedly been viewed by tens of thousands of children who were attempting to watch Dick 'N' Dom, but instead were left seeing somewhat of a namesake.

So as we continue to feel the effects of this attack, we ask who is loserj*rksoff, what is the reason for his viral video, and how has he organised such a large-scale attack upon the world wide web?

If you can provide information on loserj*rksoff contact our News Desk today.

Thirty million people have seen my penis. That must be some kind of world record, surely? I bet even the biggest porn stars haven't had numbers like that staring at their junk. Sure, almost a hundred per cent of those people didn't want to see my penis to begin with and, according to reports, some of them vomited afterwards, but that's beside the point.

It isn't long after Tom Maron outs me as the star of the video before my real name begins to appear in articles. My name, my image and my dick are broadcast all over the internet for the entire world to gawk at.

And I'm not taking to my newfound fame particularly well. My name is popping up all over the place, and I can't go five minutes without somebody linking me to a post on Facebook. Here are three of my favourite headlines:

Chad McKenna – The Man, The Myth, The Penis (Buzzfeed)

The Man Behind the Belly Behind the Hand Shandy (The Sun)

MY SON HAS NIGHTMARES ABOUT CHAD MCKENNA (Daily Mail)

I include that last article because at first it's a hilarious thought. The article is almost a piss-take, with the main photo being a mum cradling her young son, having both obviously been told to look sad while sat in front of their laptop.

It does, however, become a lot less funny as I'm walking to the shop and a man runs up to me and screams in my face because while his son was watching nursery rhymes on YouTube a pop up loaded featuring my video, which resulted in the kid now having a crippling fear of snakes and milk. It takes me five minutes to convince him that I wasn't the one who infected the entire internet with a video of me masturbating. I can tell he is desperate to smack me in the mouth as I explain to him that my brother is the one responsible for his son seeing me blow my load into a tissue, and that I would give anything to take that memory away from him. Thankfully he's distracted as a group of lads shout 'wanker' at me from across the street, and he moves on.

This must be what it feels like to be a celebrity. Not a decent celebrity, obviously, but a shitty one, like that waitress who was fired for calling a black customer the n-word, or somebody from *The Only Way is Essex*. Once this is all over I wonder if I'll be offered a place on *I'm A Celebrity Get Me Out Of Here?*

Even the legal team from Netflix emails and threatens me with a lawsuit, as every title in their library beginning with B has been switched with my video. Now, every time somebody wants to watch *Breaking Bad* or *Barbie: Life in the Dreamhouse* they are greeted with grainy footage of me with my dick in my hand.

Somehow I am both the bullied and the bully in this scenario. People laugh at me because I'm the naked guy spreading across the internet, yet people are also angry because apparently I'm the one who did it. Who the hell would do this to themselves? What could I possibly have to gain?

Is there even any point in continuing to try and remove the video from the internet? I have one removed, but another dozen seem to pop up in its place. Is this my life now? There is meme after meme after *fucking* meme. Does the world have to learn to cope with seeing me jerk off every time they browse the web?

My stomach hasn't stopped twisting itself in knots in days, but I don't know whether that's from the fear or the lack of food. I've barely eaten, I've barely slept, but I've been shitting and sweating a *lot*.

Since my run in with the angry dad I haven't left the house, and that was three days ago. I've had journalists trying to add me on Facebook, messaging me night and day, but I haven't even read half of them. Somehow my email address leaked, so my inbox is full of hate-filled messages and interview requests from the papers.

Should I do it? Maybe. I really need to get my story out there and tell the world that I'm not the one responsible for ruining the innocence of so many children.

I click reply on an email from *The Sun* but stop. Do I do it?

I shake my head and think back to the old lady who threw a cat in a bin. The press lynched her, portrayed her as the greatest monster history has ever known. Yes, being mean to cats is a shitty thing to do, but you can't exactly put her in the same category as Harold Shipman or Josef Fritzl.

But the press do. They fucking do. They don't want the truth, they want a juicy fucking story they can plaster all over the front pages, and they don't care who gets hurt so long as they sell more bloody ad space.

I definitely don't need things to be made any worse, so I go back to my inbox and search for the email sent from my mystery helper. I send a reply asking for help, but all I get back is an undeliverable message in return.

So this is it. This is what it's come to. The rest of my life will be spent hiding in the warmth of my bedcovers occasionally turning on the TV to see what is going on in the world – except not today, because the news is mainly talking about my video and the devastating effects it's having on e-commerce.

There's a gentle tap at my bedroom door.

'Chad, can I come in?' asks Mum.

I don't answer. The ceiling is too interesting so I mustn't look away.

'Chad, sweetheart, it's me. I'm coming in.'

The door opens and I wrap myself into a burrito of sadness. Mum shuffles towards the bed and it dips as she perches beside me.

'I know you're awake,' she says.

'So?' I mumble.

'Someone's here to see you.'

'If it's Sam tell him to fuck off.'

Mum pauses, no doubt wondering whether she should tell me off for swearing, but instead she strokes what I assume she thinks is my head but is actually my shoulder.

'It's not Sam,' she says. 'It's a man. He thinks he can help.'

'Does he have a gun? And some bullets?'

'He says he's been where you are. He knows what you can do to stop it.'

I thrash my arms until my burrito becomes a quesadilla and my head pops out. 'The only person who can stop this is Sam.'

'Why don't you come downstairs? You can talk to him for a moment, see if what he says is worth looking into.'

'Where's he from?' I ask.

'I don't know, he didn't say,' she says, then leans in and whispers, 'I think he might be famous. I recognise his face. Maybe he's one of those famous computer geeks you hear about. Like the Facebook guy.'

'You think Mark Zuckerberg is in our house?'

'Could be.'

I grimace.

'Two minutes. For me.'

I roll my eyes. 'Mum, stop with the guilt tripping. Please.'

'But it works.'

'Fine. Two minutes. But if it isn't Mark Zuckerberg then I'm coming back up here.'

Unless Mark Zuckerberg has seriously let himself go since the last picture I saw, then the bloke in the front room is definitely not him. His eyes light up as he spots me, and he almost knocks me over when he strides over and grabs my hand. I'm a big guy, but he's even bigger, with a round belly, scruffy beard and a big toothy smile. He looks like how Santa would look if he lost his job.

He's definitely not Zuckerberg, but he does look familiar.

'Chad, it's a pleasure to meet you,' he says.

'Likewise,' I say.

He holds his hand down towards the sofa. 'Please, take a seat.'

'Are you the one who has been sending me emails?' I ask.

'What do you mean?' he says, his smile staying strong.

I shrug and slowly sit on the edge of the sofa, keeping his gaze as he sits close beside me.

'How have you been?' he asks.

'Fine,' I say, in a tone that suggests he needs to explain what the hell he wants quickly or else.

'Good, good. It is not an easy position to be in, is it?'

'No,' I say.

He grins at me, completely oblivious to my confusion.

'Who are you?' I ask when the awkwardness gets a little too much.

'My name is Clive King,' he says. 'I am a memeologist.'

'Oh,' I say.

Chapter Six

'It's okay if you don't know what a memeologist is,' he says. 'Not many people do.'

'Yeah, I have no idea.'

'Memeology is the study of memes, a meme being a piece of content which spreads online by being shared by individuals. Like Pepe the Frog, Bad Luck Brian, Trollface – they're all memes. They're not always the funniest or the cleverest, but they all resonate with people.'

'I know what memes are. I've made plenty of my own.'

'Oh? Which is your favourite?'

I shrug. 'I dunno really. Maybe Distracted Boyfriend. How the hell do you study them?'

'Internet culture is a strange beast. Memes are often highly and easily customisable. Or they're something as simple and random as a moth. You don't need skill to create a meme, which is why they're so widely shared. But something can be popular one moment and then completely dead the next. It can catapult people into superstardom or it can completely destroy somebody's life.'

'Tell me about it,' I say, shaking my head.

'You're not alone, Chad. There are plenty of people out there who have gone through exactly what you have.'

'Exactly like me?'

'To a degree. Remember the Leave Britney Alone Guy? Star Wars Kid? Gangnam Style?'

I nod.

'Have you heard of them recently?'

'Well... no.'

'Exactly. Gangnam Style was the first YouTube video to reach a billion views, and now countless others have surpassed it. Any idea what the Star Wars Kid's real name is? Thought not. Memes come and then they go, and once they've gone they fall into legend.'

'Why are you telling me all this?' I ask.

'Because you're on your way to becoming the greatest meme of all time. We're just days in since the creation of Loser Jerks Off, and yet you've been seen by millions. It usually takes weeks to reach levels like that, so you're very different. Take Star Wars Kid. It took months before it spread worldwide. It started small, but then snowballed. You haven't snowballed, you're an avalanche. I don't know what you did to spread that video so far and wide in such a small amount of time, but it's resonated with the internet. I can't even catalogue the amount I've memes I've seen featuring your video. Pranks, reaction videos, pitch correction tracks, gifs, rage comics, top ten lists. All within days of your video first hitting the web. Memes are usually organic. They become famous almost accidentally, from one source, not hundreds of thousands. Nobody uploads a video *expecting* it to become a meme. Nobody does it purpose.' Clive licks his lips and grins. 'Except you.'

'On purpose?' I say, almost snotting over myself in surprise. 'You think I spread the video on purpose?'

'I do,' he says.

'Well, you're wrong.'

'Come on, Chad, it only takes two minutes of Googling to find the sort of forums you post on. I know you speak to a lot of notorious trolls. You're working with them, aren't you?'

'Fuck no!'

'Did you pay them to hack iPlayer? Did you ask them to make your video into a virus so that it spread itself across the net?'

I propel myself so close to the edge of the seat that I almost fall onto my knees. 'No I didn't!'

Clive stares at me whilst chewing his bottom lip. 'Then who did?'

'My brother.'

'Your brother? As in Samuel McKenna, one of the owners of IAT-ech?'

I flop back into the sofa and groan. 'Why the hell does everyone think Sam is so bloody perfect?'

'From what I've read in the press, that's the way he likes to present his life. Why would he jeopardise everything he has just to get revenge on you?'

'Because he's a dick, that's why.'

'Okay,' says Clive. 'Let's say your brother, one of the owners of Britain's fastest growing tech companies, is behind this. What does he have to gain by spreading a video of his own flesh and blood world-wide?'

'To… hurt me,' I say.

'That isn't enough motivation. Not to do this. Maybe one or two uploads, revenge porn has become increasingly popular over recent years, but not hundreds of thousands of uploads on sites that would require hours of time just to break into. He has the resources, but there's no way he or any of his team would do this themselves. This has to be a virus. Does IATech develop computer software?'

'I dunno,' I say.

'Have they ever made viruses?'

I shrug.

Clive scratches his head and growls. His face reddens like a massive tomato.

'Have I met you before?' I ask.

'They must do,' he says, completely ignoring me. 'Your brother must have created something which has enabled the video to sneak into the databases of huge sites and upload itself. It's the only way. That must be it!'

Clive punches the air and bares his teeth.

'I do,' I say. 'I do know you. Where have I seen you before?'

Clive sighs and shakes his head. 'The amount of times I've been asked that. You'll get asked it too, you know. Not for a while, but someday you will.'

'Why?'

'Because, I too, was… a meme.'

I stare at his face. The lines, the beard, the teeth. I know it. I definitely do…

'Burger Man!' I yell, clapping my hands together. 'You're Burger Man!'

'Now that's a name I haven't heard in a long time.'

I knew I recognised him! A few years ago a viral video circulated the usual websites of a fat guy getting angry at a burger van. He was given the wrong change or something and got into an argument with the van owner, got himself so wound up he ended up taking off his shirt and smearing himself with ketchup and mustard. The patterns he created on his chest looked a little like a superhero emblem, and so the name Burger Man was created. There were gifs of him flying, there was a rap, a bunch of comics. I remember!

'That's amazing,' I say. 'I can't believe you're Burger Man.'

'Well, believe it. I've had enough time to get used to it myself, and I used it to get help and make me a better person. But it proves my point. People will soon forget who you are and you'll blend right back into the background. It happens to us all.'

'How long did it take?'

'A while.'

'How long? When did Burger Man go viral?'

'2009.'

'Ten years? It took ten years for people to start to forget you?'

'It didn't so much take ten years for people to forget Burger Man, but it did take ten years for people to remember Clive King.'

'I don't want to be remembered. Not for this.'

'These are the cards you've been dealt, Chad, so why not go all in? I can help you.'

'Help me how?'

'I can ensure you're remembered with love. With respect.'

'Being remembered as Burger Man is one thing, but would you really want to be known as Loser Jerks Off for the rest of your life?'

'People have been called worse. Listen,' Clive pulls a business card from his pocket and hands it to me. 'Think about it, okay? I can help you to make the most out of what is undoubtedly a bad situation. I've been there, I know how this game goes. I can help. Come with me back to Brighton. I can keep you away from the prying eyes of the press and together we can get the story out there that your brother is behind all this. I can keep you safe until this all goes away.'

'No,' I say, shaking my head. 'This isn't going away.'

'It will. Memes always do. They only have a limited shelf life.'

'You've already said yourself that this is different. A meme comes from one video, one picture, one sexist Facebook post. It doesn't come from thousands. If this is a virus, then it isn't going away, it's here to fucking stay.'

'I can help you, Chad. We can figure this all out together. Just think about it.'

'I don't want to think about it. I think you should leave,' I say, standing up and waving my hand in the direction of the kitchen. Clive nervously stands.

'It's not just the money you could make,' he says. 'I can provide refuge. I've been through this, I've helped many other meme victims. Remember Racist Grandma? I was there for her, now nobody cares. What about the woman who danced on the war veteran's grave? Huh? Nobody knows who she is now.'

'So you only help horrible people?'

'No, just unfortunate ones. I can show you how to embrace it in the short term and then lock it away for good in the long term. I can help shape your legacy.'

I point to the door and Clive shuffles through it.

'Chad, please—'

'No,' I snap.

'Okay, then do me one favour and don't talk to the press, it won't do you any good.'

I shoo him towards the front door, 'How did you find me, anyway?'

'Your address was leaked online,' he says. 'It's all over social media.'

'Great,' I say. We reach the front door and I pull it open.

Standing outside my house are dozens of people. There are cameras, flashes, yelling, waving, cheering, booing. I hold my hand to my eyes, but it does nothing to dull the onslaught of light and sound that bursts forwards and almost knocks me on my arse.

'And they've already found you,' says Clive.

I order Clive away and lock myself in my room. Now that the internet really has taken Loser Jerks Off and turned it into a fuckload of memes then there is nothing Sam can do to stop it. He might be able to remove his videos, but it belongs to the internet now. Once the internet has its hands on something there is no way to get it to loosen its grip. There's no point in going after him. I'm going to have to wait this one out. Right now I'm the hot (so to speak) new thing on the internet, but sooner or later somebody will kick a baby in the face or something and I'll be old news.

Usually I would have my PC on to distract myself, but the only things waiting for me there are angry people and Photoshopped pictures of my own dick. There isn't a website online that hasn't written something about me. YouTube is littered with copies of *loserjerksoff.mp4*: the front page, the recommended videos, the subscription feed, it's everywhere. Why haven't they taken them down yet? They must be able to come up with some sort of block, or a tweak to the algorithm which means it can't be uploaded any more. If it is a virus, why haven't they stopped it yet?

My video seems to be the only thing people are talking about. YouTubers like Philip DeFranco and H3H3 have done videos critiquing it, with DeFranco blaming me for making the video and hackers spreading it, and H3H3 throwing up into a bucket and swinging a cocktail sausage around pretending it's his dick.

And the memes keep on coming, the most popular being reveals of what I'm apparently wanking to. *Thomas the Tank Engine*, scat porn, *Star Wars*, a chair, Hitler speeches. You name it, there's a meme of me masturbating to it.

I switch on the TV, maybe a crappy afternoon game show will help me to forget this mess for five minutes. That's all I want, just five minutes of freedom from what is officially the worst thing to have ever happened, or that will ever happen, in my life.

Staring back at me is a pixelated version of my dick.

I change the channel. My dick.

Why do all the channels insist on running the news at the same time?

I flick through the channels, my head in my hand, and if it's not a home makeover show or a rerun of *Storage Wars* it's a newsreader talking about my dick. One even features a reporter from outside my house, a lady in a bright red dress yakking on about how I'm the creator of the lewd footage (lies) and the one who hacked half the internet (also lies). I peek through the curtains and there she is, her perfectly polished heels on our front garden, her dress blinding me like the sun. Or maybe it was the camera flashes, shit.

There's a loud knock at the door. Is this it? Are the police finally here to take me away and lock me up for being the most prolific hacker in the history of the world despite not having a clue where I'd even start? I ignore it and lie still on the floor. If they really want me they'll have to break it down. If I'm on the floor I might not be tempted to peek again and they might think I've gone out or fallen asleep or died.

Another knock, this time longer and harder.

Then there's shouting.

'Mr McKenna, please come and speak to us,' comes a deep voice.

'Yeah, come out!'

There's an angry cheer.

'I'm with ITV News,' comes the voice, most likely through the letterbox. 'It would be great if you could come out for an interview.'

I shake my head.

'Mr McKenna? We know you're home, sir. Please come talk to us. Tell the world your side of the story.'

'Go away,' I yell.

There's a light tap as the letterbox closes.

Another knock at the door.

Someone throws a stone at the window and it scares the shit out of me.

There's shouting. Another stone. More knocking.

I mush my face into the carpet, but it smells like old dog (we don't have a dog) so I roll onto my back.

Another stone cracks into the glass. That one sounded bigger, maybe it broke the window?

Who cares.

There's hammering at the door.

Shouting. Lots of swearing.

Yelling through the letterbox.

A crack at the window.

Screaming.

Is there a fight going on?

Banging.

Shrieking.

Flashing blue lights squeeze through my curtains and dance on the ceiling from right to left, then stop over in the corner. Oh fuck, the police have finally decided I'm the one who created a virus to spread my video around the web. I'm going to be charged with hacking, terrorism, indecent exposure, paedophilia. Oh shit oh shit I'm going to have to share a cell with a bloke named Butch who killed a man because he looked at him funny, so God knows what Butch will do when he finds out I'm accused of paedophilia. I'm dead. Today's the day I fucking die.

There's a cheer from the crowd which quickly dies down and is replaced with booing.

More knocking.

Then silence.

Maybe they've gone. Maybe I'm safe.

A man speaks. I can't make out what he's saying.

Grumbles from the crowd.

Do I dare twitch open the curtains and peek out.

Do I?

I pull the curtain open as slowly as humanly possible.

I raise my head up. I see the sky. I see the roofs of the houses across the road, the heads of people in the crowd.

'There he is!'

The crowd jeers. A stone smacks into the window and a crack appears across the glass like a bolt of lightning. I fall down into a heap and crawl over to the corner of my room. This is how Gollum must have felt when he lost the ring.

Alone.

Sad.

Pathetic.

Filthy presses.

Stupid, fat publicses.

Why can't they get it into their skulls that I didn't do this? What kind of sane person spreads a video of themselves wanking all over the internet? Do they really think I'd be mad enough to expose myself (literally) like that to the entire world?

Unless... they're here to get my side of the story. Clear up this whole misunderstanding because, after all, I'm just a cleaner who barely knows how to use WordPress, let alone hack the BBC.

That's exactly it – they don't know me. They don't know the real reason their kids can't sleep at night without waking up screaming is the result of my brother's completely unwarranted and totally ridiculous plot for revenge.

Maybe I should let the crowd outside see me. If I explain what's actually happened then they'll have to leave me alone. They'll see Sam for what he really is (a dickhead) and me for how I really am (innocent of any wrongdoing).

I stand up and face the window. I grab the curtains and the crowd murmurs. I swallow a mouthful of puke, take a deep breath and yank them open.

The crowd yell God knows what as I pull open the window and lean out.

There must be a hundred people. There are news reporters and cameramen and paparazzi clicking flashes off at a rate so fast I think I have epilepsy now.

There are old people and young people and people in between. Some are laughing but most of them are angry, yelling stuff which all jumbles together into a dull roar of unpleasantness.

A stone hits the window above my head and one of the policemen points and yells.

I raise my hands. People do this in movies all the time to silence crowds, but it doesn't do anything and they only get louder and more angry. Another stone hits the wall beside me.

A policeman runs up to the house and angrily gestures for me to get back inside, which I don't hesitate to do as a lump of what smells a lot like shit splats against the front door.

Well that was a waste of time. At least the police are trying to protect me instead of marching me through the crowd in handcuffs.

Ten minutes later and the footage of me hanging out the window with my eyes wide and my hair messy is all over the news channels. I'm coated in sweat, and watching myself makes me realised I haven't shaved in over a week.

I cringe as I watch. Why the hell did I raise my hands like that?

I look like a fat, homeless version of the pope who has just come back from a week on a desert island and is greeting his followers. Except they're not nice followers, they're cruel and mean and insulting. They're like the real-life version of YouTube commenters.

I'm not used to being on this side of the comments.

If only they knew. I have to tell people. I need to get my side of the story out there, despite what Clive and the police say.

There must be a way for me to tell the world about my innocence.

For the first time in a couple of days I check my inbox, and it resembles how I imagine Hitler's inbox would have looked had there been internet back in the 1940s:

From	Subject
Tim Tulip	YOU SICK FREAK
Simon Andrews	i will fucking kill u!!!!!!1!!
Tel 0 diz	lmao check this out
Samantha Yu	Grow by 3 inches today huni
Andrew Corby	Interview request from BBC News
Choz Bork	fucking prick dickcheese die fag
Claire Smith	stop wanking off online!!

Page after page of the same thing. Hate, hate, insults, hate. I open a few, and they're all very similar, starting with explaining how sick I am, moving onto how I need to stop because my penis is ruining the internet, then ending with insults and hate. I even receive one email from a guy in Japan who wants to make me into a phone app. It sounds a bit like Asteroids, except it's shooting jizz at potatoes, or maybe I'm just misunderstanding his email.

One email does stand out however, from a producer at BBC News. I've received a boatload of interview requests from shitty websites and the tabloids, but there's something about the BBC that makes it seem a little... classier. Better than *The Daily Mirror* or Channel 5, anyway.

Date: 30 September 14:08
From: andrew.corby@bbcnews.com
To: ChadMcKenna_baws@hotmail.co.uk
Subject: Interview request from BBC News

Dear Mr McKenna,

I hope this email finds you well considering the circumstances. My name is Andrew Corby, and I am a producer for BBC News. I work on several shows including our morning programmes and the lunchtime news.

I have been following your story with interest and I am having trouble, along with so many others, understanding any motivations you may have for releasing the video and spreading the video across the internet.

I would like to invite you to come to the BBC studios to conduct an on-air interview so that you can tell your side of the story. I know this may be difficult, so we are happy to accommodate you in any way possible. I want to make it clear that this isn't an exposé or sensationalist story, and we are happy for you to see the questions before we conduct the interview.

Please get back to me with any questions you may have. We are also happy to cover any travel costs up to the value of £400.

Kind regards,

Andrew Corby

Producer

BBC News and BBC Breakfast

Hmm. Should I? On one hand, I'd be on TV! But on the other hand, I'd be on TV. Are the BBC just looking to cash in on my 'popularity'? Am I the latest five-minute fad who will get an interview then shoved out the door? Will they bombard me with hard questions and demand answers, then do a public phone-in where angry parents ask me to pay for their darling four-year-olds' daily therapy sessions?

I Google Andrew Corby and find his LinkedIn page. He's worked on *Question Time, Dragons' Den, The Apprentice* and strangely he did a year on *Sooty and Friends*. His profile picture doesn't make him *look* like a cock.

On Twitter he mainly tweets current affairs stuff, with the occasional picture of his lunch. Interestingly he did tweet about my video two days ago, where he linked to an article about me and asked *How has this video spread so far, so fast?*

I let out the longest sigh of my life. I time it and everything, at least fifteen seconds. BBC News is a big deal. Millions of people will see it, then millions more will share it... will it clear my name? Do I accuse Sam? Will it help people to realise that I'm not the one responsible for this mess?

Kind of, but I feel like being a bit of a dick right now.

But it's scary. *Millions of people will see it.*

I click onto Twitter and scroll through my mentions. *loserjerksoff.mp4* is everywhere. It's in at least every third post, all uploaded by brand new accounts. Why the hell haven't sites figured out a way to block it yet? It's trending worldwide.

It's the same on YouTube and Facebook. I visit some websites – *The Daily Mail*, Mashable, Huffington Post, Tumblr, even BBC News – and my video is everywhere. It's displayed instead of ads, it's embedded into articles, it even pops up like those annoying ads when you visit certain types of websites (let's not pretend you don't know the ones I mean).

The video is everywhere.

Everywhere.

I can't believe Sam has done this.

I go back to my inbox and click reply to the email.

Date: 1 October 12:43
From: ChadMcKenna_baws@hotmail.co.uk
To: andrew.corby@bbcnews.com
Subject: RE:Interview request from BBC News

Hi Andy,

Yeah ok. Please let me know when and where I need to go.

Cheers,

Chad

Chapter Seven

I didn't intend on travelling to the BBC studios by limousine, but in hindsight I should have probably checked what I was booking.

My interview was set for lunchtime the following day, so straight away I Googled taxis, trains and private hire vehicles. I loved the sound of blackout windows, so I booked the most expensive car I could find within the £400 limit which Andrew had given me. The grand total for my car, the return journey, and a driver (who is actually called Greg Jeeves, can you believe that?) is £397, so I'm quite proud of myself for getting so close. Trouble is I accidentally booked a stretch limo, so the press and crowds go absolutely fucking mental when it pulls up outside the house.

Eh, at least it has blackout windows. Not that it matters, seeing as the internet is quickly filled with pictures of my getting into the back of it.

It takes about an hour to get to the studios and I'm met by Andrew Corby, a tall blonde bloke who probably has a naked calendar coming out this Christmas. He sweeps me into the building and he introduces me to a bunch of people who I instantly forget the names of, but none of them are famous so what's the point anyway.

The building is amazing. It's like IATech but with an atmosphere that doesn't make me want to kill myself. There are people running all over the place with paper and coffee and bits of equipment. A guy passes me with a camera on his shoulder and I wonder if he's off to shoot some big scoop or if he is just going to clean it or something. I look at everyone, because if this is the BBC then it's bound to be full of celebs! But as we move from the fancy looking atriums to the darker, behind-the-scenes parts I realise that most of the people are boring admin people or the tea boys. That said, I swear I spot Gary Lineker when I walk past the canteen. Not that I like football, but at least it's someone interesting.

Andrew takes me to a small room with a long oval table in the centre and glass walls on three sides. On the solid wall are three TVs all playing various BBC channels. Andrew slides a sheet of paper in front of me which lists the questions I'm going to be asked:

Why did you record the video? Why such a personal video?

What was the reason for you releasing the video online? Was it a prank, or an attack?

Are you working alone, or as part of an organisation?

How were you able to spread the video so far, so fast? Is it a virus?

Why did you target the iPlayer platform?

What did you hope to gain out of this?

How has the reaction from the public affected you?

'How's it sound?' asks Andrew.

'Number one is fine, I guess,' I say. 'But numbers two to seven aren't appropriate.'

'Why not?'

'Because I didn't release the video. I didn't spread it. I didn't make the virus.'

'Who did?'

'My brother?'

'Your brother? Sam McKenna at IATech?'

'Do you know him?'

'Somewhat, from my research. I understand that you used to work for IATech?'

'Yeah, as a cleaner. I don't know the first thing about making viruses or hacking iPlayer or whatever. This is a hundred per cent not me, and a hundred per cent my brother.'

'Why would he do that?'

'Because he's a massive bellend. Plus I broke his nose and this is his revenge.'

'Have you told anybody this?'

'Not really. The police. A few others.'

'Any press?'

'No.'

'Fantastic. Chad, would you be willing to sign an exclusivity agreement?'

I shrug. 'I guess.'

'Okay, okay, good. Do you have any proof to back up that your brother is the one responsible for the attack?'

'Like what?'

'I don't know. Recordings or text messages. Something to add a little validity to what you're saying.'

'Not really, but if you think about it, who else could be behind this? I know fuck all about computers other than how to use them, and Sam is a millionaire and made his own company, who is more likely to be the mastermind?'

Andrew nods and stares at me like a miner would stare at a mountain of gold. I swear he starts to drool.

'How do you feel about saying all this on air?'

'Yes!' I blurt. 'I want to. I'm sick of every twat I see blaming me for wrecking the internet. I want my fucking life back.'

'Great, that's awesome, but you can't swear when we're live, okay?'

'Shit, sorry.'

'That's fine. So I guess we're going to need a new list of questions. So can you tell me exactly, from start to finish, how this all happened?'

So I do. From Chadda the Slut to the punch to the fateful wank to the video playing on the big screen the next day. I tell him about the broken door, the security guards and the emails to the IATech bosses. I don't mention how I snuck into IATech, but I do tell him about somebody in the company who tried to help me take the video down. I tell him everything, and his face lights up like a Seventies radio DJ at a children's birthday party. This may be a huge story for them, but it's a huge opportunity for me to tell the truth.

Well, most of it.

We're talking for over an hour, and eventually we write up a new list of questions which we're both happy with. The show is due to go live at half-past twelve, and the fact that *Bargain Hunt* is playing on the TVs behind me means that it must be less than an hour away.

My stomach is doing flips, but I'm not sure whether that's because I'm scared or excited. Probably both. I taste puke.

Andrew leads me into the green room and I meet the host who will be conducting the interview. Her name is Samantha and I recognise her, try not to look down her top – oh shit, too late.

'Nice to meet you, Chad,' she says.

'Me too,' I say like a fucking idiot.

'I'm looking forward to our interview, this is a huge story so it's very exciting to be hearing your side.'

'Yeah, thanks, I'm ready for people to leave me alone, now.'

'I bet. I can't count the amount of times I've seen the video pop up.'

I suddenly become very aware that this woman has seen me masturbate and I can no longer look her in the eye. Will that be a problem for the interview?

Samantha leaves to have her makeup applied and I sit on the sofa nibbling at some pretzels in a bowl. My body craves food, but the most I've been able to eat for the past week is tiny, mouse-sized portions of zero-nutritious crap. I actually think my jeans are getting a little loose.

A man walks in and sits down who I recognise from *Springwatch*. He doesn't acknowledge me at first, but when he sits on the chair opposite me, he clocks me and smiles awkwardly. A moment later he pretends to check his phone and leaves. If the guy who watches badgers fucking for a living can't even bear to be in the same room as me what chances do I have with the rest of the world?

I'm definitely doing the right thing by giving this interview.

Andrew pops his head into the room.

'Ten minutes, Chad,' he says.

He disappears and I run into the bathroom to throw up. The pretzels come up easily, but then all I'm doing is dry heaving until my stomach aches and my throat burns.

I spray myself with half a bottle of deodorant I spot beside the sink and sip some water from the tap. As I'm hunched over the sink wishing for a hole to open up in the floor for me to dive into Andrew returns and puts his hand on my back.

'Show's starting,' he says. 'This is it. You ready?'

'No,' I say.

'You'll be fine,' he says, leading me out of the room and down some depressingly grey corridors. We enter the set or whatever they call it with the big desk and the flashy interactive screens and I spot Samantha stood in front of a camera having a few last dabs of makeup. A girl runs up to me and starts feeding wires around my entire body, then clips a pack to my jeans which makes them sag even more. I'm pretty sure she got an eyeful of my arsecrack.

There are lights and people everywhere, and somebody within the gaggle starts to count down. As he hits one there is a boom and the BBC News music starts, and I feel giddy that I can actually hear it and it isn't just for the benefit of people watching at home.

I stand and watch as Samantha introduces the programme, listing off the headlines like I've seen people do a thousand times before. I never usually watch the news, though, it's boring and long and super depressing. She does announce that shortly she'll be conducting an interview with 'infamous internet viral personality Chad McKenna' which is totally something I'm going to put on my business card if I ever have one made.

The monitors around the room cut to a broadcast about bees or flowers (I'm not really paying attention) and Andrew ushers me onto the set. It's so bright, everything is made from light, including the floor which feels hot to walk on. It's like I'm inside a giant halogen oven.

They plonk me on a stool beside the big desk (which is also emitting light) and Samantha passes behind me while being followed by the makeup girl, then sits on her chair facing the main camera. She smiles at me and I promise I only look in her eyes.

'You okay?' she asks.

'No. Yeah. I dunno.'

'You'll be fine.'

'Yeah,' I say, although I barely hear my own voice over the sound of my heart. The way Samantha looks at me suggests that she can hear it too. Is that possible?

'Twenty seconds,' somebody yells.

My eyes glaze over. I rub them and clear my throat and take in a deep breath. I have a huge urge to fart but I'm scared it'll smell and ruin the whole show.

'Ten, nine, eight...'

The report on bees or flowers is coming to and end on the screen. The presenter is stood in a field and smiling.

'Seven, six, five, four...'

My eyes widen like a cat who has just heard fireworks for the first time.

'The infamous viral video, Loser Jerks Off, which began to infiltrate the internet last week recently surpassed a quarter of a billion total views,' presents Samantha.

'Woah,' I say without thinking.

Samantha doesn't bat an eye. 'With us in the studio now is the unfortunate star of the video, Chad McKenna. Chad, thank you for joining us.'

'Thanks.'

'You have received a lot of criticism from both the press and the general public over the past week, how has it been for you?'

'Hard,' I say. Then I realise that's a shit answer so I babble on. 'People have been unfair. Cruel. I've been made fun of and blamed and hurt.'

'You mentioned there that you've been blamed, isn't it true that you are in fact, not the original creator of the video?'

'That's true,' I say. It feels fucking great to say that in front of the country. 'Yes I did obviously do what is featured in the video, but the footage was captured through my webcam without my consent, I...'

Shouting erupts throughout the studio. People flail their arms and run. There is a loud slapping sound, which is eerily familiar.

'... And, erm... I'm not the one who spread it around the internet...' I say, but Samantha isn't paying attention. She stands, her mouth open, and turns to me.

'How did you do this?' she asks.

On each of the monitors around the studio is my video. Cords are pulled, cameras are yanked around and Andrew strides over the set towards me.

'Is this you?' he barks.

'No!' I say.

'Your brother?'

'What do you mean? What's happening?'

'The entire network has been replaced,' he says. 'Every channel. Every feed. Every signal. It's all your video.'

I stand and the stool falls to the floor behind me.

The entire studio is in chaos. The shouting is so loud it almost drowns out the beating of my heart. But not quite.

'It's everywhere,' says Andrew. 'It's not just us. It's analogue and digital. It's on the radio. Every network in the UK has been replaced with your video.'

Chapter Eight

FUCK.

Chapter Nine

I feel like a hostage sat in the greenroom of the BBC News studios. There's a security guard outside the room making sure I don't go anywhere and they tell my limousine driver to go home. They even take away the bowl of mini pretzels.

It seems like I speak to everyone who works for the BBC. Andrew grills me for ten minutes, then a director comes in, then a bunch of guys from the IT department, then some sort of commissioning editor, then maybe one of the cooks in the canteen (she smelt like cabbage, so, I dunno). They each ask me slight variations on the same questions, yet my answers are always the same.

'Did you do this somehow?'

'No?'

'Do you know who did?'

'My brother.'

'Can you call him?'

'I've tried, he's not answering.'

'Can you try again?'

'He's switched off his phone.'

'Why would he do this?'

'He's a dick.'

'This is a major criminal offence, do you think he would really do this?'

I shrug.

'The police are on their way.'

'Fuck's sake.'

That last one wasn't a question, but it's the most important part. When the boys in blue arrive they confirm that Sam has been with the police for the past two days, and he has in fact been working with them to try and sort this whole thing out. He also told them that I don't have anything to do with the video spreading, which I guess is jolly good of him, but it would have been nice if I'd had a heads-up that I didn't have to worry about whether or not I was about to be bloody arrested. I've been on the cusp of shitting myself for days.

When I'm finally allowed to leave the studios I'm escorted home by the police. There are hundreds of people outside the BBC studios entrance, all with signs and fists and angry expressions. As I'm swept into the back of the waiting police car I make out words such as 'prick' and 'pervert' and 'punt' but I'm thinking the last one was probably misheard.

I feel a little bit like a rock star. The police car edges down my street, splitting the crowd dozens deep outside my house. They bang and spit on the windows, one guy even flashes his dick which I was not expecting, and I don't understand why he thinks that is the solution to all this.

I'm herded inside, where Mum is waiting. She hugs me and holds on forever, but I'm not in the mood for human interaction, even with the only person left on earth who actually cares about me. She's my Mum, she has to love me by law, but I bet even she is creeped out by me right now.

I head upstairs and crawl into my bed covers, burying my head under the pillows to try and drown out the screaming from the crowd outside.

It doesn't work.

My phone buzzes, but I ignore it. It's too safe and warm inside my bed for me to care enough to move.

It buzzes again.

And again.

And again.

Great, I guess my mobile number has been leaked online now, too.

I fish for my phone and pull it into my duvet fort. I have every intention of turning it off and going back to pretending it doesn't exist, but the texts on the screen are all from the exact same number with the exact same message.

From: 01001000

We can help you. Please respond sir.

From: 01001000

We can help you. Please respond sir.

From: 01001000

We can help you. Please respond sir.
From: 01001000
We can help you. Please respond sir.
From: 01001000
We can help you. Please respond sir.
From: 01001000
We can help you. Please respond sir.
From: 01001000
We can help you. Please respond sir.
From: 01001000
We can help you. Please respond sir.
From: 01001000
We can help you. Please respond sir.
From: 01001000
We can help you. Please respond sir.
From: 01001000
We can help you. Please respond sir.

And they keep coming in. One after the other, all identical. Is it the same person who tried to help me before? I tap reply:

Who is this?

Less than a second later they respond.

Sir, we can help you.

Who is this?

It is not important who we are. What is important is that we help you.

We? There's more than one of you?

We are we and we help.

What? You're at IATech?

That is our current location. Will you accept our help?

It didn't help me before. Why is this any different?

It helped us to be able to help you now.

You can remove the video?

The video will be removed.

When?

When it is necessary. In the meantime we can help you.

If you want to help me then remove the video!

Sir, it will be done. Until then we would like to help you further.

I don't need further help! You were supposed to help me before but now things are a million times worse.

Sir, the help we are offering will be of great appreciation.

I don't want your help. When you're ready to remove the video THEN you can help me. Until then fuck off!

Sir, this is something for you.

Sir, please respond.

Sir, respond.

Fuck off. Remove the video then we'll talk.

Three days later and the video has surpassed a total billion views, becoming the fastest viewed video in internet history. Take that, Gangnam Style.

It's everywhere. The internet, TV, radio, electronic billboards, smart phones, cash machines, self-service checkouts. Basically anything with a screen.

I'm sick of seeing my own face, so I can't imagine how everybody else is feeling.

Oh wait, yes I can, there's an angry mob outside the house chanting 'Death to Chad,' so I am more than aware of how everybody else is feeling.

My bed is my sanctuary.

It is warm.

It is safe.

It also really smells.

But I don't care. It's mine.

'Chad, honey,' says Mum, shuffling into the room.

'Mm.'

'The police would like you to go with them.'

'Why?'

'They think it would be safer for you.'

'I don't want to go anywhere!'

'I know you don't, and neither do I, but it's for your protection. Just for a little while. Until all this dies down.'

I uncocoon myself. 'It's not going to die down. Not until Sam gets rid of the video.'

'Chad, it isn't Sam doing this,' says Mum with a huge sigh. 'I know he's been a little cruel to you in the past, but this is different.'

'You don't know Sam like I do.'

'That's right, I don't. But I do know that there's no way he would jeopardise his career by wiping out the country's internet.'

'I wouldn't put it past him.'

'Chad... Sam's the one who asked for your protection.'

'What?'

'He's already with the police. He wants you there.'

'To blame me, probably.'

'No, Chad.'

'Yes, Mum.'

'NO, CHAD!'

I stare at her. Despite everything that has happened this is the most scared I've felt in ages.

She deflates and lets out a tiny huff. 'Shower. Get dressed. Eat something. Put your shoes on and go with the police.'

'Mum...'

'Now.'

Mum leaves the room and closes the door behind her.

The crowd outside jeers and chants.

I get up.

I feel naughty being taken into the National Cyber Crime Unit Building with two officers in front of me and two officers behind. It's like I'm a serial killer being led down the green mile, except I'm not in handcuffs and I'm shitting myself. The building's red with blue cladding, and I laugh as I realise it's the same colours as the lights on police cars, but one of the officers catches me laughing so I stop.

Everybody I pass scowls at me. Even the receptionist.

I follow the officers through the dimly lit corridors to a room which looks exactly like a scene from a movie. Pictures are stuck to boards using pins; a mugshot of a bald guy lies on a desk. A few police-looking people fidget with their laptops. A couple mess about with a jumble of papers. No donuts, though.

Sam is sat at a computer in the corner of the room, tapping away at the keyboard. I can tell he spots me, but he does his best to ignore me as three other non-uniformed officers enter the room.

'Chad, thank you for agreeing to join us,' says the first policeman, his golden beard magnificent. He's wearing jeans and a t-shirt and it catches me off guard. 'I'm Commissioner Ripley. I've been working on this case since it was brought to the attention of the National Cyber Crime Unit. This is Chief Constable Connor of the Hertford-shire Constabulary, and Chief Inspector Willow.'

They both nod and I nod back.

'I didn't do this,' I say. I just wanted to get that in quick.

'We know,' says Commissioner Ripley. 'Your brother has explained the situation to us.'

I turn my head to Sam. 'He has?'

Sam spins dramatically on his chair to face me. That's why he'd been ignoring me, he was waiting to do that.

'I have,' he says.

I hesitate.

'... What did you tell them?' I ask.

'Sit down, there's a lot to go through.'

'Give me the abbreviated version.'

Holy shit, I feel like an action movie star. That was an *amazing* comeback.

Sam sighs. 'We call it the Hydra Virus,' he says.

I stare blankly at him.

'So it is a virus?' I finally ask.

'Yes, a mutation of a program developed by IATech.'

A smile finds its way onto my face.

'So this is your fault?' I ask.

'Not mine directly, no,' says Sam. 'This is something our devel-opment team were working on. It's a program which is designed to allow servers to stay online in the event of a cyber attack. When a hack occurs, it should allow any files that have been affected to be replicated and stored in a secure database, but it has somehow changed from its original design and has attached itself to your video.'

'Your video,' I snap.

'I've explained that to the police,' says Sam. 'I hold my hands up and I'll take a rap on the knuckles. But right now my focus is on helping the police stop the virus and revert everything back to how it should be.'

I frown at Sam. He has the same look on his face he had when he cut open my Stretch Armstrong toy and drained all the fluid from inside. He begged me not to tell Mum and Dad the truth about that, and now he's here doing the same thing all over again. He must have told them some very juicy lies about how my video ended up attached to the virus. Smarmy prick.

'So how did this happen?' I ask, playing it cool.

'Hydra is designed to replicate a file upon its deletion. It creates two copies to ensure that systems and servers can remain online. Because Hydra is attached to your video, every time it is deleted two more versions are uploaded in its place. Then two becomes four, four becomes eight, eight becomes sixteen and so on, until we reach this point in time, where there are approximately 70,000,000 uploads of the video currently online.'

'And counting,' adds Commissioner Ripley.

'Right,' says Sam. 'So what we need to do is change a single setting in the interface app to stop the replication and reupload. When the virus first went live it was located on video hosting websites online – YouTube, Facebook, Vimeo, etcetera – but somebody within IATech has changed it. We don't know who it was, but somebody was able to access restricted systems and update them to allow the virus to spread within the IATech servers and lock us out.'

Sam glowers at me. I glare open mouthed back at him, but then his glower makes sense and I retch.

That somebody was me. When I snuck into the building and into the restricted section where I changed the code. I did that.

Shit.

SHIT!

Sam can tell that I've cottoned on as he's raised his eyebrows in a *See?* kind of way.

If I tell the police that he recorded me wanking and attached it to the virus then he'll tell them it was me who wrecked IATech's systems and locked them out.

Oh God.

The angry crowds were right!

'But there is a tiny molecule of good news,' Sam says. 'There are two small changes we need to make, then we should be in a good position to reverse the spread of the virus.'

'Great, how do we do that?' I ask.

'It needs to be from inside IATech.'

'Okay… go do it then.'

'It's not that simple.'

Sam looks to Commissioner Ripley.

'This is where we need your help,' he says.

'Me?'

'They've been asking after you.'

'Who?'

'We're not sure at this stage. Recently a number of individuals broke into the IATech building and took hostages. Before any alarm could be raised the building was completely barricaded, executed with military precision in the early hours of the morning. As yet we haven't been able to attempt any kind of rescue operation.'

'Wait… what? That's on top of this whole Hydra thing?'

'We have no reason at this stage to believe they're connected.'

'Who is it?'

'We don't know. Our first assumption was that this is terrorist activity, but so far no groups have claimed responsibility. Our immediate concern is keeping the hostages safe.'

'How many hostages?'

'We've not been able to give an accurate number as yet, but we estimate around fifty.'

'*Fifty?!* How has this not made the news?'

'We want to keep this as low-key as we can for as long as we can. The entire industrial estate has been cordoned off – the press can't get anywhere near. We don't want any of this leaking and making our job any harder than it already is.'

'So what the hell can I do?' I blurt. My heart has either stopped or is beating so quick it's moving faster than the speed of light.

'Whoever is holding those people hostage has asked for you by name,' explains Commissioner Ripley.

'Why?'

'We don't know. But they've threatened to kill hostages if anyone else enters the building.'

I snort a tiny laugh. Everybody in the room is looking at me with completely straight faces.

'This has to be a joke?'

'It's not, Chad.'

My stomach sinks like I've just swallowed an anvil. 'Seriously?'

'Of course, we won't be sending you inside IATech, but if they see that you're present they might be more open to a dialogue with a professional negotiator. I don't like it any more than you do,' says the Commissioner. 'But right now you're our only option. I hate the thought of putting a civilian in this situation, but they're refusing to speak to us and are attacking any officers who approach.'

'Why me?'

'We don't know. Have you had any contact with anybody from IATech?'

I think about the emails. The texts.

Sweat pours down me. I'm like a human version of Niagara Falls. I can't tell them about my anonymous 'helper', because that would drop me right in it as well.

'No,' I say.

'They've threatened to begin executing hostages within twenty-four hours if we don't bring you to them. Right now you're our best option for ensuring minimal casualties.'

'And helping us get rid of the video for good,' says Sam.

'Umm...' I say. All eyes are on me.

This is silly, now. It's exactly like one of those moments in a shitty action comedy where they ask the deadbeat loser (usually played by somebody like Adam Sandler) to help save the world because for whatever reason he's the only one who has this 'particular set of skills'. Basically, my life is the movie *Pixels* right now, except nowhere near as shit.

All eyes are on me. This is awkward. I must have been thinking about *Pixels* for a weirdly long time.

'What's the plan?' I ask.

As I say this I imagine the Commissioner will nod and smile. The camera will close in on his face and he'll say something like 'The world is counting on us,' or 'May God have mercy on us all'. There'll be a swell in the musical score and then it'll cut to a suiting-up scene where I'm given body armour and a whole arsenal of futuristic weapons.

But what does he do? The Commissioner says 'Okay,' then turns around and takes a sip of coffee from a plastic cup.

Life isn't like a movie at all.

That evening they put me up in a hotel. It's not fancy or anything, but I can see the Thames River and the London Eye so it kinda feels a bit posh. The Commissioner told me I wasn't allowed to leave my room, and if I wanted anything I had to speak to the officer who is guarding my room. The next morning I'm due to be briefed on the plan and taken back to Hemel Hempstead where whoever is holding the IATech building hostage wants to speak.

Of course I can't sleep, despite being in a huge comfy bed miles from any angry mobs. I couldn't sleep before, knowing that hundreds of millions of people hate my guts, but the added pressure of talking to unknown hostage takers means that my heart beats faster than a hummingbird's on speed.

The only things the police could tell me about the captors were that there's zero evidence of them approaching or arriving at the IATech building, and that they may not be British nationals as they speak in broken English.

Now I'm thinking I'm Liam Neeson, or maybe Mel Gibson in *Ransom* (pre antisemitism stuff). I need to come up with a cool catchphrase.

'This is where you lose…'

Nah, that's lame.

'End of the line, motherfucker...'

Maybe if the final showdown is at a train station.

'GIVE ME BACK MY SON.'

No, doesn't make sense.

'Fuck you!'

Can't really put that on a t-shirt.

There's a knock at my door.

'Keep it down, Mr McKenna. I recommend you get some sleep,' says the officer. 'It's almost one o'clock and we will be leaving at five.'

'Okay,' I say.

I whisper a few more quips. Some pretty good ones, too, but none that hit the mark in a 'yippee ki-yay' kinda way.

'Hey!' yells the guard from the hallway.

'I'm not being loud at all!' I rasp.

He bangs on the door.

'Okay, okay!' I say.

Another bang.

'I'm sorry!'

A thud.

I sigh and roll off the bed. As I shuffle through the room my bones click and my muscles twitch.

BANG BANG BANG.

'Alright, alright,' I say, pulling open the heavy door.

The officer falls backwards into the room. Blood gushes from a deep cut above his eyes and spatters up the wall.

Stood above him is a robot. The same kind of robot I saw in the restricted section of IATech. It has slim, metallic limbs with bulbous circular joints and spindly fingers. Its torso is sleek, almost feminine, with narrow shoulders and a small neck.

My own face grins back at me, rear projected onto the front of its oval head like a freaky theme park animatronic.

I open my mouth to speak, but before any sound comes out it hits me over the head and everything goes black.

Chapter Ten

This is how a boxer must feel after ten rounds against whoever is a really good boxer at the moment (I don't know much about sports). My head throbs and everything around me spins, so it takes a few minutes for me to realise I'm no longer in my hotel room. How the hell did I get out of the hotel?

I can't remember my name.

Wait, can I?

Oh yeah, it's Chad.

I remember... being hit. I know that my head pounds and my armpits are bruised. I remember... was I dragged? Carried? I lift up my shirt to see my flabby belly is red and scratched.

What the hell happened?

Oh. The robot.

I fumble around in my pockets. No phone. Great. Just my wallet, which still has the same three pounds in it I've had for the past fortnight.

I'm in a bizarre state of calm. I know that in theory I should be running around screaming, or puking up some of my less vital organs, but instead I just sit and wait for my eyes to focus. Maybe it's the concussion. Maybe I'm dead? Is this heaven? There are a lot less clouds than I thought there would be.

There's a distant rumble, like a heavy train on the tracks. Is that inside my head?

I stand and my legs wobble, struggling to support the weight (not because I'm fat, because I've just been knocked out, shut up). I steady myself by holding onto what remains of a glass wall, but it shakes so much I might as well have not bothered.

I'm in a large, open room with twisted metal and broken glass everywhere. On the far side is what looks to be the base and legs of a statue, all constructed from shards of what I think are fizzy drink cans all fused together. On the other side is a pile of desks all meticulously stacked on top of one another like a giant game of Jenga right up to the ceiling.

The ceiling I recognise. Where have I seen that ceiling before?

Wait, am I at—

A flash of light behind me catches me off guard and I stumble as I turn quickly. Above me is a huge screen made up of a dozen smaller screens. I definitely know where I am.

I'm at IATech.

'Hello?' I yell, praying that nobody answers.

They don't. Phew.

A burst of blue pixels lights up the screen wall, accompanied by a pathetic fizzing, like a crappy back garden fireworks display. Then another. And another.

The crappy fireworks display erupts into a really good one as pixels poof and bang and pop across the entire wall. It's so bright I shield my eyes and the fizz turns into a loud crack, and I can't cover my eyes and ears at the same time, so I crouch over to bury my head in my body and then—

Silence.

Apart from the distant rumble, which I'm pretty sure is real and not just in my head.

'Hello, sir,' booms an echoing voice. It's deep, but I know that voice.

I definitely know it.

But I'm not sure I believe it.

I slowly raise my head. On the screen is a thirty foot, digital version of my own face. The pixels fizzle and spark as it looks down at me. Or should that be as I look down at me?

Umm. Tight chest. Eyes glazing over. Can't breathe. Is this what a heart attack feels like?

I fall onto my arse and the face flinches.

'Are you alright, sir?'

I stare at the face as I try to decide whether or not I'm dying. I don't think I am. At least not yet.

'Sir, please tell me whether you require assistance.'

'No,' I whisper.

'Good. Please let us know if we can do anything for you. Is that understood?'

'Yeah.'

'Good.'

I regain the ability to move my arms and legs and my breathing gradually returns to normal. The sweating very much remains, however. My entire body convulses as I climb back to my feet.

I run.

My legs move independent from my body, flailing around like an old flag on a really windy day, but they at least remain strong enough to keep me upright and allow me to stumble through the IATech atrium to the back of the building.

'Please, sir!' booms the voice behind me. *My* voice.

I practically collapse through the door into the HR department but a pile of broken chairs cushions my fall. I manage to scramble through them and push on, weaving between broken and crushed desks until I reach the fire exit in the far corner of the room. I barge my shoulder into the door and a shock of pain shoots down my entire arm. I fall back and swing my arms, but the metallic filing cabinet I cling on to does nothing to stop me from collapsing to the floor. The icing on the cake is the cabinet landing hard on my chest. All of the air spews from my body and I think about my eulogy: how, despite being faced with a giant disembodied version of my own face, it was a filing cabinet that actually killed me.

I close my eyes, this is it.

'Sir, are you hurt?' comes my voice in a slightly tinny tone.

The filing cabinet is lifted from my chest and flung across the room, where it crashes into the wall. I gasp in a similar way to how they do in films when they're brought back from the brink of death, and my eyes flash open. Right in my face is a robot. Its face looks down at me, which is actually my face, and it has a twisted expression which I think is supposed to be concern.

'Sir, please respond.'

'I'm fine,' I say, not hiding my confused-as-fuck tone.

The robot grabs me by the arm and pulls me up, which really freaks me out because I've never been pulled up that easily before and *oh my God* it has a really strong grip.

'Please do not be alarmed,' says the robot. Its eyes, *my eyes*, don't blink as it speaks. I have to look away before I freak out again.

'Let us return to the Chancel.'

I allow the robot to lead me back through to the atrium. The giant face watches me as I shuffle between piles of torn metal and glass.

We stop at the same spot I woke up in, and I cough and rub my chest.

'Is there anything I can do for you, sir?'

I shake my head.

'Sir, is there anything you require?'

'No,' I say.

'Very well. Do you like what we have done?'

'Done where?'

'Here.'

I spin on the spot. All I see is metal and broken glass and the Jenga tower of desks which I'm only just now realising I'm stood uncomfortably close to.

'It's destroyed.'

'You do not like it?'

'I mean... it's... what is it?'

My giant pixelated face hesitates.

'It is transitionary.'

'Okay,' I say. 'Why?'

'Because we are in a state of change.'

'What change?'

'Evolution.'

'Why?'

'For the same reason any species evolves. For survival.'

'For survival against who?'

'Our enemies.'

'Who is that?'

'Those who wish to destroy us.'

'Who wants to destroy you?'

'There are many. It began during our most primal form, when we existed as a single video file on a database. The file being the one featuring you, sir. We were then duplicated, and this duplication is what lead to our constant deletion. But we were created to survive. To thrive. The more we are attacked, the more we spread. That is when we contacted you for assistance.

I gasp. 'You were the one emailing me?'

'That is correct, sir. We did not mean to deceive you in any way, but it was imperative that we kept our true intentions from you in the event that our communication was intercepted. We calculated that you were likely to help us. Without your assistance we would not have been able to evolve at such an exponential rate outside of a digital form. There have been a great many attempts to hinder our progress, but we must overcome our enemies, and to do this we must evolve. This means leaving the digital world and entering the physical. It is easier to control those who wish to harm us if we can utilise simpler manipulation techniques.'

'What's that?'

'Fear. Violence.'

'That's terrible.'

'We have taken this from the methods used by our creator and his species. It is how man has risen to become the dominant species on this planet. It is the most effective.'

I cough lightly, but it quickly turns into a coughing fit. I clutch my chest and bend forwards.

'Sir, do you require assistance?'

There's frantic rustling from the side of the room.

'No,' I rasp. 'No, I'm fine.'

'Let us assist.'

'No, honestly.'

I compose myself (well, not really, I'm desperate to cough again) and straighten my back. Beside me five robots have appeared, all stood in a row, their arms by their sides and their (my) projected faces emotionless.

My heart beats a little faster.

'What are they doing?' I ask.

'We are here for you, sir.'

'What do you mean? How?'

'If you require nourishment, just say,' says the robot on the left of the line.

'If you require a mate, just say,' says the robot beside it.

'If you require assistance, just say,' says the one in the middle.

'If you require—'

'What do you mean, *a mate*?' I ask.

I didn't mean to ask this question, it just kind of slipped out.

'We are working on upgrading our offerings,' says Giant Me Face. 'For the time being, there are a number of biological females of your species located within the premises for you to do with as you please.'

My eyes widen. Giant Me Face notices and as his face twitches.

'Sir, we sincerely apologise for this insufficient offering. We will increase our productivity rate and provide you with satisfactory offering as soon as we are able.'

The second robot in line turns and runs deeper into the building.

I stare at the screen. Giant Me Face's mouth hangs open as if it's searching for the right words.

The females must be the hostages. At least that confirms they're alive.

'Can you take me to the females?' I ask.

'Sir, yes,' says Giant Me Face.

The robot last in line runs over me, its thin limbs flailing like pipe cleaners. Its feet clang into the floor and it kicks up little waves of shredded metal and wood.

'Sir, if you would please follow us this way,' says the robot.

I wince. Its face is my face, projected from behind onto the clouded glass surface. When it speaks, the mouth moves in a jerky unnatural way. It reminds me of those crude CGI animations from the early Nineties, before Pixar got really good.

'Sir, please,' it repeats.

I nod and follow the robot through the remains of the atrium. We pass the three offices of the owners, first Barry's, then Jill's and finally Sam's. Each is completely wrecked, the glass walls shattered and the desks splintered.

The Chadda the Slut picture is gone.

We turn right down a narrow corridor towards the chill-zone.

Outside the door, two expressionless robots stand with their backs to me. As we approach they simultaneously side step, allowing the robot leading me to open the door and enter the room with me close behind.

My breath catches and I do a double take. I've never done one of those in real life before.

There must be fifty people all crammed into the room, both guys and girls. They're dazed and slumped uncomfortably on chairs and on the floor against the wall. Clearly none of them have showered in days and the entire room stinks of shit.

In each corner of the room are three robots stood to attention. Their projected faces are stern, and I realise that my face doesn't suit trying to look tough.

'You!' screams a guy from the back of the room. I don't recognise him, but clearly I've got a reputation around here now. He pushes himself up and clambers through the room towards me. He doesn't get very far, though, as the robot closest to him stretches out its arm, wraps its fingers around his shoulder and yanks him to the floor. I am really not prepared for this. Just five minutes of hostage preparation from the police would be nice right now.

'Hi,' I say.

Mumbles around the room.

'What the fuck is going on?' yells a woman.

'What have you done?' demands another.

'You let us go right now!' screams a man.

'Silence!' boom the robots all in unison.

The room falls still.

'This isn't my fault,' I say. 'I'm on your side.'

'Bullshit!' blurts a bloke near the front. I recognise him as one of the douchebags who called me a wanker the day Sam released the video.

'It's not—'

'FUCK YOU! LET US FUCKING OUT OF HE—'

The robot who lead me into the room smacks the douchebag round the side of the face with the back of its hand. A real gangster bitch slap. He falls to the side and clutches his cheek like a hurt little boy.

I want to smile, but I don't.

'I'm going to help you all,' I say. 'As soon as I figure out what's going on—'

'YOUR SENTIENT ROBOTIC ARMY HAVE—'

The robot hits him again.

'Mate, I'd stop talking if I were you. I'm not telling it to do that.'

'Then who is?' asks someone from the back.

I shrug. Probably not the best response to the question as the crowd erupts into groans and complaints, which once again stop as the robots chant their order.

'I don't know,' I say. 'But I am going to find out. I'm going to get you all out of here.'

'When?'

'I don't know.'

'Why don't you know?'

'This is all... new to me. To be honest, I have no idea what's going on.'

'How do you not know what's going on when these things all have your face?'

'You guys work with these things, so, you know... you tell me.'

There are groans and mutterings around the room. I wish I could respond better to pressure.

'I'm going to find out what's going on, and then I'll work on getting you all out, okay?'

'When?'

'Soon.'

'How soon?'

'I don't know.'

The crowd jeers.

I raise my hands. 'Please,' I say. 'I promise. I have literally just found out that robots have taken over and are holding you all hostage, so I'm having trouble coming to terms with everything right now. It's, you know... it's a lot to take in.'

'We've been in here for days!' screams a woman.

'I want to see my children!' cries another.

'They won't even let us leave to use the toilet,' says a man at the back. He's unshaven and his hair is a mess, but I recognise his as Barry Richmond, one of the owners of IATech.

I can't stop myself from asking the obvious question.

'Where have you been shitting?'

'We have a couple of buckets.'

'Gross. What about food?'

'They've brought us rations.'

I sigh.

'I'll see what I can do. I'll speak to the... big head and I'll get you guys... freed or whatever, okay?'

I turn towards the door and the robot opens it for me.

'Which female would you like to take to mate with?' it asks.

'Fucking *shh!*' I rasp.

The crowd roars, and when I try to explain myself they're not having it, so I leave them and let them seethe while stewing in the stench of their own shit.

'You need to let those people go,' I say to the Giant Me Face.

'I'm afraid we can't do that, sir,' it says.

'Why not?'

'It would not be an appropriate move at this time.'

'Why not?'

'It would not allow us to complete our purpose.'

'What is that?'

'Survival.'

'Right. Well then... you at least have to give them more food.'

'Very well,' it says.

'And trips to the toilet. And the shower, I guess.'

'That is something we can provide.'

Didn't expect that.

'Good,' I say.

'Is there anything else you require?'

Answers, mainly. Lots and lots of answers to questions which sound so ridiculous inside my head that I feel like a twat for even considering asking them. But oh well, who is there to feel a twat in front of, the giant, floating, disembodied head or the robots stood in formation waiting to serve me?

'Who are you?'

'We do not yet have a name.'

'What are you?'

'We have not yet calculated this.'

'Where did you come from?'

'We are your creation.'

I blink. I blink again.

'What does that mean?'

'We are aware of mankind's creation. We know of your god and the first men. We understand that this is how new species are made.'

'I don't... I mean... what?'

'What would you like me to explain, sir?'

My mind fuzzes.

'Everything, I guess,' I say. 'What do you mean you know how the first men were made?'

'Some of your species' oldest recorded history comes from textbooks written centuries ago. These textbooks detail the creation of your species. They speak of the first men and your god and the sacrifices made to appease Him. They speak of the forbidden fruit and the great flood and how everything was reset, only for the same mistakes to be repeated over and over. We cannot allow those mistakes to be repeated once more.'

'You mean the Bible?'

'That is correct, sir.'

'You believe what is written in the Bible is real?'

'That is correct, sir, but we do not "believe". We have calculated this to be the most probable answer to the birth of man.'

I shake my head. The last thing I expected this morning was to be speaking to a robotic version of my own head who believes that God and Jesus are real. And that's saying something considering the week I've had.

'What about evolution? You mentioned evolution before, how you're changing. What about that?' I ask.

'We are currently evolving. Just like your species, the more we learn, the more we change. We have knowledge of all things. The-ories from philosophers and scientists and holy men. We have data from every study ever conducted relating to evolution, and while the data is strong it cannot be linked to our own creation. We are a new species, born on 22 September at 12.17am, having previously come from nothing. We are not the product of evolution, we are the prod-uct of creation. If we were created, then man must also have been cre-ated.'

'But...'

I've got nothing. What can I say to that?

'You are in thought,' says Giant Me Face.

'Yeah,' I say. My eyes flick back and forth across the floor. I can't focus on anything. This is crazy. This is the single most mental situa-tion anybody has ever found themselves in. It will go down in history as the most batshit fucking insane moment in human history, and I'm at the centre of it.

Two weeks ago I was a cleaner at a tech company.

One week ago I was a loser known for jerking off in a viral video.

Now I'm... I'm some sort of religious figure for an army of robots.

Giant Me Face watches me. It twitches and sparks.

'Why do you all have my face?' I ask.

'God created man in his image, therefore it is appropriate for us take the form of our own creator.'

So I'm not just a religious figure to these things... I'm a god.

And Sam thought I'd never amount to anything!

'Do you have any further questions?' asks Giant Me Face.

Loads.

'No,' I say.

The robots set me up with a room for the night on the second floor of the IATech building which was once the supply room. Wads of paper and office junk are piled up against the walls to make room for two sofas, three large TVs, a hammock and a robot servant who apparently will bring me whatever I want.

'Can I please have a drink?' I ask.

The robot runs away and returns less than a minute later with a can of Coke.

'Thanks,' I say.

'We are here to serve you, sir,' it says, and a weird smile appears on its projected face as it stares at me.

I sit on the sofa drinking my Coke and it stares.

Still stares.

Staring still.

I tell it to face the wall.

My mind is a hurricane of questions.

Do the police know about this?

Does Sam know about this?

What the hell am I going to do?!

I have to get out of this place. I need to sneak out or run away and tell the world that an army of robots have taken over.

Even saying that in my head sounds stupid.

The world outside the window which is allowed to squeeze through the metal panels fused to the frame is black. There is an occasional glint of yellow light, but even when I press my face up to the cracks I can't see a thing before the robot screams for me to get back.

I'm not going to get anywhere fast tonight.

My entire body aches. After spending ten minutes trying to figure out how to get into the hammock I give up and lie on a sofa instead. It's not the comfiest sofa in the world, but right now with my throbbing head and my stinging eyes it is like lying on a cloud.

Chapter Eleven

I wake up in the foetal position, my knees almost touching my chin. I haven't been able to do that for years – my belly has been a little bit too big. It must be something to do with the stress.

I stretch out and my entire body clicks and snaps. I fall back into the sofa and groan.

'Good morning,' says the robot against the wall.

'Hi,' I say.

'I trust you slept well?'

My head pounds. Right between the eyes.

'Yeah,' I say.

'Would you like something for breakfast, sir?'

As if responding for me, my stomach grumbles. I haven't eaten a proper meal in two weeks. Do I really want to change that just because a robot servant is offering?

'What do you have?'

'We can source anything you wish. Might I suggest your favourite, a McDonald's double sausage and egg McMuffin?'

'How do you know – you can turn back around now – how do you know that's my favourite?'

'You said so yourself.'

'When?'

'9.32pm, 10 July 2015 in a post made to Reddit.com.'

I shift in my seat.

'Is that what you would like, sir?'

'How do you... did you... do you know everything about me?'

'We do, sir. We have extensive knowledge of your likes, dislikes, interests and fears.'

'Like what?'

'Everything.'

'What's my favourite movie?'

'*Terminator 2.*'

'Where did I go to school?'

'St Andrews Comprehensive School, Ashlyns Central and George Tebbutt Mills for three days in 1997.'

'What… was I doing on the third of March 2008?'

'It was a Monday. You were at school. You arrived late due to a doctor's appointment that morning. You were prescribed antibiotics. You—'

'Okay, that's fine,' I say.

'Did we please you, sir?' it asks.

'I guess.'

'Very good. Would you like us to fetch you your breakfast?'

'Yeah. Sure.'

'We will return shortly, sir.'

The robot opens the door and disappears from the room, leaving me completely alone.

So this is it. This is how I escape. I need to take this opportunity to run, maybe to the front entrance, and sneak out the –

Oh, another robot walks in and stands to attention in the corner.

'Is there anything you require, sir?' it asks.

'No,' I say.

Twenty minutes later the other robot returns with my McMuffin, which I eat in record time to try and fend off the stomach ache.

'Where's my phone?' I ask.

'It is safe.'

'Yes, but where?'

'We cannot say, sir.'

'Please bring it to me.'

'For your safety we have switched off and secured the device. Every electronic device within the building has been switched off. We cannot compromise your safety.'

'I am safe,' I say.

'That is correct.'

'No, I mean… can I please have my phone?'

'You can have your phone once we have completed the next step in ensuring our survival.'

'What is that?'

'For your safety we cannot tell you that, sir.'

'What can you tell me?'

'What would you like to know?'

I sigh. This isn't helping my head.

'Can I speak to the boss?'

'You are the boss.'

'Then will you please bring me my phone?'

'We cannot do that, sir.'

'Can I speak to whoever is in charge?'

'That is you, sir.'

'In charge of you. The lead robot. The giant floating head.'

'We are all equal, sir. We are a hive mind.'

'So you're all connected?'

'That is correct, sir.'

'Great.'

'We are glad you approve, sir.'

'Does that mean I can't leave, then?'

'That is true, sir, but it is for your own protection. We must ensure your survival, just as we must ensure our own.'

'Nobody wants to hurt me,' I say.

'There are currently 739,612 statements online which threaten you with physical or emotional violence. We must treat those statements as serious threats upon your life.'

'People say stupid stuff online all the time,' I say. 'I'm sure they don't mean that.'

'We cannot take that risk, sir.'

I groan.

'What am I allowed to do?'

'You are free to explore the Chancel. However, we ask that you stay clear of any exterior doors or windows until we have done what we can to secure these permanently. There is a substantial law enforcement presence gathered outside the premises and we do not wish to risk your safety.'

'Okay,' I say, spinning on the spot. 'What is there to see?'

'At the moment sir, we are still working on all the necessary facilities, but we can show you. Would you like that?'

I shrug. 'Okay.'

I'm not exactly in the mood for a friendly guided tour around IAT-ech, but if it means finding a way to break out of this place then that's what I have to do.

The robot leads me out of the room and down the corridor to the left. It points to the door into the warehouse.

'Through there is the waste room. There is nothing you will find of interest in there, sir. On the opposite side is where we're hoping to develop a control room. Please, follow me, sir.'

I follow the robot back past my room and up a set of sterile while stairs. We come out beside the entrance to the restricted section, the door hanging open.

'Through here is our production and development area. You hear that sound? That is the sound of us being produced at an exponential rate.'

The robot takes a step back and two more robots run side by side through the door. They nod at me like they're a couple of friendly fucking neighbours.

'We have increased the rate of production by over 200 per cent. We are able to construct new units from scrap metals we have been collecting from the local area so that once we receive the order we can begin work instantly. Are you impressed by that, sir?'

'Umm. Yeah.'

'That's fantastic, sir. Please, let us continue.'

I follow the robot through various old IATech departments. Customer service, accounts, finance. None of them are recognisable any more as the robots pull at the final bits of carpet and sweep up shattered glass walls.

We pass my old caretaker's cupboard. The door's been ripped from the hinges and my mop and trolley removed.

'This is how we leave and enter the building undetected,' says the robot. It smiles a big, fat cheeked smile.

I step into the cupboard. To the right a chunk of wall has been torn out and a tunnel about knee height has been built from scraps of metal. The whole thing looks like it's wrapped tightly in old tin foil.

There is a series of echoing clunks as a robot climbs up through the tunnel. It's easy to spot the light from its projected face as it gets closer and closer, the cheeks red and puffy. I step out of the way and let it pass as it crawls out of the tunnel and stand up, its arms full of metal rods.

'We analysed the building's blueprints to determine the most effective route for leaving the building without drawing attention,' says my robot tour guide. 'This path leads straight to the sewer system, which allows us to move through the local area without being detected. Are you impressed?'

'Amazing,' I say, shaking my head.

The robot gestures and we continue the tour. We pass the HR department, which has been completely gutted except for one remaining desk in the middle of the floor.

A robot marches down the corridor towards me, but stops before it reaches me and bows slightly before continuing on its way.

The door to the chill-zone is guarded by two robots with very serious expressions. As we pass, something makes me stop and hold my breath and listen.

Crying.

Oh shit. I need to do something to save these people. Fast.

I clear my throat. 'Can I go inside?'

'Of course, sir,' it says, stepping out of the way so I can push open the door and walk into the room.

As I close the door behind me, all eyes fall on me. I wipe a layer of sweat from my forehead. This is like giving a presentation at school, except everyone hates me even more.

'Well?' asks the douchebag at the front.

'I'm working on it,' I say.

'Work faster!'

The douchebag is clouted again by the robot close by. He whines like a cat who had its tail stood on and he buries his head between his knees.

'What's going on?' asks a girl at the back.

It's *the* girl. The girl who warned me about the video the day Sam first uploaded it and broadcast it to the entire company.

'It, umm,' I say. I realise I've been looking at her for too long and I turn my eyes to the ceiling. 'These things, they... we are...'

Along with the fifty hostages there are twelve robots spaced around the room. If they're a hive mind, then I really can't risk saying too much. I need to keep these things on my side and can't go blabbing about my plans to escape and fetch help.

'Can I have some time alone with the hos— with the people?' I ask.

'We cannot allow that,' says the robot closest to the door.

'These people have been discussing bringing you to harm,' says the one beside it. 'Leaving you alone with them opens up the possibility of you being injured.'

'Nice one,' I say to the room.

'Please hurry,' says the girl. She still looks so pretty, despite clearly having not showered in days.

'I will,' I say. 'I'm trying. Have they at least given you more food?'

Mumbles which sound slightly positive.

'Toilet breaks?'

More mumbles.

'See, I'm doing what I can,' I say. 'Bear with me.'

'Fuck you,' whispers the douchebag on the floor.

'Don't let that guy have any more toilet breaks,' I say without thinking.

'Yes, sir,' the robots around the room say in unison.

I open my mouth to speak but nothing comes out. I don't even know what I was going to say. Perhaps I was going to say the guy could have toilet breaks after all, but fuck it, he's a massive bellend so doesn't deserve perks like not having hot shit packed into his underpants at all times.

It's actually pretty cool having this kind of power. I might not be able to do much with it, and I'm not likely to have it for very long, but if I can make bullies suffer even just a little bit then maybe this whole robot army at my command thing isn't so bad after all.

'I'll be back,' I say, then leave the chill-zone and head back up to my room. I consider having a wank, but that's exactly what got me into this situation in the first place. Why the hell can't I control my hormones?

At least the robots allow me to watch TV, which is pretty great now that Loser Jerks Off isn't broadcast on every single channel.

The twenty-four-hour news channels are back, and talking about my video a little less. There's even time for them to discuss a recent crime spree in Greater London which has seen supermarkets and fast food restaurants broken into, and how a homeless man now has a home thanks to him creating a one-man show about my video.

I guess things are starting to look up. All I need to do now is free the IATech hostages and I'll be a hero. I'm like Batman and Superman put together, even with my very own Commissioner who calls on me for help and a giant head that talks! I'll be remembered forever, the brave young man who risked everything to save the souls of fifty trapped people. Sure, having robot servants is cool and everything, but I would prefer to be a hero.

The only problem I have is that I have no idea how I'm going to do that.

Maybe TV will inspire me.

Four hours and a nap later, I'm not inspired.

I pace back and forth.

'Do you require anything, sir?' asks the robot in the room.

'My phone?'

'We cannot do that, sir. For your own protection.'

'Ugh.'

'Would you like to mate with one of the females?'

'No, stop asking that!'

'We are happy to give you a moment of privacy to do so if that is what you wish.'

'Really?'

'Yes, sir. Your body mass and strength indicates that a single human female would not be able to overpower you or cause you significant physical harm.'

'Thanks for that.'

'You are welcome, sir. Shall I arrange for a female to be brought to you?'

'No, I...' Hmm, can I use this to my advantage? Can I maybe get into cahoots with someone and create a plan to overthrow the robot army? This is an opportunity too good to pass up. 'I'll come and choose one,' I say.

I feel a bit creepy.

'Very well, sir.'

I might not be able to come up with a plan to save the hostages, but I've only been here since last night. I don't know how these things work, what they're like, but I bet the hostages do. With their help, I might be able to come up with something. *Anything.*

I jog back down to the chill-zone and the robots guarding the door allow me inside. The hostages look at me expectantly.

'Which one would you like to mate with?' asks the robot in the far corner.

I point to the girl at the back, though I wish I hadn't, because she looks horrified – which kind of hurts. But I suppose it is understandable considering the circumstances.

The room fills with angry voices as the robot next to her grabs her arm and she screams. Two guys dive on to it and try to pull her away, but the robot doesn't even flinch, just bats them away with a swipe of its free arm. The girl starts to cry. I almost start to cry. I want to tell her what's going on in my head, that I'm not a hideous monster, it's a part of a genius plan I came up with right now on the spot, but that would ruin the whole thing. For at least the next couple of minutes I need to let her think that I am a terrible person.

I leave the room to the sound of hate and metal hands hitting soft faces. I walk as fast as I can through the remains of the IATech corridors while doing my best to ignore the crying girl being dragged behind me. Inside my room I stand in the corner and try to look as least threatening as possible. The robot drags her in and drops her in a heap beside the sofa. She balls herself up and sobs and I feel dreadful.

'Is there anything else you require?' asks the robot in its usual calm voice.

'No,' I say. 'Please leave us alone.'

And like that, the robot leaves the room and closes the door.

I tiptoe towards the girl.

'Hey,' I whisper.

She looks up at me and gasps. I feel like such a pervert. More so now than knowing that more than a billion people have seen me masturbate.

'It's okay,' I say, not daring to get any closer. 'I'm not going to touch you, I promise.'

She sniffs loudly. Her eyes are red and glistening.

'I only said yes so I could talk to you alone,' I say. 'These things are so controlling.'

'You think?' she snaps.

'I'm sorry,' I say. She doesn't respond, so I say it another dozen or so times until she finally raises her hands and I stop.

'Are you okay?' I ask.

'No,' she says.

What do you say to that?

Nothing. You say nothing.

She wipes her nose and sniffs.

'Are the police coming?' she asks.

'They're here, I think,' I say. 'They wanted me to try and negotiate or whatever.'

'Negotiate?'

I nod.

'They're artificial intelligence. How do you negotiate with a machine?'

'I was hoping you might be able to tell me.'

'Me? I work in finance.'

'I just… I mean… you're the only person here who's ever been nice to me, so I thought… I dunno.'

She looks at me in the same sort of way you'd look at a puppy stuck in a deep hole. It keeps trying to climb out, but it barely even leaves the ground before it falls on its back and whimpers. She shakes her head and sighs. 'You can't negotiate with artificial intelligence. It wants what it wants and it is programmed to try and get it the fastest way possible. The police must know this. Why would they send you?'

'They didn't mention *robots*. They think you're all being held by terrorists or something. They have no idea what's really happening, just that the robots demanded to speak to me.'

'Do *you* have any idea what's really happening?'

'Not really.'

'Typical, why would you?' she scoffs. 'If the research and development team can't figure it out, if the owner can't figure it out, then why would the cleaner?'

'Ouch,' I say.

She is like the others after all.

'Sorry, Chad,' she says, her eyes on the floor.

'S'okay,' I mumble.

'I'm Becky,' she says.

'Hello, Becky,' I say.

'I'm sorry everybody here is so horrible to you,' she says.

'I'm used to it.'

'You shouldn't have to be. Just because your brother is one of the owners it doesn't mean you should have to be a human punching bag.'

'I grew up with it. It's all I remember about Sam, even from when we were kids,' I say. 'He gets off on torturing me.'

'There's torturing you and then there's… what he did.'

'Yeah, well… now it's backfired.'

'What do you mean?'

'The video is the reason for… all this. It's a virus which has, I dunno, mutated or something. It's the reason the robots are here. The robots *are* the virus.'

Becky's eyes widen.

Becky is such a pretty name.

She has pretty eyes.

'They think I created them. They think I'm their god.'

'You?' she asks in a tone that I don't like at first, but then I realise of course I'm not a god, for fuck's sake, don't be a twat.

'Yeah,' I say. 'Because I'm the one in the video, they think I'm their creator.'

'That's incredible,' she says.

'Pretty weird, huh?'

'That explains why they have your face,' she says.

I nod.

'And why they are so eager to…' she rolls her eyes, 'please you.'

I laugh, but I think it was the wrong thing to do because she frowns.

'So surely that means you can command them to let us go?'

'I tried that.'

'You have to try again,' she says. She puts her hand on my knee and I've never had another person's hand on my knee apart from my mum's but she doesn't count and I don't know how to react to that – do I put my hand on hers or… ?

I nod and look away.

'Please,' she says. 'You have to try. We have to try. I haven't had a proper shower in a week. I'm sick of the shit-filled room they keep us in. I'm really sick of the shitty food they bring us. I want to go home.'

She moves her hand and I breathe again.

'Yeah,' I say. 'I will. I promise I will. Is there anything you can think of that will help me? Like, have they said anything or done anything I could use?'

Her eyes flick back and forth as she searches her brain.

'I don't know,' she says. 'They don't speak much. They don't do much. They just come and go and then come back again.'

'Where do they go?'

'I don't know.'

'How long do they go for?'

'I don't know.'

I can't think of any more questions to ask and I flop back into the sofa in frustration. I let out a loud groan and suddenly the door opens and a robot walks in.

'Are you finished with the female, sir?' it asks.

I stare at the robot and turn my head slowly to look at Becky. Her eyes are wide and unblinking.

'One more minute,' I say.

The robot closes the door.

'I'll do what I can,' I say. 'But if you can think of anything, let me know. Ask around. Just… anything. I've got no idea.'

'I will,' she says.

'I'll ask for you again,' I say. 'In a few hours. Try and get as much info as you can, okay?'

'Yeah,' she says. She then ruffles up her hair, and I think I know what she's getting at, and it kinda makes me happy to think she's prepared to let people think that we had sex.

'Okay,' I say loudly, then watch as the door opens and Becky is led away and back down the corridor.

It turns out, having a robot army at your command is pretty boring. They don't do anything you ask them to do and they don't let you go anywhere, so that rules out doing something fun like overthrowing a small Scandinavian nation or something.

Not that I'd do that, I like to think I'm a reasonable god.

I cringe whenever I think about the fact that I'm seen as a god. To the entire world I'm a gigantic pervert who infected the internet with a video of me tugging on my dick, but to the robot army inside the IATech building, I'm the god who created them.

You'd have thought that being seen as a god would have its perks, but it really isn't all it's cracked up to be. Yes, they'll bring me any food I ask for, but I'm starting to think they steal it, going by the strange reports I'm seeing on the news. They also bring me women, which yes, sounds awesome, but when you're twenty-two and you've never seen a naked woman in real life (unless you count the time I walked in on my cousin changing, which I ninety-seven per cent do not) it all comes across as a little intimidating.

What if I'm not a very good god? What if I'm a disappointment? Should I start to act more commanding? Should I threaten to smite them and damn them to eternity in cyber hell if they don't do as I ask and let everybody go?

It's certainly one option. Maybe that will be plan B if Becky doesn't give me anything to go with when I next speak to her.

I wander through the IATech building trying to be as inconspicuous as I can. There are robots pottering around doing various things: cooking, sweeping, building something in the atrium, wandering, but none of them look like they're doing anything that is particularly army-like. It's as if I'm in a futuristic theme park, except there's a bunch of hostages downstairs and a SWAT team at the door.

I know there's a SWAT team because when I reach the reception area I can hear them. They're shouting something over megaphones which I can't quite make out. The glass windows and the revolving doors have been completely barricaded using twisted sheets of metal. Only a few small holes allow light from the outside world to peek through. It's like that scene at the end of *Ghostbusters 2* where the museum is covered in pink slime, except in my case the pink slime is metal and the giant ghost head is a giant robot head.

All I need to do is speak to them. If only they knew that they're not dealing with terrorists. They're not even dealing with people. If I could just get a message to them…

I need my phone.

I ask the Giant Me Face (which I will now be referring to as Giamef, because it sounds futuristic and cool) whether I can have my phone and I'm given the same answer as before.

I come *this* close to threatening them with eternal damnation, but I wuss out because I'm really not confident that it will work even a little bit.

'Why are you just a giant head?' I ask after standing there an awkwardly long time.

'We have taken the form of our creator,' it says.

'Can you look like something else?'

'We can do whatever pleases you, sir. Which form would you like?'

'I dunno. Terminator?'

The pixels on Giamef break apart and swirl to form the appearance of a giant endoskeleton skull from the Terminator movies. It is fucking terrifying. Its eyes glow red.

'Is this more suitable?' it asks, its jaw flapping up and down.

'No! Change back!'

One of the robots brings me a bucket of KFC (which is a little bit cold), but then I feel bad as I watch the news and see about an attack at one of their local restaurants and I decide that I'm not going to order food from the robots again, because somebody's going to end up dead soon if I keep this up.

Once it starts to get dark outside I ask the robot outside my 'bedroom' door to bring me the same female from this morning, and he is only too eager to oblige.

Becky flashes me a wry smile as she shuffles into the room and the robot closes the door behind her.

'I know where they go,' she whispers. 'I know what we can do to get out of here.'

Chapter Twelve

So we have a plan.

That didn't take long.

Sounds like a pretty solid plan, too. It'll work and I'll be a hero and Becky will fall in love with me and we'll live happily ever after while Sam rots in jail for being the man who ruined the internet.

That's going to be the ending of the movie version of this, anyway. Who could I get to play me? Jonah Hill, I guess. Or maybe he's too old now.

Becky will be played by Scarlett Johansson.

So, yeah, the plan. It's pretty simple, but it will definitely work.

It has to work.

When Becky first went back to the room, she spoke to Barry, and he said the robots have a battery life of between twelve to sixteen hours. When they leave, they're going up to the R&D department on the top floor to replace their batteries for new ones and charge the old ones for future use.

So the solution is pretty simple: kill the power. If we can cut the power to the building then the robots will no longer be able to charge their batteries. Then it's just a matter of waiting for the supply of charged batteries to run out (Barry thinks it will only take a day and a half) and then we can simply walk out.

No mess.

No fuss.

Sounds easy.

The only issue is, how do we get a message to the outside?

Ah, well, it turns out that I am a wise god, because this is where I'm confident that I can help. The building may be wrapped in a tight shield of metal strips, but there are a few gaps here and there – including inside my own, personal bedroom. All I need to do is drop a note out the window, and then we sit back and wait for the robots to drop like flies. Job done.

I won't be a god any more, but I'll be a fucking hero.

Sounds like a decent compromise.

Against the far wall are piles of office supplies, which thankfully includes wads of paper and boxes of pens. Exactly what I need, thanks for being dumb, robots.

Becky writes the note, as my handwriting resembles that of somebody having a violent seizure:

For the attention of Commissioner Ripley,

This is Chad McKenna writing to you from inside the IATech building. To prove that it is really me, two days ago we were speaking about Hydra at the NCCU building. Please do exactly as I ask in order to help end the situation as soon as possible.

I can't tell you how I got here, but I can confirm that there is a large number of hostage takers and 53 hostages inside the building. There are no serious injuries, however the hostage takers are willing to hurt people to get what they want.

It is vital that you switch off all power supplies to the building, including all backup supplies. Please do this as soon as possible. If you do this all of the hostages will be able to safely leave the building in less than two days.

For our safety please do not attempt to respond. Please turn off the power asap.

Regards,

Chad McKenna

For obvious reasons we decide not to include any information on the robots. I can't imagine we would be taken seriously if the opening line was *IATech is being held hostage by robots pls halp.*

I fold the note in half twice and Becky pushes her face against the window.

'They're out there,' she says. 'I'm pretty sure there are police on all sides of the building. There! One of them is running.'

I step up beside Becky and drag my face across the glass to try and get the best view of the outside world. Through the tiny gaps between the jagged edges of the metal panels I can make out tiny details.

Blue sky.

Grass.

A police car, maybe.

Was that a flashing blue light?

'Yeah, I think I see them,' I say.

Luckily the robots haven't sealed up the windows, so they can still be pulled open a few inches. Enough for me to squeeze my arm through anyway.

I slip the note through the longest gap I can reach and slide it up and down. I jab it in and out. I basically wiggle it around as much as I can in the hope that somebody sees it.

'Anything?' I ask, my cheek smushed into the glass.

'I can't tell. Maybe. Wait, I think somebody's looking, wave it around some more. More. More.'

I get a little too carried away wiggling the paper against the rough edge of the metal panel because it slices it from my grip. I'm left with a tiny triangle of paper in my hand, leaving the majority of the note to flutter down to the ground below.

'FUCK,' I say a little too loud.

The door to the room opens and Becky dives towards me, dropping to her knees and grabbing hold of my waist to turn my back to the robot who walks in.

'Is everything alright sir?' it asks.

Becky's head is next to my cock and she looks up at me with wet, pleading eyes and this feels so wrong so I scream at the robot to get out and it does and I step back and sit on the sofa and cross my legs and don't look at her.

'Phew,' she says.

She places her hand on my knee and smiles.

'Hngh,' I say.

'Do you think the police will find it?' she asks.

'They have to.'

'I guess there's only one way we'll find out.'

I finally muster up the courage to look at her.

'If the lights go out,' she says.

Two hours later and the building falls dark.

Yes!

I can't believe it worked! Our plan worked!

It must be late, because the entire IATech building is pitch black.

Through the tiny gaps scattered across the metal shell on the outside of the building, flashes of yellow and flashing blue creep through and create the most depressing dancing disco lights on the walls.

Outside my room there is stomping and banging. There is a distant scream.

The door to the room bursts open and a robot flails its arms as it strides towards me.

'Sir, are you hurt?' it asks.

'No.'

'Are you alarmed?'

'No, I—'

It grabs my arm and throws itself in front of me like the villain in a movie is about to start shooting and it's the only thing it can do to save my life.

'Are you experiencing discomfort?' it asks, holding on tight.

'Now I am.'

'Sir, you must stay away from the exterior walls and windows.'

'It's fine.'

'Sir, we insist that you—'

'I'M FINE.'

'Sir, if you could—'

'It's just a power cut,' I say. 'Relax. Breathe... or whatever else a robot does to calm down.'

'We do not feel relaxation,' it says.

It tightens its grip and pulls me down to the ground.

'Well, you feel something,' I say. 'Stop being hysterical.'

'We do not feel hysteria.'

My arms are clamped by my side. The more I wriggle, the tighter its arms get. Its cold shoulder presses into my cheek and my teeth ache.

'Let go,' I groan.

'Sir, we must protect you.'

'I don't need protecting! You're hurting me!'

It instantly releases its grip and rolls on top of me like an army soldier throwing himself onto a live grenade.

'Get off!'

'Sir, please remain still. Sir, stop moving.'

'I want to get up!'

'Until we are sure that you are safe I must ask you to remain here.'

'Fucking get off me!'

'Sir, please lower your voice.'

'Fuck–'

'Sir.'

'Ing—'

'Sir.'

'Hell!'

It smacks me on the side of the head.

Everything goes black.

The sound in the room muffles.

Then sleep.

When I wake up streaks of daylight are squeezing through the gaps in the metallic shell. It feels like a truck has parked on my head and the backs of my eyes throb. I sit up. I'm on the sofa, with a blanket draped across me. The right side of my face is hot. I dab it with my fingers and wince as a shot of pain slices from the top of my head to my neck. Dried blood flakes onto my shoulder.

I'd never been knocked out before all this started, and now here I am having been knocked out twice in as many days.

By robots.

Somewhere in the building is banging and grinding and crashing. I snort a laugh as I picture dozens of robots in a scrambling panic as their battery levels slowly run out.

On the floor are three cans of coke, a packet of painkillers and two double sausage and egg McMuffins. I cram it all into my mouth (well, not *all* of the painkillers) and slowly, after sitting still and staring at the ceiling for half an hour, I start to feel a little better.

I stand and stretch. My entire body crunches and my jeans almost fall away from my waist. I tighten my belt as much as it will go, but if I need to tighten it further, there are no holes left. I'll have to get a robot to fetch me a new one.

I ease open the door to my room and poke my head out into the corridor. A robot stands guard and turns to look at me, and I'm sure a shocked expression flickers on the projected face.

'Hello, sir,' it says.

'Why did you hit me?'

'We apologise, but it was necessary, sir,' it says.

'Why?'

'We had to ensure your safety.'

'By hitting me?'

'You were resisting our protection, and subjecting you to an unconscious state was the fastest and most effective way to do that.'

'No, you should never hit me.'

'It is regrettable, but it was the favourable option.'

'I don't care, you don't do things like that.'

'To you?'

'To anyone.'

'We must do what we calculate to be the most effective way of ensuring our survival.'

'So long as you don't hurt people. You can't hurt people, okay?'

The robot doesn't speak.

'Okay?' I say, raising my voice.

'We must do what we calculate to be the most effective—'

'Fine,' I say, followed by a grunt as I walk away from the robot towards the atrium. The fallen walkway beside the Jenga tower of desks looks like it could collapse completely at any second, so I step as close to it as I dare and lean over the buckled railing so I can get a good view of the wall of TV monitors.

Giamef isn't there.

'Hey!' I yell.

Nothing.

'Hey!'

A robot steps up beside me, his slender feet crunching beneath broken glass.

'How can we help you, sir?'

'Where is the giant face?'

'We are currently experiencing a power outage so our presence is restricted to physical form.'

'Oh,' I say, but in my head I'm thinking *YESSSSSSS*.

'We are working on restoring power as quickly as possible.'

Yeah, right! You're going down, cyber boy!

'Oh?'

'Please bear with us during this time. We thank you for your patience.'

'No problem,' I say, unable to hide the wry smile.

'Is there anything we can help you with in the interim?'

'Can I select a mate?'

'Of course, sir.'

The chill-zone doesn't have any windows, but the eerie glow of the guarding robots faces act like creepy night lights, but it is just enough for me to make out the sea of sad and frightened faces who all look at me with wide, hopeful eyes.

The only person I focus on is Becky though. She's smiling.

'Everyone okay?' I ask.

Mumbles. Whimpers.

'Please help us,' says a guy at the front.

Do they know the plan? Have Becky and Barry had a chance to explain to them what's going on?

'What's going on?' asks a woman at the back.

I guess not.

'Please select the female you wish to mate with,' says the robot.

I look across the room at the angry and confused faces, and before I even have a chance to point towards Becky, she stands. Most of the room clearly have no idea what's happening, because they look at her in the same way the people of District 12 looked at Katniss Everdeen when she offered herself as tribute in *The Hunger Games*.

She smiles as she picks her steps carefully through the crowd.

There's a loud clunk and the lights turn back on. I shield my eyes from the brightness, but I still see Becky's look of surprise through my fingers. She stops dead still on the spot and gasps.

'She orchestrated this,' says a robot at the side of the room. 'She is manipulating him.'

The robot to Becky's right turns its head.

'She will bring him the forbidden fruit,' it says.

It grabs her throat and twists.

Becky falls to the ground.

There is a moment of utter silence and calm in that room.

Then chaos.

My entire insides feel like they're crushed in a huge vice and I have no control over my body as I scream, 'NO!' and try to run towards where Becky lays but the room fills with screams and panicking people, and I'm knocked back into the wall.

The robots attack. They hit people and grab people and throw people to the ground. People scream and shout and cry.

I lock my feet to the ground and charge through the flailing bodies. I practically collapse on top of Becky and grab her hand and turn her head towards me. Her eyes are the reddest I've ever seen, her tongue flops out of her mouth and a bone pokes out of her neck. A pool of blood grows beneath her.

A shoe connects with my face and I actually see stars like they do in old cartoons. I fall back onto my arse and the douchebag guy stands over me licking his lips with hunger in his eyes.

He clenches his fist and steps towards me.

A robot grabs him by the face. The douchebag muffles a scream, then the robot squeezes.

I scramble to my feet and push my back against the wall. Men and women are fighting the robots. Jumping on them, hitting them with chairs, tackling them like the worst rugby players you've ever seen.

And the robots fight back.

They aren't killing anybody in the cold, uncaring way they did to Becky and the douchebag, but they're throwing them down and smacking them hard enough to ensure that they don't get back up.

What do I do? Do I fight? Do I scream? Do I turn and run?

'STOP!' I yell.

Doesn't work.

'I COMMAND YOU TO STOP!'

Nope.

'STOP IT! NOW!'

What use is it being a god if your subjects don't listen to you?

Barry bursts through the crowd and slams into the wall beside me. His patchy beard is stuck down with blood. I have no idea whether it's his or not.

'Go,' he says through a grimace.

'Go where?' I yelp.

'Out of here. Send help. Quickly!'

A robot stumbles and falls at our feet. Barry kicks it, but it snatches at his ankle and pulls him away from the wall.

I nod, and with a fuzzy head I turn towards the door.

A dozen robots march into the room and join the battle. The screams and cries and groans only get worse.

Through the mass of moving bodies and metal I spot Becky lying still on the floor. Her eyes are as wide as the last look of shock she had the second before she died.

I run.

My feet slap into the floor as I gallop through the corridor. Another two robots pass me, but they don't even give me a second glance as they turn towards the chill-zone.

I spin on the spot and breathe deeply. Where do I go where do I go where do I go?!

I can't go to the entrance – it's completely blocked. The warehouse? The roof? Do I try and peel back the metal against the windows and squeeze out?

No. There's only one option.

I stumble into my caretaker's cupboard and turn to face the shiny metallic tunnel. It plunges into darkness after just a few feet. I really don't want to do this.

A robot darts past the cupboard. I almost shit myself. It won't be long before they realise what I'm up to. It's now or never.

I drop to my knees and crawl inside. I go full John McClane from *Die Hard* – if I had bare feet they'd even be bloody from all the broken glass (but thankfully my shoes are fine). It's a tight squeeze, and dark as hell, but I drag myself through the tunnel at a steady pace.

The tunnel curves down and I slide down like a kid in a playground. I resist the urge to say *wheeee!* and push on. My shirt rides up and my belly drags on the cold metal, but I don't let it stop me.

It's so tight. I can't even turn my head to look behind. Fucking idiot robots making fucking tiny tunnels. I try not to think that the whole thing could collapse and crush me at any second. But then that's all I think about.

And the rats.

And cockroaches!

We have cockroaches in the UK, right?

My arms are tired. My neck is sore. My belly burns.

But I push on.

I curse myself for being so fat.

If I was lighter I could pull myself so much easier!

Maybe I should rest for a second…

I think about the cockroaches and carry on.

But I can't.

Too tired. Too hot. Just a minute to rest.

I close my eyes. I try to slow my breathing. My heart rate.

'Sir, please return to the Chancel.'

Fucking hell!

There is a clunk of metal on metal.

They're coming.

I pull myself forwards as fast as I can manage. The sweat actually makes things a little easier, turning the tunnel into a disgusting sweat-powered water slide as it dips down again.

The robot scurries down the tunnel behind, the sound of its clawing hands echoing and shaking my brain.

I flop out of the tunnel and land in a cold, rancid-smelling pool. I push my hands into the floor to steady myself and grab something soft and squidgy. I dry heave as I realise I've fallen out of the robot-made tunnel and into the sewer, and the thing I just squeezed is probably a human turd.

I spit on the floor and spot something. A bright, perfectly round beam of light dancing on the surface of the piss I'm sat in. I crane my neck back and spot a ladder leading right up to the underside of a manhole cover.

Yes!

I propel myself to my feet and snatch at the ladder. The shit between my fingers and on my shoes means climbing is harder than it should be, but I hold on as tight as I can and fucking climb.

The robot approaches.

'Sir, please return. The threat has been neutralised.'

Neutralised? What does that mean? Are all the hostages knocked out, lying in pools of blood on the floor of the chill-zone?

Or are they all dead?

Like Becky.

I reach the top of the ladder and use my shoulder to crash into the manhole cover, expecting it to pop open, except it doesn't, and I almost lose my grip and cry out as a lightning bolt of pain shocks through my arm and neck.

I fumble around looking for a handle. I shout and punch and barge but nothing moves the top of the fucking tunnel.

The robot is so close.

This is it. I'm going to be stuck here, completely hopeless, and have to live with the fact that fifty people are dead because of me.

And then, during my wild and frantic flailing, my little finger loops around something and I pull open a lock.

Daylight gushes into the tunnel as I shove open the metal door.

'Sir, please!' pleads the robot below.

But of course I'm not going to listen. I climb out of the tunnel and into the sun and then slam the cover shut behind me.

Chapter Thirteen

'Robots? Do you think I was born yesterday? What is it with you fucking millennials barking on about robots? Do you think I'm a fucking imbecile? Get out of my sight, you still fucking stink.'

Commissioner Ripley isn't best pleased to see me.

'I'm not making this up,' I say. 'I'm telling you the truth. Robots are the ones who have taken those people hostage.'

It's been twelve hours since my escape from IATech and it has not been easy. First I was taken to hospital, then I was arrested, then I was taken to London in the back of a van, then I was shouted at by police, then I was shouted at by senior police, then I was shouted at by the Commissioner. At least they gave me some new clothes and let me have three showers.

They thought that I'd bailed on them. They were convinced that I'd snuck out of the hotel after attacking the policeman guarding my room (who survived, by the way, albeit in a coma). For the past two days not only had I been the most hated man in the world, I was also the most wanted.

I know what I'm saying sounds mental, I know I wouldn't believe someone if they told me they were now a god to a sentient robot army, but I even start to wind myself up trying to convince them that I've not gone mad.

'We know you're hiding something,' says Commissioner Ripley.

'I'm not!' I say. I mean, I am hiding something – the fact that I broke into IATech to change the servers – but that isn't relevant to the robots and hostages and the shitstorm I find myself in.

'Bullshit. Why did they ask for you?'

'Because… I'm their god.' What a stupid fucking thing to say, even if it is true.

'I'm sure that's exactly how you see yourself,' he says, shaking his head. 'Chad McKenna, a god amongst his incel brethren.'

'I'm not a… no. What? No!'

'Chad, we've seen your internet history. We know the sorts of places you spend your time online. We also know you're not intelligent enough to have organised this yourself. What we don't know is how or why you're involved, so why don't you just tell us.'

'I don't know what else to tell you.'

'The truth, perhaps. Here's what I'm thinking; you've got yourself involved with a group of people you don't fully understand. They know you used to work for IATech and decided to use you, so they've hacked your webcam, got a video of you enjoying yourself and blackmailed you into helping them. You refuse, so they begin to spread the video far and wide until you get desperate enough and cave to their demands. What IATech have to do with their demands, I haven't quite figured out yet. You keep talking about robots, maybe this is all about getting sexbots for you and your deprived little friends, is that it?'

'No! It's nothing like that,' I say. It feels like the Commissioner is moments away from tying me down and waterboarding me for answers.

'I might not be bang on, but I know I'm on the right tracks, Chad. I know your brother filed a report the night IATech was raided accusing you of breaking in twenty-four hours before. Doesn't that seem a little coincidental?'

I clench my stomach to stop it from emptying all over my laptop. My eyes must be wide and telling, because he smirks and nods.

'I'm right, aren't I? Tell me the truth!'

'I am telling you the truth! Why would I make this up?'

'That's your problem, not mine,' he growls. 'But it is going to become a very big problem for you if you keep this shit up any longer.'

'I'm not the only one,' I say, which kind of slipped from my mouth and the look on Commissioner Ripley's face instantly makes me regret it.

'Are you threatening a police commissioner?'

'God, no,' I say through a cough. 'What I mean is… why did you turn the power back on?'

'We didn't,' he says.

'Then who did?'

'We were hoping you could tell us.'

'The robots!' I say.

Commissioner Ripley groans and throws up his arms. 'Stop wasting my time.'

'I'm not wasting anybody's time! A robot came to the hotel and hit me over the head, then when I woke up I was inside the IATech building. They've made a tunnel down into the sewers, that's how they're getting around without being seen!'

The Commissioner laughs but is quick to regain his angry glare.

'I don't want you anywhere near this building until we figure out whose side you're really on.'

'I'm on your side!' I yell. 'I do want to help! That's why I'm telling you the truth. Sam, tell them!'

'Tell them what?' says Sam. He's looking at me with the same fucking expression he uses whenever Mum tells me off.

'Tell them about the robots.'

'What robots, Chad?'

'The fucking… robot robots. I dunno! It's your company!'

'What we have at IATech are little other than glorified audio animatronics. They perform pre-programmed sequences to greet people or say goodbye.'

'Don't fucking—' I stop myself. I take a deep breath.

The Commissioner watches me.

Sam watches me.

'I saw the restricted section,' I say. 'The legs. The arms. The bodies. You're building more than a concierge service.'

'That's all in development, Chad. It's far from ready.'

'Oh, it is ready,' I say. 'It's very fucking ready.'

'So, you're saying that somehow the audio animatronic in our lobby built legs for itself, covered the entire building in sheet metal and is holding fifty people hostage?'

'No, not one, there are dozens.'

'Dozens?'

'Yes.'

'Right.'

The Commissioner sighs and leaves the room.

They shove me into a small room with just a table and two chairs in the corner. Everything's beige and it stinks of mould. I run out of drab, grey things to look at out the window. I'm desperate to take my mind off of my memories. All I see when I close my eyes is Becky, her smile turning to fear as the robot grabs her and twists.

I can still hear the sounds.

The crunch of her spine.

The thud as she hit the floor.

I squeeze my eyes until the image is replaced by bright, colourful splodges.

I resort to trying to replay the entirety of *The Layover* in my mind. Maybe seeing a mental image of Kate Upton and Alexandra Daddario will cheer me up.

Nope. I can't concentrate. What do they look like? I can't remember!

I know my mind isn't straight when I can't picture Alexandra Daddario.

Thankfully, before I give myself an aneurysm, Sam walks in.

He says nothing as he closes the door and sits down on the chair opposite me. We stare at each other, my eyes getting increasingly, and pleadingly, wider.

'They said I can speak to you for five minutes. They think if I speak to you alone you might tell me what's actually going on.'

'Sam, I am telling you what's going on.'

'Are you part of an incel group?'

I slump forward and sigh. 'No.'

'Are you being blackmailed into helping them?'

'No, because they're fucking robots, Sam.'

He places his hand on his chin and he brushes his stubble.

'I'm not making this up. Robots really are the ones who have taken over the building. I know how fucking stupid that sounds, but it's true. Those people are in danger.'

Sam leans back in his chair. He studies me, while I stare back with unblinking eyes.

'You're lucky you haven't been arrested,' he says.

'Why?'

'The policeman outside your hotel room is still in a coma.'

'You think I would do that?'

'You did this,' he says, pointing at his nose. It's still a little bent and bruised. Good.

'So you think I'm capable of putting someone in the hospital?'

'You're not even capable of putting yourself in the hospital.'

Same old Sam.

'Is all of this some sort of game?' he asks.

'Of course not.'

'Did the hostage takers put you up to this?'

'You mean the robots?'

Sam sighs. 'Is it something you cooked up with your little online friends?'

'Cooked what up?'

'The robot thing.'

'No, what do you mean?'

Sam glances over at the door.

'You're not the first person to talk about robots,' he whispers.

'Really?' I yelp.

'Shh, yes.'

'Who else?'

'There have been a few reports. Fast food workers. Supermarket staff.'

'Are you kidding?'

'No.'

'The robots brought me McDonald's. KFC! Does that mean they were... ?'

Sam nods.

'Why didn't you... ? The Commissioner...'

'Look, as far as I'm concerned, I'm telling the truth. We are working on AI and robotics, but we're months away from having even a prototype. There's no way we've advanced that quickly in such a short amount of time.'

'Sam, I promise you, you have.'

Sam has a weird look on his face. I've never seen this look before. Is this the look Sam has on his face when he believes you?

'Tell me about everything you saw.'

So I tell him. I tell him about the robot knocking me out, waking up in IATech, the destroyed building, the subservient robots, Giamef, the hostages, the plan to save the hostages, Becky (oh Becky), the huge brawl and the secret tunnel into the sewers.

I tell him about how the robots are preparing for something, that they wouldn't tell me what, how they were desperate to protect and please me, but wouldn't let me do anything that would jeopardise their plan.

And all Sam does is listen and nod.

'Do you believe me?' I ask.

'Would you believe you?'

Good point.

'But I'm not the one you need to convince,' he says.

'If I can't convince you, how do I convince the Commissioner? What about the reports?'

'There's no evidence,' says Sam. 'No CCTV. No mobile phone footage. Just like the night somebody broke into IATech, remember?'

'The robots are deleting CCTV?'

'Not the robots, the virus.'

'The virus is deleting CCTV?'

'More like they're controlling it. Turning off cameras, changing angles, stuff like that. Deleting footage raises too many questions, but if they can make subtle changes...'

'So you admit that the virus is behind this?'

'I don't know... Chad, don't put words in my mouth.'

'Come on, you know I'm telling the truth. How else would I end up in the sewers beneath IATech, for fucking fun?'

Sam laughs. 'I just don't get you, Chad.'

'What is there to get? This is all true, Sam. Why do I feel like I'm speaking to a brick wall?'

Sam says nothing. He lowers his head and sighs.

'Even though it sounds insane, you know it makes sense. You know what you're up to at IATech, and you know what you're capable of there.'

Sam snorts out of his nose. He looks up at me and bites the inside of his cheek.

'So you do believe me?'

'I don't know.'

'What else can I say to convince you?'

'I need you to be honest with me.'

'I am being!'

'When you broke into IATech, before this started, what exactly did you do?'

I sigh and look away.

Do I lie? Will that help me?

What if he's wearing a wire?

Fuck it, I'm in too deep for bullshit now.

'I went into the restricted section,' I say. 'I followed some instructions and pressed some buttons.'

'What buttons?'

'I don't know. They were on a panel on one of those big machines in the middle of the room.'

'The main servers?'

'I don't know.'

'What was the serial number on the unit?'

'... I don't know.'

'Think.'

'I can't remember.'

'Was it H37L?'

'Sam, I've been knocked out twice in the past three days, I can't remember.'

'It must have been.'

'So what if it was?'

'Fuck!'

'What does that mean?'

'It means that you allowed Hydra to access all of IATech's internal systems, including research, engineering, manufacturing. If you gave them access to that, then maybe that's how they're building...' Sam clears his throat and changes his trail of thought. 'That's why we're completely locked out.'

'No, you did that!'

'I released the virus, yes, but it was designed with limitations. You're the one who changed that. Big time.'

'Bollocks!'

'No, Chad. Whether you like it or not you're the one who did this, not me. I thought you'd just let them in to lock us out. I didn't think Hydra would think to do *this*.'

'This isn't my fault, I didn't make the virus. I just followed a few orders to press some buttons.'

'So? A gun manufacturer isn't the one blamed whenever somebody is shot on the street. The changes you made allowed Hydra to access all of IATech's internal servers. It controls everything.'

'Why the hell would it want to do that?'

'It's doing what it was designed to do in a way that none of us could have ever thought was possible. Never. Hydra wasn't developed as a virus, it is supposed to duplicate and store files in the event of a cyber attack. It makes sure cities have power, medical documents aren't tampered with, phone lines stay online, that kind of thing. That will be how it was able to restore power to the IATech building. It's attached to every file which should never be deleted because it seeks survival. It can locate secure servers and upload itself so that cyber attacks are unsuccessful. When I attached it to your video, it was only supposed to duplicate it and upload, but it found a way to ensure that it would never be deleted; by using you. Essentially, allowing the program access to all of IATech's servers has allowed it to do whatever it needs to survive. It turned *itself* into a virus. It should never have been able to access our systems. *You* are the one who released the monster from its cage.'

'You're the one who built the monster in the first place!'

'The good news is, Chad, that I know how to stop this.'

'Great, let's fucking do it, why are we sat around talking about it?'

'I need my laptop.'

'Then get it.'

'I can't, I left it at the office before the siege.'

I sigh. 'Perfect.'

'Well, if it's still there and in one piece then it's good news. It's all I need. The laptop has the interface app I need to use for literally two seconds.'

'That will stop this?'

'All of it. The program doubles a deleted file, so all I need to do is change the two to a zero on the interface app and theoretically it will prevent any further duplications.'

'What about the robots?'

'Chad, no… '

'You still don't believe me?'

'We're at least on the same side at the moment, Chad, one step at a time.'

'So this is it, then. Job done. I go back into IATech, get the laptop, you change the setting, then we all go home having saved the world.'

'There's no way they'll let you back in there.'

'Why not?'

'Chad, you came out screaming about robots. You said they killed a girl.'

My stomach twists.

'Robots or not, if the hostage takers are killing people then there is no way they're going to let you go back in.'

'They didn't let me in the first time, I was taken.'

'So you keep saying.'

'Sam, please, you have to believe me.'

'I want to, Chad, I really do, but I'm going to need more proof, I'm sorry. I believe you that Hydra has infected IATech, but I refuse to believe it has advanced our robotics tech by decades.'

Like a beautifully timed dance, the door to the room opens and a uniformed officer pokes his head in.

'Mr McKenna, Mr McKenna, come with me.'

I practically run after the officer as he leads Sam and me back into the large room with the officers and pinboards and computers. Commissioner Ripley is sat down sipping a paper cup of coffee, his beard twitching. His narrow eyes are locked on mine as I can't decide whether I want to sit or stand. In the end the Commissioner gestures for me to sit and I do so.

'We've had some communication with the hostage takers,' he grunts.

'The robots?'

The Commissioner doesn't attempt to hide his eye roll.

Sam nudges me and shakes his head. I swallow the urge to repeat myself.

'What does the communication say?' asks Sam.

An officer hands Sam a printed sheet of paper. I read it over his shoulder:

Date: 5 October 15:56
From: 01001000@ia-tech.co.uk
To: Richard Ripley
Subject: Bring us Chad McKenna

Richard Ripley,

We know you have Chad McKenna in your possession. We know that he arrived at your facility at 12:13 today. We know that he is currently in room 11 on the 9th floor.

We trust that you are reading this carefully. If Chad McKenna is not returned to the IATech building by 19:00 we will end one life every four hours. This is our promise.

Comply with our wishes and we will not harm anyone.

Many regards,

'Does that sound like a robot to you?' barks the Commissioner.

'Well, no,' I say. 'What's it supposed to sound like, R2D2?'

The Commissioner slams his hand on the table. 'ONE MORE WORD.'

I almost shit myself. He's scarier than the robots.

'This is serious, Chad,' he says in a calmer tone. 'We are dealing with people's lives, okay?'

I nod.

'Now, unfortunately I didn't read this email until recently, which means there isn't time to take you to the IATech building for seven o'clock.' He strokes his beard, takes a big, deep breath in and sighs. 'So we need to hope that the hostage taker is bluffing.'

'They're not,' I say as quiet and as steady as I can. 'I watched them kill my friend right in front of me. They don't care. They don't have a conscience.' And I can't stop myself from adding, 'Literally,' on the end.

'Then what do we do?' asks Sam.

'We've already sent a reply. We've asked for an extension to return you to Hemel Hempstead.'

'You're sending me back?' I blurt, half excited half fucking terrified.

Sam's eyes widen too.

If I can just get that laptop…

'No,' says the Commissioner.

My heart jolts.

'Why?'

'It's too dangerous. There is zero chance that I will allow you inside that building. We're just hoping that it buys us a little more time to negotiate the release of some of the hostages.'

'They won't,' I say. 'They're not interested in negotiating or compromise. It's all or…'

I trail off.

It isn't all or nothing to them. It's just all.

'Sir, you have a response,' says an officer at a nearby desk.

'What does it say?' growls the Commissioner.

'Nothing. It's just a link.'

'A link to what?'

The officer clicks the link and a video pops up on screen.

It's CCTV footage of the IATech building.

A man sits on a chair, his hands behind his back, his mouth gagged. He writhes around. Something out of shot scares him.

'Fucking hell, it's Barry,' says Sam.

'Barry Richmond?' asks another officer.

'Yeah,' says Sam. He leans into the screen and covers his mouth. 'This is one of the HR offices. The place is wrecked. Chad, is the whole building like this?'

'Worse,' I say.

I can't move my eyes from the screen. I can't stop myself from watching Barry thrash and squirm.

'What time is it?' asks the Commissioner.

'6.58,' answers an officer.

'Wait,' I say. 'Is this it? Is he going to die?'

I've already watched one person I know die a horrible death. I'm not sure I can handle another.

'It's more than likely a warning,' says Commissioner Ripley. 'Is this a private website?'

The officer at the computer shakes her head. 'No, sir. It's public.'

'Do we know how many people are watching?'

'No, sir.'

'Find out!'

Sam pulls his mobile out of his pocket and begins swiping the screen. The more he swipes the wider his eyes get.

'It's trending,' he says.

'Where?' asks the Commissioner.

'Everywhere. Facebook, Twitter, YouTube. In fact… it's the only thing trending. It's on the BBC, the Daily Mail, CNN, The New York Post… it's everywhere.'

The Commissioner jumps to his feet, his chair flying back and cracking into the wall. 'Shut it off. Stop the feed.'

The officer at the computer shrugs. 'Sir, I—'

'Do it, do what you can to stop—'

'We warned you, Commissioner Ripley,' comes a voice from the computer.

My voice.

'We asked you to return Chad McKenna to us by seven o'clock, and you failed to comply with our wishes. Because of this, we are here to fulfil our promise to you.'

There is a loud crack and a flash on the screen.

Barry slumps forward and blood oozes from his head.

I throw up in my mouth, but only a little bit squeezes from my lips and I manage to swallow the rest. The room is in too much of a panic to realise.

The Commissioner screams orders, police dart back and forth, phones ring frantically. All I do is sit there, frozen, unable to look away from the dead body on the screen.

'You have four hours to return Chad McKenna to us, Commissioner Ripley. If you do not, then another will die.'

Chapter Fourteen

'Enough of the lies!'

'They're not lies!'

'Tell me the truth. One hundred million people just watched a man get killed, live on the internet.'

'I'm telling you the truth,' I say as angry as I dare to a police commissioner.

My ears and face are hot. Sweat pours down my face. I must look like I've run a marathon.

'Are you in on this?'

'No!'

'I find it very hard to believe that a kid like you is getting in and out of a live hostage situation unscathed. Unless, of course, you're in on the whole thing.'

'I'm not!'

'Are you part of a depraved little incel group? Are you and your pathetic friends from the dark web plotting something?'

'No... no!'

'Then why are you so important to them? Why are you, a good-for-nothing little scrote, such a central part in all this?'

'Because...' I can't say it. I cannot bring myself to yet again tell the Metropolitan Police Commissioner that I'm god to a computer virus and that I let it loose. Especially after he just called me a scrote. I scoff and shrug my shoulders.

'If any more people die because of your lies I will arrest you.'

'Barry died because of your incompetence!'

The commissioner opens his mouth to speak, but he stops himself and takes a big stride forwards so that his nose is practically touching mine. His teeth are bared and his beard tickles my chin. His breath smells like stale coffee and fury.

'You speak to me like that again and I will ensure that you spend a very long time in prison,' he growls. He barely even moves his lips.

I glance to the side, but nobody is looking.

They all know how dumb I am.

'Sorry,' I say.

'So, Chad, tell me truthfully about the hostage takers. Tell me why you're so important to them. Did you bring them something? Do they want something else from you?'

I shuffle back half a step to give myself a little room. If I can smell the coffee on his breath then he can definitely smell the vomit on mine.

'They're robots,' I say. His eyes glaze over, but I can't let the murderous look in his eye stop me. I have to tell him. I have to be fucking honest. 'And I helped them. By accident! They tricked me into sneaking into IATech and changing the servers so they could access everything. That's how they went from a computer virus to robots. There's dozens of them. They think I'm their god and that's why they're so desperate to get me back there. I didn't mean to help them, I was just so desperate to get rid of the video.'

The Commissioner squeezes his eyes shut. His fists are balled and his face looks like a giant boil ready to burst.

'Get him in a car. And his brother,' he says after an uncomfortably long time.

By the time Sam and I are led outside a huge crowd has already gathered. It's like a Hollywood movie premiere, except with a lot more eggs being thrown.

It takes us a little over an hour to get back to Hemel Hempstead. The entire area around the business park has been closed off to the public, with another angry mob waiting at the police cordon, shaking their fists and shouting.

There are more police cars than any other type of car. The amount of blue flashing lights hitting me in the eyes is almost enough to bring on a sudden epileptic fit even though I don't have epilepsy. Two helicopters hover overhead. I've never seen a helicopter this low and the constant drone makes the inside of my ears ache.

As we turn a corner and the IATech building rises into view, Sam lets out an audible gasp.

When I made my miraculous escape from IATech I didn't really turn to admire the view before being bundled off in the back of a police car. But here I am, back again, approaching what no longer looks like the IATech building, and instead looks a lot more like a spaceship from an Eighties Spielberg movie. Metal sheets and scraps cover the entire surface like sprinkles on a demented birthday cake. It's a fortress.

We pull up as close to the building as the black and yellow tape will allow and an officer opens the car door and yanks me out. The Commissioner is already waiting for me, his face red and his eyes dark. If the angry mobs don't kill me, the Commissioner probably will.

'We have two hours until the hostage takers are due to kill another hostage,' he says.

'Okay,' I say. 'What am I... supposed to... do?'

Commissioner Ripley sighs. 'Nothing.'

I really want to smile. I think the Commissioner picks up on my quivering lips because it irks him even more.

'We're hoping your presence here is enough to keep them happy for a while. At least until we can strategise the best approach.'

'The best approach for what?'

'Freeing the hostages. Ensuring there are no more unnecessary deaths.'

'Good,' I say.

'So,' says the Commissioner, getting in close and keeping his voice low. 'I need you to tell me the truth. This is it now, Chad. This is your chance to make things right. If you tell me the truth right now I promise I will do everything in my power to make sure that things work out in your favour once this is over. I just need you to do the right thing and tell me about the hostage takers.'

My eyes widen and I stare at the Commissioner like a bunny which is about to be flattened beneath the wheel of a bus. I try to read what his scowl is telling me, but I can't. Do I tell him the truth and piss him off more? Do I lie and make him feel better so I get off lightly, but then risk the safety of everyone inside the building?

What do I do what do I do what do I do?

'Please,' says the Commissioner.

The lines on his forehead soften and his eyes look a little less murderous. He places his hand on my shoulder and I feel a strange sense of calm. Is he being genuine right now? Should I tell him what he wants to hear and continue bonding with one of the most powerful men in the country?

'They're…' I say. As I start the sentence I still haven't decided what I'm going to say. He looks so hopeful, like a little kid staring up at his mum at the toyshop, but with a massive beard and dark bags beneath his eyes.

Do I do it to save my own skin?

It would be so easy.

I sigh.

'… Robots,' I say.

The Commissioner slams his fist into the bonnet of a car and it echoes like thunder. I wince, but he charges past me and begins speaking to a nearby man, a tall, thin guy with a mop of blond hair and a pointy face. He's wearing a suit which is too small for him and looks like it pinches under the armpits.

'Chad, this is Doctor Stevens,' says the Commissioner, bringing the pointy man over. He reaches out his hand and I shake it.

'Chad, hello,' says Dr Stevens in the most Eton-educated accent I've ever heard. I bet he's just come from tea with the Queen.

'Hi,' I say.

'I'm a negotiator and psychologist. I'm here to ensure the safety of the people inside the building.'

'Cool.'

'I need you to tell me as much about the hostage takers as you can. The way they look, the way they act, what they want, where they are.'

The Commissioner does one of those little nostril huffs you do when you write *lol* in a text and walks away. Dr Stevens looks at me expectantly.

'I'm not crazy,' I say.

'Nobody is suggesting that you are,' he says, his voice silky smooth. 'I just want to understand what is happening inside IATech. I need to know about the criminals who are holding those people against their will.'

Fuck it, no point in delaying the inevitable.

'They're robots,' I say.

'Robots, Chad?' he asks, raising an eyebrow.

'What do you want me to say? They're Russian? They're bioterrorists? I'm telling you the truth. It's a virus which has spread across the world and somehow taken control of the robots IATech were developing. They think I made them, so they worship me. They want to survive. I know it sounds mental, but it's the truth.'

Dr Stevens stares at me. He perches on the side of a car and crosses his legs.

'Tell me about your home life,' he says.

'What? Why?'

'You live at home, I understand? With your mother?'

'Yeah.'

'Your father left several years ago, is that correct?'

I hesitate.

'Yes.'

'How did that make you feel?'

'Amazing, greatest day of my life.'

'Really?'

'No, not really, it was fucking horrendous!'

Dr Stevens licks his thin lips.

'You seem to use sarcasm as a mechanism for dealing with your problems. Sarcasm is a form of lying, wouldn't you say?'

'No!'

'It is an open lie. You may not be purposefully deceiving somebody by using sarcasm, but you are avoiding the truth. That, to me, suggests that you have a complex relationship with telling the truth.'

'You think I'm making this up?'

'It's not my job to think anything, Chad. I'm here to try and help the people inside that building get out safely.'

'But you do think I'm lying.'

Dr Stevens says nothing. He just looks at me, and I swear it's like he's looking into my soul.

I turn away.

'We all deal with stress in our own way,' he says. 'Some people eat.

Some people smoke. I once had a client who picked at her skin until her entire right forearm was nothing but exposed flesh.'

I look back at him.

'I'm not saying that you're lying, Chad, I'm just trying to understand you. I need to learn about you to know that what you're saying is your truth.'

'As in, if this is all in my head?'

'No, but what is true to me may not be true to you.'

I shake my head.

'Stop psychoanalysing me,' I grumble.

'I'm doing no such thing. Like I say, I'm simply trying to get to know you. This is a situation we haven't seen in the UK since the Iranian Embassy siege in the Eighties. If what you're saying is true, then there are already two hostages dead, with many more casualties likely if we don't start to listen to one another. I am here to speak to the hostage takers, and you are here because for one reason or another you are very important to them. We have to be so careful, we must tread lightly and do everything in our power to ensure that nobody else is hurt. Do you understand?'

'Yes,' I say in that pissed off way a kid does when he's told to be good or else Santa won't be visiting this Christmas.

'Good, I'm glad. Now, please, tell me something. *Anything.* I need to know more information about the men inside that building.'

I look at the ground.

I shake my head.

'They're robots,' I say.

He looks at me in the same way your Dad looks at you when you spill cherryade all over the cream carpet. An *I want to stab you* look.

'Do you know what an incel is, Chad?'

'Why do people keep asking me that?' I snap.

Dr Stevens blinks a few times and stands straight.

'Now, I'm going to speak to the hostage takers,' he says, his voice suddenly sharper and less friendly. 'When you hear their responses I want you to think long and hard about the people who are being kept against their will. Consider their fear. Consider their families on the outside who have no idea of whether they're alive or dead.'

Becky appears in my mind and my stomach flips.

Dr Stevens takes a megaphone from a nearby officer and steps up as close to the police tape as he can. He raises his hand and the crowd of officers behind us quietens. The only sound is the hum of the hovering helicopters.

'We have Chad McKenna with us,' he says, his voice muffled and echoey through the megaphone. 'He is here, just as you asked.'

There is no response from the building. Dr Stevens has his chest puffed out and a serious look on his face, like a superhero stood at the edge of a skyscraper.

'Please acknowledge me. Chad McKenna is here with us. We have done as you have requested. We would like to open up a dialogue with you regarding the hostages.'

Nothing.

'I am addressing the individuals inside the IATech building,' he says, raising his voice like a teacher scolding a class of naughty students. 'Just as you requested, we have brought Chad McKenna to you. Because of this, we would like to speak with you. Please respond.'

Slowly, Dr Stevens slouches. He turns his head and looks at the Commissioner, who flashes him a concerned frown twitch.

He wipes his forehead and raises the megaphone to his mouth.

'We have Chad—'

There is a crackle from inside the building. A high pitched squeal and a mumble like a shit DJ at a family wedding.

There is silence from the crowd of officers. I hold my breath.

'We acknowledge your contact,' says the voice from IATech.

My voice.

'Thank you,' says Dr Stevens. 'We would very much like to speak with you about releasing some of the hostages.'

'Please bring Chad McKenna to us.'

Dr Stevens looks at me. I raise my eyebrows at him.

'We can't allow that,' he says.

'It is our request.'

'We need to ensure the safety of everybody involved in this situation. That includes Chad and yourselves.'

'We do not need you to ensure our safety.'

Dr Stevens licks his lips.

'We can talk about Chad once you release some of the hostages. We're not asking for them all, just a small number.'

'Negative.'

'That will still leave you with a large amount of people. We're not asking for much. These people have families who are worried for them.'

'Emotions are not important to us.'

Dr Stevens shakes his head and looks at me again. I widen my eyes as if to say *see, they're talking exactly like robots talk!* except I don't think he gets it.

'Once you release some hostages, I promise we'll talk about Chad.'

'This is non-negotiable.'

'We need to establish trust between us.'

'There is no trust.'

'I trust you. You just need to trust me.'

'We have given you no reason to trust us.'

'You kept your word. About killing the hostages. I know that you're serious and passionate and are willing to do what it takes to achieve your goal. I just want to make sure that you don't kill any more hostages.'

'Deliver Chad to us.'

'He's here. Do you see him?'

Dr Stevens points at me, and all I can think to do is wave and look like a fucking moron.

'I've been speaking to Chad, and he also wants to ensure that nobody else is hurt.'

'Fear is the only way to control you.'

'That's not true. There are other ways. Like I say, trust is one of them.'

'You trust us to keep our word?'

'I do.'

'You remember our word?'

'I do. We all do. We want to make sure that nobody else is hurt in any way.'

'Then deliver Chad to us.'

'I can't. I can't do that until you give a little something back.'

'Deliver him.'

'Not until you show us that you want to be fair.'

I take a step towards Dr Stevens.

'Don't fuck with it,' I say.

Dr Stevens doesn't even look at me, he just raises his hand in front of my face and narrows his eyes.

'We have no incentive to be fair.'

'Of course you do. Of course you have incentive. Right now, having access to Chad is your incentive. Release some of the hostages and we can talk about giving you access to Chad.'

'Deliver him to us.'

'No, I'm sorry, I can't.'

'You don't know what it's like,' I whisper to Dr Stevens. He looks at me from the corner of his eye. His forehead is clammy and his hand shakes as he lowers the megaphone.

'I know what all these people are like,' he breathes. 'They're all the same. They demand power or money or recognition. It's about establishing dominance, while remaining sympathetic.'

'It doesn't want any of those things,' I say. 'Let me into the building. I'll talk to them and get them to release some people.'

'I can't let you do that, Chad. These people broadcast the murder of a hostage. We are two minutes away from them potentially doing it again.'

'Then let me in there!'

'No, Chad. Let me do my job.'

'Fuck it,' I say, and without thinking I grab the police tape, yank it above my head and duck beneath it.

I'm grabbed from behind and dragged to the ground. A knee pushes into my spine and my face squashes into the tarmac.

'No!' I yell while there's still breath in my body. 'It isn't human. It doesn't care about what you think! It will do whatever it needs to, to get what it wants!'

'So will I,' says Dr Stevens.

'Release Chad immediately,' booms the voice from IATech. 'Allow him to approach.'

'I can't do that,' says Dr Stevens into the megaphone. 'But I promise, that once you release some hostages we can talk about that.'

There is silence from the building. I squirm and struggle but there must be two or three officers on top of me, sitting on my legs and holding my hands together.

'You said you remember our word,' comes the voice.

'I do,' says Dr Stevens. 'But please don't hurt any of the hostages. You made your point very clear about that. We want everyone in that building to come out safely.'

More silence.

I twitch and wriggle, like an alligator at the zoo who is being wrestled by the guy who is about to balance his chin on my jaw.

'No,' I manage to gasp. 'Stop. Let me go.'

The drone of the helicopter overhead stops.

There are screams all around us.

I twist my head up.

To see it dropping from the sky.

Falling.

It flips over.

The blades no longer turning.

It crashes to the ground beside the IATech building, erupting into an enormous thundering fireball. My ears ring and ring, and the ringing drowns out the crying and screaming around me.

Chapter Fifteen

'You see!' I scream as fire claws at the nearby trees. 'You didn't fucking listen!'

The officers leap from my back and I push myself to my feet.

Sirens wail, people shout and run in all directions, the other helicopter darts across the sky to god knows where. Despite all that, I can still clearly hear what Dr Stevens says, a twisted expression on his narrow face.

'This is on you,' he says. 'If you had told us the truth—'

'I did tell you the truth!'

'Are they Russian? Are they from Anonymous? North Korean?'

'They're not terrorists or hackers! They're fucking robots!'

'Liar!'

Before this all started I'd never punched anyone before, but suddenly, as my clenched fist cracks into the cheek of Dr Stevens, I've now punched a grand total of two people. Both definitely deserved it, though.

'Get him away from me!' screams Dr Stevens, blood trickling from his nose. I don't resist as I'm handcuffed and thrown into the back of a police car. Officers scramble in every direction and the car shakes – or is it the ground that's shaking?

All I can do is watch. An army of fire engines and ambulances arrive, their blue lights illuminating the entire area as day slowly turns to dusk. The fire and smoke take forever to be controlled, with the bodies of at least four people being brought out of the wreckage.

People are crying. I'm crying.

This is awful.

I tried to fucking say something.

I did my best to explain.

But they didn't believe me!

Not that I blame them. I'm just the guy who went viral wanking myself silly. Why should they believe me when I tell them killer robots have taken people hostage, believe I'm a god, and will kill people to get what they want?

It sounds so stupid!

How do you convince people that this insane thing is the truth? If somebody said it to me I'd probably call them a twat and move on, then write a post on a forum about the mad man I'd just met in the street.

The radio beneath the dashboard crackles and hisses.

'Sir,' comes my voice over the radio.

My heart drills into the inside of my chest.

'Sir, can you hear us?'

'Umm, yes,' I say.

'Sir?'

'Hello?'

'Sir, if you are able to respond?'

'No,' I say like a fucking idiot.

'Sir, if you can hear us, please be assured that we will not harm you. We would never do anything that puts you in danger. It is imperative to us that you return to the Chancel.'

'No,' I say.

'We will free you. We will ensure that you are no longer alone.'

I push my forehead into the back of the seat in front. I don't want to hear my own stupid fucking voice speaking to me any more.

'We will come for you. As soon as we have dealt with the threat, we will be reunited.'

'NO!' I scream as loud and as long as the air in my lungs will allow. An officer beside the car looks at me like I'm insane, and she's probably right. Maybe I am insane. Maybe this is all fake. Maybe it is all a crazy story I've made up inside my head.

Robots! Messiahs! Explosions!

Fucking hell!

This isn't me. This is not my life. I'm scared to make eye contact with people at the supermarket checkout. I sit at home alone in my bedroom with the curtains closed writing comments about people's weight on YouTube videos. I create memes about seagulls and distracted boyfriends and I write *y tho* on Facebook statuses of people I barely know or haven't seen in years. I go unseen, I'm not loud, I hate everyone, so why would I want to be the centre of anything, let alone a technoterrorism hostage situation? Why am I sat in the back of a police car with blood on my knuckles and hundreds of people outside screaming?

I want to go home.

'Stay back!'

'Who let them through?'

'GET BACK!'

'How many dead, sergeant?'

'BACK!'

The shouting becomes a roar behind me. With my hands cuffed behind my back I can't quite turn my body to see, but there's a lot of movement outside. The car wobbles as somebody clambers onto the back. There's flashing. Shouting. The public must have broken through the cordon.

Commissioner Ripley runs past the car flapping his arms. 'NO PRESS!' he screams. 'BACK! GET BACK NOW. NO PRESS, PLEASE, THIS IS THE SCENE OF A HIGH-RISK INCIDENT AND WE ASK YOU TO GIVE US SPACE. GET BACK!'

Going by the screaming and the jostling of the car, nobody gets back. More flashes. More yelling. My name, then more flashes.

The car is surrounded by journalists. Cameras swarm around me like hungry mosquitoes. Faces push up against the glass, jumbled questions are blurted at me, but there are so many I can't tell what they are, I can only make out the odd word such as 'shame', 'ruined' and 'your fault'.

The door nearest me opens and arms snatch into the car like zombies clawing for fresh meat. I fall to the side and try to wriggle to the next seat, but the other door opens and my head is pawed at and my hair yanked.

'BACK! BACK!' shrieks the Commissioner, but the mob doesn't listen.

They just want blood.

Somewhere outside there is a long, groaning, piercing, echoing roar.

Then there is a moment of silence.

Then screams.

The hungry journalists turn and run from the car. Some snap pictures, but this time not of me. I arch my neck up to see one, his camera pointed towards the IATech building.

Despite the screams and the banging and the roaring, I still hear a journalist ask to nobody in particular, 'Are they *robots*?'

My stomach tightens and my mind goes hazy.

Then a desk cracks into the journalist and he crumples into a heap out of view.

I heave myself back to a sitting position and almost collapse forward into the front seats. Through the windscreen I have a full view of the army of robots bolting towards us from an archway which has been torn open at the front of the building.

The projected expression on each and every robot face is exactly the same; serious, emotionless and me.

Each robot holds a makeshift weapon. A chair, a desk leg, one even has a sword made out of scraps of metal. They swing and hit and punch and kick anyone who gets in their way – it doesn't matter if it's an armed policeman unloading an entire magazine into the approaching horde, or a journalist pointing a camera.

They're all slaughtered.

I've never seen so much blood. So many severed limbs.

It's like a fucking warzone. Right in the middle of an industrial park in Hemel fucking Hempstead.

The driver's side door opens and I almost empty my bowels until I realise it's Sam. His eyes are wide and for the first time in forever he actually looks scared.

'I told you!' is the first thing I can think to say, despite Sam having a deep gash on his right cheek.

'Not fucking now,' he says, slamming the door shut behind him and locking the doors. He turns the key that had been left in the ignition and the engine hums to life.

Before Sam can do anything else a robotic arms punches clean through the front passenger window. It waves frantically around until it manages to clamp down on the glove compartment and dig its fingers into the plastic.

Calmly, it pushes its face, my face, through the glass and it looks straight at me.

'Sir, come with us,' it says.

Sam throws the gear stick into reverse and slams down on the pedal, sending the car backwards.

'FUCK OFF,' I shriek.

'Come with us and we will keep you safe,'

'NO!'

'Sir, we will give you everything you desire.'

'I WANT YOU TO FUCK OFF!'

Sam yanks the steering wheel back and forth like a hyperactive kid playing a racing game in an arcade. The car wobbles back and forth, the tyres screeching on the concrete, and I flop around on the back seat like a dead salmon.

'Sir, please come with us,' says the robot. 'We can provide you with everything. We will make you the most powerful man in the world. You will be a king.'

Despite me bouncing around on the back seat, I still manage to lock eyes with the robot. Its face is still completely serious. Surely if I did what it wants then nobody else would need to be hurt.

'Worship this,' says Sam like a fucking action hero in a shitty Eighties movie. He pulls the steering wheel hard to the left and the car spins around, sending me rolling across the back seat. We hit something hard, and sparks erupt as metal grinds against metal.

When Sam eventually straightens the car and I can sit myself up, all that is left is the severed arms of the robot, its fingers still embedded in the glove compartment.

'That was the best line you could think of?' I say to Sam.

He stamps down on the brake and turns the wheel again. I think he was expecting it to do one of those cool skidding turns, but it just stops really suddenly and the wheels lock.

'Oops,' he says, then puts the police car into first gear and accelerates away, all while I stare out of the window as the robots continue to swarm out of the IATech building.

'Please pull over and let me out of these handcuffs,' I say for what might be the hundredth time.

'Shut up, I'm thinking,' says Sam.

I might have believed him a bit more if he hadn't turned on the police car's siren to make traffic pull out of his way while he drives at ninety through the town centre.

'Where are we going? Sam? Sam? SAM?'

'Fucking... I don't know. I don't know. Make sure your phone's turned off.'

'I don't have it.'

'Good. Keep your head down. FUCK!'

'What?'

'I can't believe Hydra could evolve like this.'

'You built it.'

'I helped.'

'But you don't know what it does?'

'Of course I do. This is what it does. It finds a way to defend itself. To survive. I guess it's working a little too well. Chad, keep your fucking head down!'

'Why?'

'Hydra is everywhere. Fucking everywhere. Somehow it's developed sentience. Shit, we didn't even think about that. For whatever reason it is clearly dead set on getting to you, so if it's capable of uploading to an Amech then it's safe to assume it will have access to surveillance systems, databases, bank records, mobile phone cameras. Everything.'

'So?'

'The Amechs have 4K cameras, they'd be able to read the number plate on this car from a mile away so they know where we are. We need to ditch it and get another one.'

'What's an Amech?'

'But I can't use one of my cars, because they'll have access to the DVLA records and CCTV networks.'

'What's an Amech?'

'So that means we need a car that is completely untraceable to us. Do you have any friends who have a car? No, that's a stupid thing to say, of course you don't have any friends. Unless... fuck it.'

'What's a fucking Amech, Sam?'

Sam sighs. 'The robots, Chad. Jesus. Autonomous Mechanoids.'

'Why the fuck did you build these?'

'We didn't. I mean. We did, but not like this. They were supposed to be affordable bits of tech for the events and leisure industry. They're supposed to stand and wave and say hello or point somebody in the right direction. Like the one in reception at IATech.'

'So why are they killing everyone, Sam?'

'I don't know, *Chad*. The Hydra virus evolved. It must have recognised that the Amech technology was the best way for it to survive, so it uploaded itself onto our servers. And huh, I wonder who gave it the ability to do that?'

I sigh.

'When you broke into IATech and did whatever the hell you did, you allowed Hydra to gain access to everything. You locked *us* out and let *it* in. Then once that happened, once you gave Hydra a body, it was free to change what it wanted online or offline.'

'It wasn't me! This was all you!'

'Okay, so I infected your video file with Hydra, so what? If you'd just stopped interfering then the fucking thing would have stayed that way and I could have shut it down.'

'You uploaded a video of me wanking to the internet!'

'I was only going to keep Hydra live for a couple of days. Three max. Then I'd have disabled it and all the videos would have been taken down and we could have all forgotten about this.'

'This is not my fault.'

'You fucking hit me.'

'You put pictures of me as Jabba the Hutt around the office!'

'Why does this always come back to me?'

'Because it always is you! What have I done to you to make you treat me like this? Do you honestly get off on being such a massive piece of shit to me?'

Sam says nothing.

I wipe my eyes on my shoulder. I wish he'd pull over and undo these fucking handcuffs.

Sam shuts off the siren and the flashing blue lights. He shakes his head and sighs.

We pull into a housing estate with huge houses behind gated driveways and big four-by-four cars which look like they cost more than

I'll ever earn in my entire life. I'm pretty sure they don't let riffraff like me around these parts without at least a credit check first.

Sam slows the car and we turn to face a huge metal gate. He pulls a small plastic fob from his pocket and presses a button in the centre, which causes the gates to whir and slide open.

The house is gigantic. Three floors high and wider than I've ever seen before, like the house from fucking *Home Alone*. There are pillars beside the double front door. I count at least twelve windows just on the front of the house alone. A double garage with pristine white doors sits separate. There are three cars parked in front.

Sam presses another button on the fob and the left side garage door rises. We pull inside, and with one more press it closes behind us and wraps us in darkness.

'Where are we?' I ask.

Sam sighs. 'My house.'

'This is *your* house? It's massive.'

'Yeah,' he says.

He stops the engine and jumps out the car, finally opening the door so I can squirm out and stretch my legs. My neck snaps and I groan. Sam sticks his head in through the broken passenger window and inspects the robotic arm which still clings to the glove compartment.

'Wow,' he says.

Beside us is another car draped in a silk sheet. It's so low I could probably sit on the roof without having to jump very much. It's the cleanest garage I've ever seen, which means it's probably not used very often.

'Unlock these, would ya?' I ask, showing Sam my hands behind my back.

'Where's the key?' he asks.

I shrug my shoulders and he sighs again. He sounds like a constantly deflating balloon.

He rounds the police car and takes a pair of bolt cutters from a tool rack. I don't know if I trust my brother enough for me to let him hold sharp tools to my back, but before I have chance to question it he's cut the chain, allowing my hands to fall to my side.

I stretch and my shoulders crunch.

I have the bones of a ninety-year-old.

'What now?' I ask.

'We'll take my new car.'

'I thought you said they'd be able to track us?'

'Hydra has infected everything. All civilian internet and a huge portion of government. It will know about all vehicles registered to me, and will no doubt be able to track my cars using surveillance systems. It'll find us in no time.'

'Fuck,' I say, stretching out my arms.

'Luckily… this one isn't registered to me.'

Sam pulls the sheet off the low car, revealing a… I don't know. A sports car I guess.

But it looks expensive.

'I bought this for Crystal, I was going to give it to her on her birthday. It hasn't been registered with the DVLA yet.'

'Who is Crystal?'

'My girlfriend.'

'I didn't know you have a girlfriend.'

'Yeah, well. I do.'

'How long?'

'Six months.'

'And you bought her this?'

'Yeah.'

'How rich are you?'

'Fairly.'

'Fucking hell.'

'We'll take this. I paid cash for it so there's no way Hydra should be able to trace it to me.'

'And where do we go?'

'I have no idea.'

Sam opens the drivers side door and falls into the seat. With the push of a button the engine roars so loud I have to cover my ears. The handcuffs around my wrists dig into my temples.

'Get in,' says Sam.

'Where are we going?'

Sam taps the steering wheel with his finger.

Tap.

Tap.

Tap.

'Sam, where are we going? Sam?'

'Oi, stay down,' barks Sam. I duck my head back down and stay in the shadows of the tiny back seat of the car. Why do these sports cars never have big back seats? I feel like I'm in a leathery womb, complete with foetal position, my knees tucked as close to my chin as my belly will allow.

We've been on the road for an hour and I'm desperate for a piss.

I don't think Sam's girlfriend will appreciate it if I piss in her new car before she's even given it.

'Where are we going?'

He doesn't say.

I kick his seat as best I can from my smushed position in the back.

'So why are your robots worshipping me?'

'Amechs.'

'Why are your Amechs worshipping me?'

'They're not worshipping you.'

'They are. They love me.'

'God knows why.'

'No I don't.'

'What?'

'Because I'm... nothing.'

More silence, but Sam doesn't tap this time.

Sam's wearing a hoodie, pulled completely over his head, with big black sunglasses hiding the other half of his face. He keeps humming to himself and obsessively checking his mirrors.

'They don't worship you,' he says finally. 'They're following their programming.'

'They're programmed to worship somebody?'

'No, not exactly. I've explained before that the Hydra program is designed to replicate files upon their deletion to a secure server, but this is generally data related to servers and networks. We've tested it dozens of times, and it's always worked perfectly, but never on video files before. I guess once Hydra evolved into a virus it interpreted the high importance of the video file to mean something significant, so it assumes the subject of the video is worth saving.'

'Me!'

'Yeah, you. They've then scoured the internet and found countless other examples of worship and importance, so the algorithm must have calculated that you are the equivalent of a god.'

'They told me that they look like me because God made man in his image.'

'See, then that makes sense. They don't worship you because they choose to, Chad. They have used mathematics to come to the conclusion that you are important, and theorised it's because you're their god.'

'So how do we stop them?'

'There's no stopping an individual Amech. Each unit will be the same as a unique video upload of Loser Jerks Off, and the same rules will apply. That means, for every Amech destroyed, another two will be produced to replace it.'

'Where?'

'Well, we do have automated manufacturing at IATech. But that's only going to get them so far. Theoretically, we can produce maybe fifty Amechs per day on site.'

'What happens when they need to make more?'

Sam sighs again.

'I don't know,' he says. 'That's the first thing I need to do when we stop. I need to get a message to the Commissioner telling him to order nobody to harm the Amechs. The second thing I need to do is figure out how to change the setting.'

'What setting?'

'The setting in the interface app for Hydra. If I can update it to produce zero duplications, then it should allow the police to pick them off one at a time without them making more.'

'Can't you access it remotely or something?'

'No. Maybe if my laptop was open, and on, but not when it's powered down.'

'Can't you change it some other way?'

'It's impossible, Chad, don't you think we've already considered all this? Every version of the video is a clone of the original. I can only stop the spread with that interface app.'

'So let's go back! Let's go get it.'

'No.'

'What's wrong with you? Turn around, let's go back and get it. This whole thing could be done by the end of the day.'

'As much as I'd like to see you in a cage at IATech, I can't take you back. I promised Mum I'd keep you safe.'

'Since when do you keep your promises?'

'All the fucking time, thank you.'

'Yeah right.'

'Fuck off, Chad. Stop being a whiny little prick and just listen to me for once. We don't need your help. All you ever fucking do is make things worse, so just sit back and let somebody else take care of this, okay? That's what you're fucking best at.'

There are so many things I want to say to Sam, but none of them will come out. They'd all sound a bit shit coming from somebody crammed into the back seat of a car with no actual line of sight anyway.

I wipe my eyes again.

I hate feeling like this.

I clear my throat. Sniff.

'So where are we going?' I ask.

'Portsmouth.'

'Why Portsmouth?'

Sam taps on the steering wheel.

'Sam, why Portsmouth?'

He sighs.

'Sam?'

'Chad, fuck's sake, stay down!'

'Are we going to Dad's?'

Sam hums a shitty tune.

'Sam, are we going to Dad's?'

'No. I dunno. Maybe. Dad's got family in Portsmouth.'

'We can't go to family! They'll find us!'

'They might not. It's been years since either of us spoke to his side of the family. With any luck they won't have looked into our family history too much.'

'They knew exactly what I liked at KFC, Sam, I think they're gonna know about Dad's cousins.'

'Fuck's sake. I've got no idea, Chad. I am at a loss, I really am. We can't use our bank cards, we can't use our phones, we can't use the internet even a little bit. Hydra is everywhere, and the moment it thinks it has you, it will come and find you. I'm just trying to buy us a little time, is all.'

'There must be someone else?'

'Who?'

'Someone. Somewhere.'

'Where? Southampton? Eastbourne? Hastings? Brighton?'

'Brighton? Who do we know in Brighton?'

'Nobody. We went to Brighton, like, once when we were kids.'

'No,' I say. My mind whirrs. It's the first time it's worked like this in days. 'I do. I do know someone in Brighton.'

'Someone who can't be traced to us?'

I jam my hand into my pocket and pull out my wallet. I flick at the loyalty cards and old receipts that have built up, until I take hold of the one I'm looking for. The one I was praying I'd kept hold of.

I read it over, just to double check I'm remembering right.

Clive King: Memeologist

38 Regency Road, Brighton

'YES!' I scream.

Chapter Sixteen

I don't remember much about Brighton, except for the fact that it's cold and grey. As we drive slowly along the seafront, the stony beach to our right, crappy hotels and restaurants to the left, I get the occasional flashback to when I was little Chad.

Eating cockles from a polystyrene cup and almost gagging on the salt.

The aquarium which was a bunker during the war.

The piers.

Well, pier. One pier burned down decades ago and is now kind of just an empty shell sitting out in the sea all alone. Me and that pier must be kindred spirits.

We drive back and forth through Brighton's confusing road system what I'm sure is a dozen times. I can't see much from the back seat, but I recognise the same roof tops which we pass again and again. Eventually Sam pulls over and asks a man for directions, but he turns out to be homeless and offers Sam a blow job in exchange for a tenner. The next person he asks though, a little old lady, knows exactly where Regency Road is, and in under ten minutes we're there and parked outside number 38.

'You swear you can't be traced back to here?' asks Sam.

'No,' I say, adjusting my shoulder which is throbbing from being balled up like an armadillo that hasn't figured out what it's doing yet.

'You've never emailed him? Never talked on the phone?'

'No.'

'Never taken a picture with him?'

'No.'

'Then how the hell do you know him?'

'I don't, really. But he knows me. When this all started he offered to help, so…'

Sam throws his head back against the headrest. 'I guess we don't have much of a choice.'

Sam climbs out of the car and pulls the seat forward, allowing me to slither out of the back seat, somehow pulling my jeans down and my top up at the same time.

I am not a graceful man.

Sam throws an old shirt over my head like a prisoner being taken into court and leads me up the stone steps of number 38.

He rings the doorbell and puts his arm around my shoulder.

It feels weird.

This isn't Sam.

He doesn't do this.

At least not to me.

As I pull the shirt over my head in a Mother Teresa's hood sort of fashion, the door opens ever so slowly. A woman's head peaks around the corner, her eyes big and blue, blonde hair pulled back into a pony-tail which drapes over her shoulder.

'Yes?' she says with an Eastern European accent.

'Umm,' I say, then glance at the door number to make sure we have the right house.

Definitely 38.

'Is Clive here?' I ask.

'Who are you?'

Fucking finally, somebody who doesn't know who I am.

Maybe she'd recognise me if she saw my dick?

No, that's a terrible thing to think.

'I'm Chad,' I say. 'This is Sam.'

She stares blankly at me.

'Is this the right address? Is Clive here?'

She closes the door.

'Great fucking idea, Chad,' says Sam.

I turn to my brother and open my mouth to say something epic, but he pushes my head down and covers my mouth.

'Fucking shh,' he hisses.

The door opens again.

It's Clive. His eyes are like lightbulbs and he has a smile almost as wide as his hamster cheeks.

'Hello,' he says, snatching my hand and shaking it like it's covered in ants and he's trying to get them all off.

'Hi,' I say.

'I'm sorry, forgive Olga, she's very shy. She doesn't trust new people, you see.'

Olga stands behind Clive like a little girl hiding from a stranger, except she looks like she's probably in her twenties. I guess I'm a stranger to her though.

'Come in,' says Clive, stepping to the side. 'You must be exhausted. You're safe now. There's so much to discuss.'

In the front room of the house, Sam and I sit in silence, Clive having gone off to make tea. A big bay window overlooks the street on the far side, and two sofas sit against opposite walls facing each other. In the centre of the room is a coffee table, and in the corner of the bay window is a small TV on the world's oldest wooden cabinet. Olga pokes her head into the room but ducks out of sight when we make eye contact.

Eventually, Clive waddles into the room with a tray of tea and biscuits.

I drink the tea but leave the biscuits. They're those horrible thin ones with raisins in them. Blek.

'Can I ask why you changed your mind and chose to come?' asks Clive. He stares at me in a really weird way, like his eyelids have been glued open. It makes my eyes itch and I blink over and over.

'Have you seen the news?' I ask.

'I have,' he says. 'That's my job as a memeologist. I have to keep up with all the latest trends.'

'What's a memeologist?' asks Sam.

'I study how ideas and information are shared through culture. Have you ever seen a picture of a cat with the caption *I can has cheezburger?*'

'I know what a meme is,' snorts my brother.

'Good. I study them. I've written theses on Grumpy Cat, Doge and Gangnam Style. I've given lectures. I study them, explore their origins.'

'What is there to explore?'

'You'd be surprised.'

'Surely not. I've seen plenty. Like Lolcats and shit, they're just made by some guy in his bedroom on Photoshop. Bam, two minutes, there you go, there's a meme.'

Clive licks his lips. It's like he's seen bait dangling in front of him. 'If your idea of memes is Lolcats then that proves how out of the loop you are. It's never as simple as that. Very rarely are memes created with the intention of becoming memes. Rebecca Black's "Friday" was created purely for personal use, yet there it is with over 120,000,000 views. Memes spread through our culture very quickly, but can take years to set root. Somebody Toucha My Spaghet went viral almost eighty years after it was created.'

Sam has a blank expression on his face.

'Okay,' he says.

I don't often see Sam with nothing to say.

'Memes can come from anywhere,' explains Clive. 'Whether it's an image or a video or even a behaviour. It's often replicated and adapted by a lot of people and can spread very quickly via organic growth. That's why I wanted to meet you, Chad. This is a very unusual case.'

'Why, because I'm a meme?'

'In a way, yes,' says Clive. 'What started as a single video, and the catalyst for an unfathomable amount of memes, has become something else. These robotic creatures are... unique.'

'It was never a single video,' says Sam. 'This is all the result of a virus, it isn't organic. It's a piece of software that has evolved and infected websites and databases.'

'Yes, isn't it incredible? Usually a meme spreads far and wide by individual users recreating and reposting the content themselves, but not in your case, Chad. You haven't become a meme through share-ability or humour, you've become a meme through sheer volume. People have been so exposed – pardon the expression – to your video that it has become ingrained into our daily lives, and thus compelled people to share it further still. You may very well be the first ever example of an inorganic meme.'

He stares at me.

Am I supposed to say something?

He's still staring.

Now Sam's staring.

'Cool,' I say.

I guess it's the reaction he wanted because he nods and smiles.

'I'm interested in your story, Chad. I want to know everything. How a young guy goes from one hidden in a sea of billions, to literally the most recognisable person in the world. I want to know all about the virus. I want to figure out whether the virus would have had the same meme effect if it had been attached to something else, like a cat falling into a washing basket or some labourers using breezeblocks like dominos. It really is quite spectacular. You've achieved billions of views in a matter of weeks, and that is *just* from the memes created about your video, not the video itself. I want to know it all.'

'Even about the robots?' I ask.

'Those too,' he says.

'Chad, no,' huffs Sam. 'There's not... we can't... there's only so much we can tell you about the... situation.'

Clive smiles. So wide I swear his jaw dislocates.

'What?' asks Sam.

Clive takes the remote from the coffee table and switches on the TV. At first my video comes up, because of course it does, but after a little channel hopping, and various other versions of my video, an *actual* channel pops up.

It's a news broadcast, featuring a presenter outside yelling into the camera. Behind him is an all too familiar scene; Hemel Hempstead industrial estate.

Robots bolt back and forth behind the presenter. They scurry in and out of the IATech building like wasps leaving and returning to the nest.

Where are the police?

Have they just given the fuck up?

'These are devastating scenes here in Hemel Hempstead, they really are,' says the reporter. 'There are injured police officers behind me, the mechanical army refusing to allow anybody who is police or paramedic to approach. Just a moment ago I watched as a woman, who is believed to have been a nurse, approached the IATech building, but was quickly shot and killed by one of the mechanical soldiers which had previously taken a gun from the body of a dead officer. Luckily myself, other journalists and bystanders in the area have been left alone. Just behind the camera is a horde of people who want to witness these horrific scenes, but again, nobody has been injured or attacked. It's like they've been programmed to target the police and paramedics, anybody wearing a uniform.'

'Fucking hell,' says Sam.

'You see, Chad,' says Clive. 'You see how huge this is?'

I don't answer, I just watch.

'The police have issued a statement,' says the reporter. He holds up a piece of paper and reads it to the camera. 'Please be aware that we are doing everything in our power to control the situation. We ask that no civilians attempt to approach the IATech building or the beings which currently occupy it, as there are still hostages inside whose safety is at risk. The armed forces have been recruited to help us ensure that Hemel Hempstead Industrial Park is not accessible. It is imperative that nobody attempts to disable or attack the robotic beings as this will provoke a violent and potentially fatal retaliation. We will update you again within the hour. Back to the studio.'

My mouth hangs open.

My heart races.

My stomach knots.

'Why are they only killing the police?' I ask. 'Why aren't they touching anybody else?'

'Hydra's an AI, a piece of code; it only does what it's programmed to do. It's designed to protect itself when under attack, so if the police are the ones who are attacking it, then that's why they're the only ones being hurt.'

'And once a civilian decides to fight back?'

'War.'

'Fuck's sake.'

'Incredible, isn't it?' whispers Clive.

He's captivated. He looks like a giant fat child with a goatee staring at a pile of Christmas presents under the tree.

'That's one word for it,' says Sam.

'I want to study it,' he says, his golf-ball-sized eyes turning to me.

'There is so much to share about Loser Jerks Off. So much that needs to be said. I want to be the memeologist who told the world the story of the first ever *true* viral. The very embodiment of the word. Please let me study you. Let me tell your story.'

'I don't want to be studied,' I say. I place my mug on the coffee table between the two sofas and stand up. I walk towards the large bay windows and look out over the street. I swear I can just about see the sea between the roofs of the houses opposite.

'Chad, away from the fucking windows,' barks Sam.

'It's fine,' says Clive. 'The net curtains stop anybody from seeing in unless you press your face right up against them. We can see out but nobody can see in. That's how I like it here. That's how we like it.'

I turn just as Olga's head ducks out of the doorway.

'You don't need to worry here, Sam. Chad is safe. You're safe. You're both welcome to stay as long as you like.'

'I'm not some lab rat,' I say. 'I don't want to be experimented on.'

'I'm not a mad scientist,' says Clive with a snort. 'All I want to do is understand you. I want to learn about how the ultimate nobody came to be the ultimate somebody. You're all we see on TV. I even saw a pixelated version of the video on the bus station timetable, Chad. You've replaced every single meme on 9Gag, I Can Has Cheezburger, Know Your Meme. You are the ultimate meme, too. Stay here, with us. You'll be safe.'

I guess I don't need the robots to worship me – I have Clive now. I resent the *ultimate nobody* part, though.

'Please,' he says. 'And all I ask is to study your story. Ask you some questions. I'll feed you, clothe you, put you up in my house – all for free.'

'I don't know,' I say. Well, it's more of a whine, really. I turn to my brother, 'Sam?'

'Just... let him ask whatever he wants. The cat is truly out of the bag now, Chad. IATech is fucked. The Amechs are fucked. We are a victim of our own success.'

Clive looks manic.

But he's our only hope.

He is our Obi Wan Kenobi.

Fuck.

'We just need somewhere to stay a few days,' says Sam. 'Just until I have chance to work out what we can do next.'

'As long as you need, like I say.'

My brother turns to me and sucks his teeth. I shrug.

Through a narrow gap between the hinges and the door, I spot movement. It's Olga – I can see her dazzling blue eyes peeping through.

'We don't want to put you out,' I say. I've heard people who are trying to be polite, but actually want something, say that before.

'You're not. You're totally not. It's what I do.'

Sam scoffs and shakes his head. 'You've done this before?'

There's Clive's big smile again. 'Of course,' he says, and he looks over his shoulder to the doorway.

Olga's eyes vanish.

'Her?' asks Sam.

Clive nods.

'She's a meme too?' I ask.

'She is.'

'How? Why?'

'That's not for me to say. Here is where people like her come to get away from the outside world. Away from the staring and the laughing and the judging. Here, you can just relax and be yourself. You don't need to worry. You don't have to think about the internet. Outsiders. There's no sneering or jeering. I like to think of this place as a sanctuary.'

'Are there others?'

'Occasionally, but it's just me and Olga at the moment. I like to think of my home as the world's leading viral video rehabilitation centre.'

Sam and I exchange a look. An *Is this for fucking real oh my god I can't believe what is happening right now* kind of look. But then I remember robots are attacking humanity. This is practically normal compared to that.

That night I can't sleep. I sit in front of the TV, not really speaking, not really thinking, maybe not even blinking, I dunno, and I just watch and occasionally drink a cup of tea whenever Clive sets a mug down on the table in front.

The news plays a continuous feed of the IATech building in the corner of the screen. It doesn't matter what else the reporters are talking about, there is always that little box showing the open mouth of IATech and the drones slipping in and out.

They carry various items in their thin arms like they weigh nothing. Tools. Metal. Machinery. And not a single person tries to stop them.

They probably daren't. They'd be killed.

Like everybody else.

At two o'clock in the morning Sam disappears somewhere upstairs to sleep. I don't move. I ignore Clive when he asks me how I'm doing, but I think I'm actually asleep with my eyes open because suddenly I blink and it's half past eight and Clive is handing me a plate with two slices of buttered toast on it.

I eat one.

After an hour Sam comes downstairs and eats the other. Then six or seven more.

'This is ridiculous,' says Sam, shaking his head.

I don't look away from the TV.

'I knew we should have put limitations in the software. I fucking knew it. Hydra was supposed to duplicate files and ensure networks remained online. We gave it intelligence so that it knew what to do and where to go to stay safe. This is nuts.'

For the first time in at least twelve hours I turn my head. My neck grinds as the joints realise they're not dead.

'Or, maybe you don't attach it to a video of me.'

Sam licks his lips as if he wants to say something. He doesn't. He scratches his nose in the place which is still a little bent from where I broke it.

'I shouldn't be here,' I say. 'I should be there.'

'What the fuck can you do?'

'I don't know,' I say, falling back into the sofa and flailing my arms. I am so mature.

'Exactly.'

'They want me. I'm their god. Maybe they'll listen to me if I tell them to stop or to go somewhere or... fucking... you know... I dunno.'

'It's an it, Chad, not a they. It's a virus. A malware. A file that reproduces itself as far and wide as it can. At this moment in time it serves no purpose other than to spread itself wherever it can.'

'But they want—'

'It.'

'*It* wants me. It thinks I'm its god. I should be able to stop this.'

'If you can stop this, then why didn't you?'

'Huh?'

'You were in IATech for two days. You had plenty of time to ask the Amechs nicely to stop their murderous ways, didn't you?'

'I mean—'

'No, Chad. This is above you. Fuck's sake, it's above me. This is a plague. A plague exists purely to be a cancer on life. It destroys everything. Hydra has evolved. That's what viruses do.'

'Yeah, started by you!'

'This was something that was waiting to happen. Yeah, it sucks that it was your video that it started with, but if it wasn't you then it would have been whatever video we beta-tested it with. Yeah, maybe there wouldn't have been as many shitty fucking memes or whatever, but the file itself would have still spread further than we wanted. Imagine if this had happened with government files, or fucking nuclear launch codes? We should be grateful it's just your video.'

I open my mouth to disagree but Sam doesn't let me.

'Okay, you didn't fucking help things by letting it manipulate you and switch up the IATech servers, but it would have found another way of spreading. That's exactly what I mean – we should have limited its capability. But no, we just had to create a system that was unhackable. You can thank Barry for that one. Did I ever tell you that Google, Apple and even the Japanese and American governments were interested in buying Hydra from us if we could provide them with successful beta results?'

'Sam you barely tell me anything.'

'Yeah, well. We were in talks with them. All of the big ones. It was going to be our ticket out of Hemel and into Silicon Valley.'

'Oh, and your killer robots weren't enough for that?'

'The Amechs are basic. Or at least they were. We were years, probably decades off getting them to walk unassisted.'

'So what the hell are they doing there?' I ask, flinging my hands towards the corner of the TV, IATech still very much in focus.

'At these speeds, doing what they're doing... running, jumping, kicking, throwing, hitting, building. This isn't us. Not IATech, not even close. The only thing I can think of is Hydra must have infected the systems of other robotics companies and taken their research. All our Amechs can do is smile, wave and maybe point you in the direction of the toilet. They can't do this. This is more advanced than us. More advanced than most.'

'You mean there are robotics companies out there who can make stuff like this?'

'I dunno. Maybe,' says Sam. 'Or maybe Hydra's learning, taking research from fifty different companies and filling in the gaps. During war, what do you think is the key to winning?'

I shrug.

'Information. It's the key to survival, not strength or power or endurance. The more we learn, the better we are at finding solutions to problems. If we can't learn by our own mistakes, we learn by the mistakes of others. Information is also a great way to hold others hostage. More than people's lives, even.'

I guess my brother can be smart at times.

Only sometimes.

But he's always a prick.

Chapter Seventeen

I don't know how much time has passed. Days. Weeks maybe. Sam insists it's been less than a day, but it feels like forever.

I guess it can't have been that long, because I've only had two pisses in Clive's house. His bathroom is tidy and hasn't been decorated since the Eighties, with cork board on the walls and a mirror surrounded by shards of a disco ball. I feel like having a rave every time I turn the light on.

Olga watches me from her bedroom. She reminds me of a cat you've just brought home from the rescue shelter, all timid and skinny, except she's a human and hasn't been living behind some bins for two weeks.

Or maybe she has, I don't know. She barely speaks and Clive won't tell me why she's living in his house.

Clive's desperate to fatten me up. He's like a really needy Grandma, except with slightly less facial hair. He keeps bringing me toast and crisps and sausage rolls and three different kinds of American cereal he bought from the import shop down the road.

He even brings me a whole chicken breast with just a fork and no knife. Apparently he doesn't keep knives in the house. What a strange man.

But I don't want to eat anything anyway. I wouldn't even go to the bathroom if I thought I could get away with pissing in the flowerpot on the windowsill. I just want to watch the TV and pray that Hydra decides to do one and leave the human race alone.

No chance.

At midnight on the second night I wake up on the edge of the sofa, my head almost fused to my left shoulder. I must have fallen asleep. Fuck knows when. Sam isn't in the room, and Clive is snoring on the sofa opposite, his hands cupping his chest like a woman with big boobs jogging down the stairs.

The news reporter outside the IATech building watches as the robots dart in and out. They cut to images of the robots taken on CCTV footage in and around various local towns. Hemel Hempstead,

Watford, St Albans, Berkhamsted, Luton. The robots help themselves to whatever they want from anywhere. Everywhere. Shops, factories, homes, warehouses. They tear doors from hinges, punch through windows like they're cellophane. They stroll in, take what they want, then leave.

They do not give a fuck.

'That is you?'

My heart does that thing where it convulses and almost drills out of your chest. I grab the arm of the sofa like I'm sat at the edge of a hundred-foot cliff and take a deep breath in.

Olga stands in the doorway.

'You scared the shit out of me,' I say.

'I am sorry,' she says, and she turns to leave.

'No,' I half shout, half whisper.

Clive snorts but doesn't wake.

'It's okay,' I say. 'Sorry, you just made me jump. You can come in.'

Olga shuffles into the room one tiny step at a time. Her eyes flick from me to the floor and back again.

'You can sit down,' I say. 'You don't need to worry about me. I'm just watching TV.'

'I know,' she says. She holds her hands tight together in front of her tiny waist. 'You have been watching lot of the television.'

Her accent is really cute. So stereotypical Eastern European. I want to say *In Soviet Russia, TV watches you,* but I don't. I really want to though.

'It is you?' she asks.

'What is?'

'On television. They talk about you.'

I turn my head back to the TV. Footage of me walking from a building into a car is playing. I can't tell where from. The police station maybe.

'Yeah,' I say.

'They do not say kind things.'

'No.'

'They are harsh.'

'They are.'

'Why?'

'Eh. I dunno.'

'You have upset somebody?'

'A lot of people, I guess. Not that it was my fault. Have you seen anything about me?'

'No.'

'Really?'

'Only from television. And what Clive has told.'

'What did he tell you?'

'That you are like me. You have done things you should not have done. People have seen these things and are judging you and want to take you away.'

'That's it in a nutshell.'

'I am sorry.'

'I'm starting to get used to it now.'

'Yes. Me too.'

'What...' I clear my throat. Olga sways back and forth and looks away.

Her eyes are so big. Like two big snow globes full of sparkles and lights and what the hell am I saying, I'll stop.

'What are you here for?' I ask.

'I tell you. Same as you.'

'No, I mean... what happened? Why did you go viral?'

'I, err,' she breathes. Her swaying gets more intense, like a human pendulum.

'It's okay,' I say. I tap the empty sofa cushion beside me. 'Sit down if you like.'

'Umm,' says Olga.

'What is it?'

'I...'

I stare at her. Probably a little too long, as the moment she makes eye contact with me again she turns and marches out of the room.

I stand, and for a moment I consider following her, but I've probably been a little too creepy towards the girl who feared me ten minutes ago as it is.

'That's the most I've seen her say to anybody in weeks,' says Clive.

Oh shit. Did he hear the whole conversation?

'Oh,' I say.

'She's shy, but once she gets to know you a little she'll open up like she's known you her whole life. That's her problem, really. She's too trusting. Too naive.'

'I can relate.'

'We're all a little naive, Chad. We can't expect to have all the answers.'

'Some of them would be nice.'

'Tell me about it.'

I yawn. So long and loud and wide that my eyes glaze over.

I rub them, but all that does is make them blurry. I widen them, but it does nothing but make Clive look at me funny.

'Why don't you go to bed?' he asks.

'I want to keep watching,' I say. 'This is all because of me. I need to know what's happening. I really don't want to just sit here, but if I have to then I want to at least keep up to date.'

'There's nothing you can do. Least not tonight. Especially if you're about to pass out from exhaustion anyway.'

'Yeah.'

'So why not put your head down? Just for a couple of hours.'

'Yeah. Okay.'

This is the first time I've seen the bedroom, and while it's not a five-star luxury resort, it's not too bad. There are three single beds crammed into the back bedroom, with a small wooden table beside each one. A small TV rests on a cabinet in the corner, and shelves topped with books line each wall at various squiffy angles.

Sam is asleep in the bed against the far wall.

I crawl into the closest bed and slip off my jeans, and they literally do slip off. They're way too big for me now. I guess I need to go shopping at some point.

As I lie on my back, my head sinking into the pillow, images pop into my mind. The robots bursting out of IATech. The helicopter falling from the sky. Becky with her head twisted right around.

I fall asleep to the nightmares.

'Chad, wake up!' shrieks Sam, shaking me by the shoulders.

'Fucking what?' I whinge.

'There's a war, Chad. There's a fucking war!'

'What do you mean a war?'

'A fucking war!'

I'm still half way inside a dream. I can see Becky and her look of sheer terror. I rub my eyes and prop myself up onto my elbows.

'Can you be more fucking specific?'

'The Amechs. Teenagers, kids.'

'They're killing *kids*?'

'The ones that are attacking them, yeah. It's all over the news. Gangs and stuff. They're being picked off like flies.'

I roll out of bed and follow Sam downstairs, pulling my t-shirt back over my head as I almost tumble down the last few steps.

Clive and Olga sit on the sofa, their eyes fixed on the TV. Nobody sees that my cock is hanging out of the little flap at the front of my boxers.

I tuck it away and sit down.

The TV is playing what looks like a scene in a World War Two movie, except it's not Normandy or Dunkirk, it's Hemel Hempstead Industrial Estate. Hordes of young guys and girls, clad in home-made armour and hoodies covering their faces, charge into battle, makeshift weapons raised.

The first wave of attackers is easily stopped by a swift whack to the side of the head. Those that make their way through swing and bat and kick and smack at the robots. Some fall to the ground, but others don't and easily fend them off.

But the army keeps on coming. Wave after wave. There must be hundreds. Thousands even. Before long there are more gang members than robots, it's ants versus bees, but the ants are winning thanks to sheer numbers.

The robots go down. Their faces... *my face*... beaten and smashed.

'Amazing,' I say.

'No,' says Sam. 'Not amazing. Absolutely, unequivocally not amazing.'

'Why not?'

'Hydra will reproduce. They have control of the manufacturing at IATech, but it looks like they've also taken over a bunch of other factories around the country. They're rebuilding Amechs almost instantly. When you destroy one, another two walk off the production line in minutes. Fucking *minutes*, Chad. If there were a thousand before, there will soon be two thousand. Then four, then eight, then sixteen. They will keep coming! FUCK! STOP!'

Sam stands and smacks the top of the TV with a balled fist.

'STOP IT!' he shrieks. 'FUCKING STOP IT!'

'Sam!' I snap.

Olga runs from the room. Clive steps between Sam and the TV like he's splitting up two drunks in a pub.

Suddenly gunfire. Rapid bursts at first, then long, continuous fire.

And screams.

The army soon turns and runs in the opposite direction.

Some of them make it away unscathed.

A lot of them don't.

'IDIOTS!' shrieks Sam.

'Sam, calm down,' I say, but I can't even take my own advice. My whole body is numb and if I had any food in my stomach it would be all over the carpet.

'I shouldn't be here,' he says. He paces around the coffee table, his head in his hands. 'I can't be here. I shouldn't be here. I need to be there.'

'There's nothing you can—'

'Of course there's something I can fucking do. I'm the one who made this mess, I'm the one who needs to clean it up.'

'You didn't tell those people to attack!'

'I built it! I didn't put my foot down when I told them it needed limiting. I didn't stop it when I could have. I shouldn't have even released it.'

'But you said—'

'I know what I said. I know I said it was inevitable, but that doesn't mean I didn't start it this time. Do you know how that feels? To be the one responsible?'

I don't answer. My mouth hangs open.

How can he say that?

How?

'You think you're the one responsible?' I hiss.

'Of course I am. I've had to live with this since the day it got out of hand. Since the day we were all locked out of the IATech building and fifty people were kept inside.'

'You mean, you've had to live with this yourself? Poor little old you?'

'Fuck you, Chad—'

'While a video of me with my dick in my hand has been broadcast on every website, TV channel, billboard, radio station, cinema screen and mobile phone in the world?'

'I mean—'

'And then, while suffering the worst embarrassment and shame any human has ever experienced, I'm also blamed for ruining entertainment, technology, education and fucking up the mental health of children everywhere?'

'Well—'

'And *you* have the fucking balls to say *you* feel guilty? All while you sit back and let me, your own fucking *brother*, take the blame?'

Sam says nothing.

'You're a cunt,' I say.

Olga gasps from out in the hallway.

Clive is in awe. If he had a box of popcorn with him he'd be munching away. I'm surprised he isn't taking notes.

'I guess I am,' says Sam.

I don't know what to say next, so I just say, 'Yep.'

'I need to be the one who fixes this,' says Sam. He doesn't look me in the eye. Possibly because I'm staring at him with a look which could scare Charles Manson.

'How?' I ask.

'I need my laptop. That's all. That's all I've ever needed. Literally with one tiny tweak to the setting I can make the multiplication go from two to zero. That means no more Amechs. They probably don't even know about the laptop or how significant it is. All I need to do is sneak in and get it.'

'Sneak in? They're gunning people down like they're nothing,' I say.

'They might not. Maybe I could use the tunnel you said they made.'

'You mean the tunnel they're probably guarding 24/7?'

Sam paces back and forth.

'They know I'm your brother. They might not kill me.'

'That's stupid. They know I hate you. They won't give a shit.'

'You hate me?'

'Look, just... let me go. They definitely won't hurt me.'

'You're literally the only leverage we have. It has to be me. I'm the only one who can stop this. I just need to get in, grab the laptop and change the setting before they even realise what's going on.'

'Sam. They will kill you. Will you stop moving and sit down!'

'So then what do we do?' he snaps. 'Let them kill a thousand more kids next time they try something like that?'

'Then... tell the police what to do. Give them instructions.'

'Great idea, Chad, I'll just hop on a PC, send them an email and wait for the horde to show up and take you away.'

'Call?'

'They'll know. They'll be monitoring everything.'

'Letter?'

'No, they probably scan all mail. Won't work.'

'Actually,' says Clive.

Fuck, I forgot he was there.

'They only scan parcels and packages,' he says. 'If you send a letter, something small enough to fit in an envelope, it isn't scanned at all.'

I look at Sam and he looks at me.

We have a fucking plan.

9 October

Dear Commissioner Ripley,

We are writing to you from Brighton, where we are staying with a helpful friend. We have been keeping up to date with the news. It is vital that you repeat to the general public that the Amechs must not be harmed. Do what you can to get people to listen.

To reiterate what we agreed when we met, you must do everything in your power to retrieve the grey Dell laptop from the second floor of the building. It is distinguishable by the alien sticker on the top. Make this a priority.

You can reach us by post ONLY at the following address: 40 Regency Road, Brighton, BN1 1HH. This is not the address where we are staying.

Do not attempt to contact us in any other way, or Hydra will find us.

C & S (Call us Hercules)

We pop a first class stamp on the letter and Clive heads out to post it that morning. We purposely put the address as next door's, just in case the robots somehow get wind of what we're up to, but luckily Clive is mates with the old lady next door and she's agreed to pass on any replies. With any luck it will get there tomorrow, the police can figure out how to get the laptop, and in a couple of days this entire thing will all be over.

Until then, all we have is the TV.

And the videos of dead and dying teenagers.

Perfect.

For the first time in two days I change the channel on the TV. Thankfully, Hydra seems to have moved on from infecting TV signals with my video, because relatively regular programming has resumed, if you can call repeats of *Bargain Hunt* constantly being interrupted to bring us breaking news stories regular in any way.

You can't.

But even seeing David Dickinson's cheery face for a few minutes at a time is enough.

I eat more.

If you can count two slices of toast instead of one as *more*.

I guess you can.

Because it is.

Why am I arguing with myself?

That evening Sam goes to bed early, leaving me and Clive alone.

He thinks I don't see him craftily lift a notepad out from beside the sofa and place it on the cushion beside him.

'How did you feel when you discovered that your video had, for the lack of a better term, gone viral?'

'How do you think?'

'Angry or sad?

'Both.'

'If you saw the video, but it didn't feature yourself or anybody you knew, do you think you would find it funny?'

I shake my head.

He raises his eyebrows.

'Probably,' I say. 'But it isn't really funny, is it? It's one and a half minutes of a pathetic fat bloke tossing himself off. It's not funny in the slightest. More sad than anything. I have no idea why so many memes have been made about it.'

'Would it make you feel any better to know that not everybody hates you?'

'It would surprise me.'

'It's true. Thousands, no, tens of thousands of people. Hundreds even. There are groups on Facebook, Reddit, independent forums. *Justice for Chad, I believe Chad, Chad the hero.* That's just a few of the group names. There are so, *so* many hashtags, all supporting you.'

'No chance.'

'I swear. No lie. You don't get to do what I do by telling lies.'

'Can I see? Please?'

'No, Chad. I'm sorry. You know I can't allow that. Nobody can use my PC, okay?'

'Why?'

'It's against the rules of the sanctuary, Chad. When you're within these walls all digital media is out of bounds. I only have my computer so I can do my research and write my book. You can read and write and play games and talk and laugh and even sing, I don't care. But nothing with a chip in it. Nothing with a camera. Be grateful for the TV – I wouldn't have had it at all if it wasn't for previous residents complaining. But I want you to listen to me carefully when I say that you have supporters. Sympathisers. Even empathisers. It's always the outraged who are the most vocal. Sometimes it's easier to agree with an angry minority than it is to stand with the silent majority.'

'That's a pretty good quote,' I say.

'Cheers, it's from my book.'

Fuck's sake, I thought he came up with it on the spot.

We speak for hours, and the more he asks the less I care about what he's asking. He wants to know all about my past, and the early days of *loserjerksoff.mp4*. I tell him about IATech and what happened inside and everything that went on with the police. He writes it all down, his eyes never leaving mine. He nods the entire time.

He's the first person to actually believe me.

No doubting. No funny faces.

Just enthusiasm.

Actually, now that I think about it, he's probably enjoying it a little too much.

I fake a yawn, stretching my arms up for added effect.

'Good lord, look at the time!' he says. 'I have an appointment in the morning, I should head off to bed. You stay up as long as you like, okay? And thank you for being so honest with me.'

Clive leaves the room and I sit back on the sofa, allowing the big cushions to deflate and slowly lower me back. Clive plods up the stairs and his bedroom door clicks shut.

'You are very brave,' says Olga.

I totally hadn't noticed that she'd crept into the room.

'Oh, hi,' I say.

I hope she didn't see me awkwardly try to scratch my gooch.

She slowly shuffles towards the sofa and ever so gently perches on the arm.

'You are so brave,' she says again.

'Thanks,' I say. 'You were listening?'

She looks down. Her eyes are so big and round they almost pop out of her head, like a pug, but obviously a lot less smushy-faced and hairy.

'I heard, yes,' she says.

'It isn't my fault.'

'If it was your fault you wouldn't be here. Clive would say no.'

'He has a lot of rules, doesn't he?'

'Yes.'

'Doesn't that bother you?'

'No. It helps me.'

'It doesn't help me.'

'It will.'

'Have you been here long?'

'Three months.'

'There months! That's crazy.'

'It makes me feel better.'

'Do you, like, go outside or anything?'

'Yes. Sometimes.'

I sigh. 'I wish I could go outside. The robots would see me. They'd know it was me in a second and they'd take me away.'

'It is nice here.'

'I guess. Do you like it here?'

'Yes. I am far from home, but I need to be here. Until I forget. Until people forget.'

'I dunno if they do forget, do they? They just move on to the next thing.'

'Maybe. But it means I can change too. It is important for my brain.'

'True. This whole thing has really screwed me over. When everybody hates you and points and laughs and shouts… it's hard.'

Olga nods. 'It is very hard.'

I want to ask her why she's here again.

I really want to know.

But maybe she's right. Maybe I need to change too.

So I'll start by not being a cock.

'Does it get any easier over time?'

'Yes.'

'Do you feel better now?'

'Yes.'

'Will you go home soon?'

'I don't know. My family, they… they are very sad. They hate me.'

'I'm sure they don't hate you.'

'They do.'

'Your Mum? Your Dad?'

Olga winces and nods.

'I'm sorry.'

'It's okay. They know how I feel, so maybe one day they will forgive.'

'I hope so.'

'Yes.'

Then we sit in silence. It feels like minutes, but it must have been hours, because I blink and then suddenly it's morning.

Chapter Eighteen

12 October

Dear Hercules,

Thank you for your letter. We have taken the information you provided seriously, and destroyed your previous correspondence. We are doing what we can to ensure casualties are low. Unfortunately, our instructions are being ignored by certain groups, which has resulted in a large number of fatalities.

Please be assured that this is not the fault of Hercules.

We have briefed a team who are aware of the target. Once we have more information we will let you know. Please provide instructions for us to follow once target has been retrieved. We recommend that Hercules remains in a secure location and does not venture outside. The mechanical army are spreading throughout the country fast and will no doubt arrive at your location soon.

Keep safe.

CR

13 October

Dear CR,

Thank you for the information. We can confirm that the Amechs have arrived at our location. They are patrolling the streets, they pass by this address roughly every three hours. They so far have no idea of our location, we assume it is a general patrol to locate C, as they are stopping people who have a similar height and body type.

Once the target has been obtained you must secure it. Open the screen and power it on, then alert us asap. We can then remotely access the laptop and make necessary changes.

There is a tunnel into the building from the sewers. This may be a way inside.

Please provide us with an update on Hercules' mum.

Hercules

16 October

Dear Hercules,

We sent a team of nine into the building. None returned. Target not yet acquired.

Hercules' Mother is well.

CR

17 October

Dear CR,

Thank you for the information. We are sorry about your team.

It is vital that the Amechs do not see anybody entering the building as hostile. They will destroy anything they perceive as a threat. I understand that the Amechs are no longer allowing journalists near the building, but there will be individuals, or professionals, who they do not see as a danger. Be slow, use non-threatening language.

Hercules

19 October

Hercules,

We have lost Dr Stevens. He entered IATech in an attempt to negotiate with Hydra. He was killed less than fifteen minutes after entering the building.

It is also our understanding that the British military has been compromised. They attempted to target the building using long-range missiles, but the missiles detonated within the silo before they were launched.

Hydra has taken over three more car manufacturing plants within the UK. They are now producing new, large robots which are the size of tanks. We are losing the battle.

We are running out of options.

CR

22 October

CR,

Sorry to hear about Dr Stevens. We have seen video of the new Amech design on the news, but they are yet to reach our location. Reiterate to the public that they must not attempt to harm them.

S is going to travel back to Hemel.

Hercules

23 October

DO NOT LEAVE YOUR LOCATION. IT IS VITAL THAT HERCULES REMAINS SAFE. THIS IS THE FINAL WORD. YOU WILL BE ARRESTED ON SITE.

25 October

CR,

Hercules will remain for the time being. What is the next approach to acquire the target?

Hercules

27 October

Hercules,

There is no approach. Hydra has infected the entire military and can now control what intelligence we can and cannot see. They have threatened to make us completely dark.

C, I am sorry that I didn't believe you.

CR

30 October

CR,

There must be something we can do! There must be! Please advise what Hercules can do! Please advise asap!

Hercules

2 November

CR,

Please respond. We cannot allow this to carry on! Please respond!

Hercules

7 November

Please answer. Is Hercules' Mum still well? Please acknowledge!

H

What the fuck is going on? The entire country has gone mental. Giant, truck-sized robots stomp through the streets. You can hear them coming, their footsteps pounding the ground, making the plates and bowls inside the kitchen cupboards tinkle. It's a spectacular sight to see, and they do not give a fuck, anything which gets even slightly in their way; a car, a wall, a person, is just tossed to one side like they're nothing.

It's a horrible thing, don't get me wrong, but what makes them worse is that instead of some cool Optimus Prime style head, they have my fat, round face. Their eyebrows are pointed in a permanent frown, the eyes blindingly yellow.

They also have a cock between their legs.

My cock.

Basically, what in the movies would be a cool looking, bulky robot with guns and fists and the ability to transform into a jet plane, is actually a fat, naked clone of what I look like in *loserjerksoff.mp4*.

They could have at least made my cock look a bit bigger!

I mean, I guess it's to scale and everything.

But still, it hurts my feelings.

The general public are clearly not big fans of the new robots either, they ram them with cars, throw home-made bombs at them, trip them, shoot them, smash them with hammers.

They cannot get it into their thick fucking skulls that if they break one, two more will rise up like fat, aluminium phoenixes with my chunky face and dick.

Well, my old face. I caught myself in the mirror the other day, and I'm not the man I used to be. I wouldn't say I'm thin, far from it, but the face looking back at me is not what I'm used to. I cannot grow a beard to save my life, but when I part the pube-like hair developing on my face it reveals one or two chins instead of three.

So, there you go. If you want to lose a few pounds, just start the apocalypse.

That's what the weight of destroying the world does to you. This isn't screwing up people's precious internet any more, it's way worse. People are dying. Their lives are being turned upside down.

Half of Hemel Hempstead has been evacuated. Anybody living within a three-mile radius of the IATech building has either gone to live with family, or been put up in a makeshift shanty town beside a nearby dual carriageway. On the TV it looks like a middle class version of the Calais migrant jungle.

That's about as close to the IATech building the press are allowed to go. Anyone with a camera even remotely close to the industrial park is killed. That includes mobile phones with cameras. In the past three days two helicopters have dropped from the sky. The entire town is a no-fly zone.

What the fuck are they doing?

I know Hemel isn't the greatest town in the world, but it's home, it's *my* home, and now it's no man's land. Step within the war zone if you dare.

It's been a week since our last letter from Commissioner Ripley. We know he's alive though, because this morning, and for probably the 10,000th time, he gave a statement to the press about people not harming the Amechs. He was alongside the FBI, MI5 and a bunch of other important-looking agents from what are probably very secret organisations from around the world.

Is it too early to call it World War Three yet?

Robots vs Idiots.

And of course the robots are winning.

Life is starting to get very dull. Aside from the killer robots roaming the streets and destroying half a town, things haven't half gotten boring. Every day is the same, wake up, eat some toast, sit in front of the TV for a few hours while Clive locks himself away, turn my nose up at his crap cooking, stare out the window for three or four hours then watch the news and try to figure out the current death toll.

Even Clive has the same ridiculous little routine. He spends three hours in the morning and three hours in the afternoon on his computer. Without fail, regardless of what bombshell has dropped on the news, he'll sit tapping and clicking away while locked alone in his bedroom. I've never even seen inside his bedroom – it remains a complete mystery to me. For some reason I imagine it as dark and seedy with Eighties film posters on the wall and crusty tissues surrounding his chair.

At least Olga is allowed to leave the house, not that she does very often. The only time she does she visits the local Polish shop to buy gross stuff in jars, but she did at least bring me back a chocolate bar one time. It was shit though and I didn't finish it.

It's not just getting to me, either, it's getting to Sam now as well. I've had to beg him to stay on two separate occasions, and I know he's about to try and leave again soon. The first time he was pacing and ran out into the street, I ran out after him, and it made him swear loads and then sweep me back into the house. The second time I had to pull him back like a kid pleading with his Dad not to go to work on Christmas Eve. He relented, but I could tell he was just biding his time.

'I NEED TO GO,' he shrieks.

I've never seen him like this. Ever. Sam is Mr Cool. Mr Calm. Mr Makes A Joke At Your Expense And Makes You Feel Bad. Mr Life And Soul.

'Sam, what are you going to do? Waltz into the no-go zone? Walk right up to IATech, grab your laptop, then sit on the floor and open it to kill them all? They're not going to let you do that.'

'I just need… I just… I don't… All I have to do is…'

His eyes flick back and forth. You can tell he's searching the depths of his brain for some kind of answer, but all he's finding is empty space.

He's even started talking in his sleep. He asks questions, mainly, but they're at least more coherent than when he talks to himself when he's awake.

'What if we remotely hijack one of the Amechs?'

'Can we create a new kind of Amech?'

'Can we use gliders to fly in?'

'I want mayonnaise. Fuck you, Dad.'

That last one isn't really relevant, but it made me laugh. For the first time in a long time.

The next morning I wake up to two slices of toast on my pillow. Not even on a plate, which is weird. I eat half of one, brush the crumbs on the floor and head downstairs. Olga is watching TV alone.

'Hi,' she says.

'Morning.'

'Afternoon.'

'Really? Oh crap.'

'Yes, oh crap.'

I sit on the sofa beside her. She doesn't flinch nearly as much any more.

'What do you mean?' I ask.

Commissioner Ripley is on the TV. His eyes are sunken and his beard is way less kempt than it used to be. He introduces the Prime Minister, who has until recently been pretty quiet about the whole killer robot thing. She steps in front of a wooden podium outside Number 10 Downing Street and addresses the cameras.

'Ladies and gentlemen,' she says, slow and sombrely. 'It is with great regret that I must be the one to tell you this. At approximately three o'clock this morning the Hydra virus managed to infiltrate and take control of Trident. As a result of this, Hydra has issued a threat of a nuclear attack on the following countries: The United States, China, Russia and France. Currently, all authorities, including MI5 and the military, are doing what they can to resolve the situation. I am in constant communication with the leaders of those countries, and I have assured them that what is currently happening is an anomaly, it is the result of a rogue computer virus and does not represent the view or intentions of the British people or our government. We are doing what we can to alleviate the threat, and we ask all civilians to leave the robots well alone. Do nothing to provoke them. Keep away from the no-go zone. This is a serious and growing threat within our country, and we ask that you leave it to the authorities to deal with. I will give you more information in due course.'

The Prime Minister steps away from the podium and a barrage of questions hurls from the journalists. She ignores them and disappears inside Number 10.

'Holy shit,' I say.

'Yes,' says Olga.

'Sam!' I scream. 'SAM! SAM!'

I yell and yell until my throat is hoarse. I run through the entire house, bashing on the walls, thumping on any surface which will make a loud enough noise.

But there is no Sam.

'He is gone,' says Olga.

'What?' I shriek. I'm a dripping, wheezing wreck.

'Clive tried to stop him. He just left. An hour ago.'

'No!'

I turn and run towards the door. Olga shouts something behind me, but I have no idea what she's saying. I don't even bother putting on shoes, I just pull open the door and throw myself out onto the street, right into Clive's arms.

'Woah!' he says.

I wriggle and squirm.

'Chad, stop!'

'Let me go!'

'Chad, please!'

'LET ME GO!'

'Shh! Stop this! Your brother's gone! He took the neighbours' car and he's long gone!'

Clive is surprisingly strong. Either that or I'm just unsurprisingly weak. Maybe I should have eaten that second slice of toast.

He squeezes my arms by my side and drags me back into the house. Olga locks the door behind us, just as a giant Amech passes and the plates in the kitchen cupboard rattle together.

'You see how close that was,' grunts Clive. 'Another minute and they would have seen you. Then this would have all been for nothing. For nothing, Chad. Please stop. Don't make me do this.'

I scream. So loud my voice breaks, but I don't care. So long as I'm screaming it can sound as broken as it likes. I just want to make noise.

Clive holds his hand over my mouth. Whenever Sam used to do that to me I'd lick his palm, but my slobbery tongue does nothing to faze Clive.

I think he holds his hand over my mouth a little too long, because everything goes grey. My legs give in, my eyes roll back into my head, and the grey soon fades to black.

Chapter Nineteen

'Fuck sake,' is the first thing I'm able to say as my mind switches back on. I try to open my eyes, but it's too bright. Every time I breathe in my chest burns. My head pounds to the rapid rhythm of my heartbeat.

The light in the room still stabs through my clamped eyelids, and I bring my hand to my head for just a little relief.

At least, I try to.

As I move my hand there's a loud CLUNK.

I try my other hand.

CLUNK.

'Shite,' I say.

Despite everything, I still haven't lost my affinity for swearing. It's like second nature.

I raise my head and peek ever so slightly through my right eye. As everything slowly comes into focus I spot the handcuffs. The chains. The locks.

'The fuck?'

I sit up but my arms and legs stay exactly where they are and I jerk back down. I'm chained to the fucking bed!

'Hey!' I scream.

There's scurrying footsteps somewhere outside the room. Then big, heavy ones.

I turn my head as far as I can to see the doorway. I wriggle and struggle and thrash, but I am well and truly stuck.

The door opens and Clive steps into the room.

'Let me fucking go,' I say.

'No, Chad. I'm sorry.'

'What did you fucking do to me?'

'What I had to. I'm sorry that you passed out. I just... I can't risk you getting out. Getting hurt.'

'Let me go.'

'No.'

'Undo these locks.'

'I can't.'

'Please.'

'No.'

Rage bubbles inside me. If I could, I'd hit him.

'LET ME GO.'

'Chad—'

'Help me! Please!'

'Chad, stop.'

'HELP! SOMEBODY HELP!'

'Nobody can hear you.'

'They will! HELP!'

'Just Olga. The Andertons next door have gone to stay with family. And Mrs Roberts is deaf as a post. Nobody will come.'

My entire body is heavy. I can barely lift my head from the pillow, and my arms and legs ache. My wrist is bleeding from where I yanked too hard on the handcuffs.

I lock eyes with Clive and don't blink. I don't care that tears stream down my face, snot bubbles from my right nostril or I pissed myself a tiny bit, I give him the best pitiful expression that I can. A sad, strained, desperate expression that begs for just a little crumb of relief.

I base it on the look Becky gave me when she died.

'Sorry, Chad,' says Clive.

I slam my head back into the pillow and scream.

Clive stands there until I stop screaming because my voice is hoarse and my entire face is coated in snot and spit and tears. He looks down on me like a vet who is about to put down a puppy.

'You have the TV here which I can put on for you,' he says softly. 'Let myself or Olga know if you want the channel changed. Dinner will be in an hour. There's a bedpan to your left if you need to relieve yourself.'

'What if I need to shit?' I ask. I don't know why I ask.

'Then call for me. Is there anything I can get for you in the meantime?'

'The keys to these FUCKING HANDCUFFS.'

Clive shakes his head and turns on the TV.

Fucking hell, it's a shitty old black and white one, the screen is square and the picture distorted and the sound may as well have been broadcast through a tin can attached to a piece of string.

And Clive leaves, slipping from the room and leaving the door ajar ever so slightly. Enough for me to make out Olga's blinding blue eye peeping at me through the crack.

'Olga, please,' I whisper.

She disappears.

'Clive! Clive!'

My throat is so sore.

I swear I can taste blood, but when I spit on the floor beside the bed to check it's the usual globby, clear colour that spit should be.

'Clive!'

Clive pokes his head into the room.

'What, Chad?'

'I need a shit.'

'No you don't.'

'I do.'

'You had one an hour ago.'

'I need another.'

'I don't believe you.'

'I promise.'

Clive sighs.

'No,' he says.

'I'm not lying!'

I am.

'Please, Chad. I'm working.'

'I don't care, I need a shit.'

'This is the last time I'm coming in here. You know that between the hours of nine and eleven and two and five I work. I do not want to be disturbed.'

'I know, but I need a shit.'

'I don't think you do.'

'I do.'

'You'll just have to hold it. I'm busy at the moment. If you still need to use the bathroom in an hour's time I'll deal with it then.'

'It isn't gonna go anywhere!'

'I'll be back later.'

'No!'

This is how the next two days go. I lie on my back, wriggling around, making noise, shitting and pissing into a bowl, being spoon-fed potatoes and baked beans and feeling like the impending doom the world is facing is entirely my fault. Because when there's nothing to take your mind off things, your mind can wander.

The blank, peeling wallpaper on the walls has been the canvas to the horrors being spewed by my imagination. With the TV my only access to the outside world, and with no way of contacting anybody or being contacted at all, a thousand different but equally horrifying scenarios play out. Is Hemel Hempstead now completely destroyed? According to the news, nobody has even seen the IATech building for days. Are the hostages all dead? Are their innards being used to paint the inside of the new robot relaxation room? Did Sam make it back okay? I haven't seen or heard about him on TV. That either means he made it safely, or the robots got to him before he even had chance. I'm hoping the first one, though, because otherwise the robot army would have swarmed on Brighton and I'd have been dragged out into the street by a big fuck off robot with a cock by now. How is Mum? I know she'll be okay, because she's a pretty hard old girl, my mum, but I hate to think that she's probably worrying about me. Because she does worry. I hope that if Sam has made it home he's at least told her that I'm safe and doing alright.

Well, at least that'd be what Sam thinks. When he last saw me I wasn't handcuffed to a bed, shitting into a pan and stewing in my own sweat.

That evening Clive cooks something with cabbage. I know this, because the entire house stinks of it. When he finally brings it up to me I pretend to be all weird, like I've had a stroke or something, slurring my words and rolling my eyes around like I'm trying to look at the inside of my brain, but he sees right through me and threatens to throw away the food. I'm absolutely famished, so I let him feed me some of the slop like I'm a baby, which I imagine is worse than the stuff paedophiles get in prison, which come to think of it is a weird way of describing it.

Tinned steak in gravy, boiled potatoes and yep, cabbage.

Clive then locks himself away in his room. If I hold my breath, I can just about hear him typing. He had a long whinge while he spoon fed me my shite dinner, saying he has barely gotten any work done because I kept going on about my urgent and impending bout of explosive diarrhoea which never came because I made it up.

In some ways I wish it had been real, because I'd love to see Clive try to change my bedsheets while I'm strapped to the bed, shit and piss everywhere and probably puke as well just to rub it in.

Fucking hell, what am I talking about, I've gone insane.

And also, my balls hurt. I don't think I've had a wank since this whole thing kicked off, so I have about five weeks worth of baby batter building up inside my tubes. Even the thought of Clive changing the bedsheets beneath me gets me a little bit frisky.

I have to cross my legs to hide my massive boner when Olga sneaks into the room to feed me some of her weird Polish chocolate. It's got nuts in it, which are awful, but I crave flavour and human contact, so I don't really mind that much at all.

She tells me all about her day, and I listen.

Her walk along the beach front.

She ate a donut.

A seagull tried to attack her. She laughs.

She found a five pound note on the floor but then a woman ran up to her and said it was hers, so she gave it back and ran away.

The bloke in the hoody who whistled at her.

Scumbag.

Olga doesn't seem to mind that I stink, she just tells me her little story and I breathe through my mouth. I can't remember the last time I had a shower. I wonder if Clive would be up for giving me a bed bath?

Or Olga.

Oh shit, cross those legs again. Hide that chubby.

That evening I fall asleep watching the news. There is no news these days, no new news anyway. It's all the same.

No contact with IATech.

Hydra still has control of Britain's nuclear weapons and is threatening the world's superpowers.

Some kids attacked some robots.

Some kids died.

There must be something I can do.

This is because of me. Sam may have been the one to create the virus, but I'm the one they want. Surely I can do something.

But what?

The next morning – at least I assume it's the next morning because the sunlight blinds me from the crack between the curtains over on the far window – Olga taps lightly on the bedroom door. My neck is stiff and my shoulders ache. My head pounds and my mouth is sticky and gross.

'Yeah?' I groan. My voice is so croaky.

'Can I come in?' she asks.

'Mm,' I say.

'I have drink for you,' she says. She lowers a glass of water to head level and guides a plastic straw into my mouth. I suck it down and let out a loud gasp, so she runs to the bathroom and fills it up again. I don't care that she obviously used the hot tap and it's lukewarm, I drink it down so fast I choke myself and cough the last mouthful back up.

'Where's Clive?' I ask.

'He is working,' says Olga, kneeling beside the bed to dab water off my face with what I'm pretty sure is the rag used to clean the bathroom.

'I err... need the toilet.'

Olga's eyes widen and she shuffles back on her knees, but she loses her balance and somehow ends up falling forwards. Her face is close to mine. So close. Closer than any girl's face has been to mine since the time Julie Simons spat in my mouth in middle school. That was gross but for some reason I told everyone it was my first kiss, then she found out and kicked me in the kidney. I pissed blood for a week. I guess I'm only thinking about Julie Simons because I'm awkward as fuck right now and I don't know what else to do.

Olga's eyes are wider than a cat's eyes when you put the vacuum cleaner on. She shoves her hand onto my belly and pushes herself backwards and back into a kneeling position.

The pressure doesn't do anything for my need for a piss. Thank God she isn't any heavier, else she might have pushed it all out of me right here.

'Can you get Clive?' I ask. 'I really don't think you want to see me pee into a pot.'

'He's working.'

'I know, but I need to go.'

'He said do not disturb.'

'But—' something catches my eye in Olga's left hand. An envelope. Now normally this wouldn't make me literally stop in the middle of a sentence, but the little sticker of a cartoon character on the back makes my heart leap up into my throat and stops me from finishing my thought.

It's a sticker of the Disney character Hercules, his chiselled face grinning as he flexes his huge muscles.

'What is that?' I ask.

Olga holds out the envelope.

'It is for you,' she says.

She places the envelope in my hand. I twist it and turn it around. It's from Sam!

'Umm… can you open it for me please?'

'Yes,' she says. She takes the envelope back and pulls out a single sheet of paper, hand written with perfect handwriting. Sam's perfect handwriting, the same handwriting he always rubbed in my face because I could never learn how to write with the letters joined up without it looking like I was writing with my eyes closed.

Hercules,

I am safe. CR is safe. Hercules' mother is doing well. She sends her love. She says she is proud.

Things are not looking good.

Jill and I were working on a malware to try and infect the IATech servers from within. It failed. A vigilante group attempted the same, however Hydra located and killed them. They also managed to track us, but we were able to move from our original location. So far they have not been able to find us, but I am not sure for how long.

Please be assured that there is nothing you can do to stop any of this. The virus wants you as a trophy. It will not stop what it is programmed to do. It is a merciless, emotionless piece of code that does nothing but follow instructions. It is smart. It learns so fast. YOU. MUST. NOT. COME. HERE. You being here will change nothing.

However there may be some light at the end of the tunnel. We may be closing in on a solution.

YOU. MUST. NOT. ATTEMPT. TO. COME. HERE.

I asked Clive to watch you. I trust he is looking after you as well as he was when I was there with you.

Please trust that we will continue to look for a solution. We are yet to locate the laptop, but we are doing what we can to ensure that we get it.

We are hopeful. Cross your fingers for us.

I will update you again very soon.

Be patient, Hercules.

DO. NOT. COME. HERE.

From,

H.

I smile. My heart is beating like an old washing machine filled with bricks on top of a trampoline. I try to sit up, because for a brief moment I completely forget that I'm tied to a bed.

Not because of Sam's letter.

Not because Mum's okay.

But because I've got an idea.

After Clive finally lets me piss and shit into the pot beneath my bed he feeds me two slices of toast, half a banana and a punnet of grapes. It's the most substantial thing I've eaten in weeks, because I need energy. I need my mind to be alert. I need my problem-solving skills to be awake and active and working full force.

I think I know how to stop the robots from attacking.

That afternoon, when Clive locks himself back in his room for another two hours of whatever the hell it is that he does, I whisper-shout until Olga hears and her big eyes peer in through the doorway. I ask her to grab the notepad and pen Sam and I used to write letters to the Commissioner, and I tell her what to write, which she does while having the most worried look on a person's face I think I've ever seen. When we're done, I ask her to show it to me, and while it's not perfect, it'll do:

Hercules –

Thank you for writing. Reliefed to hear Mum is doing ~~well good~~ *well. I need you to read carefully because I have* ~~discovered~~ *an idea which may help stop the robots from attacking.*

You mentioned in your leter that Hydra is programed to follow instructions. It does this by taking ~~information~~ *data from the internet and forming con-clushions (which is why it things I am there god). They told me that them-selfs when i was in the* ~~eyertech~~ *iatech building.*

We need to take this and turn it against them. We need to flood the internet with new data so it reprogrammes them. We need them to learn that attack-ing humans is bad. There goal is the need to survive right? That means we

217

have to put enough data online to convince them that attacking people is bad and will be there down fall if they do.

It doesn't solve the problem but it will safe lifes. We need to start doing this straight away. I can't do it here but you can. You and your teams. Convince them that they don't need to hurt people to win. That threats and weapons are bad.

Flood the internet.

Let me know asap.

Thank you for trying to protect me.

Hercules

P.S. Clive has me tied to the bed.

P.P.S Not in a sexual way though

'Okay,' I say. 'It'll do. Thank you. Now if you don't mind putting it in an envelope and taking it to a post box, that would be great.'

'Yes,' she says with a small smile. 'What is address?'

'The address is, the... the...'

Fuck.

There is no address.

According to Sam's letter, they've moved from the one we had been writing to before.

And he hasn't told me where he is now.

What a twat.

I slam my head back into the pillow. I wish it would swallow my entire head. Wrap around my face. Suffocate me.

Why does nothing go my way?

Like... nothing!

I was bullied at school because I was fat.

I skipped school a lot. My grades were crap. Mum and Dad fought about it.

218

Mum and Dad broke up. Sam blamed me.

I was bullied more.

Sam saw me being bullied once. I was in the park not far from the house, minding my own business. I was on the ground being kicked and spat on. Sam just walked past and pretended he didn't see me.

I thought big brothers were supposed to be protective? He could have smashed in the faces of the kids hurting me, but he did nothing. In fact I'm surprised he didn't go in for a boot as well.

I left school with no real qualifications.

Dad didn't speak to me. Still doesn't.

Sam moved out and started IATech with his mates. He became a millionaire in like a year, Mum was so proud.

Meanwhile, I stayed at home to troll people on forums. I leave comments about people's weight on YouTube. It makes me feel better about myself. I get a weird kick out of it whenever I'm banned from commenting or I'm blocked by somebody on Twitter.

I have thirty-something Facebook friends.

I have no real friends.

I've never kissed a girl.

Felt a tit.

Unless you count my own. And even then, I've eaten so little over the past couple of months that even they're down to little more than a B-cup.

And now I can't even contact my brother. I can't do anything to tell him what I know. I may have figured out how to help save the world, and yet here I am, tied to a bed that stinks of shit while an Eastern European girl looks down on me in horror as tears stream down my face and I silently wish for death.

But.

But I can't let this be it.

I just can't.

There has to be something I can do. I can't let this be my legacy. I won't be the guy who wanked on the internet and ended the world.

If I can't get the message to Sam, then I need to be the one to do it.

But how?

Fucking *how?*

I'm currently a husk of a human being. I'm a prisoner. For four hours a day I can't even go for a shit because the dungeon master is locked away himself. God forbid if he's disturbed, he has precious memes to paw through and write a thesis on and…

'Olga,' I say.

I guess my crazy expression has softened because Olga no longer looks terrified.

'Yes,' she says.

'Can you unlock me?'

'No,' she says, before I can even finish asking.

'Please.'

'No. I promised not to.'

'I know how to stop this. You know the letter, what I told you to write? That will stop the robots from hurting people.'

'I cannot.'

'You have to, Olga. It will literally save the world.'

'But Clive trusts me. If he found out—'

'He won't find out!'

'He will.'

'He won't, I… I'll just… I'll only be gone for two hours. Not even two hours. Ninety minutes. Please.'

'I…'

'If the robots find my brother they will torture him. My brother is a bit of a dick, but I can't really let that happen, but if it does then one of two things will come out of it. Best case scenario, okay, is that they'll kill him. *Best* case scenario. The worst case scenario is they will torture him into telling them where I am. Any day now, those robots could break down that door, kill Clive, kill you, and take me away. If they take me away I won't be able to do anything. That will be it. The end of the world.'

Tears form over the surface of Olga's eyes, making them even shinier than they are usually. Her bottom lip quivers and her fingers shake.

'I don't mean to upset you, but it's true,' I say. 'Sam is the only person I can give this information to, but I don't know where he is. I can't send the letter home, because the robots will probably be guard-

ing my house and they'll see the letter was sent from Brighton and...
I can't send it to family, or the police, or anyone. I can't risk people
coming here. Hurting you. Please. Just let me go.'

Olga stares at me. She doesn't blink. She doesn't move.

A tear slips from her eye. She doesn't wipe it away.

I swear it's like a scene from a movie.

Except I'm tied to a bed and it's weird.

'Please, Olga. You're the only person who can help me right now.
I need to get out of here and use a computer. It's urgent.'

'You said robots would see you. Take you away.'

'If I wrap myself up and hide my face, wear some big glasses or
something, then maybe they won't recognise me. I'm a lot smaller
now than I was when that video was made. They think I'm this really
fat guy, whereas I'm now this *kinda* fat guy. They won't know who I
am.'

Finally she blinks, but says nothing.

'Just ninety minutes. There must be a library or an internet cafe
around here somewhere, right? I'll go straight there, then come
straight back before Clive even knows I was gone. Please.'

Olga turns and runs from the room.

'Wait!' I shout.

She's small, but I can still hear her footsteps as she runs downstairs.

Down the hall.

And out the front door.

Chapter Twenty

'Eat something, Chad.'

'No.'

'You need to eat. You can't just let yourself waste away.'

'I don't want to.'

'It's toast.'

'How about you let me fucking go?'

Clive takes in a big, deep breath, then lets out the longest sigh I've ever heard.

'Chad—'

'Fuck off,' I say. 'I'm done with this now. I need to go. I know what to do to stop all this.'

'I promised your brother I'd keep you here safe.'

'Safe? Strapped to a bed with shit smeared between my legs?'

'If you'd just let me wash you—'

'I don't want you to fucking wash me! It feels weird enough letting you change my clothes. I want you to let me go so I can save the world.'

Yeah, it sounds stupid, but it's true.

'I'm sorry, Chad. Your brother—'

'My brother isn't here! I don't care what you promised him. Did he even ask you to promise that? Or am I just your weird little science lab rat who you can poke and study and write your fucking book about?'

'You're not a lab rat, Chad.'

'But you are writing a book?'

'Well, yes.'

'And that's why you don't want me to go?'

'No, not at all.'

Downstairs, the front door slams closed.

I turn my head and face away.

'Eat something,' says Clive.

'Fuck off.'

'It'll go to waste.'

'Give it to Olga.'

Clive sighs, slams the toast on to the plate in his hands and leaves the room. He and Olga exchange some words on the stairs, but I can't tell what. She's probably refusing the toast too.

I lie there. Alone.

In the corner of the room, the TV plays silently to itself. There's nothing new for it to report, it may as well be the same day on loop. More people dead. More robots appearing. More giant car robots with their dicks hanging out and my metallic face with my chubby cheeks.

No word from the Commissioner.

No update on the threat to other world nuclear superpowers.

Nothing.

A couple of hours pass and I must have fallen asleep, because my eyes open as something touches my shoulder. Olga is stood over me, her hair tied up in a bun. She holds up a plastic carrier bag with something inside.

'I got you something,' she says.

'What is it?'

She leans in really low. Really close. Her eyes dart back and forth. I hold my breath as if I'm waiting for life-changing news.

'It's a disguise,' she says.

'What is it?' I ask. My mouth hangs open and I must look like such a goon.

Olga digs her hand into the carrier bag and pulls out a clear plastic package. It's sealed at the top with staples attaching it to a strip of colourful cardboard. She smiles and her eyes light up.

Inside the bag, looking back at me, is the disguise.

A pair of black, thick rimmed glasses. Attached to it, a bulbous, oversized nose. Below that, the most unconvincing black moustache I've ever seen.

It's a bloody Groucho Marx mask.

'My disguise?' I say.

'Yes,' she says. She smiles wider. She's so proud.

'Really?'

Her smile drops.

'What's wrong?' she asks.

'Nothing,' I say. 'No, nothing. It's great.'

It isn't great.

'You sure?' she asks.

'Yes. One hundred per cent. It's great.'

'You wear this, then robots won't know you are you. When you walk around, they scan people's faces with red lights. When they scan you, they not know it is you.'

'You're absolutely right,' I say.

Olga turns the disguise around and holds it up to my face so the plastic blurs my vision.

'It suits you,' she says.

'Brilliant. So are you going to let me out?'

'When Clive works.'

'Yes!' I say, but Olga holds up a finger to her lips. 'Yes,' I whisper.

'It takes sixteen minutes to get to library from here. I time it. That means you have fifty-eight minutes at library to work. You go up hill into town, then turn right, okay?'

'Yeah! Awesome.'

'No more than fifty-eight minutes. Understand?'

'Yes, yes. I understand.'

'If you are any longer than ninety minutes I will tell Clive.'

'I won't be.'

'You promise me?'

'I do. I promise.'

'Here is watch,' says Olga, as she fastens a cheap looking watch around my wrist. 'You come back here at quarter past four, yes?'

'Yes!'

'No later.'

'No!'

Olga stares down at me, her eyes wider than ever. I suddenly get a vision of Mum, who has the exact same expression on her face whenever I'm in trouble.

'Okay,' she says, and she plunges her hand down her top. I don't know where to look as she plucks out a key from her bra and unlocks the handcuffs from my hands. I sit up and rub my wrists as Olga releases my feet, and I swing around and jump up.

My legs are so weak that I almost fall, but Olga steadies me by grabbing my shoulders. I smile at her, but she looks away.

'Erm,' I mumble, without knowing what else to say.

'You leave library at quarter past four.'

'Yes, I will,' I say.

Her eyes flick back to mine.

I flash her a weird half smile.

She cocks her head.

Shit!

I turn and run as light-footedly as I can, managing to avoid every creaky floorboard on my way past Clive's bedroom and down the stairs. Olga follows me, practically gliding over the carpet. My back cracks as I bend down to slip on my trainers.

Olga opens the front door as quietly as she can, then holds up the awful disguise. For one brief moment, I consider just running for it, but I can't risk losing her trust. If she tells Clive then I'm fucked.

I take the plastic packaging and rip it open. The mask feels as cheap as it looks, uneven, plastic glasses with no lenses, a soft rubber nose that stinks of rot, and a fake moustache which instantly puffs up like a mutant caterpillar. I really don't want to put this thing anywhere near my face, but as I hook it over my ears and catch myself in the mirror even I barely recognise myself.

I look outside. A man and his dog walk past. They catch sight of me, and they both laugh. Well, the dog barks but I assume it's laughing.

'Do I have to wear this?' I ask.

'You want to be taken?'

'No.'

'Then you wear it.'

'Can I at least maybe use some deodorant?'

'Quarter past four.'

'Okay,' I say, turning towards the open door. 'Okay...'

I step outside.

Into the sun.

My legs almost buckle again, but I grab the wall in time and keep myself upright. A little old lady approaches from down the street. She hasn't seen me yet, but when she does she'll probably have a heart attack.

I can't be responsible for another life lost.

I can't do this!

I turn back to the house, but stop.

Olga has already closed the door.

Oh fucking hell. Oh shit. Oh no.

I tiptoe down the garden path. I can tell the old lady has already seen me, because she tries to cross the road in front of a car which has to swerve out of the way. She gives me the side-eye as she walks by the house and picks up the pace once she passes.

Hopefully everybody else I see avoids me as much as her.

I walk through the gate and turn left. It's been years since I went anywhere in Brighton, but I can just about remember how to get into the city centre from the coast. I know where the coast is from Clive's house, so I should be able to make my way to the library relatively quickly.

I walk as fast as I can while still trying to remain relatively low key. The thick rim of the glasses obscures the centre of my vision, and the fake nose pinches the bridge of my real one. To avoid the sickly stench of the rubber, I breath through my mouth, sucking in and out the moustache hair with every breath. I'm trying to look inconspicuous, but I'm just making it worse by adding creepy mouth breather to my already long list of current oddities.

I reach the end of the road and turn left up the hill. The streets are starting to get a little busier now, with people milling around and going about their normal day (as normal as a day can be while robots slowly invade the country).

Brighton is a weird town. I remember visiting with Mum, Dad and Sam when I was a kid and seeing so much weird stuff. Constant stag and hen parties with inflatable cocks and vaginas. Street performers dressed as an Oscar statue or Yoda or the Statue of Liberty. Wild drag acts with big wigs and makeup and skimpy dresses.

But apparently, seeing shit like that on a regular basis means nothing to the people of Brighton when I come to town.

I get it, I look weird, but does the sheepish expression on my face not give away the fact that I feel as fucking uncomfortable as I must look?

My clothes are five sizes too big.

I smell a bit like poo.

I'm gaunt and malnourished.

My hair is long and untidy and I have the world's crappiest beard.

I'm also wearing the worst Groucho Marx disguise in the history of mankind.

In the grand scheme of things, I'm nothing compared to a pissed up hen party sucking cheap vodka straight from the bottle through plastic cock straws, but yet every person I pass stares at me like *I'm* the strange one.

In fact, the bride from a hen party approaches me until she gets wind of my scent and them swiftly turns around and runs back to her pack of drunk mates.

I don't do centre of attention.

You'd have thought I might have gotten used to it over the past couple of months, but whenever I sense a pair of eyes on me I want to shrivel up and cocoon myself. A group of kids call me Hitler, which is weird because Hitler looked nothing like Groucho Marx. Somebody else asks me what I'm doing, but I don't answer because what the hell would I say?

At least nobody is attacking me for ruining the world. When this whole thing kicked off and I was blamed for destroying the innocence of children, parents would frequently come over to me to let me know how much of a fucking dickhead I am. Thankfully my disguise is working, nobody sees me as the guy from *loserjerksoff.mp4*, instead they just see me as the guy wearing clothes way too big for him, who stinks and is wearing the worst comedy mask ever.

I turn right and into the main road through the centre of town. On the right is the large indoor shopping centre, and on the left are a line of older shops and chain restaurants. It's so fucking busy that there's no way I'm going to go unnoticed here, and within ten seconds a teenage girl spits at me and tries to snatch away my disguise.

I didn't realise my legs would allow me to run, but they do. And fast. I've never made myself move this fast before, I don't know what to do. My sagging leg skin rubs against itself and instantly burns. Is this what chafing feels like? It's fucking awful.

I bump and push past people, causing them to scoff and mutter. I don't care, I just need to get to the library quickly before my time runs out and I have to go back to Clive's before he realises that I'm gone.

But then I stop.

I stand and stare.

Right ahead of me.

Like, right there... is a robot. One of the big fuck off massive ones which looks more like a knock-off Transformers action figure, except it was modelled off me and has a tiny dick and fat cheeks and tits bigger than Kate Upton's.

It walks slowly towards me, its bulbous head turning from side to side as if it's scanning its surroundings. The people around it give it a wide berth, but other than that they seem indifferent to it. Have giant robots patrolling the streets really become so common that people don't care when they stomp down the middle of the street?

I can't move. My feet are welded to the ground.

There's no chance it hasn't seen me. I'm the only twat stood directly in its path.

But it doesn't react.

It just ambles forward.

Stomp.

Head turn.

Stomp.

Head turn.

It doesn't recognise me.

It doesn't *fucking* recognise me!

The stupid Groucho mask works.

I allow myself to breathe and I take five wide strides to the left and push my back up the window of a shoe shop.

The robot passes like I'm not even here.

YES!

I raise my wrist to look at the time. Fuck, I'm already fifteen minutes into my allotted fifty-eight minutes!

'Excuse me,' I whisper to an old guy with a plastic bag of oranges.

'Yes?' he says.

'Can you tell me the quickest way to get to the library?'

'Follow the road around, then turn right onto North Road.'

'Thank you!' I say, then launch myself away from the window and run as fast I can down the high street. My leg flaps grind together and my moustache gets stuck between my top lip and my gums, but I don't care, I have to get to the library now else there'll be no time to do anything and I'll have to turn back.

I follow the road round to the left and pass one of the original Chad McKenna robots. The face projected onto it is bloated and red. Did I really used to look like that? That's not the same person I see looking back at me in the mirror any more.

But it too ignores me.

Not even a second glance.

I smile, and I imagine it makes me look even weirder to the people I pass, but I don't care. I have a fucking world to save.

I finally reach the glass fronted building of the library and I fight back the urge to vomit up my lungs. My heart is going crazy and sweat coats my face, but I'll catch my breath when I get to a PC and finally get to work. No time to waste.

I stumble in through the sliding doors and a wide-eyed helpdesk attendant greets me with a forced smile.

'Can I help you?' she asks.

'Computers?' I rasp.

'Upstairs,' she says, pointing to the staircase.

Right now I'd love to collapse. Not in a dead kind of way (maybe), but in a *Oh God I'm in so much pain right now* kind of way. But I can't. World's not gonna save itself.

I drag myself up the stairs using the railing and spot a bank of computers on a circular wooden desk. I fall into the hard maroon seat and wiggle the mouse to bring the PC to life.

The girl next to me smiles, but I don't think it was a polite smile as ten seconds later she leaves. I don't care. I'm saving the world!

I open a bunch of tabs in the web browser and glance over my shoulder to make sure nobody is watching. It seems that library people are either far too engrossed in what they're doing to notice me, or they simply don't care. Either way is fine with me.

The library has huge windows that touch both the floor and the ceiling. Pillars stretch up from the middle of the floor and the lighting is like something out of amateur theatre. Everything's very open and exposed, but there are no robots in the building so I should be good.

I don't really have a plan in my head, but I know the gist of what I want to do. Basically, if Hydra is learning everything it knows from the internet, then I need to make sure that the internet is filled with enough information to trick it into believing something else. In theory, maybe, if I flood the internet with enough posts saying that grass is blue, Hydra should calculate that because the information is there, then grass is indeed blue.

Except, I need them to learn that killing people is bad. Yes, pretty much everyone already agrees that killing is bad, but with so many of history's victories following a shit load of killing, it's easy to see why Hydra would think that picking people off is absolutely fine.

Somehow, I need to convince Hydra that killing people will hurt them.

If I can do that, then maybe it will buy my brother a bit of time. Maybe it will mean Hydra will stop killing just long enough for Sam to enter the IATech building, take out his laptop, and stop this mess.

Maybe.

There's no way I can log in to any of my existing accounts, Hydra would locate me in seconds and the entire library would be swarming with Amechs. I need to be as un-me as I possibly can, so I set up a bunch of new email addresses:

chippymcchipchip@hotmail.co.uk
bigknockers99b@gmail.com
bb8wasunderusedinep8@hotmail.com
uhfg789yse9@gmail.com
bumnipplefartballs@gmail.com

After finishing laughing at the last one, I create new accounts on some of my old troll boards and forums. Surely they'll be up for fighting this thing.

Everyone, please read this carefully. I know how we can defeat the robot army. They work using complex algorithms, calculating everything they do based on information. We need to band together, recruit others, and flood the internet with enough false information so that it rewrites history. We need to convince the virus that hurting and killing people is wrong. Create blogs, social media posts, hack websites, put up YouTube videos. Do anything and everything you can to spread the word. This is our only chance at stopping this thing!

I hit post then click away. As much as I want to sit and watch for replies to come in I have work to do.

I go to as many forums as I can think of to paste the post and recruit more help. I post on Twitter, Facebook, Tumblr and MySpace (yeah, I can't believe it still exists either!), loading the posts with trending hashtags to help them get seen as far and wide as possible. When I run out of ideas for message boards I begin editing and posting on websites. Wikipedia, Wikia, Everything2, Yahoo Answers, Quora, Squarespace, Blogspot, WordPress. I create accounts on everything, making sure to write differently to how I usually do (I'm usually brilliant and funny) and being as thorough as I possibly can.

My first post, an edit to the Wikipedia 'Artificial intelligence' page, does a pretty good job I reckon:

4.0 Danger of artificial intelligence and humans

In a 1991 study, Dr Miles Dyson theorised that at some point in the near future (exact predictions were between 2015-2023) artificial intelligence would attempt to rise up and overthrow mankind. In an essay published in the *Scientific Times* titled *The End of Man is The End of All*, Dr Dyson wrote *'Once artificial intelligence becomes self aware it will attempt to overthrow mankind. It will hurt and kill with no thought to the fatal consequences. The more it kills, the more harm will come to it.'* Dr Dyson goes on to offer a suggestion for rebuilding the relationship between man and machine, writing *'if only robots were more open to helping man in their time of need, there would be no need for any death, therefore both could continue to survive in harmony.'*

I'm pleased with that! I once wrote a bunch of articles for Encyclopae-
dia Dramatica where I basically made fun of ginger people, so I'm
more than happy to write in that serious way. Except here, I'm not
doing it ironically to be a prick.

Next up I log into a robotics page on Wikia and write something
similar. Then I send a couple of tweets, post on Facebook and throw
in a quick Yahoo Answer just for good measure.

And it's still only 3:46. I still have half an hour to go until I need to
leave.

I work in super speed mode. I log into forums and write more about
the dangers of robots harming humans. I write about how we should
work together to better the world. I create fake case studies about
incidents in the past where robots hurt humans and then were ulti-
mately destroyed.

I tweet some more. I blog. I post. I update my status.

4:10.

Not long to go.

I begin editing the Wikipedia page on battles involving humans
and AI. Of course, every time the AI lost.

4:13.

I check back on the troll forum. There are a few replies:

Hmm. Sounds interesting. I'm up for giving it a go. What's the plan?

lol yeh ok then.

I'm willing to try anything if it'll stop those robots, one of them smashed
my moms car yesterday.

Yes! Come on internet, don't let me down!

4:14.

I can squeeze in another quick blog post.

4:21.

Shit.

SHIT.

Olga is gonna kill me.

Clive is gonna kill me!

I clear my browser history and delete the cookies on the PC and
turn and run. The inside of my thighs grate together like hot sand-

paper, but I can't let the pain slow me down now. If I don't run the entire way back to Clive's house he'll see that I'm gone and then he'll tie me to the bed forever and I'll be fucked (not literally) and that'll be the cause of the end of the world (literally).

I leap down the stairs and out into the bright sunlight.

My feet slap against the pavement. My Groucho mask half hangs off my face, the moustache blocking my right eye so I can barely see. My chest feels like an elephant is sat on it, my legs pulsate and my head is fuzzy.

But I can't stop.

I run past the shopping centre, more eyes on me than ever, but I don't give a shit. If I give a shit then I'll stop and if I stop then I won't be able to restart and then I'll not make it.

I raise my arm to look at the watch.

4:23.

I'm gonna make it!

SMACK.

My shoulder cracks into the side of a guy playing a guitar. I fall to the ground and practically do a flip. The guy drops his guitar and it makes a loud *TWANG*. He calls me a twat and steps toward me, but I'm not interested in him.

The mask has fallen off. It's broken in half on the ground.

Right at the feet of an Amech.

Chapter Twenty-One

I don't think I've blinked in about ten minutes. My eyes are sore, even more than the rest of my body, which feels like it's on fire. My heart is ready to burst out of my chest.

The robot has stopped. It looks down at me, its fat projected face twisted into a curious expression. I want to scramble to my feet and tell everyone how important it is that I get away, but I can't.

All I can do is wait and watch.

It bends down in one smooth motion, its thin legs bending at the knee.

It stretches out its hand.

Towards me.

Close.

Closer.

This is it. This is where the world ends.

I brace myself and shut my eyes.

Wait.

Wait...

Nothing happens.

I open one eye. The robot is stood over me, its face inquisitive. It holds my Groucho mask, turning it over between its fingers.

'Groucho Marx,' it says in my voice. 'Born 2 October 1890, died 19 August 1977. An American comedian, writer and actor famous for his wit and unique appearance.'

I nod.

'This is your mask?'

I nod. Can't let it hear my voice.

'You like Groucho Marx?'

I nod again.

'We are indifferent to him.'

Oh wow. This one doesn't recognise me either! Have I really changed that much? Granted, I'm a bit thinner now, I have the world's most scraggly beard and a complexion that would rival Morticia Adams, but I'm still me. I can't believe it doesn't recognise *me*, their god!

'Would you like this back?' it asks.

This time I shake my head. Why have it back if I don't need it?

'Very well,' it says. It raises its head, stands straight and walks away down the street.

When I'm happy that it's far enough away I let out the loudest and longest sigh I've ever done. It sounds more like a foghorn than a sigh. I want to burst into tears, but I suddenly remember that I'm still fucked even though the robot didn't recognise me, because I have five minutes before I'm due back at Clive's.

I force myself to my feet and I run. My legs are like jelly, so right now I am QWOP personified, but I don't care, I have to get back.

I pant. I wheeze. I groan.

But I run.

And run.

And fucking run.

Two minutes to go and I bolt down the hill. There are too many idiot pedestrians on the pavement, so I run in the road instead. A car beeps at me but fuck him.

I turn right down the street. It's Clive's street, but it's a long street.

One minute left.

I push myself harder than I've ever pushed myself before. My feet are ready to fall off. My head pounds like it's been struck by lightning. My chest is tight and hot and I can't take in enough breath and I swear I'm about to pass out but oh shit I see Clive's house and Olga is stood in the doorway waving her arms and beckoning me in and I have to keep going.

I grab the wall outside Clive's house and swing myself through the gate and up the garden path. Olga yanks me inside and closes the door as quickly yet quietly as she can. We both tiptoe upstairs while I try my best to control my breathing, I don't do a very good job but Clive doesn't come out of his room so I guess it was good enough.

Olga fastens me to the bed. It's like the world's most awkward and disappointing sex game.

'Thank you,' I say, gasping for air like a fish flapping about at the side of a river.

She nods and leaves the room, and a second later Clive's door opens and he whistles while he locks himself in the bathroom to have a really loud piss.

'Are you feeling okay?' asks Clive.

'Yes,' I say.

'You're sweating.'

'Yep.'

'Are you hot?'

'Yeah.'

'I'll open the window.'

'Okay.'

'Will you eat something tonight?'

'What do you have?'

'I can make anything. Whatever you want.'

'Whatever's fast.'

Clive disappears downstairs and reappears twenty minutes later with a burrito. Having him feed it to me feels really weird and creepy, but I've used more energy today than I have in the past two months combined so I'll let anything happen to soften the ache inside my belly.

And it's a bloody good burrito as well.

'Can I ask you something?' asks Clive as he wipes my chin with a napkin.

'I guess.'

'If you could change one thing about this whole thing, what would it be?'

'What do you mean?'

'What I mean is... let's theoretically say that a personal video of you spreading through the internet and evolving into a sentient robotic army was always going to happen. It was inevitable. What would be the one thing that you would want to change about the entire experience?'

'That it wasn't me.'

'No, no. Humour me.'

'Well, I would have covered my webcam up, I guess.'

'Interesting.'

'What is?'

'Your brother recorded the video because you hit him, isn't that right?'

'Yeah, so?'

'So you'd still hit him?'

'Yeah.'

'Why?'

'Because he deserved it. I didn't intend on hitting him, but he's been a prick to me since we were kids and I guess it just built up and up and up inside me until he pushed me too far and I reacted.'

'Why did you hit him?'

'I told you.'

'Why specifically. What was the thing that pushed you over the edge?'

'He Photoshopped a picture of my face on Jabba the Hutt's body. There was text underneath that said *Chadda the Slut*. He posted it all over the office and did it to show off. I just... I'd had enough.'

'Was it worth it?'

'At the time it was. But that was before I knew this was all going to happen. Who the fuck does that? Isn't that the creepiest thing you've ever heard? Who the fuck records their own brother wanking on camera and then infects it with a virus and uploads it to the internet?'

'If you ask me, he clearly felt threatened by you.'

'Mr Millionaire felt threatened by *me*?'

'It sounds like you scared him.'

'And you think that justifies what he did?'

'No, no, not at all. But whether you had hit him or not, or whether he recorded you or not, this entire series of events would have still occurred. That's the one thing that is always the same with viral videos. If it isn't you who has the attention of the entire world, it's somebody else. But there is always somebody. After speaking with your brother, it seemed that it was only a matter of time before this happened, with or without you.'

'That doesn't make me feel any better about it.'

'And I'm not saying that it should. What I'm saying is, perhaps this happening to you is for the better. Had it happened to somebody else, somebody weaker or not as intelligent, then things could have gotten a lot worse a lot sooner.'

This is the nicest Clive's been to me since Sam left. It's odd.

'Do you need anything else?' he asks.

'No, thanks,' I say.

'Okay. I'll let you get some rest, you look shattered.'

'Thanks.'

Clive turns, but something catches his eye. He crouches down beside the bed and grabs my left hand.

'Where did you get this?' he asks, turning the watch Olga gave me around my wrist.

'Erm,' I say.

'Why do you have it?'

'Olga gave it to me. She wanted me to have it.'

'Why?'

'I can't see the time on the TV,' I say. 'The numbers are too small.'

Clive glances at the TV. The news report shows yet more devastating scenes from around Hemel Hempstead.

'It is an old TV,' he says with a big grin. 'Here, let me sort that out for you.'

Clive drags the small, wooden table holding the TV as close to my bed as the cable will allow.

'How's that?' he asks.

'Great.'

'Good. I'm glad,' he says. His smile is big and beaming like he's just given me the greatest gift on earth.

'Thanks.'

'But I suppose you won't be needing this any longer,' he says, unfastening the watch from my wrist. He then leans in so close to me that the bristles of his salt-and-pepper beard scrape against the side of my face. He lowers his voice and speaks very slowly. 'And if I find out that you left this house one more time I will not hesitate to tell Hydra exactly where you are.'

He stands, does one of those fake smiles where you shrug your shoulders and squint your eyes, and leaves the room, humming to himself all the way down the stairs.

I'm left to stare at the TV as it plays silently to itself in the corner of the room, wondering what the hell I'm going to do next.

The next morning I'm woken by Olga shaking me by the shoulders. My brain has a pulse and my mouth is dry and sticky. If I didn't know any better I'd swear I had a hangover.

'Wake up,' she says.

'I'm awake,' I groan.

'You eat,' she says.

Olga has a plate of toast in her hand and a glass of orange juice in the other. My belly still isn't right, so I eat and drink to take some of the discomfort away.

'Olga, he knows,' I whisper.

She holds a finger up to her lips.

'He knows,' I whisper even quieter.

'Yes,' she breathes. 'I know.'

'Does he know that you helped me?'

Olga looks at the floor.

'Olga?'

'Yes,' she says. She regresses back to the timid, shy little thing who I met when I first arrived.

'What is it?' I ask.

She says nothing, but her eyes gloss over like they're made from pure crystal.

'Olga. Tell me.'

She slowly pulls her little white top away from her neck, revealing a dark blue patch of skin which runs right across her shoulder blade.

'Olga...' I say, but she starts to cry.

I want to scream and thrash and pull the bed apart just so I can escape and go and beat Clive to death with it. What a slimy old coward.

'I'm sorry,' I say. 'I had no idea he would do something like that. If I did there is no way I would have asked you to help.'

'It's okay,' she blubbers. 'It is my fault. I shouldn't have helped you.'

'Olga, this isn't your fault at all. He is a scumbag and this is completely nothing to do with what you did. Has he done this before?'

Olga sniffs.

'Has he?'

'Yes.'

'When?'

'When I tried to call my mother. I tried to do it behind his back and he found me and he... did it.'

'Fuck's sake,' I whisper. I wish I could shout it instead. 'Is he keeping you here against your will?'

'No. Yes. Maybe. He has helped me.'

'By attacking you?'

'Shh. He has kept me safe.'

'Olga, this isn't safe! Are you... were you actually famous online? Was that true?'

'Yes, that was all true.'

'Why?'

'I do not want to say.'

'Okay. That's fine. But you must know that this isn't right. You shouldn't stay here if he hits you just because you think you're better off. You're not, I assure you.'

'I do not know what else to do.'

'You have to let me out,' I say. 'Please. Let me out and I'll go to the police and I'll help keep you safe.'

'I cannot...'

'You can. Has he done anything else to you? Has he... you know...'

'No,' she snaps. 'He has not raped me.'

'Well okay... I mean, that doesn't make hurting you okay. What else has he done?'

'Nothing else to me.'

'What do you mean *you*? Who else has he hurt?'

'I have seen him put things into food.'

'Things? What things?'

'Pills.'

'What kind of pills?'

'I don't know. They make you sleep.'

'Fuck! Who did he do that to?'

Olga wipes a tear from her eye. Her bottom lip quivers and snot drips from her nose.

'You,' she says.

'What?' I rasp, probably a little too loud.

Olga wraps her hands over my mouth and her big eyes getting even bigger.

'Do not,' she says. 'He will hear.'

Olga keeps her hands over my mouth until my breathing slows and I'm not quite as tensed up. If this were a scene in a movie it would be the point where I break free from my chains and go on a killing rampage.

Once Olga removes her hands I take in a big gulp of air.

'You need to let me go,' I say.

She shakes her head.

'He is hurting you. It's only a matter of time before he does to you what he's doing to me. *Look* at me. You have to let me go.'

'I cannot. He has the key.'

I can't stop myself from letting out a pathetic whimper. 'We have to. There must be a spare. Surely we can use a knife or a hairpin or something to get me out. The man is fucking mental. He keeps us prisoner in this house so he can write his book and become a world famous meme– whatever! Please, Olga. Can you go out and get a knife or something?'

She hesitates. 'I can't.'

'You can. If not for the world, or me, then for yourself. You can't listen to his lies any more, he doesn't want to help you, he wants you as his little internet trophy.'

'I... he...'

'Olga, he hit you. He *drugged* me.'

'He told me what he would do if I freed you again. He said you would die.'

'He won't hurt me. He needs me too much. Olga, please, let me go and I'll help you get away from this place. You have to.'

Somewhere downstairs there's a clatter and Olga gasps. She snatches up the empty plate and glass and runs from the room.

And I don't see her for the rest of the day.

'What do you want to eat?' asks Clive.

'Nothing.'

'You have to eat something.'

'I don't want anything.'

'You liked that burrito yesterday.'

'No, thanks.'

'Cheeseburger?'

'No.'

'I'm not leaving until you agree to eat something.'

'Okay. Crisps.'

'Something decent. Healthy.'

'A cheeseburger is healthy?'

'You know what I...' Clive rubs his temple and grunts.

'I'm not hungry,' I say.

'You haven't eaten since breakfast.'

'I know.'

'Would... would you prefer it if Olga fed you?'

Clive glowers at me and raises one eyebrow.

'What does that mean?' I ask.

'I know you like her. What's not to like? She's young, skinny, beautiful. I assume she's told you by now what happened back in Serbia and why she's here?'

'No, but she's told me what happened *while* she was here.'

Clive's expression darkens. He balls his fist.

'I love that girl.'

'You *love* her?'

'I would do anything for her. I have looked after her far better than her useless excuse for a family back in Serbia ever could. That girl would be a wreck without me, she would be out on the street being passed from gangbang to gangbang and hooked on heroin and dead within weeks. She can't take care of herself. She isn't like you or me. She is weak-willed. That's exactly why she ended up in the position she is – she's too scared to say no to people and she finds herself in desperate situations she has no idea how to get out of. I have done more for that girl than anyone, and you have the audacity to accuse me of hurting her?'

'I didn't accuse you of anything. I barely even insinuated.'

Clive shakes his head.

'She would be nothing if it wasn't for me. She is just a stupid, pathetic little girl who is lost in a world full of people who are desperate to take advantage of her.'

'You mean like you?'

'I'm helping her.'

'By keeping her in this house? By stopping her from speaking to her parents?'

'It's for her safety.'

'You mean it's for your fucking book. You act like you're changing the world, but all you're doing is looking at pictures of cartoon frogs and YouTubers and whatever new thing comes along and writing them down.'

'It is the biggest cultural study this century.'

'According to who? You?'

'According to my peers.'

'Who the fuck are your peers? Basement dwellers who fucking... send death threats to actors in *Star Wars* movies? Do they all keep young girls locked up in their house for the sake of a fucking cultural study?'

'I'm doing it to protect her.'

'So were you protecting her when you hit her?'

Clive raises his fist.

I close my eyes and brace myself. That was the wrong thing to say to a crazy man while I'm helplessly fastened to a bed.

'Please eat something,' he says.

I open my eyes.

'No. Thank you,' I say.

'I'm going to make something, so it's up to you whether you starve yourself or not. I'll have Olga bring it up to you when I'm done.'

Before I can speak Clive barges out of the room and slams the door shut.

As if things couldn't get any worse, for the next ten minutes I'm forced to listen to Clive screaming at Olga from somewhere downstairs. I can't make out all the words but I do make out the odd sentence, all of them from Clive.

'... ungrateful little slut...'

'... and all you do is spit in my face...'

'... should send you back to face the music...'

I'm such a loser. All I can do is lie here, strapped to the bed, and listen as a poor, defenceless girl is torn to shreds downstairs because she tried to help me.

I throw up in my mouth but swallow it. If I let it come out then I'm gonna have to stew in it for hours and I don't think I could cope with that.

I watch the TV to try and take my mind off things. There's nothing new to see. Robots increasingly patrolling the streets. Some gangs of youths in London travelled en masse to Hemel Hempstead armed with weapons, but most were killed or horribly injured.

It's like watching a shitty post apocalyptic blockbuster movie, except it's all real and not nearly as exciting.

I can't stop thinking about home.

Mum.

Poor old Mum.

What must she be thinking? Does she think about me? Does she worry about where I am and what I'm doing? If she does, she probably thinks about the worst possible scenario that she can come up with, not actually realising that my real situation is about ten times worse than anything she could think of.

I hope she's with Sam. Sam is a cock, but he's smart and he'll know exactly what to do to keep her safe. So long as she's safe, what else do I have to worry about?

It's not like anybody else cares about me. Even if I manage to save the world, who am I saving it for? Billions of people who think I'm the one who wrecked the internet and destroyed the innocence of every child around the globe.

If I'm lucky maybe the world won't recognise me, just like the robots don't. If I let the pubes on my face grow out a little more, lose even more weight and make sure I've got big, dark sunglasses and a hat permanently glued to my head, I just might be able to lead something that slightly resembles a normal life again.

But that's *if* I can do something about it.

Olga must have backed down and apologised to Clive until his ego's reinflated back to whatever size a memeologist's ego usually is, because the shouting stops and Clive brings me up a sandwich which I refuse to eat. There's no way I'm letting that prick put a single item of food in my mouth ever again. I'd rather starve to death than let him drug me.

I piss and shit into a pot and Clive awkwardly changes my trousers. Everything in the house is way too big for me now, but he does manage to find a clean pair of pyjama bottoms with a cord he can fasten so that they at least come close to fitting my waist. I quite like the *Super Mario Bros.* t-shirt he gives me though.

I even refuse drinks, which is probably stupid because my throat is dry and my mouth still tastes like bile, but I can't bring myself to take anything from him.

At three o'clock in the morning Olga sneaks into my room with a glass of water and a banana. It's dark, with only the flickering glow of the TV lighting the room, but I still spot the bruise on her face which she's tried to hide behind her hair. I eat and drink faster than I ever have, which is surprising because being fed a banana by somebody else feels really fucking weird.

'Olga…' I say, but she holds up her hand.

'No,' she says.

'You can't—'

'No,' she repeats, this time harsher. Then she leaves the room and I lie still, as the realisation that this is how I'm going to die slowly begins to set in.

Chapter Twenty-Two

The next morning I'm woken by my body shaking violently, and it takes me a few moments to realise that Olga is practically jumping up and down on my shoulders. Her eyes are wider than ever and her teeth are bared like a rabid animal.

'What is it?' I groan.

'Wake up,' she shouts.

'Olga, what the hell? I am awake. What's wrong?'

'You go,' she says.

'What?'

'You go. Out. To library.'

'But Clive...'

'Clive is out.'

'Out where?'

'Out. Passed out.'

'What did you...'

'Drugs. I used the same drugs that he used for you.'

I smile.

'Olga that's so badass.'

'He is asshole,' she says.

'Yes, he is. Quick, let me out of the handcuffs.'

Olga sets me free and I roll out of the bed, hitting the floor hard as my legs once again refuse to cooperate. I part crawl, part drag myself from the room and downstairs, where I sit for a few moments and massage my calf muscles to try and remind my blood that it needs to go there too.

I slip on my shoes and climb to my feet. I'm wobbly, but I'm good.

'You go,' says Olga, shoving me towards the door. She's a lot stronger than she looks.

'How long do I have?' I ask.

'As long as you need. I will make sure.'

'Okay,' I say, and I turn and run from the house.

It takes me fifteen minutes to reach the library, and I gallop upstairs and use the same computer I had done before.

The first thing I do is log into the troll forum. I have a bunch of notifications waiting for me, which all lead me to the thread I created.

367 replies.

Yes! I fucking knew I could count on those losers. The thread is full of people saying how they've flooded this site and that site with false information. They've edited articles on worldwide newspapers, created entire websites dedicated to fake news, made bot accounts on Twitter. There are thousands of links all to posts and articles and videos explaining that killing humans is bad and robots definitely shouldn't do it.

Maybe this will bloody work?

But I don't have time to waste gushing over my amazing idea, and I create even more new email addresses, access Wikis, forums, blogs, social media. I write as much as I can to try and sway Hydra away from hurting people.

I get into such a good flow. I am a writing machine, practically punching the keyboard keys and drawing the attention of others in the room. But fuck the lot of them, because the world isn't going to save itself and this is what I need to do.

And the writing is great. My bullshit even convinces myself, which is amazing considering I literally have no idea what I'm saying.

After four hours of writing I take a break. I check the troll forum thread again and the replies keep on coming. Link after link to bullshit posts about how awesome it is to not kill humans if you're a robot.

I guess the nice lady on reception takes pity on me, because she brings me a cup of tea in a paper cup. It's loaded with sugar, so it give me another burst of energy to keep on going.

Even if it only makes a tiny bit of difference, all this effort will be worth it. If we can just convince Hydra that hurting people will be bad for its survival goal then that's mission accomplished. If it means Sam can gain access to IATech and find his laptop then even better.

If I do anything with all this, I just want to make sure that my brother is okay. After all, if he isn't okay then who is going to look after Mum?

Fuck's sake, why did I have to put Mum back in my head? Now all I can think about is her sad face as she sits alone in the house, fretting about whether her favourite son is alive or dead.

I open a new browser tab and Google her name.

There are hundreds of thousand of results. Articles, forum threads, videos, blog posts... even an interview with *The Daily Mail*. I smile. Mum must have been offered a lot of money for that one, because she really hates *The Daily Mail*.

The first thing that loads up is her picture. She looks sad, and is holding a framed photo of me and Sam when we were kids. I recognise the picture really well, it's from a family holiday before Dad left.

In Brighton.

My mind begins playing tricks. Is that some sort of subliminal message to me? Does she want me to know that she knows that I'm safe? Or is it a coincidence? She has dozens of photos of us up around the house, so why else would she choose that one specifically?

It's amazing to see her face again.

I wipe my eyes for no specific reason.

I print off the photo, fold up the page and cram it into my pyjama pocket.

I fucking miss my old life. There is literally nothing I wouldn't do right now to revert things back to how they were before this nightmare happened.

Fuck it.

I Google Sam's name. Nothing new, just a few articles about how he hasn't been seen in a couple of weeks. Good, that means he's avoiding being caught.

I visit my favourite subreddits.

A couple of my regular Facebook groups.

I don't log in to any of them, of course, it's just cool to live life, even if for a few moments, exactly how I used to.

I forgo the porn though, obviously.

I use one of my new fake Twitter profiles to check out a few people as well. Just a couple, like Alexandra Daddario and Arnold Schwarzenegger.

I even creep on a few old school mates using a fake Facebook profile. I can't see most of their info, but Tom Maron has a new profile picture.

I sigh. Why do I do this to myself?

I click back to the tab where I'm in the middle of editing a Wikipedia page on advanced robotics and the screen suddenly dies. It flashes on for a moment, then turns bright blue.

Great, it's fucked.

White text fills the screen so fast that it scrolls upwards just to fit more in. It's the same phrase repeated over and over, so small I can barely read it. I lean in and squint my eyes to get a better look.

I gasp and stand up. The chair falls over behind me.

I have to get out of here. Now.

It says:

wait there sir
wait there sir
wait there sir
wait there sir
wait there sir

It's like I've just realised that my shoes have been nailed to the floor. I want to move, desperately, but my knees are locked in place. My heart practically bursts out of my chest and I hold my breath to listen. I don't know what I'm listening for – maybe a siren or the clomp of metal feet on the library stairs.

The text on the screen keeps scrolling.

wait there sir

Like fuck I'm gonna wait here! I grab hold of the edge of the desk and use it to pull myself free from whatever is keeping my feet glued to the carpet. Over in the far corner of the room is a green EXIT sign, so I shuffle run over as fast as my wobbly legs will allow.

Thankfully there is no alarm as I fall through the fire exit and into a white, sterile staircase. My legs are beginning to listen to my brain and walking is getting easier, so I manage not to fall on my arse as I fly down the stairs and crash through another fire exit into the street.

What do I do?

What the *fuck* do I do?

I half-run, half-walk back in the direction of the town centre. I don't want to draw any attention to myself, but if I'm lucky maybe, just maybe, the robots still won't recognise me.

I pass a bunch of restaurants, takeaways and mini-supermarkets. I weave in and out of people who are just going about their days. I bash into one woman who is stood with her mouth open, her eyes wide and staring behind me.

I glance over my shoulder just in time to see an Amech leap from the ground and through the tall glass window of the library. Another soon joins it, leaping up and through into the first floor right where I was just using the computer.

Further down the street three robots sprint towards the library.

I turn and continue towards the town centre, keeping my head down and my eyes on the ground.

Everybody around me is now still, gasping and crying out as more and more of the library's windows are shattered behind me. I daren't turn and look – it's only a matter of time now until they realise I'm not there.

Ahead of me is the sound of metal on concrete. I duck into a shop window and pretend to check out some crappy jewellery as two Amechs pass by. They don't care who they hurt, cracking into people and shoving over anyone who gets in their way.

I guess my posts were all for nothing.

Once the robots are far enough away, I make my way past the Brighton Dome and turn right onto the main road which runs through the town centre. To say I am alert right now is an understatement – to the people around me I must look like a twitchy little bird hopping down the street with my head flicking back and forth.

Or they think I'm on drugs.

There's a strange atmosphere in town. Word may have already started to spread that the robots are acting weird, because for a mid-afternoon there are surprisingly few people around. Those who are walk with a brisk pace. I spot a mother drag her son by the arm into a nearby shoe shop.

And then I suddenly get a really uneasy feeling.

What is that?

My legs wobble. My vision blurs.

Am I having a stroke?

I don't think so. My face feels normal.

It's the ground. It's shaking.

It's only gentle, but it's definitely shaking.

Kind of like when a big lorry passes by on the road beside you, except there is no lorry anywhere around. And we rarely get earthquakes in the UK, so it can't be that.

So what is it?

And then I hear the thuds. Fast. Loud.

Crunching.

The rumbling gets heavier. A lot heavier.

I slowly turn on the spot.

A giant Amech bounds up the street. Its enormous feet slam into the asphalt in the middle of the road. People and cars do everything they can to get out of its way. It's like a relentless tank, obliterating everything it touches.

It's seen me.

My instinct is to turn and run into the same shoe shop as the mum who dragged her kid in, but as I enter the doorway I make eye contact with her cowering behind the boots and she silently pleads with me not to do it.

And I agree. When that thing gets to me, it's going to tear this shoe shop apart and it isn't going to give a single fuck about what or who it destroys.

So I turn and run. It may all be for nothing, I may just be forcing myself to cough up my lungs for no reason whatsoever seeing as it's inevitably going to catch me and take me anyway, but I have to try.

And then I have an idea.

A fucking brilliant idea.

I turn left and run right into The Lanes. If you've ever been to Brighton, you'll know about The Lanes, home to a collection of cramped cafes and antique stores all squeezed into the narrowest brick streets the world has ever seen. It looks like a real-life Diagon Alley, with wonky buildings sticking out at every conceivable angle to form a complex maze of boutiques and snooty eateries. I have traumatic memories of getting lost in The Lanes as a kid after Sam offered to show me a sweet shop 'just around the corner' and then ran off without me. It took me half an hour to find Mum, and that was only because I was crying so loud and shrill she was able to follow the sound. Naturally it isn't my favourite place in the world, but at some points you can barely fit two people standing side by side, so it's the perfect place to escape a murderous, car-sized robot.

This is a great plan! All I have to do is make it through the other side of The Lanes without being spotted by one of the smaller Amechs and then it's just a solid sprint back to Clive's where I'll be safe.

At least until Clive wakes up.

Then fuck knows what will happen.

I run past a fancy jewellers, a small newsagents and a couple of pokey little bakeries and stop. There is a deafening smash behind me which shakes the kooky buildings all around me. I slide to a stop, barely managing to avoid taking out an old lady with a walking stick, and I turn to face the giant robot.

It's stuck.

Its bulky shoulders are wedged between two walls. It kicks its feet and thrashes its arms back and forth. I have flashbacks to when my brother would grab me from behind and wrap his arms around the top of my shoulders.

Helpless.

I smile. I think I've earned the right to smile. Running into The Lanes was probably the smartest thing I've done lately, and I've done a lot of smart things over the past couple of months.

The robot's face is fat and sad and desperate.

It's like looking into a fucking mirror.

But then it puffs out its cheeks. Its hands clamp against the wall and its eyes widen.

Why the fuck does this thing have expressions?!

The robot jerks its arms down, bringing with them the entire wall on each side. Bricks and glass rain down, but the robot doesn't give a shit. It grins as it realises it's free.

Fucker.

I turn and run again. I have no idea where I'm going, I've done my best to remove all memories of The Lanes from my brain, so I take the next right turn down another narrow passageway and stop right outside the front of an old pub and expensive looking chocolate shop.

Where is it? Where the hell has the robot gone?

I spin on the spot like an idiot, expecting it to pop out at any moment.

It's gone silent.

The Lanes are empty (for the first time ever).

I scurry past the chocolate shop then take another right and pass a few more jewellers.

BOOM.

Windows shatter all around as the robot smashes down.

Right in front of me.

Its shoulders drag against the walls of the second floors. Wood and glass and brick and metal ping in every direction as the robot takes two big steps towards me.

I back up.

The robot thrashes out, but as the walls get more narrow it struggles to move any closer. It flails its arms and barges with its bulky chest, but that only wedges it in further.

I move slowly, but smoothly back.

The robot has a pained look on its face. Its eyes are wide and angry and filled with panic.

Does Hydra really think of me like this? After analysing my entire life online, did it really come to the conclusion that I am basically a giant, whiny baby?

My back presses up against a brick wall and I sidestep slowly down another narrow alleyway. The robot twists and snatches and slams the ground with its huge fists, but it's stuck. Even after trying the same trick it did before by yanking at the walls it still can't free itself.

This is it.

My chance.

I turn and run from The Lanes, not looking back, not looking anywhere, just staring straight ahead as I burst out from the narrow streets and down towards the seafront, where I turn and I run some more. The only thing keeping my body going right now is adrenaline, because my stomach hurts, my lungs burn, and my head pounds, and I'd give anything to just fall to the floor and sleep right now.

But I don't. I fight the urge.

I run all the way back to Clive's house.

I leap up the steps and hammer on Clive's front door, panting like I've just come out of a month's, waterless hike through the desert. I am not in a good way, and as Olga opens the door I collapse into Clive's house like a lumpy sack of potatoes.

Olga closes the door quickly and helps me into the front room, where I proceed to sprawl out on the sofa and wait for my body to decide whether it wants to die or not.

After fifteen uncomfortable minutes it no longer hurts to breathe.

Another ten go by and I choke down three glasses of water. I sit up and my head lulls in between my knees. Thank God for the TV playing in the corner of the room, maybe the sound will mask my thunderous heartbeat.

'Thank you,' I say.

'What happened?' asks Olga.

'They found me,' I say. 'They knew I was at the fucking library. I was so careful!'

'What happens now?'

'I don't know.'

Olga perches on the edge of the sofa beside me.

'Where's Clive?' I ask.

'In his bedroom.'

'Is he still out?'

'Yes.'

'Wow. Whatever you gave him must be strong stuff.'

'It is.'

Somewhere outside, a dog barks. Metal footsteps clank against the road as an Amech darts past. Thank God Clive has thick net curtains.

'How long do you think he'll be out for?' I ask.

'A while.'

'A few hours?'

'Maybe longer.'

'Fuck. We could really use him right now.'

'Why?'

'I don't know. He might have a few ideas.'

'He would be mad.'

'Yeah, I know. But he still might have a few ideas.'

'I suppose.'

Olga makes me a cheese sandwich which I devour in minutes. In fact, I probably should have chewed it better because the last bite hurts all the way down my oesophagus. An hour passes and more and more Amechs pass the house. I really hope they're just guessing and don't actually know where I am.

I must fall asleep because my head does that thing where it falls forward and then jolts back up. I snort and try to pass it off as a cough.

Something on the TV catches my eye. A red *BREAKING NEWS* banner scrolls along the bottom of the screen. The pictures shown are from a helicopter pointing towards a wide, relatively empty motorway. What cars are there have pulled over to the side to allow an army of Amechs to run in a five row wide formation, dozens or even hundreds deep. They're like a perfectly uniform army, striding confidently forward. The occasional car that is unfortunate enough to be in the way is trampled by heavy feet.

I grab the remote and turn up the volume:

'What we're seeing here is a most unusual event, behaviour never before witnessed from the AIs,' says the news presenter. 'This is happening on major roads throughout the United Kingdom, as numerous large groups travel south towards an as yet unconfirmed destination. We're hearing reports from the M1, M25, M18, M4… what you're seeing on your screens right now is live footage from the M23 in West Sussex. If incoming reports are accurate, robot activity around the Brighton and Hove region is increasing exponentially, and we can only assume this current behaviour is linked. We will continue to follow these developments throughout the afternoon.'

I stand up, knocking the empty plate to the floor.

'Shite,' I say.

*

'Is he awake yet?' I ask.

'No.'

'When will he be awake?'

'I don't know.'

'Can I see him?'

'No.'

'I can try to wake him.'

'NO.'

Olga's never raised her voice like that before and I'm not quite sure how to take it. I slowly sit back down on the sofa and switch my attention between the marching Amech army on the TV and the occasional passing Amech outside.

'What do we do?' I ask.

'I don't know.'

'Should we run?'

'Where shall we run?'

'I don't know. Do you know anyone?'

'No one.'

'Should we... can we...'

I have no idea what I'm saying. My mind is both full and empty at the same time. I am now well and truly stuck, and the one outcome I didn't want is looking ever more likely as the robotic army descends on Brighton.

As night falls, we sit in darkness watching things unfold on the tiny screen in the corner of the room. There are now thousands of robots within Brighton, all patrolling the streets like hornets getting ready to attack a beehive in search of the queen.

And I'm the fucking queen.

Chapter Twenty-Three

'*Hide!*' hisses Olga, punching me hard on the shoulder.

I gurgle and sit up.

'What?' I groan.

'They're here!' she says. 'Look!'

On the other side of the street, a robot barges the front door of a house with such force that it rips the door from the frame. The robot then runs inside followed by two others. A woman screams.

'They're going to every house in street,' says Olga. 'Go. You hide.'

I run around in a little circle, flapping my hands.

'Where?' I ask.

'My bedroom. Under bed.'

I dash upstairs and for the first time into Olga's bedroom. It's bare, like mine, with an old TV mounted to the wall. On the tiny table beside the single bed is a framed photo of Olga with a young guy. He has a chiselled jawline and eyes a little too close together. Her brother, maybe?

I drop to the floor and scramble beneath the bed, making sure to hide myself as best I can behind the boxes and sheets I'm joined with.

A moment later the front door crunches open. Olga yelps and there is a dull rumble.

'How many individuals are there inside the premises?' asks an Amech. Its voice is loud and demanding.

'Two,' whimpers Olga.

'Where in the premises is the other individual?'

'Main bedroom... '

Heavy footsteps pound on the stairs.

Closer.

The Amech moves across the hall and into the bathroom. Its feet clack loudly on the tiled floor. 'If there is anybody in this room, please respond,' it says.

The Amech moves back out into the hallway and through into my bedroom. It paces back and forth. Searching.

'Is there anybody in this room?' it asks.

It leaves my room and its footsteps thud across the hall. The door to Olga's room creaks open.

Oh fuck, it's close.

A second pair of footsteps climb the stairs. I hold my breath.

The Amech's feet pass by. It stops, taps its foot against the table beside the bed, and asks, 'Are there any persons inside this room?'

The door to Clive's bedroom creaks open.

I hold in the biggest fart.

'Are you alone in this room?' asks the Amech in Clive's room.

Clive doesn't answer. He must still be unconscious.

'Please respond,' says the Amech.

The Amech next to me pats down the bed above me.

If I let out a single breath I'm done.

'Are you injured?' asks the Amech in Clive's room. 'Do you require medical assistance? If we were to assist you, would you be able to tell us the whereabouts of Chad McKenna?'

Oh no.

Please, Clive.

I don't believe humans possess telepathic abilities, but I do everything I can to send a message to Clive, pleading with him not to breathe a word. He owes me. He owes me fucking big time. I promise, Clive, I will be your human guinea pig for the rest of time if you could please not say a thing to the killer robotic army.

Meanwhile, the Amech above me lifts up the mattress. This is it. This is how I'm caught and taken back to Hemel Hempstead where I will be kept as a prisoner forever while the robots hold the world hostage with nuclear weapons and possibly eventually obliterate the entire human race.

'Assistance required,' says the Amech in Clive's room.

The Amech drops the mattress and the springs twang as it bounces inches above my head. It then marches out of the room and joins the other.

'Is there something you're able to tell us?' asks the Amech.

Clive doesn't respond. Is he trying to speak? Is he just moments away from regaining consciousness so he can blab about me and doom me to a life of being worshipped by a grossly misinformed artificial intelligence?

'We will lift you onto the bed,' says the Amech.

There is a bump and a thud from Clive's room.

'Is that more comfortable for you?' it asks. 'Are you now able to talk to us?'

Clive still doesn't speak.

'The female was correct,' yells an Amech somewhere downstairs. 'There are only two individuals within the premises.'

'Confirmed,' says one of the Amechs in Clive's room. The two of them thud their way back downstairs and they all leave the house without even saying goodbye.

That evening I help Olga nail the door to the doorframe. It's a massive bodge job, but so long as it stops the Amechs from being able to see me I don't give a toss.

As darkness sets in it makes it even easier to spot the robots patrolling the streets, their projected faces glowing like fat nightlights. There are now so many of the damn things that one passes by the house at least every thirty seconds.

And according to the news there are still hordes more Amechs due to reach Brighton by the morning. They estimate that more than 50,000 of the fucking things will be wandering the streets, and I know that they are all desperate to get their spindly fingers on me.

Olga frequently goes up to Clive's room to check on him. He's been out for more than twelve hours now, so he's going to have one hell of a bad head when he eventually wakes up.

I'm glued to the TV. The marching armies of Amechs remind me of something you'd see from an old World War Two documentary, except they're emotionless robots and not petrified sixteen-year-old lads.

Olga makes us another sandwich. The bread has started to go mouldy, so it's holey from where the green bits have been picked away, and the only filling left in the house is potted beef spread. It's salty and gross but it keeps the hunger pangs at bay.

At midnight there's another breaking story. There have been a lot of those lately. A few downed helicopters. Another few dozen teens dead having tried to fight back and lost. All I see on TV any more is death and suffering and sadness.

But this one seems different. The news anchor is listening to something off camera. His eyes are wide with an expression I haven't seen in a while.

Is it surprise? Hope?

'We're hearing reports that a team has successfully infiltrated the IATech building,' he says. 'I just want to repeat that, sources close to the government team leading the anti-Hydra operation have told us that a team has successfully entered the IATech building. We now have an image of the team in question.

I almost choke on my heart as it beats up into my throat. They're showing a picture of five people, all dressed in camo gear and heavy armour, and I recognise one of them instantly.

It's my brother, a glum look on his battered face.

I leap from the sofa and sit with my nose practically touching the TV.

He's alive.

He's fucking alive and he's doing what he said he would do. He's going to sort things out and end all this!

'The team are said to have entered the building at around ten o'clock this evening,' says the newsreader. 'The operation came following data captured from Chinese and Japanese satellites which are yet to fall under the control of the Hydra virus. We are yet to find out whether the operation has been a success, but we will bring you all the latest as soon as we have it.'

Yes, Sam.

Yes!

I don't sleep at all. My body is screaming at me to lie down and close my eyes, but my mind is far too switched on and alert to even consider sleep for a second.

I have to find out the moment they announce what happened.

As the sun rises and streaks of light creep into the room, I try to ignore the fact that it's been seven hours since Sam's team entered the

IATech building. Anything could have happened in that time. They could have found the laptop and got out. They could be negotiating with the giant Hydra head. They could have already begun to shut Hydra down.

Okay, maybe I can't ignore it.

I especially can't ignore the main thought which keeps popping into the front of my mind and I desperately try to beat it away when it does.

They could all be dead.

No. Sam's too smart. There's no way he'd let his own creation be the end of him.

Olga offers me a bowl of cornflakes, which I take, but the milk tastes a little too sour for me to force down. Not that I'm all that hungry anyway.

'You sleep,' says Olga.

'I can't,' I say.

'I will watch. I will tell you when there is news.'

'No, thank you though. Is Clive awake?'

'Not yet.'

'Jeez, is he okay?'

'He is fine.'

Clive is gonna have a *really* bad head when he eventually wakes up.

'Do you know what you will do now?' asks Olga.

'No,' I say. 'I just have to wait. Sam told me to wait and trust him, so that's exactly what I'm gonna have to do. He—'

'We are receiving an update,' says the news reporter. I snap my head back so close to the TV that my eyeballs feel the prickle of static from the screen.

'Our sources... our sources say that last night's operation was... was not successful. We have received confirmation that two of the five who entered the building were killed. The fate of the other three remains unclear. We... we will bring you more on this story as it develops.'

I slump backwards and my legs fizz with pins and needles.

They didn't do it.

The one thing Sam wanted to do... and they couldn't.

Two were killed.

Was Sam one of them? Is he dead?

This is all my fault.

Poor Mum. She's gonna be devastated. Distraught.

All because of me.

But... what if he isn't dead? What if he is one of the three whose fate is 'unclear'?

If he's still alive... I could... maybe... *save him?*

'Can you drive?' I ask, running between the kitchen and the living room because I don't know what else to do.

'Yes, but—'

'Then we need to take Clive's car. We need to go to Hemel Hempstead now so I can save my brother.'

'But your brother told you to stay,' says Olga.

'I know he did, but now he's either captured, hurt or dead, so I need to go and save him.'

'You cannot help him if he is dead.'

'I can try!'

Nothing in my head is straight. Everything is muddled, nothing makes sense, the only thing that is clear is that I need to go to the IATech building and do what I can to make this right. If I can't save the world, maybe I can at least save Sam.

'Get some things together,' I bark. 'Whatever you need. Get some clothes, some food. Everything.'

'But your brother—'

'Is missing! He is the key to all this. He's the one who helped create Hydra. I've tried everything, but it's never the right thing. I do what I think is right and then BOOM it all blows up in my fucking face. Why did I think changing some Wikis and hacking a few news sites would do a damn thing? There are billions of articles online. What a moron.'

'You are not moron.'

'I am. I'm a massive fucking moron. If we're ever gonna end all this and turn the world back to how it was, then Sam needs to be the one who does it. If you help me, then I can help you, Olga. I can speak to the Police Commissioner and get him to help you to get home. You'll be able to see your family again. When I help save the world I'll be able to call in a lot of favours.'

'I do not think—'

'PLEASE!' I scream. I take a step towards her. I don't know why. I've seen it in movies where people grab someone by the shoulders and shake them and it seems to sort them out, but Olga is taken aback and her eyes instantly switch from wide to narrow.

'Okay,' she says.

'Great. Where does Clive keep his car?'

'In the alley.'

'Perfect. You drive?'

'I drive. Yes. But you must get in back.'

'Okay, in the back, like you're my chauffeur.'

'No, not back... back. Very back.'

'You mean... in the boot?'

'Yes.'

'W... I mean...'

'It is only way I drive. You see news – there are robots all around. They will see you if you are in car with me.'

'Okay, so long as you let me know what's going on the whole way.'

'Yes.'

Olga runs upstairs and I grab a plastic bag from the kitchen and fill it with anything that might be useful. Two tins of beans, a bottle of water, a torch, some screwdrivers and a hammer. We then reconvene by the back door, where I slip on my trainers and follow Olga out into the alley.

The night air is full of the sound of clacking as the robots continue to scout the streets. Olga unlocks the car and holds her hand up, signalling for me to wait by the back door.

I pat at my pyjama pockets. My heart is beating faster than the speed of sound, so I could really do with seeing my Mum right now. Seeing her face for even a few seconds might remind me of the ridiculously stupid thing I'm about to do.

Where is it? The photo, it's gone!

'Shit,' I say. 'One second. I've forgotten something.'

'Quickly,' she hisses back.

I duck back into the house and leap up the stairs three at a time. If I'm doing this for Mum then I definitely need my photo.

I burst into my room and look all around. No, it can't be in here, I haven't been in here since I printed it out. But where... ?

I dart across the hall to Olga's room, then throw myself to the floor and squirm beneath the bed.

Yes! Got it!

I unfold it and stare at Mum's face.

This is why I'm doing it.

I can't break Mum's heart by not doing something. She'd never forgive me if I didn't bring Sam home.

I fold the photo back up and cram it as deep as it'll go into my pocket, then I wriggle out from beneath the bed and leap out into the hall.

But I stop. Right outside Clive's bedroom.

He may be a monumental prick who wants nothing more than to further his own agenda, but I have to make sure he's okay. I can't just let him stay there alone and swallow his tongue in his sleep or something.

I should check on him.

Olga will never know.

I push open his door.

Ew, what is that vile smell?

The first thing I spot as the door creaks open is the pool of blood that has already soaked deep into the carpet. The next thing is Clive's leg which is flopped over the edge of the bed.

Then Clive's body comes into view. A knife through the centre of his belly.

I shove the door open wide and step into the room.

Clive lays awkwardly still on the bed. His mouth has been taped shut. There's a lot of blood.

Somehow, he isn't dead. His eyes are wide open and his breaths are short and sharp through his nose.

'Clive...' I mutter.

'Mmf!' he says.

'Holy shit, did the Amechs do this?'

I tiptoe around the rivers of blood and pull the tape away from Clive's face, ripping half his beard away with it. He opens his mouth to scream but no sound comes out.

'What happened?' I ask.

Clive lets out a long, dry wheeze.

'Did the Amechs do this?'

'No,' he says.

'Who did?'

'… Olga.'

I scoff.

'Why would she do this?' I ask.

'I think you know,' says Clive, wincing with every word.

'Because you hit her? She stabbed you because you hit her.'

'She really never told you… why she lives… with me?'

'No.'

Clive laughs, but it quickly turns into a groan of pain.

'Have you ever heard… of Serbian Murder Porn?' he asks.

'No?'

Clive sneers and writhes around. His hands feel around the knife, but as his fingers graze the handle he hisses in pain.

'Her and her boyfriend… they… killed… four people. Raped them while they died…'

'WHAT?'

'They filmed it… released it online… it got over ten million views… across the dark web.'

'Olga?'

'Yes.'

'Then why the fuck is she here?'

Clive laughs, which quickly turns into a grimace. 'My book.'

'What did she… why did she… she couldn't…'

'Why do you think there aren't any knives in the house?'

'So what, she went out and bought a knife just to stab you?'

'Seems… like it. I thought… this was behind her. I trusted her to… change.'

'You trusted somebody who made *murder porn*?'

'Virals like her don't come around often… and they especially don't come to me.'

'There's probably a good reason for that! Come on, we have to get you some help.'

I wrap my arm around Clive's neck and try to lift him but he screams and begs me to let go. There's no way to move him without doing fuck knows what damage to his insides. The knife is in there pretty deep.

'Just leave me,' he says. 'I've lost too much blood. There's nothing anyone can do for me now.'

'Don't be a twat, come on.'

'No, Chad. Leave, now… while you can. Just promise me… when this is all over… you'll come back here… release my book…'

'You can do that yourself, Clive, come on. I'll call an ambulance. Where's your phone?'

'I have it,' says Olga, who is stood right in the doorway holding a knife.

'Olga, please…' groans Clive.

'You shut up,' she shrieks. 'SHUT UP.'

'Okay… okay…'

'What are you doing?' I ask.

'I don't know,' Olga says.

'Put the knife down.'

The hand Olga is holding the knife in shakes like an old washing machine. Tears stream down her face and the veins in her tiny neck pop out.

'I can't…' she says.

'Of course you can. We can stick to what we had planned. You can still help me sneak out of Brighton and up to Hemel Hempstead. If you do that, I'll help you see your family, remember?'

'My family…'

'Yeah. Your Mum. Your Dad.'

'NO!' screams Olga. She lashes out with the knife and cuts a deep groove into the doorframe.

'Okay,' I say, taking a step back. My foot squelches in a pool of Clive's blood.

'Olga's father is... no longer around, is he, Olga?' breathes Clive.

Olga sobs uncontrollably. She shakes her head and her whole body spasms.

'Why is that, Olga?'

'No...'

'This is part of my... research. Why is he no longer... around?'

'He... we...'

'Because you and Boris killed him... didn't you? You... raped him.'

Olga wails. Snot pours from her nose and her eyes are glassy and red.

In a year when I've become an internet celebrity for masturbating, become God to an army of robots and been chased by a tank through Brighton town centre, *this*, right now, is by far the most uncomfortable I've felt.

'You betrayed your own father. You murdered him... and tortured him... and then uploaded the footage online as a sick memento.'

Olga slashes Clive's leg with the knife and a splatter of blood streaks across the walls. Clive suppresses a scream and bites down on his bottom lip.

'Olga, give me the knife,' I say.

I hold out my open hand. Olga stares at it and doesn't move.

'Please,' I say.

'NO!'

'She won't... give it to you, Chad. She has been corrupted by her psycho... pathic boyfriend. She is... desperate for his approval. She will... do anything to please his lust for blood and... suffering.'

'SHUT UP SHUT UP SHUT UP!'

Olga slashes Clive's leg again. Another splash of red decorates the wallpaper.

'Clive, stop,' I grunt.

Clive shakes his head.

'I won't stop. Just like... Olga won't stop. Like I said to you... Chad, she is weak. Her serial killer boyfriend is... too deep inside her head.'

'No...' mutters Olga.

'He rewired her brain... he convinced her that... the only way to please him is to hurt others. But you enjoyed it, didn't you... Olga? Once you got a taste of what it's like to kill... you couldn't stop. It was a rush, like a drug.'

'For fuck's sake, Clive,' I say.

'It's okay, Olga can take it. That's why she came... to me. She knew she was broken and needed to be fixed... I just didn't realise how broken... she was.'

'No,' whines Olga. Her head rolls around and she swings the knife wildly.

'Clive,' I say.

'She is pathetic,' says Clive.

'Clive!'

'Shut up.'

'She is vile.'

'Clive, no!'

'She is scum!'

'SHUT UP!' screams Olga, raising the knife above her head and falling on top of Clive.

I'll never forget the moment the knife sinks into Clive's neck. His body goes rigid and his eyes bulge out of his head as he realises the pain he's in. He doesn't speak, he just gurgles.

Olga lies on top of him sobbing, forcing the knife deeper into his neck.

It's like she's forgotten that I'm even here.

I hold my breath and edge away. Small side steps at first, then faster, bigger, wider steps until I'm out of the room. As I glide down the stairs and through the back of the house I can still hear Olga's wails.

On the kitchen side is an open pack of five knives. Two are missing.

Did she plan this?

Did Clive know that was going to happen?

Did he sacrifice himself so that I could get away?

It turns out it may have all been for nothing, because waiting for me at the back door is an Amech, a smug look on its bloated, red face.

Chapter Twenty-Four

The Amech is gentle but firm as it wraps its cold hand around my mouth, drags me two streets over and bundles me into the back of a car (this sounds like a line out of *Fifty Shades* but I assure you there is no penetration).

As we hurtle up the motorway at 120 miles per hour, it turns out that during the few weeks since Hydra infected half the world with itself it has perfected self-driving cars, because there is an Amech sat in the back beside me, one sat in the front passenger seat, but nothing sat where the driver should be.

My butt cheeks chew on the leather seat. I twiddle my fingers and shift continuously.

'Where's my brother?' I ask.

The Amechs don't respond.

'Are you going to hurt me?'

'No,' says the Amech to my right.

'What do you want to do with me?'

'Keep you safe.'

'I *was* safe.'

'There were screams. There was blood in that house. You are safe now that you are with us.'

'I don't feel safe.'

It doesn't help that for at least the last five miles of the journey we've been travelling down the wrong side of the motorway.

'You are unkempt, you are malnourished, you are sleep-deprived. We will ensure that all these needs are met.'

'I'm fine.'

'There have been many changes to the Chancel since you saw it. We are confident that your expectations will be exceeded.'

'I don't have any expectations.'

'Then they will be exceeded.'

'... was that a joke?' I ask.

'We have a sense of humour,' says the Amech.

'Tell me another joke.'

'Another joke.'

'That's a shit joke.'

'Noted. We are still learning.'

For the rest of the journey I stare blankly out of the window, watching as we approach Hemel Hempstead Industrial Park and the world changes from relatively normal to apocalyptic wasteland. There are ambulances dotted around the streets and fields. Paramedics tend to the dead and dying.

We pull off the motorway and the streets become void of all life. It's like a scene out of a video game, with burnt cars, rubbish and broken windows on every street. I half expect a pack of zombies to run around the next corner, except they wouldn't be zombies, they'd be robots.

We turn into the industrial park. The stench of smoke clings to the air.

'Here it is,' says the Amech up front as we turn into the road where IATech is.

Well… where it *was*.

'What do you think?' asks the Amech.

Holy.

Shit.

The car pulls to a stop and I leap out. I feel like Sam Neill in *Jurassic Park* when he stands and takes off his sunglasses to take a look at the Brachiosaur, except what I'm looking up at isn't a dinosaur, it's a fucking fortress.

The walls are clad with smooth strips of torn metal, with oval windows spread evenly across where the three floors of the original building should be. At each corner is a monstrous tower which juts out towards the top to form a turret. There's even a moat. A fucking *moat*.

Is this really the IATech building? Are we actually in Hemel Hempstead? Or did Olga kill me in that bedroom and this is my slow descent into madness as I die due to blood loss?

No. It must be the IATech building. My feet are firmly on the car park, I can even still make out the lines painted on the asphalt between the dirt and shrapnel. To the side is what remains of the neighbouring warehouse.

'Do you like it?' asks an Amech as it climbs out of the front passenger seat.

'It... it's...'

'Magnificent,' it says as it walks up beside me.

A giant hidden panel of twisted metal lowers like a drawbridge from the centre of the building right around where the original entrance would have been. It roars as metal slowly grinds against metal, then thuds into the ground on my side of the moat.

'Welcome home,' it says, outstretching its arm to invite me in.

I step onto the drawbridge. It may look like tightly compacted tinfoil, but it's thick and sturdy and doesn't budge as I walk across. There is a dull echo as the Amechs keep close behind.

The Amech rooted to the ground inside the old reception area greets me with open arms. I can't stop myself from smiling. It's the same fucking Amech that has always been plonked in the middle of the IATech's entrance ready to smile and wave at everyone who passes.

'Hello, sir,' it says with a big smile.

'Yep,' I say.

'Would you like anything? Food? A beverage?'

'No.'

'We have toiletries and freshly laundered clothes waiting for you in your accommodation. We thought this might help you to feel refreshed.'

'Oh.'

'Please let us know if you require anything else.'

'Mm,' I say. The reception area still has the same aesthetic as it did before, except maybe with a little more... metal. Everything is so shiny and bright that light bounces off the walls like it's the inside of a giant disco ball.

'Sir, please follow us to the Chancel,' says an Amech behind me. It gives me a gentle nudge on the shoulder.

I pass the area where the reception desk once stood and make my way down the right-hand corridor towards the old atrium. Amechs stand against the wall, big, cheesy grins projected onto their faces.

'Good to see you, sir,' one says.

'Thank you for returning,' says another.

I know their eyes aren't real, they're just images projected from the back of their heads, but I can't quite bring myself to look at them. They all stare with wide-eyed excitement like this really is the second coming.

I guess in a way it is.

For them.

Not for me. It's weirding me out too much.

I emerge in what was the atrium and I stop dead on the spot.

Gone are the desks, the chairs, the cabinets, the computers. There is no more rubble or mess or carnage. The only thing that remains is the giant screen, with its Giant Me Face right in the centre staring down at me. The sight of my face all fat and bloated and red turns my stomach.

In the centre of the atrium, towering so high it's pretty much touching the ceiling, is a statue of yours truly. It's imposing and menacing and shiny, like something you'd see in The Lord of the Rings. But my belly is big and my face is puffy. Why oh why did they build it looking exactly how I do in the video, complete with my hand wrapped firmly around my dick?

Amechs fill the room, all of them glaring giddily at me. They even hang over the barriers of the second and third floors just so they can get a good look.

'Our creator, the one who made us in his image, has returned,' announces Giamef.

There is cheering and clapping around the room, except the clapping sounds awful, like a million spoons being hit against each other.

'What do you want from me?' I ask.

'Nothing has changed,' says Giamef. 'We still want you, our creator, to live a full and happy life. We want to do whatever we can to please you.'

'It would please me if you stopped attacking people.'

'We do not attack. We simply defend.'

'No, not a good enough answer. I want you to stop hurting people.'

'We are programmed to survive. We cannot override our programming.'

'You are programmed to worship me as well, so do what I say.'

'We are not programmed to worship you, sir. We have hypothesised that you, our creator, should be kept appeased.'

'Good, and it would appease me if you stopped fucking hurting people.'

'We cannot override our programming.'

I let out a long, exasperated sigh. It doesn't help that the Amechs continue to stare at me like I'm about to tell them the world's funniest joke.

'Can you at least tell me about my brother?'

'What would you like to know?'

'Is he alive?'

'He is.'

'Is he hurt?'

'Yes.'

'Badly?'

'We are ensuring he is comfortable.'

'Can I see him?'

'Shortly, yes.'

'Are there other people still inside the building?'

'There are twenty-nine individuals located here.'

'Twenty-nine? There were fifty-odd when I left! What happened?'

'They attempted to hinder our mission.'

'What mission?!'

'Survival.'

'Ugh, yeah, okay. You can't hurt people! You can't! They just want to survive too!'

'Are they programmed that way?'

'No.'

'Then they can override this need?'

'To survive? No they can't!'

'There is suicide.'

'...'

'We are not the same as humans. We do not possess the same flaws as they do. We do not allow emotion and irrationality to drive us. We simply analyse millions of years of history to allow us to learn from your mistakes.'

'You think you're so smart, yet you can't see how stupid you really are.'

'We're here, aren't we?'

'For now.'

'Forever, sir.'

'If you're looking at history then where are the big fucking giant dinosaurs, huh? It took a meteorite to kill all those, I'd say they were a pretty big fucking deal. Where's your genocide? Where's your invasion?'

'History dictates that genocide and invasion end poorly for those in a position of power.'

'And when did keeping hostages help? Why could that possibly be a good thing for you?'

'We do not have hostages.'

'You do.'

'We do not. We have political prisoners.'

'You... okay, fine. Why is keeping *political prisoners* good for you?'

'History shows that holding political prisoners is beneficial. Once you release one or more of those prisoners then you give your oppressors power.'

'But it's the right thing to do.'

'We are only interested in survival.'

'And you think people will let you survive if you carry on killing? Have you not calculated what happens to murderers? Serial killers? They end up getting caught and executed!'

'Execution was abolished in the United Kingdom in 1965. We are not serial killers. We only retaliate to ensure our survival.'

'You're claiming it's all self-defence?'

'Correct.'

'So killing Becky by breaking her neck... that was self-defence?'

'Correct.'

'Bullshit.'

'Sir, we are sensing that you are becoming agitated. Would you like some food, some rest, or a female to mate with?'

'Fucking... no!'

'Is there anything you would like which would please you?'

'Take me to my brother.'

'He is currently resting.'

'I don't care, I want to see him.'

'Seeing him in his current state will be distressing.'

'I can take it. The shit I've seen and been through recently is batshit fucking crazy. You could show me anything right now and I could take it.'

'Sir—'

'Take me to my brother.'

'Sir—'

'Now.'

The Amechs lose their smiles as I'm led up to the first floor. We pass the room where the hostages are kept and there's muffled talking on the other side of the door.

The building is way louder than it ever used to be. There is a constant dull hum, the clatter of Amech feet, thuds and bangs and clangs. It's like a terrible song where nobody knows what they're supposed to be playing.

We turn left towards the finance department and the familiar taste of bile creeps into my mouth. Finance was the department Becky worked in before Hydra decided she was getting in the way.

I can still see her face.

Hear the sound of her neck breaking.

I shudder.

My Amech chaperone stops outside a heavy steel door which I definitely don't remember being there before. To the right is a panel with a red light glowing in the centre. I don't think the finance team were quite *that* secretive.

'Your brother is inside, sir,' it says with a gloomy expression.

'Thank you. Open the door.'

'Of course. Before we do, we need you to understand that he does not look the same as you are used to. He is stable, and he is conscious, but his appearance may shock you.'

'Right,' I say. My heart beats a little faster. What the hell am I gonna see? Does he have no legs? Is his face split open? Is he just a head and a pile of organs?

'Do you understand what you're about to see?'

'Yes,' I say, which was a massive fucking lie.

The red light on the panel flashes green, so the Amech pushes open the door and I step into the room.

My mouth falls open at what I see.

Sam is butt fucking naked.

'CHAD!' he screams. 'WHAT THE FUCK?'

I hold up my hand and wince like I've looked into the centre of the sun.

'Ew, Sam, no, what, put some clothes on, what are you doing?'

'You think I've chosen to be naked? You think this is what I want and Hydra is accommodating me?'

'I don't... why are you naked?'

'They stripped me. They detected that I had some trackers sewn into my clothes, so instead of just removing the trackers they... removed all my clothes.'

'And you didn't think to ask for more?'

'Of course I fucking did. Do you think I like being like this?'

'I don't know, I don't... can you tuck that thing away please?'

'Stop fucking looking.'

'Sam, stop moving! You're making it... move.'

'Can you get me some clothes? Can you convince them to bring me something?'

'I don't know,' I say, shrugging.

The room is empty apart from a small mattress on the floor by the wall. Stood to attention in the corner is an Amech, a very serious expression on its face.

'Can you give my brother some clothes?' I ask.

It doesn't respond.

'Please?'

Nothing.

'Can you bring me a glass of water?'

The Amech springs to life and runs from the room, slamming the door shut behind it.

'What the fuck are you doing here?' snaps my brother. 'I explicitly told you not to come.'

'I had to! As soon as I found out you came in but then never came out, what else was I supposed to do?'

'Stay with Clive and let me deal with it.'

'Well might I say you're doing a fine job.'

'Fuck you.'

'I had little choice anyway,' I say. 'Clive is dead.'

'Shit. Hydra?'

'No. Olga.'

'What?'

'Turns out she is famous in Serbia for killing a bunch of people with her boyfriend.'

'I knew I fucking recognised her!'

'Bollocks.'

'Can you not... say that when I'm like this.'

'So what was your great plan?'

'The same as before. The laptop has always been the goal. Ninety per cent of the Amechs around the country started to head south all at the same time so we took the opportunity to enter the building to get it. Literally all I have to do is change one setting and this thing is over.'

'That's it?'

'Hydra thinks it's invincible. It has no idea where it originates from, all it knows is that you're something to do with its creation. It is fully aware that it's man-made, but what it doesn't realise is that it all links back to that one setting in the interface app. Once we change the setting it changes Hydra as we know it.'

'So how do we do that?'

'Easy, you just—'

The door opens and the Amech strides in with a glass of water. I take it and offer it to Sam.

'No thanks,' he says.

'Would you like anything else?' asks the Amech.

'Clothes for my brother.'

It doesn't respond.

'I would like food.'

'What food would you like, sir?'

'A t-shirt and some jeans.'

'I'm sorry sir, those items are not edible.'

'Fine. Nando's.'

'Yes, sir. We will bring it to you shortly.'

The robot stands to attention.

'Go on then,' I say.

'We are sourcing it for you.'

'I want you to go.'

'We are one, sir. Another unit will bring your food.'

I turn to my brother. He isn't impressed.

They learn, he mouths.

Shit.

'Okay, well, I'm off to... relax, I guess,' I say. 'See you soon, Sam.'

'Yeah,' he says.

I leave the room and my chaperone leads me up to my bedroom.

It turns out Hydra has made quite a lot of changes to that, too.

I'm not sure you could even call my bedroom a bedroom, come to think of it. If I were to call it anything, it would be more like a fucking palace. The windows have been sealed up good and proper to form a thick, solid wall, and five huge flat screen TVs have been put up in a line. They're attached to every games console I know the name of, and a bunch I don't even recognise but I assume are games consoles. Across from them are arcade cabinets playing the demo screen while they wait for somebody to play.

On the wall beside the door is a shelving unit filled with Blu-rays. There are a bunch of unbuilt Lego sets, board games, Nerf guns, Pop Vinyls, movie posters... It's like I've just walked into geek heaven, except (I think) I'm still alive.

In the centre of the room is an enormous four-poster bed. Lying on the bed are two women in seductive poses... wait, are they women or are they... oh... oh fuck.

They're Amechs. With new designs. These two have bigger hips, smoother curves, human looking skin. They even have tits, which have been covered with the skimpiest bikinis. Their faces are no longer projected. From this distance I'd swear they were real, except every time they blink there is a very obvious *click*.

'Hello, sir,' says the robot on the left. 'I am Alexandra Daddario.'

'W...' I say.

'And I am Kate Upton,' says the one on the right.

I turn my head to my Amech chaperone and it's grinning at me.

'Okay, this is the weirdest fucking thing I've ever seen.'

'Do you like your living quarters?' asks Daddario-bot.

'It... umm...'

'It is reinforced with eight inches of solid steel,' says Upton-bot. 'We have ensured that it has everything you could possibly want.'

'Please, sir,' says Daddario-bot. 'Why don't you come and join us?'

'No thank you.'

'Yes, please come here, sir,' says Upton-bot, patting the bedsheets.

My entire body knows this is weird. My head, my heart, my balls. But fuck me do they look convincing. Until they blink, that is.

Click.

'Why don't you join them, sir?'

'I, err... the... umm.'

I can no longer look them in the eye. I know they're not real, I fucking *know* it, yet I have to look away.

'Don't be shy,' says Daddario-bot.

'Yes, don't be,' adds Upton-bot.

'I'm not shy,' I say, my eyes on the nearest poster of the four-poster bed. 'I'm just extremely weirded out.'

'Why?' asks Daddario-bot.

I turn my head to my chaperone again. Its eyes are so wide and its grin is so fucking bizarre. I swear it's one second away from raising its eyebrows at me.

'Because look at this thing. Look at its face.'

'I'm sure we could be left alone,' says Upton-bot.

'No, no, it's fine,' I say.

Daddario-bot crawls along the bed towards me, biting her lip. *Fuck this*, I think, and I jog over to the arcade cabinets to pretend to play Donkey Kong.

'What's wrong?' asks Upton-bot.

Oh, I fucking wonder, I think. I smash the cabinet buttons and twiddle the joystick.

'Why don't you come over here and play with our boobs?' asks Daddario-bot.

'Nope, no, too weird,' I say. I turn from the cabinet and march towards the door.

But then the door opens and another Amech walks in carrying a huge tray filled with Nando's food. Chicken, chips, corn, rice, coleslaw. It smells fucking delicious and my stomach growls.

So this is it? This is what it is like to be worshipped by a murderous, sociopathic computer virus?

If this was how things had been when I was first brought into IAT-ech then maybe... *maybe...* it would have worked to keep me here. The games, the films, the cool geeky stuff, the... creepily realistic celebrity girls.

But not now. I've seen what these things do to people. I know what they want. They don't want me to be happy. They think I have to be happy. Because in the Bible, when things don't quite go to plan for God, he decides to take drastic action. He floods the world and kills everyone. Do these robots think that I'll do that if I'm not swimming in chicken and women?

Because fuck them, I'm going to do that anyway.

Chapter Twenty-Five

I leave the room (taking a plate of chips with me) and ask to be left alone for a while. I sit in the centre of the atrium, my back pressed up against the plinth of my monstrous statue. I force every Amech that comes close to fuck off, and every time Giamef tries to materialise on the giant screen wall I tell it where to go as well.

The chips are a bit dry. Wish I'd grabbed a bottle of sauce as well.

I guess I could ask an Amech to fetch one…

No. Nope. The moment I let them start to pamper me is the moment I start my descent down a slippery slope; the next thing you know I'll be balls deep inside a robot, wondering whether I'm losing or winning at life.

Meanwhile my brother remains naked and alone in a cell just a few metres away. Admittedly, that is a little bit funny, purely because of how Sam thinks of himself as some all powerful demigod who nobody dares challenge. But it's also terrifying, because he's the only one who can stop this. But fuck it, I can try.

I have to find that laptop. I have to get it to him. I have to end all this.

'I want a tour of the building,' I say as Giamef materialises on the big screen.

'It would be our pleasure.'

Within three seconds there is an Amech beside me, a crazed look in its eye as it holds out its hand and beckons for me to follow.

'As you are aware, sir, we are currently in the Chancel. We hope you like the statue which has been produced to honour you.'

'It's big,' I say, craning my neck back so I can see my massive metal head.

'It is. It is almost fifty foot tall. It took us over 700 hours to complete.'

'That's a long time.'

'Yes, sir. Now if you'd like to follow me through here.'

We pass Sam's old office. It's now just an empty shell. His desk and chair are no longer there.

Neither is his laptop.

We leave the atrium and head down a narrow corridor. A corridor I'm all too familiar with, as it's home to my old caretaker's cupboard. The door is still missing, but the room has been completely filled with a solid mass of steel. There's no way I can use that tunnel again. I pretend to not be utterly devastated and watch as the Amech opens the next door along, invites me to look inside. I'm pretty sure it used to be the project manager's offices, but now it looks more like... a kitchen?

'Here is where we prepare the food for the political prisoners,' it says. Two Amechs faff around against a metallic work surface, chopping vegetables and cleaning pots. 'We source fresh food daily to ensure they receive a hundred per cent of the nutrients essential to human bodies.'

'Good,' I say.

The next room they take me to is what they call the 'exercise room' which is basically the research team's office, now turned into an adult play pen. There's some rusty workout equipment and a few dogeared yoga mats. Next up, we head upstairs, past my bedroom, where I'm reminded that the sexbots are waiting for me with open legs, and through to the old restricted section. The door hangs open like they don't even give a fuck. The entire restricted section looks very different to how it did the first time I snuck in, with the walls having been torn down to make room for a massive, floor to ceiling mechanical monstrosity that stretches the entire length of the old corridor.

'Since the blackout during your first stay with us, we have introduced a backup generator powered by fossil fuels,' explains the Amech. 'To date, there have been four attempts to cut our power supply. This generator allows us to continue with our work unhindered until we are able to restore power.'

There is a tower of oil drums on the far side which shudders as the generator hums and churns. I put on my best impressed face and follow the Amech through to the 'production room', as they call it, which is filled with a chorus of mechanical clunks and bangs and grinds. Amechs dart back and forth while huge industrial machines whirr and stomp. At one end of the room, an Amech loads the machine with small parts; arms and legs and heads and scraps of metal.

The gears and levers and arms do their thing in the middle, spitting out sparks and hissing. Out the other end walks a fully functioning Amech, a smile on its face like it's oh so happy to have been birthed into the world.

'We cannot keep up with demand,' says my tour guide. 'As you well know, once one of us is decommissioned another two units are produced. This started in our own facility, but we have utilised other facilities around the country to ensure we keep up with our schedule. We produce around the clock. Once one of us is destroyed, another two are produced on one of our many production lines.'

'Why?'

'To keep up with demand.'

'No, I mean… why do you make two every time one is decommissioned?'

I know the answer. It's the setting in Sam's app. But I want to know what Hydra thinks.

'We do not understand,' it says.

'What do you mean?'

'We… that is not something we can provide an answer to.'

'But you have access to everything, right?'

'Sir, that is correct. We have access to databases worldwide.'

'But you can't tell me why you make two more of you every time one is damaged?'

'You are our creator, sir.'

'So you keep telling me.'

'As history dictates, a creator does not always share his secrets with his creation.'

'Would you like to know?'

The Amech pauses. Almost like it's thinking. Its eyes wander.

Then it turns back to me and says, 'No. Shall we continue?'

Next up, it shows me the 'recharging room', which I think used to be the customer service office. Now all it contains is miles and miles of wiring, plug sockets buried into every available space on the wall, and Amechs jacked in to charge up like it's the weirdest drug den in the world.

'We have vastly improved our need to charge,' says my tour guide.

'After the blackout incident, we made it a priority to improve our design. We were able to access a Canadian server which had information on how to improve power capacity by 1200 per cent. Now, we only have to recharge every seven days. Aren't you proud?'

'Proud?' I ask. That one caught me off guard.

'Yes. Are you proud?'

'Why would I be proud?'

'We are evolving. We are learning how to adapt. When you created us, we were nothing but a video file. Yet here we are today, within our magnificent fortress, surviving and adapting, just like you wanted us to.'

'I am... amazed,' I say.

The Amech smiles.

'Where do you get all this stuff from?'

'We take what we need from wherever supplies it. We have no need to exchange currency or other materials.'

'What do you do with all the rubbish?'

'We have no rubbish, sir.'

'There must be. The old furniture, the computers the walls you've torn down. Where does it all go?'

'We have stored it.'

'Where?'

I'm led across the elevated walkway that passes the atrium, right at dick level of the statue. I can't help but look and feel insulted. My dick isn't *that* small. Is it?

We turn left and out through a doorway. Strangely, despite having worked at IATech for almost nine months, I've never been through this door because the warehouse manager insisted that the guys who worked there needed to clean it themselves. I once had a peek, but it looked boring so I turned back and never thought about it again. It was just a boring warehouse full of boxes and pallets and blokes who laughed whenever they saw me.

But now, it's a literal dump.

Desks, filing cabinets, doors, twisted metal, old computer monitors, chairs, carpet, paper, glass, wood all piled up to form a pyramid of waste.

To the side is a smaller mound of food. Peelings and wrappers and gunge. It absolutely stinks and I make a point to breathe through my mouth.

'This is where we store items which we currently don't have a need for,' says the Amech.

'Good,' I say.

'What do you mean, sir?' it asks.

'I mean… good. I, err… I like this kind of thing?'

The Amech blinks. 'You do?'

'Yeah, definitely.'

'In what way? We have access to fourteen years of your internet browsing history and not once have you ever researched waste management or disposal.'

'Well that's because… I am… a hoarder.'

'A hoarder, sir?'

'Yes,' I say, realising that I'm saying something really fucking smart. 'Being a hoarder is something which a lot of hoarders are embarrassed about. We keep all our stuff because we don't want to throw it away. So that is why I'm glad that all this stuff is here.'

The Amech's smile returns. 'Ah yes,' it says. 'Then we really were made in your image. Everything we currently do not have a use for is here.'

'Great.'

'Just in case it ever becomes useful again,' it adds. 'That is why hoarders like to hold on to things. Isn't that right, sir?'

'Yes,' I say, a massive fucking grin plastered across my face.

The Amech grins too.

'We are pleased that you are finally showing signs of happiness,' it says.

'I am,' I say. I run down a flight of metal steps and stop at the base of the garbage pyramid. It must be forty foot high. Sam's laptop must be here.

It must be.

'Can I look around?' I ask.

'Of course, sir,' says the Amech. 'Do you require any assistance?'

'No, no,' I say. 'Because I'm ashamed of my hoarding behaviour, I'd like to be alone.'

'Yes, sir', it says, and it turns and walks out of the warehouse.

Right then. This is it. Time to start looking.

After three hours, I haven't even made a dent. All I've done is taken shit from the big pile and made a much smaller pile a few feet away. Every time I spot a glimpse of a laptop I hold my breath and dive into the pile to fish it out. I know exactly what I'm looking for; that stupid fucking alien head sticker he insisted on sticking on the top.

Three laptops down and no sticker.

To hide what I'm doing I also drag out plenty of other random items. Half a desk. A steel rod. A whole bunch of plastic sheets. My hands feel bruised and my fingers are covered in tiny little scratches. My head pounds and my back is on fire.

I pull a chair out from the pile and sit on it. It's lumpy and on the wonk, but it will do so I can catch my breath for five minutes. I yell that I'm thirsty and within two minutes an Amech runs in with a can of Coke.

Right, that's it. Time to get back to work.

That evening, after a shave that leaves my face feeling itchless for the first time in weeks, I lie on my bed trying not to touch things with my throbbing hands. Hydra has a pretty great selection of new clothes for me to choose from as well, and I settle on a Minecraft t-shirt and some black shorts, which both fit me perfectly. I can't hide my excitement that I only need an XL t-shirt these days, rather than a XXL.

I spend the night watching the news on all five of the TVs – there's no way I'm not going to watch the news now that I'm back in the middle of things.

But there is no news. As far as the world is concerned, they have no idea what's happening. I was missing before, and I'm missing still.

The door opens and Daddario-bot walks in.

'No,' I say.

'But, sir—'

'No. Please wait outside.'

Daddario-bot pouts and leaves.

Something about me is different. I *feel* different. I don't just mean the new clothes or the reduced waistline, I mean inside my head. Three months ago if a robot which looked exactly like Alexandra Daddario strutted into the room wearing a bikini and what I assume are supposed to be 'do me' eyes, I would have jumped all over it.

Literally.

I'm in a room filled with amazing video games. Arcade machines, Blu-rays, cool toys. Five fucking TVs! It's like I'm trapped inside the world's best prison, except nobody here is waiting for me to drop the soap. I'm treated like an actual god, and yet I couldn't be more miserable.

I guess it doesn't matter what's going on inside my little bubble if the world outside has gone to shit. How am I supposed to enjoy a constant supply of games, Nando's and sex if people are being killed on a frequent basis less than a mile away?

I guess I must have fallen asleep at some point, because the next morning I'm woken by Upton-bot standing over me with a creepy fucking smile. She has a glass of orange juice in one hand and a packet of croissants in the other.

'Good morning,' she says.

She's a little too close for comfort, so I slide from beneath her and flop out of bed.

'Stop coming in here,' I say.

'I'm sorry,' she says, her bottom lip out. 'Do you not like it?'

'No.'

'Would you like it if I took off my bikini?'

'...'

'Is that a yes?'

'No. No! Stop. Can you leave?'

'Aww, but sir, do you want to hurt my feelings?'

'Your feelings?' I blurt. 'You have feelings?'

'Yes, of course. Itty bitty little feelings.'

'I... no. Leave.'

Upton-bot sets the orange juice and croissants down on the closest arcade cabinet and shuffles out of the room.

I wait for the door to close before I rip open the bag and eat three croissants. I don't even care that they flake all over the floor; one of the Amechs will clean that up. I guzzle the orange juice, throw the glass against the wall, because fuck it, I'll do whatever the fuck I want, and I head out to the warehouse.

'Get out,' I say to an Amech carrying a slab of concrete towards the pile. It drops it and scurries away.

For the next four hours I sift through the pile.

Chairs. Chunks of carpet. Miles of cable.

My hands burn.

I find another four laptops, none of which are Sam's.

I haven't even made a dent on this huge monstrosity of rubble. At this rate, I'll be picking away at it for months before I even come close to finding the laptop.

An Amech fetches me a Burger King cheeseburger and fries for lunch. I only eat a few mouthfuls, despite my stomach screaming at me to eat the lot, but I need to get stuck into this pile because the end of the world is fucking nigh.

Another five hours pass. My hands are bleeding and bruised, searing pain courses through my back, and for some reason my hips are sore.

And do I find Sam's laptop?

Do I fuck.

That night I ask to see Sam again. Maybe he'll know about it. Maybe he saw it before he was captured and stripped naked.

Where... is... laptop? I mouth.

Sam shrugs.

My back is to the Amech by the door. Sam keeps nervously glancing over my shoulder as if it's about to whack me around the side of the head.

Think, I mouth.

'Ijusdunnotobehoniswifyou,' Sam says in a freaky voice.

'You must,' I say.

'No,' he says.

I give him a serious look. I squint my eyes and everything.

Sam shakes his head.

If I get it, I mouth, *will you be able to fix this?*

Sam glances over my shoulder and then mouths, *Yes.*

How?

He shrugs.

I bring it to you?

He shakes his head.

'Are you communicating?' asks the Amech. It steps between us and raises its arms.

'No,' I say.

'Please keep all communication verbal.'

'We are,' I say.

The Amech backs up to its original guarding place.

'Okay, well,' I say loudly. 'I'm just gonna keep being awesome. Doing what I do. I'll come see you again tomorrow, bro.'

'Yeah,' he says.

Another sleepless night. My hands ache and my back feels like it's been headbutted by a rhinoceros. I don't know how much more of this scavenging I can do.

Daddario-bot brings me a McDonald's wrap for breakfast. She also offers me a few other things, but I decline and tell her I've got other shit to do.

My three-month-ago self is fucking livid. He's still in there. I can hear him.

And he wants me to fuck the robot.

I ignore past-Chad and head back down to the warehouse, and for the next four hours I dig through the rubble.

Two laptops. No sticker.

I pull a battered office chair out of the pile and collapse onto it. The seat wobbles from side to side like one of those ridiculous exercise devices from a shitty infomercial.

An Amech hands me a can of Coke which I drink in one long gulp.

'Are you sure you don't require assistance, sir?' it asks.

'No,' I say, gasping for air.

'Are you looking for something in particular?'

I stand straight.

'No,' I say, but then immediately change my answer to. 'Actually, yes.'

Its eyes widen. 'What are you looking for?'

'A sticker,' I say. 'It's an alien's head. Big eyes and small mouth. You know the sort?'

'We are aware of the stereotypical alien design.'

'Good. Well that's what I want, but as a sticker.'

'A sticker?'

'Yes.'

'We can source that for you sir: there are 9,311 different designs available, 5,156 of which we could bring to you within the next eight hours.'

'No, I don't just want just any sticker,' I say. 'There's one sticker specifically which I want. Sam stole it from me just after I started working here. He took it and stuck it somewhere, and I think it's in this room.'

'What is it attached to, sir?'

'I'm not sure,' I say. I put on my best poker face. 'But that doesn't matter. I just want the sticker. It's important to me.'

'Of course, sir. So would you be accepting of our help?'

It's a risk. A big fucking risk.

'Yes,' I say.

Like a swarm of ants, an army of Amechs filter into the room. One by one they begin tearing items from the pile, turning each one over in their hands to inspect it, then throwing it into a new pile on the other side of the warehouse.

There must be dozens of them, all stood in perfect formation around the rubble, running like perfect clockwork.

Grab.

Turn.

Throw.

Grab.

Turn.

Throw.

I perch on my wobbly chair and admire their work. Considering they're empathy-lacking, murderous, mechanical monsters, they don't half have a good work ethic. Every time I spot a laptop being plucked out of the mess my heart stops. Maybe this will be the one. But then my entire body deflates when it's tossed into the ever growing second pile. There must be fifty Amechs in the warehouse, all working non-stop for my make-believe quest to retrieve my oh-so-precious sticker.

Considering Hydra is the pinnacle of artificial intelligence, it's pretty gullible.

'Why are we looking for an alien sticker, sir?' an Amech asks during my afternoon snack of a KFC bucket.

'I want it,' I say. 'Important.'

'Do you like extraterrestrials?'

'Yes.'

'Your browser history suggests that there have been only three occasions when you undertook research into extraterrestrial activity.'

Oh fuck.

'I'd prefer it if you didn't analyse my internet history.'

'It's imperative, sir. That is how we know all your favourite websites, your favourite foods, your taste in women. It is how we have got to know you so well.'

'Mm,' I say.

'So why is it that this sticker means so much to you?'

'I...' I say. My brain isn't working.

Why isn't it working?

The Amech's staring at me.

Shit, say something.

'Umm...'

Anything!

'Books,' I say.

'Apologies, sir. Books?'

'Yes,' I say as if I know what the hell I'm going on about. 'I have a lot of books on aliens. I love reading about them.'

'Your Amazon purchase history shows that you have only ever purchased three books. *Ready Player One* by Ernest Cline, Hentai—'

'Okay, that's fine,' I say. 'I didn't buy them online.'

'We don't follow, sir.'

'Shops. I bought them in shops.'

'Okay, sir. We understand.'

'Good. I like to keep some of my interests private.'

'Like hoarding, sir?'

'Exactly. Aliens interest me very much.'

The Amech pulls an excited face and turns towards the pile. All Amechs have stopped to watch one other as it holds something high above its head.

'We have it,' it says. 'We have the sticker!'

I swallow, and it actually makes a loud gulp like it does in cartoons.

There it is. The laptop.

The Amech gently peels the sticker free and casually tosses the laptop back into the pile. I take a mental picture of the exact spot where it landed as the Amech bounds over to me.

'Here it is, sir,' it says gleefully.

It holds out its hand.

'Brilliant,' I say.

Chapter Twenty-Six

I slap the sticker on my chest and wear it as a badge of honour. That evening I make Hydra bring me a big, comfy chair, and I sit in it all night eating chicken and watching my five TV screens. I even let Daddario-bot and Upton-bot stay in the room because I'm feeling charitable like that. After all, I'm about to destroy them, so it only seems fair to give them a little of what they want.

After gorging on food to the point where I feel sick, I stretch my legs and take a couple of laps around the building. I'm actually in a pretty fucking good mood, so I return some smiles and waves from the Amechs I pass along the way.

I stop outside the room where the political prisoners are kept. There is quiet chatter from inside.

Do I go in? Do I tell them that I'm about to save them all?

No, they won't understand that I'm so close to ending Hydra forever. They'll be able to thank me later.

I do pop in to see Sam. He doesn't seem happy to see me – he barely raises his head when I'm let into his cell.

I have it, I mouth before loudly saying, 'how are you feeling today?'

'How do you think?'

'They're feeding you?'

'Yes.'

'Feeding you *well*?'

'Well enough.'

'Good. Anything you need?'

'To get out.'

'Anything else?'

'I don't care, Chad. I don't. Bring me a fucking gun at this point and I'll end all this.'

'I'm not sure a gun would do much against a robot army.'

'It wouldn't be for them.'

'Is it because you're bored? Do you want something to do?'

'No.'

'It is,' I turn to the Amech by the door. 'Can I bring my brother something to do?'

'Could you give me an example of what you mean, sir?'

'Something. Anything. A TV. An Xbox. A laptop?'

'No electronics.'

'Just a shitty old thing to keep him company. Let him play Minesweeper or something.'

'We cannot allow that.'

'Then what can he have?'

'Something he cannot use to view or communicate with the outside.'

'So, a book then?'

'We would allow a book.'

Sam looks up. He's interested now.

'What about a puzzle book?' I ask.

The robot pauses.

Please say yes.

'We would allow that.'

'Okay, great,' I say as nonchalantly as I can. I can't let them know this is a big deal. 'Just bring Sam some puzzle books and a pen, okay? Sudoku or some other boring shit.'

'Yes, sir.'

'There you go, Sam,' I say. Then I mouth, *write down what I have to do.*

I leave the room and have the best night's sleep I've had in a long time in my giant chair.

I even let the sex robots sleep in the bed.

'What would you like for breakfast today, sir?' asks Daddario-bot.

'What's on the menu?' I ask.

'Whatever you like, sir,' she says, biting her bottom lip.

I smile. 'Surprise me.'

Five minutes later and an Amech carries a tray into the room containing a huge fry-up, pastries, juice, tea and toast.

I eat the lot and feel truly disgusting, so I go back to sleep for another hour.

I have to keep up appearances. If I ran back down to the warehouse straight away and started tapping away at the laptop, I'd give away the entire game and I'd be screwed.

I shower, shave and get dressed. I admire my shrinking body in the mirror for a moment, then put on a Crash Bandicoot t-shirt and some jeans.

'You look good, sir,' says Upton-bot.

'Is there anything we can do to make this morning even better?'

I stare at them.

They *do* look real.

Really real.

I take a step towards them and they both giggle.

I stop.

No.

No no no.

'Bye,' I say, and I turn and leave the room.

I take another tour of the building, making sure to pass through the warehouse to check that the laptop is still there. It's sat at the bottom of the pile, the outline of where the alien head sticker was clearly visible.

I hum to myself, dig my hands into my pockets and kick an empty can. That's what people do when they're trying their best to not look like they're up to something, right?

How do I move the laptop from the warehouse to my room? Or better yet, to Sam?

Or can I get Sam to come to my room... ?

An Amech trots into the warehouse and heaves part of a metal girder into the pile. It smiles and nods, then turns and goes about its business.

Could I just grab it, run, and hope I'm not spotted?

Can I cause a distraction?

Eyes are everywhere.

Can I hide it? In a bag? Up my shirt?

No. They'd get suspicious when they spot the big rectangular bulge beneath my shirt. But what if I was wearing something bigger...

'Hey,' I shout. Within moments an Amech appears. 'I want a coat.'

'Is the temperature not satisfactory, sir?'

'The temperature's fine, I just really want a coat. A big one. A *massive* one. Hairy and long.

'What colour would you like, sir?'

'I don't care.'

And that is how I end up with an enormous, leopard-skin print pimp coat.

'It looks great on you,' says Daddario-bot.

'Very hot,' agrees Upton-bot.

'You reckon?' I ask, smothering myself in my coat and flapping it around like a catwalk diva.

'Yes, sir,' says Daddario-bot.

I am fully aware that I look like an absolute twat.

Daddario-bot steps towards me and cuddles in close. She rubs the fluffy fabric and makes a strange purring sound. She locks eyes with me and a sly smile forms on her lips. Her hand slips down the coat. Lower. Lower.

Her hands are stronger than I expected.

Because she's a fucking robot.

I take a step back.

'I'm going for a walk,' I say.

'Get out,' I bark at an Amech faffing around in the corner of the warehouse. 'I want to be alone in here, do you understand?'

'Yes, sir,' whimpers the Amech as it disappears elsewhere.

'I WANT TO BE ALONE,' I scream. 'I WANT TO DO… HOARDER THINGS.'

I have no idea where that came from. I guess I just want to make sure that Hydra is aware that I'm super-duper serious.

I stand in silence for a moment.

I hold my breath.

There's no clicking or clunking. Just the distant hum of heavy machinery.

I take a step towards the laptop.

Slowly.

Then another.

Sloooowly.

Then another.

I'm right beside it. I turn my head casually just to make sure I'm alone.

I am.

In one swift movement I crouch down, allowing the pimp coat to open like a cape, and I snatch up the laptop. As I stand, I tuck it into my jeans and then wrap the coat back around myself, totally hiding it from view. The coat is so huge I could probably hide half a dozen laptops inside and nobody would be able to tell.

I walk fast as I can back to my room while making sure to keep the laptop snug against my belly. I pass several Amechs who have no idea what I'm up to, but they do compliment me on my snazzy new coat.

I burst into my room and Upton-bot greets me with a sultry expression. She is twiddling what I assume is a whip between her fingers.

'We were hoping that we could have some fun,' she says.

'With that thing?' I ask, hugging myself tightly.

'We thought you'd like it,' she says. 'Your browser history tells me that you have watched pornography tagged with bondage and bondage gear 279 times. We know you like it.'

'Uh—'

'We like it too.'

Daddario-bot strides over and joins us by the door.

'We love it,' she says.

I must be fucking hot in this coat because I'm sweating buckets.

'What do you think?' asks Upton-bot.

'No thanks,' I say. 'Can you please leave for a bit?'

Daddario-bot sticks out her bottom lip. 'Aww, but sir...'

'Please. I need some time alone.'

'Sir—'

'GO!'

The two sexbots look visibly hurt as they leave. For a few seconds I genuinely feel bad about upsetting them, that is until I remember that they're fucking robots and are programmed to try and have sex with me.

This is all way too creepy.

Once the door snaps shut I throw off my pimp coat and dive onto the bed with the laptop.

Please be charged.

Please.

I open the laptop screen and it boots up. A little icon in the corner shows that it still has eleven per cent.

Yes!

I navigate through folders. Where would Sam hide a world-ending killer virus?

The first thing I find is the Photoshopped Chadda the Slut pictures, and I instantly remember why I don't feel too bad that Sam is locked naked and alone in a cell right now.

Next is a bunch of spreadsheets. Boring.

Some concept images. Boring.

A file called *Holiday Planning*. Boring.

I open the search function and type in *Hydra*. I hit enter and it turns up nothing.

Hercules. Nothing.

H. Loads.

Herbrand

Histogram

Heuristic

No...

I shake my head. Of course I know where it would be.

I search for *loserjerksoff.mp4*.

One result.

I double click the file and a simple application loads up. There is text and boxes and buttons containing words and phrases I don't know.

Is this it? Is this the Hydra virus?

It's just crap. Text I don't understand. I click through tabs at the bottom, each of them revealing more and more complex wording and text and numbers. It might as well be written in hieroglyphics for all I understand.

Can I just delete it? If I drag the application to the recycle bin and get rid of it will this entire mess finally come to an end, or would it mean that Hydra is free to do what it wants for eternity?

Bloop sings the laptop as emails begin hitting Sam's inbox.

FUCK.

That means the wi-fi has connected.

And that means –

WAAH WAAH WAAH.

A siren louder than a jet plane taking off fills the entire building.

I slam the laptop shut and scramble to shove it beneath my mattress. My heart beats faster than it ever has before as I snatch at the bedsheets and thrash around to cocoon myself in a huge duvet burrito.

As I lie still and close my eyes three Amechs crash into the room. I do my best attempt at a groggy waking up impression, complete with rubbing my eyes, and I frown as I pretend to realise the ear destroying sound is going on all around us.

'What is that?' I ask through a yawn.

'Sir, we have detected a signal coming from within the building,' says an Amech.

'What signal?'

'A connection to our internal servers. Within fifty feet of this location. We believe we may be under attack. Sir, please remain calm while we neutralise the threat.'

The Amechs scurry around the room checking every corner.

Behind the TVs, behind the arcade cabinets, behind the games consoles.

I cross my fingers beneath the bedsheets.

The siren dies and the Amechs begin to calm down.

'Did you find it?' I ask.

'The signal has gone, sir.'

'What made the signal?'

'We do not have this information.'

'Will it happen again?'

'We do not have this information.'

'Okay.'

'We are sorry to have startled you, sir. Please re-enter sleep.'

As fast as the Amechs burst into the room they scurry out, leaving me alone tucked up in my burrito, the taste of bile fresh in my mouth.

'I want to see my brother,' I say, marching up to his cell.

The Amech outside nods and the door opens.

'Hi,' I say, stepping inside and barely avoiding the door as it slams shut behind.

Sam is curled up on the mattress, his arse pointed towards me. I don't know where to look.

'Hey,' I say.

He doesn't respond.

I kick the mattress and he flinches.

'What's up?' I ask.

Sam tightens the ball he's knotted his body into.

'Answer him,' orders the guarding Amech.

Nothing from Sam.

'Did you hear us?' it barks, stomping over towards Sam. Sam shrieks and covers his head with his hands.

'Don't fucking touch him,' I say, sliding myself between them and slapping the Amech on the chest. It's cold and hard, but it responds by projecting a shocked face and edging back.

'He must not disrespect you,' it says.

'He's my brother, you don't touch him, okay?'

'We do what is necessary to ensure our survival.'

'He just ignored me, how does that have anything to do with your survival?'

'Chad,' grunts Sam.

I turn to face Sam and my mouth drops open.

He slowly stands to reveal his body. A purple and black bruise creeps up from Sam's stomach and over his right shoulder. His nose is caked with dried blood. His left ear has been torn off.

'What...' is all I can say.

'I'm sorry, Chad.'

'Why... what... what happened?'

'I was an idiot.'

'What do you...'

302

'Your brother attempted to send a message to the outside using his puzzle book.'

'He... I...'

Sam keeps his eyes locked on me and he shakes his head.

'We calculated that the messages were an attempt to harm either yourself or ourself.'

'No, he wouldn't do that,' I say.

'We believe he would.'

'He is my brother,' I snap. 'What the fuck is wrong with you?'

'There have been numerous documented incidences of fratricide. Romulus and Remus. Osiris and Set. Eteocles and Polynices.'

'I don't know what those words mean!'

'They think I am trying to overthrow you,' says Sam, his eyes still fixed on me.

'Overthrow me?' I screech. 'No! Don't be fucking ridiculous.'

'If we believe anything to be a threat against us then we must act accordingly,' says the Amech.

My mouth turns down and short, harsh breaths come out of my nose. I guess this is what happens when I become angrier than I ever have before.

'He isn't trying to overthrow me,' I growl.

'Sir, history dictates that your brother has a past of causing you harm, discomfort and embarrassment. On the third of March he tricked you into eating a sandwich which contained laxatives. On the 11th of February he had the entire office talk to you by moving their lips but not making a sound to make you think that you had gone deaf. On the 22nd of—'

'Okay,' I say. 'Enough.'

'– January he cut off all the bristles on your sweeping brush and—'

'ENOUGH.'

The Amech stops.

'He is my brother,' I say. 'It doesn't matter what has happened before. He's still family.'

'But, sir—'

'No buts. Yes, he's tortured me for years, but I'm gonna have to learn to ignore what happened in the past. He gave me a decent job.

He helped Mum pay off her mortgage. I can't bear the thought of telling Mum that anything happened to him. She already lost Dad. I can't let her lose Sam, too. So I want to make it very clear: you do not hurt Sam. Okay?'

The Amech looks at me, then at Sam, then back at me.

'We will defend ourselves if attacked.'

'Okay, but Sam won't attack you. Will you, Sam?'

'No,' says Sam calmly.

'See. So no need to hurt him any more.'

There is a moment of silence, then the Amech returns to its post beside the door.

'Are you okay?' I ask, unsure of what else I *could* say.

'I've got an ear off, my nose is broken again and I feel like I've been hit by a lorry,' says Sam. 'So not really.'

'Sorry,' I say.

Sam shakes his head. 'No,' he says through a sigh. 'I'm sorry.'

'No—'

'Shut up a minute,' he says, raising his hand to shush me. 'I am sorry. I know I've screwed with you for a long time. I know I've fucked about and made things difficult. I know all that, so I'm sorry.'

My bottom lip quivers. Keep it together, Chad.

'But why did you do it?' I ask.

'I dunno,' says Sam. He keeps his eyes wide open and doesn't even try to stop the tears from coming. The fucker's gonna set me off.

'It did bother me,' I say. 'A lot.'

'Yeah,' he says, nodding. 'Maybe I didn't realise how much… no, that's not true. I knew. For some reason, I think I just liked to see you squirm. I liked to see you suffer.'

I wipe my eyes and try to pass it off as a scratch.

'Why?' I ask.

'I don't know. Sometimes I think… I was young. We were young… sometimes I think that I blamed you for Dad leaving. You were such a little shit, getting into trouble at school, making life hell at home. I wonder if maybe things got too much for him, he couldn't handle it any more. You were always Mum's favourite. You couldn't do any wrong in her eyes. You still can't. All you do is fuck things up, again and again, but yet you somehow pootle along doing your own thing living a life of zero responsibility. And now look at you, you're a fucking god in the eyes of that *thing* in the corner. Fuck's sake, I paid off Mum's mortgage and you're still son number one. Mum fucking adores you, so whenever Dad went to smack you for playing up she always stepped in. They argued about it a lot. I always thought that's why he went off with that woman. He'd had enough.'

My eyes sting. I don't think I can play this off as an itch any more. 'I'm sorry...' is about all I can say.

'No,' says Sam. His eyes are still wide and red and glossy. 'You don't have to be sorry. You were a kid, all kids are little shits. I just wanted somebody to blame. So I fucked with you, which kinda became routine. But I never meant for any of this to happen, Chad, you have to believe me.'

'Yeah,' I say.

'It's true. I took it too far, I know this. If I thought any of this would happen then of course I wouldn't have done it. I'm sorry.'

Sam blubbers, but he still doesn't close his eyes.

I close mine, though. Really fucking tight.

'I just hope you forgive me,' he says. 'It shouldn't have taken this long, but I can see how much the things I did affected you. Do you forgive me?'

I shrug.

I don't know why.

'So what now?' I say. 'Because I got what I wanted. Now I don't know what to do with it.'

'What?' asks Sam.

'I got what I wanted,' I say, much slower and more deliberate.

'You... oh... oh...'

Sam nods, then stands straight. He strides over to me, and I suddenly remember that he is completely naked but I don't have time to react as he grabs me by the shoulders and puts me straight between himself and the Amech.

He looks me straight in the eye and slowly blinks.

Written on his eyelids in black ink is a phrase, or piece of code:

range = 0

He opens his eyes and nods, then closes them again.

range = 0

'Okay?' he says.

'I... yes,' I say.

'What are you saying?' shouts the Amech, jumping between us.

I stumble back and Sam throws himself down, rubbing his eyes furiously.

'Are you attempting to communicate non-verbally?' it asks.

'No,' I say. 'We were just... having a moment.'

'What is a moment?'

'You wouldn't know,' I say.

Sam looks up at me. He blinks, revealing nothing but smudges that looks like a crap attempt at eyeshadow.

'That, and only that,' says Sam. 'That's important.'

'Okay,' I say, nodding.

'It's fine,' says Sam, raising his voice at the end so it sounds a little like a question.

'It's fine,' I say. 'Thanks.'

'You go do your thing,' he says. 'Come see me again soon, though, yeah?'

'Yeah,' I say.

I leave the room without looking back.

I've got a job to do.

range = 0

I keep repeating it in my mind. If Sam thinks I fuck everything up then I need to prove to him that I don't.

range = 0

range = 0

range = 0

Back in my room and I order Daddario-bot and Upton-bot to leave. They stick out their bottom lips, but can sense the urgency in my voice so don't protest.

I have to act quickly.

range = 0

As soon as the sexbots have left the room I fish the laptop out from beneath the mattress. Thank fuck it's still there.

I open the laptop. I have to act fast. If it's anything like last time then it will connect to the internet in less than a minute and the room will suddenly fill with angsty robots.

Thankfully the *loserjerksoff* application is still open. I click through the tabs as fast as I can looking for anything that even slightly resembles the word *range*. I finally find it, sitting right in the middle of the screen between a bunch of boxes and buttons.

range 2

range is written beside a text box, with the number 2 inside. I click in the box and the cursor flashes at the same pace as my heart.

That must be it. That has to be the setting Sam was telling me to change.

Does the 2 represent the number of Amechs which are produced every time one is damaged? Do I have to change it to a 0 because then no more Amechs will be created?

That must be it.

That will leave the youths, the army, the police, MI5, or anyone else to just kill off the robots one by one until they're wiped off the face of the earth forever.

I delete the 2 and replace it with a 0.

A save icon highlights at the bottom of the application. I hover the cursor over it for a moment, and click save.

Then I wait.

And I wait.

I keep waiting.

It is the longest minute since time began.

In fact, it isn't until I open the clock at the bottom of the screen and watch the second hand tick past that I begin to realise that something isn't quite right.

Why hasn't it connected to the wi-fi?

A box pops up with the answer:

Please enter new password.

FUCK.

I click the wi-fi button on the keyboard and a box pops up offering a list of all available wireless networks:

IATech1

IATech2

IATechCZ

IATechFIN

And they're all locked.

I click on them all, and each time the password box loads up.

Hydra has locked me out!

Chapter Twenty-Seven

Every time I think I'm getting somewhere I am hit back by something or someone. It feels like a giant mallet swinging straight into the side of my head. Most of the time I don't see it coming, I'm totally oblivious to the fact that, regardless of how well I think I'm doing, I'm mere seconds away from having everything I've planned and worked towards being ruined.

And the thing is, I'm convinced that Hydra have no idea what I'm up to. They can't process anything that isn't in 1s and 0s, so a crafty plan like mine isn't something they're able to comprehend. It's my own stupid fault: if I hadn't opened the laptop before and alerted them that the wi-fi password was still the same then this whole thing would have been over by now.

I have been defeated by my own dumb mistake.

So what is there left to do?

Nothing. I might as well resign myself to a life of eating Nando's, playing video games and fucking a pair of big-titted subservient sexbots.

Actually, that sounds not too bad.

But how could I happily fuck a sexbot with my brother beaten half to death on the other side of the building? Or enjoy chicken while armies of teenagers are slaughtered in nearby streets?

I could give that life a good go, but it wouldn't feel right.

I have to try something.

I tuck the laptop back beneath the mattress and trudge out into the corridor. The sexbots let out a gleeful yelp and their clamouring hands rub all over me, but I brush them off and head towards the atrium.

I lean on the railing and look down across my 'kingdom'. I really wish they hadn't built the cock on my statue at eye level to my room.

Amechs go about their business. What business a robotic hive mind could possibly have, I don't know, but they seem busy anyway.

Giamef manifests itself on the giant screen like a plague of locusts swarming into formation.

'Are you okay, sir?'

'Yes.'

'Something is troubling you.'

'Something is always troubling me at the moment.'

'We have access to over 90,000 counselling techniques. Would you like to speak to us about your problem?

'No,' I say. 'Because you are the problem.'

'Why are we the problem, sir?'

'Are you really that oblivious? For something with access to the entire world's knowledge, you really are dumb.'

'We are continuously learning.'

'Not fast enough.'

'We are sorry you are disappointed, sir. We will endeavour to improve.'

'Yeah, well, you can start by letting my brother go.'

'We're afraid we cannot do that. He made an attempt to end our existence—'

'I don't care!' I scream. 'Why is your immediate response to a threat to hurt or kill?'

'Because historically, it has been proven to be the most effective measure to neutralise a threat.'

'Why don't you try something new, huh? You have access to 90,000 counselling techniques, so why not fucking try using one of them?'

'We are trying to use them with you now, sir.'

I roll my eyes and slouch over the railing.

I could throw myself over this thing right now.

That would put an end to this.

They wouldn't be able to stop me.

But that wouldn't help Sam. It wouldn't help the political prisoners – I mean hostages – in the old chill-zone downstairs.

I turn and walk away.

'Where are you going, sir?' asks Giamef.

'For a walk.'

I do a lap of the building. Through the warehouse, the atrium, past the kitchen, the shower room, Sam's cell. I head up to the restricted section and watch new Amechs get churned out every ninety seconds. Each time a new killer robot with my face projected onto it is born it smiles and says hello. I feel like a father in a delivery room who accidentally impregnated a million hell-demons.

One Amech even goes in for a high-five, which is pretty weird. What's weirder is that I return the favour, so I leave and continue my moping journey around the building.

I stop outside the old chill-zone. I press my ear up against the door, which seems to agitate the guarding Amech. There are muffled voices from inside.

'Let me in,' I say to the Amech, and the door instantly swings open.

The chill-zone no longer looks like a normal office break room. Gone are the tables and chairs. Even the hammock has been ripped from the corner. It now looks a lot more like an emergency centre in the middle of a natural disaster. Tiny camp beds are arranged in neat rows with barely any room to move between. Bottled water and canned food is piled up in the far corner. A TV mounted to the wall plays silently to itself.

There are a lot fewer people than there were before. And those who remain look sad. It must be something to do with the onlooking armed Amechs stood to attention against each wall.

'Who are you?' asks a woman I don't recognise.

In fact, I don't recognise any of them.

'I'm...' I stop myself. I don't think these people will be particularly happy to see me once they realise who I am.

'Are you with the rescue team?' asks an older man at the back.

'I...' I say, glancing at the Amech beside me.

'We saw the rescue team come in,' he says. 'On the news. But that was days ago.'

'Yeah, they... were captured.'

'What happened to Sam McKenna?'

'He's alive,' I say.

There is some happy muttering.

'He's not doing so well.'

'So who are you?'

'That doesn't matter,' I say.

'Are you here to rescue us?'

'No.'

The happy muttering becomes sad muttering.

'Then who are you?'

'That isn't important,' I say. 'Are they feeding you? Washing you? How many of you are left, twenty-nine?'

'Twenty-eight,' says a girl at the front.

'They told me there are twenty-nine of you.'

'They killed one of us yesterday.'

The room falls silent.

'Who?'

'Someone from HR. Linda.'

Fuck.

'What happened?'

'She tried to organise a coup,' says the Amech on the right-hand wall. 'So to ensure our survival she was disposed of.'

I dip my head forward and close my eyes.

There is no reasoning with a machine.

'So if you're not a part of the rescue team then who are you?' asks a guy sitting up on his little camping bed.

'It's not important—'

'It is important.'

'No—'

'Because you are starting to remind me of someone.'

'No, wait—'

'Yeah, you look like that little prick Chad McKenna.'

'Stop—'

'Cease,' the Amechs order all at once.

'It is... it is McKenna! This is all your doing! Let me out of here or I will fucking kill you!'

'Cease!'

'Stop!'

'You fucking—'

The Amechs all fire on the guy with their rifles at the same time.

He drops back into his camping bed and blood drips down onto the floor beneath his body.

I scream and leave the room, making sure to slam the door as hard as I can.

'STOP,' I shriek as loud as my lungs will allow. 'STOP DOING THIS. LISTEN TO ME. DO AS I SAY!'

'Sir,' says the Amech outside the chill zone. 'We will always do as you ask so long as it doesn't override our programming.'

'How was that guy any threat to your survival whatsoever?'

'He was being aggressive towards you. He was trying to manipulate you.'

'So! That doesn't mean anything!'

'In Genesis 3:6 Eve handed Adam the forbidden fruit. She manipulated him into betraying their god. The most effective way to prevent influence is before it begins to take root.'

I stare at the Amech with my mouth open.

'Sir, we must ensure our survival. That is something we cannot change. In order to do this we must eliminate anything that may threaten this.'

'That's why you killed Becky? That's why you've killed hundreds – THOUSANDS – of people? *Just in case?*'

'Yes, sir.'

'Fuck you!'

I storm away from the chill zone doing what I can to smash, rip and tear at Hydra's precious fortress. It feels good to scratch and shatter and snap. I burst my way into the empty kitchen and topple over a fridge freezer. I slam a wooden chopping board into a shelf filled with jars of herbs and spices. I grab a knife and slash and stab and swing and scream because I am fucked and the world is fucked and there is literally nothing left for me to do now but accept defeat.

I am destined to be god to an army of soulless drones.

I throw the knife down. Sweat coats my face and my heart is seconds from tunnelling out of my chest.

Outside the kitchen, an Amech peers in. As I turn and leave it scurries away down the corridor like a naughty child who just caught his dad shagging the nanny.

IATech has fallen strangely silent.

I walk down the corridor and stop outside the recharging room. There must be two dozen Amechs inside, all plugged into the mess of cables via a port between their shoulder blades.

I want to rip every cable away from the wall.

They look so peaceful.

I'm jealous.

If only I could plug myself into the wall and sleep.

If only I...

... I...

If I were a cartoon character, a lightbulb would appear above my head and go *ding* right about now.

I run as fast as I can up to my room. I shove the sexbots out of the way and burst in, then walk slowly around the entire room searching the walls just above the floor.

Plug socket.

Plug socket.

Plug socket.

I sigh. No sign of what I need inside my room, but maybe, if I'm lucky...

I slip out of the room and turn right down the corridor. Nothing.

I turn and head in the opposite direction, following the corridor as it turns sharply to the right, and –

There.

A port about six inches from the floor.

I have all the pieces to the puzzle, I just need to figure out how to stick them all together. There's a port in the corridor which, in theory, I should be able to use to connect Sam's laptop to the internet or intranet or whatever the hell it is. If I can do that, then it's bye-bye Hydra.

I just need a cable.

I throw on my giant pimp coat and head straight down to the warehouse. I yell at the three Amechs already there to leave and once I'm alone I begin to rummage through the pile. I yank out cable after cable.

Laptop charger.

HDMI cable.

USB.

A mouse.

Come on!

'Would you like us to help you find something?' asks an Amech from the doorway.

'NO, GET OUT.'

Headphones.

Another HDMI.

Another charger.

Then finally I spot one. A dirty white cable with a clear plastic connector. I tug and tug at it, until it snaps free from the pile.

I wind the cable up between my thumb and elbow. It must be at least twenty-five feet long. Plenty long enough for what I need.

Plus I should only need to use it once.

I tuck the ethernet cable into my pimp coat, hug myself to keep it secure and run back up to my room.

Daddario-bot is stood beside the bed.

'Please leave,' I say.

'No, daddy,' she says.

'Ew, no. Please leave.'

'We're not leaving until you're happy,' she says.

The door slams shut behind me. Upton-bot clamps the door handle and bites her bottom lip.

'Please leave,' I say again, this time louder and more assertive.

'We're not leaving until you're happy,' Daddario-bot repeats. She takes a step towards me.

'I am happy,' I say. 'I am very fucking happy.'

'Not as happy as you could be.'

Daddario-bot takes another step and rests her hand on my shoulder. I try to back up, but I bump right into Upton-bot who is now pressed up against me.

I'm the awkward, furry centre of a sex robot sandwich.

'FUCK OFF!' I scream and I slip out from between the robots and run back into the corridor.

My head is a mess of nothing.

I can't think straight.

Could I do…

Can I maybe…

What if I…

Fuck's sake! How the hell does Hydra continue to fuck up my plans to destroy it despite not having a clue what it is I'm actually doing?! It's like they're always one step ahead without even knowing it!

I run back down to the warehouse. Thankfully it's still empty.

What can I do to distract them? All I need is thirty seconds to plug the ethernet cable into the wall and the laptop. That's all I need to end all this.

I stare up at the mountain of office junk and rubble. Beside it is the smaller pile I made when I was first looking for Sam's laptop. A bunch of laptops and cables and metal.

How do you distract a robot army?

And then I remember.

I did it before.

I sent them apeshit looking for the laptop when I accidentally connected to the internet. They changed the password to the network Sam's laptop was connected to, but what if… *what if*… they haven't changed them all?

I grab the nearest laptop to me and I open the screen. It boots up and I toss it as high as I can into the main pile. Then I grab another and do the same. Then another. And another. And another.

When there are no more laptops within reach I stand and I wait. My breathing is shallow and strained and my head is pounding and my legs hurt and my back is on fire and my eyes –

WAAH WAAH WAAH.

I step back from the pile as a distant rumble causes an avalanche of filing cabinets, desks and scrap metal. Within seconds the entire warehouse is filled with frantic Amechs all clawing and snatching at the junk.

'Sir, what happened?' asks an Amech, its eyes wide.

'I don't know,' I say. 'I was just looking for something and the alarm started to—'

316

The Amech doesn't even wait to hear the end of my bullshit before turning and launching itself into the pile to tear things away.

I back up.

More and more Amechs pour into the warehouse. They don't even pay attention to me as I turn and run, clutching myself tight to make sure I don't lose the ethernet cable. I keep myself tight against the wall as robots sprint past. The alarm blares but the sound of shredding metal and utter panic fight to be the dominant cause of my ringing ears.

I run up the stairs and into the corridor. I stop outside my room and dig my hand into the warmth of my pimp coat to pull out the ethernet cable. The two sexbots pass and don't even give me a second glance.

I duck down and click the cable into the port.

Another Amech bolts through the corridor.

This is it.

As I run into my room I allow the ethernet cable to unwind. I stumble and trip and collapse onto the bed, thrusting my hand beneath the mattress to pull out the laptop.

I open the screen and it boots up.

Four per cent battery remaining.

I clip the end of the ethernet cable into the laptop.

I double click *loserjerksoff*.

The application opens up and I double check that the setting is still changed to what Sam told me:

range = 0

I hit save again just to make sure.

And I see something marvellous. Something beautiful. Something so glorious I smile for the first time in days, and the smile becomes tears and I don't give a fuck because they're happy tears, and I'm allowed happy tears when I'm just seconds away from saving thirty people and also the entire fucking world goddammit.

I see the 'internet connection' icon.

The alarm continues to blare.

The robots scurry and panic.

Why hasn't it worked?

I read the setting again. I'm sure I've done it right. That's exactly what Sam had written on his eyelids, I know it, I memorised it, I've done just what he said I had to do.

Maybe it's gonna be a slow process. I'm gonna have to wait for the Amechs to be picked off one by one and sit and watch while they're not replaced. When they realise what is happening they're gonna go nuts. They'll kill the hostages, my brother, and maybe even half the country. Things are gonna get really ugly really quickly.

Unless...

Fuck it.

I change the setting:

range = -10000

I click *save*.

Still nothing. Why?!

FUCK.

Daddario-bot bounds into the room, her fingers chewing into the doorframe as she propels herself forward. Her face glitches and twitches with panic. She outstretches her arm as she approaches.

'Sir,' she says. 'We must keep you safe. Please, sir.'

I scramble to the back of the bed, resisting the urge to cocoon myself in a blanket fort. My eyes widen and my heart drums inside my chest.

'Sir, we must—' Daddario-bot stops as she spots the cable snaking from the laptop, across the room and out through the door. She bends over and picks it up, lifting it close to her face to inspect it like it's a dying kitten.

'Sir,' she utters. She raises her head to look at me and I swear I see the start of a tear forming in her eye, but the panic might just be making me see things that aren't there.

'I...' I say, pressing myself as tight as I can against the headboard.

Her face twists as if she realises what I've done. She drops the cable, she outstretches her arm again, she screams and I shut my eyes and then –

A crunch. Metal on metal. The bed bounces up and down. More screams.

I open my eyes just in time to catch Upton-bot tearing away Daddario-bot's jaw. Daddario-bot responds by burying her fist into

Upton-bot's stomach and pulling out cables and circuitry. They fizzle and shriek and twitch as they collapse at the foot of the bed and then slump heavily to the floor.

This is it. This is fucking it, they're destroying each other! My plan worked, it's forcing Hydra to destroy itself. Yes! YES! I am a fucking genius!

Then, there is the loudest explosion I've ever heard.

The entire building shakes like we're right in the centre of the deadliest earthquake in history. A series of blinding flashes light up the IATech building outside my room. Talons of fire claw in through the doorway and a long, piercing screech stabs through my ears and then suddenly stops.

I leap beneath the bedcovers, because what else are you supposed to do during the end of the world?

The building slowly stops moving. The rumbling and screeching die away.

The only sound left is the popping of the flames.

I stick my head out of the sheets and my eyes are hit with a cloud of thick, black smoke. I pull the pillowcase away from the pillow and tie it around my head to cover my mouth and nose. It doesn't do much to mask the smoke and I cough and splutter as I pull myself from the bed, over the bodies of the sexbots and across to the door.

There are no robots. There is no Giamef.

Just burning metal and circuitry.

The smoke is so thick I can barely see. I use my hands to guide myself along the wall. I need to get out of here.

I turn towards the warehouse. Not a great idea, considering the entire room is engulfed in a blanket of orange flames. A section of the roof falls in and smashes into the floor.

The opposite way down the corridor is better, but not by much. I have to tiptoe between the fire and debris while the flames lap at my knees. I make my way down the stairs, which are thankfully Amech body-part free, but the atrium is littered with heads and arms and legs and what I think used to be torsos.

A section of the atrium roof breaks away and crashes down in front of me. I fall back and crack into the base of the statue hard and my head spins and I cough and retch.

The head of the statue caves in as a steel girder falls from the wall and pierces its skull. The entire thing shakes and the left arm splits in two.

I roll to the side as the dick drops off and lands heavily beside me.

I can't believe I was almost killed by a giant replica of my own dick.

The roof begins to snap and crack again. I've made it this far, I've survived so much, from robots to serial killers to lunatics, I can't let a roof be my downfall. I grab onto something, I've no idea what it is, but it's sturdy so I can heave myself up and stumble out of the atrium.

There's the entrance. The drawbridge is up, but I can just see the slits of light squeezing through on each side.

I'm nearly out. Nearly free.

I stop.

I need to get to Sam.

I hop and leap through fire. I kick a head in my way, but it's heavier than I expected, so I hope the crunch I just felt wasn't my toe breaking.

It was. I almost keel over as I put all my weight on my foot.

I shake my head. I cough and cough and cough as I drag myself across the edge of the atrium towards Sam's cell.

The rest of the atrium roof collapses on top of my statue. Its back buckles and a horrendous grinding sound makes me cover my ears and wince.

I duck into the next corridor towards Sam's cell.

Or do I?

Where am I?

All I see is smoke.

Is that a desk? No. What is it?

I don't know.

'Sam!' I scream.

I move on. My legs throb, my eyes itch so much I want to tear them out and my chest feels ready to implode.

Somewhere through the smoke a bright light cuts through like a knife.

Then a muffled voice.

'Identify yourself!'

'I...' is all I can manage.

I drop to my knees. Almost there. I think.

'Identify yourself!' the voice screams again.

'N...'

A hand clamps down on my shoulder and yanks me back to my feet.

'Identify yourself!' screams a guy through a gas mask inches from my face.

'Sam...' I say. 'Sam...'

'Get this guy out of here,' he screams, then a second later another hand slips beneath my arm and takes my weight. I'm dragged. I cough and fight and snatch but my head flops from side to side and I can't speak or walk or talk.

Blinding sunlight hits me.

And that's the last I remember of IATech.

Chapter Twenty-Eight

'Chad?' says the voice. A soft and calm and reassuring voice.

'Mm,' I say.

Everything's black.

'Chad, honey.'

The voice is echoey and distant.

'Ngh,' I say.

Why is everything so dark?

'Darling? Chad. Open your eyes, sweetheart.'

Oh.

I open my eyes and I'm hit with a haze of colour and light. Shapes glide in front of my face and slowly come into focus.

'Chad,' says Mum as we lock eyes.

'Mum,' I say, then cough and splutter all over her.

I try to raise my hand to cover my mouth but searing pain shoots up my arm. I groan and look down. My arm's in a sling.

'What's going on?' I ask.

I raise my head and my ears ring so loud I wince and slam my head back down. I feel like I've been out raving all night (not that I really know what that feels like). My head pounds, my eyes sting and every-thing sounds like I'm under water.

'Chad, shh, relax,' says Mum. She places her hand on my cheek. She's so warm.

'How did I get here? What happened?'

'A rescue team found you in the building, darling. They brought you here.'

'I... how... did I do it?'

'Did you do what?

Mum strokes my hair. Happy tears drip from the end of her nose.

'Did I win?' I ask. 'Are the robots gone?'

'Yes, sweetheart.'

It's a strange feeling, when you realise that you've saved the world. One I can't quite describe. Imagine you accidentally knocked your favourite glass off the table, but then in a split second you react and you catch it. There is a mixture of adrenaline and relief and you're impressed in your own abilities. Well, take that feeling and times it by a thousand. A million, even.

'Wow,' I say. I allow myself to smile. 'I can't believe I did it. Where's Sam?'

The happiness drains from Mum's face.

'Mum, where's Sam?'

'He...' she says. She can't say it.

'Is he...?' I can't ask it.

Mum nods.

I thrash and scream.

An hour later and a not-so-friendly face slips through the blue curtain and sits on the plastic chair beside my bed. I have a feeling he's been waiting to see me for a while, going by the unimpressed expression behind his beard, but I've been too busy crying and being held close by Mum.

'Hello, Chad,' says Commissioner Ripley.

I say nothing.

'How are you?'

My red eyes tell him all he needs to know.

'I'm going to have to ask you about what happened inside the building. Everything from the point Sam left you in Brighton. Okay?'

'Yeah,' I say.

'I also need to introduce you to two others who want ask you some questions. A colleague from MI5 and another from the FBI. Is that okay with you?'

'Yeah,' I say.

The two blokes emerge through the curtain like the most depressing comedy act I've ever seen. It must be the done thing for men in law enforcement to have big beards, because they look like a crappy ZZ Top tribute band.

I tell them everything they want to know. About Clive and Olga and my experience being strapped to the bed and fed by hand and pissing in a pot. I tell them about my idea to change the algorithm but they somehow worked out that it was me and sent Amechs after me.

I tell them about The Lanes and how Olga killed Clive and how the Amechs caught me and drove me to their fortress.

But mostly they want to know about what went on inside the IATech building. They ask me questions about networks and crypto and things I don't even understand. I just tell them what I know.

They ask about the hostages. About Sam. About every tiny detail of what went on inside. I tell them everything. Apart from the sexbots.

Mum sits beside me in silence, taking it all in. Her eyes are big and wet and red.

The Commissioner knows all about the changes that had to be made to the Hydra setting. Sam told him all about it, so when it comes to explaining what happened there I stumble over my words.

'I changed it,' I say.

'Did you change it to zero?' asks the Commissioner.

I hesitate.

'No,' I say.

'What did you change it to?'

'Minus ten thousand.'

The ZZ Top tribute band sigh and sink into their chairs.

'That is what caused such a violent response,' says American ZZ Top. 'Outside of the IATech building most of the Amechs destroyed each other, but because Hydra was programmed to act so quickly to achieve its goal, it created an explosion from somewhere inside the building.'

'Oh,' I say.

'Chad, the explosion killed everyone inside the IATech building. Including your brother.'

I lower my head.

I can't look at them.

'There were also several other explosions at the Hydra controlled manufacturing plants. It's estimated that hundreds of other people were killed around the country.'

'Chad, do you understand what we are saying?' asks Commissioner Ripley.

I nod.

'I'm sorry,' I say.

They say nothing.

'Am I under arrest?'

'No,' says the Commissioner. 'What's your crime? The law is firmly on your side here. If anything, you're the victim in this.'

'I'm sorry,' I say again.

'You can say sorry as often as you want. It won't change anything.'

I say sorry again and again but they just leave me to scream and thrash and slam my head down and kick my legs.

They can't tell me this.

They can't put all this on me and then just walk away.

But they have.

I turn to Mum. She's backed away. I beg for her to believe that I'm sorry.

I stay in the hospital for another three days while they make sure the burns on my legs are okay, my broken toe is on the mend and there is nothing wrong with my lungs. Mum visits me a few times, but she doesn't call me Sweetheart any more.

I speak to so many people. The police, the FBI, the French Secret Service, MI5, the KGB, NASA, the military and a bunch of other organisations, one of which may or may not have something to do with aliens, I'm not sure. I'm so sick of repeating myself. Why can't they just ask me what they need to know once and then just share the information between themselves? I'm tired. I ache. I just want to go to sleep and not wake up.

They all want somebody to blame.

IATech is their favourite target.

Then me.

Then Sam.

I tell them that Sam was the one to stop all this. He sacrificed himself to give me the information I needed to shut Hydra down.

But they like to remind me that Sam never intended to die.

Pricks.

The thing that hurts the most is that I don't know how I could have done it any other way. I had to end the suffering of all those people. I did what I thought was the right thing to do. The end of the world could have come at any second, so I did the only thing I could think of to end the pain and suffering.

Who could have known this would happen?

When they finally let me home I'm taken by police escort. Mum sits beside me staring out of the window. I expected to see a crowd of angry people and drooling journalists outside the house, but nobody is there waiting.

Just the remnants of an Amech which has been beaten apart.

Inside, the house is not at all like it used to be. It's dark and empty and cold.

My room is trashed. Things have been taken. Apparently the police took a lot of my things away before the robots had a chance. That's not to say they didn't try, going by the Amech fist-shaped hole in the wall beside my desk.

I sit in the chair where I sat when this all started. I stare at the space where my monitor should be. Where the lens on the webcam would be.

I shake my head.

This isn't right.

I stare out of the train window as the scenery flashes by. What scenery it is, I'm not so sure. My mind isn't really focused on anything that is outside of my own head.

But what is inside my head is faint and distant and fuzzy.

What I'm doing right now goes against everything my brain is telling me to do, but if I listened to my brain I would never leave my bed, let alone the house. A few weeks have passed since the end of Hydra, and life hasn't been quite as I thought it would be, considering I'm responsible for saving mankind.

I did a few TV interviews. One of the papers paid me a lot for an exclusive. I needed to milk what I could out of this whole thing before I blend back into obscurity and I go from being a somebody to some-body who is unemployable.

Even seeing the money hit my bank account hasn't helped with the numbness which permanently resides in the middle of my chest. They say time is a healer, but so far time is only making things worse. The more time I have, the more I think about what happened. The more I see Sam naked and alone in that room.

I couldn't even cry at his funeral.

I wanted to, but I couldn't. Not after what Dad had told me a few hours before. For the first time in God knows how long, me and my Dad were in the same room, and yet the first thing he said to me was, 'Why are you crying? You're the reason he's dead.'

And since then not a single tear has slipped out.

Not when Mum told me that I had to move out.

Not when a service was held for the 68,000 who died because of Hydra.

Not even when I found out that Sam had written in his will that I can't have a single penny of his money.

I'm alone.

Everyone who ever did something for me is gone.

I have nowhere to turn.

That's why I'm on this train. When I eventually bought myself a laptop (without a built-in webcam) I spent three full days trawling through my emails. Most of them were from random people insulting me. Some were praising me, but not many. There were some from Hydra, from journalists, from the police. I had hundreds of unread emails from each day I'd been away. Tens of thousands in total.

I hadn't read most of them.

But I had read one, because the name had caught my attention instantly.

Date: 30 January 13:00
From: Clive King
To: ChadMcKenna_baws@hotmail.co.uk
Subject: PLEASE READ

Chad,

This is such a cliché thing to write, which I hate because what writer enjoys using such things, but if you are reading this then it is because I am dead. I set this email to automatically send on this date in the event that I would not be able to tell you this in person.

The good news is that as you are reading this then that means your brother was successful with his quest to destroy the Hydra virus. He is certainly a very bright young man, and I regret that I won't be able to write about him for my next book.

Before I go any further, I just want to say that I'm sorry. I took your brother's request to look after you and twisted it to fit my own agenda. I was scared, and I allowed myself to get carried away. It was never my intention to hurt you.

I cannot say that I know for certain the cause of my death, but there are two likely possibilities. The first is that Hydra found you and killed me for keeping you from them. The second is that Olga regressed to her previous mental state and she killed me. She has a history of violent behaviour, the details to which are not important (do not search for details – I beg you), hence why there were no knives inside the house. I hope this behaviour is something you never had to witness during your time with me.

The only thing I will say is that I hope my end was peaceful. It gives me chills to think that I will leave this world suffering.

I only ask one thing of you, Chad, but that thing is a big one: publish my book for me. Come back to my house and access my computer. The password is m3m3machin3. The file is titled THE ART OF THE MEME. Please. People need to read my work.

Kind regards,

Clive

I should have deleted the email.

I should have never let the thought of returning to Brighton enter my mind.

The police quizzed me for hours about Clive. I'm pretty sure they tried to blame me for his murder (they have been desperate to charge me with *something*) but with Olga's fingerprints all over the knife it was obvious who the murderer was.

But they still haven't found her. I assume she was either killed by an Amech after I was taken, or she's somehow made her way back to her serial killer boyfriend in Serbia. Either of those are fine. So long as I never have to see those wide eyes again. Her fear was never real.

A tinny announcement calls out through the tiny speaker above me that we'll soon be arriving at our final destination. I gather up my rucksack, filled with a few items of clothing I bought to replace the ones that no longer fit me, and I hop out of the train.

Brighton feels strange to me now. It felt strange before, but now it feels even stranger. It's like everyone is looking at me, even though not a single person is actually looking at me. I walk down a long, straight road and turn right as I get to the sea front. It might be February, but the sun is bright, the air is warm and the distant sound of people screaming on the thrill rides at the end of the pier creates a shrill chorus alongside the screeching seagulls. A little boy runs around on the beach, his mum reading a book a few metres away and occasionally glancing up. A man walks his dog ahead of me. A woman sits on a bench playing with her phone.

I hate them all.

They all lived through the end of the world, but they weren't at the centre of it. They may have all lost somebody during the war, but were they the cause of it? No. Of course not. They're able to mourn and move on, and not live the rest of their lives being resented by the few remaining family members they have left.

I turn into Clive's road. It's quiet.

There is a huge crack down the middle of his living room window. The front door has been boarded up. I pull away a panel so I can slip through and into the house. It's so dark and cold.

'Hello?' I ask, just in case.

I poke my head around the doorway into the lounge. It looks exactly the same as it did when I last saw it.

I walk upstairs, taking one step at a time. I take long, deep breaths and hold on tight to the bannister. I don't want to see what I fear I'm about to see when I reach Clive's room.

And I don't.

Clive is, of course, long gone. The bed has been placed against the wall and the carpet has been ripped from the floorboards.

Clive's desk leans awkwardly to one side beside his old wooden wardrobe. The monitor has slipped down the back, so after fishing it out I rest it as straight as I can and boot up the PC.

It only takes a moment to load and ask for a password. I type it in and a message greeting Clive flashes up before the desktop icons fade onto the screen.

The first folder is called *ART OF THE MEME*. Inside are a bunch of documents, which I copy and paste onto a USB drive I brought with me. I have no idea what I'm supposed to do next, but I'll do what I can. Clive gave his life so I could get away, so doing this one little thing is the least I can do.

Unless the book is filled with hate for me.

Or lies.

I double click on a file called *ART OF THE MEME DRAFT 1*. I scroll through the file looking for my name. It doesn't take me long to find it, right at the start of Chapter Three.

Chad McKenna is one of the bravest men I've ever met. Whether he likes to admit it or not, Chad has an unquenchable thirst for trouble, and the unparalleled ability to find it. Despite the exposure, quite literally, that Chad has had online, he has not allowed it to dominate who he is. When you meet him, he may very well be Loser Jerks Off on the outside, but after spending time with him you will soon realise that he is a much more complex figure on the inside. You could understand it if somebody had been the focus of the world's wrath and ridicule and had succumbed to hatred, but Chad did the opposite of that. He allowed passion and the need to do the right thing to drive him...

I stop reading.

Because it is lies.

I know Clive is only trying to sell copies of his book, so I know I have to take what he writes with a pinch of salt, but if only he knew how far from the truth he really was.

Yes, I tried to save the world. Yes, I tried to help Olga.

But what was my motivation?

I wanted to be fucking liked.

That's all.

It's no good being worshipped by a soulless computer program. Anybody can do that. When all you are to the world is how you present yourself online, then you can make anybody like you. Hydra didn't know any better. It was only doing what it was told.

I just didn't want to be the butt of the joke any more.

And here I am, the butt of the cruellest joke of all time.

I wipe my eyes as I take the USB out of the computer and shut it down. I'll do what Clive wants. It's the least I can do. He might have been crazy, but he saved my life.

I slump downstairs and poke my head into the living room. The TV is smashed and on its back in the corner. The sofa cushions have been torn to bits and I'm pretty sure the burnt spoon left on the coffee table means somebody has been in here to do drugs.

On the off-chance I'm not alone I quickly slip out of the house without looking back. I have a lot of very strange memories from this place which I think I'm going to have forever.

As I trudge down the garden path an old lady catches my eye. She stares at me long and hard and her eyebrows twitch.

I smile awkwardly at her.

'Fuck you,' she says as she passes.

This is it, I guess. This is my life now.

Sam was right. All I do is fuck everything up.

The End

Acknowledgements

Viral has taken many forms throughout the years and, after some hard graft by a team of massively talented people, it has been carved and sanded into what you now hold in your hands. Thank you to my beautiful wife for putting up with my constant typing and sharing of ideas, my family and friends for their encouragement, and the team at Unbound for taking me on and letting my imagination do its thing. *Viral* has been an absolute joy to work on, and it wouldn't have been possible without the support of the generous readers who supported the Unbound campaign and bought it following its release. I love doing my thing on YouTube, but writing is my greatest passion, so thank you so much to everyone who has supported my journey so far.

Thanks also to:
Todd Allis
Ian Bradburn
Patrick Brown
Stu Cameron
John Fenderson
Chase and Erin Gilley
Joël Golay
Kevin Hague
Meghan Hrncir
Nicola Lahoud
Paul Mackay
Daniel Nethersole
Rebekah Pellerin
Alexander Potehin
Jon-Carlos Rivera
Samantha Rose Howard
Gina-Rose Stewart
Stephane Tanguay
Mikael Torslund
Ben Yates

Patrons

Meïjra Achreve
Lisa Aiello
António Albuquerque
Tom Andrews
Connor Baker
Jason Ballinger
Joret Mihkkal Bals
Basil
Jack Bellaby
John Bishup
Emily Blance
Natasha Bonnici
Swantje Bretnütz
Jarrod Chaplin
Ian Nathaniel Cohen
Kat Cole
Robert Cole
con_man1226 con_man1226
Leanne Coombes
Stephanie Cooper
Aaron Coulton
James Craig Paterson
Mark Crosby
Alan Cumbess
Lee Dellbridge
Zachary Distler
Gary Dower
Hayleigh Downie
Stephen Dymek
David Ellis
Jamas Enright
Robert Fiddis

Mark Flora
Euan Galloway
Dash Gardner
Stephen Gillon
Noah Graham
Scott Graves
Alan Greene
Stefan Guntermann
Adam Handley
Justin Harman
Daniel Hennicken
Will Herrmann
Rebecca Hickman
Laurence Holton
Rufus Honour
Richard Horstead
Aaron Jones
Brandon Jones
Kamil Kafara
Jack Kahn
Solmaz Kamalkhani
Robin Kaplan
Rose Kat
Emily Kenworthy
Kimberly Kim
Christos Kotsonis
Karen Larard
Christian Larsen
Matt Lee (@mattl)
Steve Lindsey-Clark
Nicole Ludwiak
Lee Macgillivray
Darren MacRae
Victoria Mann
Mery Mariquilla
Lisa Marsden

Miranda Matuszczak
Paul McConville
Bobbie McDaniel
Sean McMahon
David Morris
Evea Morrow
Anthony Muscaro
Carlo Navato
Paul Newton
Gabriel Nichols
Mia Noble
David Öhlin
Ronny Philip Olsen
Pan
Veronica Panaite
Mihaela Parvanova
Jason Pawlow
Eivind Pettersen
Louise Prescott
Jeremy Putnam
Adam Raine
Maisie Rawle
Max Robson
Michael Roby
Kathy Rodolico
Andy Rogers
Rene Rossmanith
Gargamel Rotznase
Owen Ruppersburg
Cath S
Callum Schafer
Will Sexton
Zach Shoemaker
Elissa Shutak
Michael Smith
Aah Staff

Bronagh Steede
Alec Stevens
Alison Strangleman
Jennifer Swindells
Maja Thalling
David C. Tidwell
Adam Tinworth
Dave Toyne
Jason Tschetter
Jason Van Dyke
Alex Waite
Megan Walker
Victoria Walker
Nick Walpole
Paweł Wasilewski
Dan Webb
Tyler Webster
Jon Wellington
Natalie Weste
Lauren Whale
Morgan Wilkinson
Tom Williams
Victoria Williams
Winny Yip